BETTER THE DEVIL

ERIK J. BROWN

STORYTIDE
An Imprint of HarperCollins*Publishers*

Also by Erik J. Brown

All That's Left in the World

The Only Light Left Burning

Lose You to Find Me

HarperCollins Children's Books,
a division of HarperCollins Publishers,
195 Broadway, New York, NY 10007

HarperCollins Publishers, Macken House,
39/40 Mayor Street Upper, Dublin 1, D01 C9W8, Ireland

Storytide is an imprint of HarperCollins Publishers.

Better the Devil

harpercollins.com
Library of Congress Control Number: 2025943835
ISBN 978-0-06-333832-6
Typography by Chris Kwon
25 26 27 28 29 LBC 5 4 3 2 1
First Edition

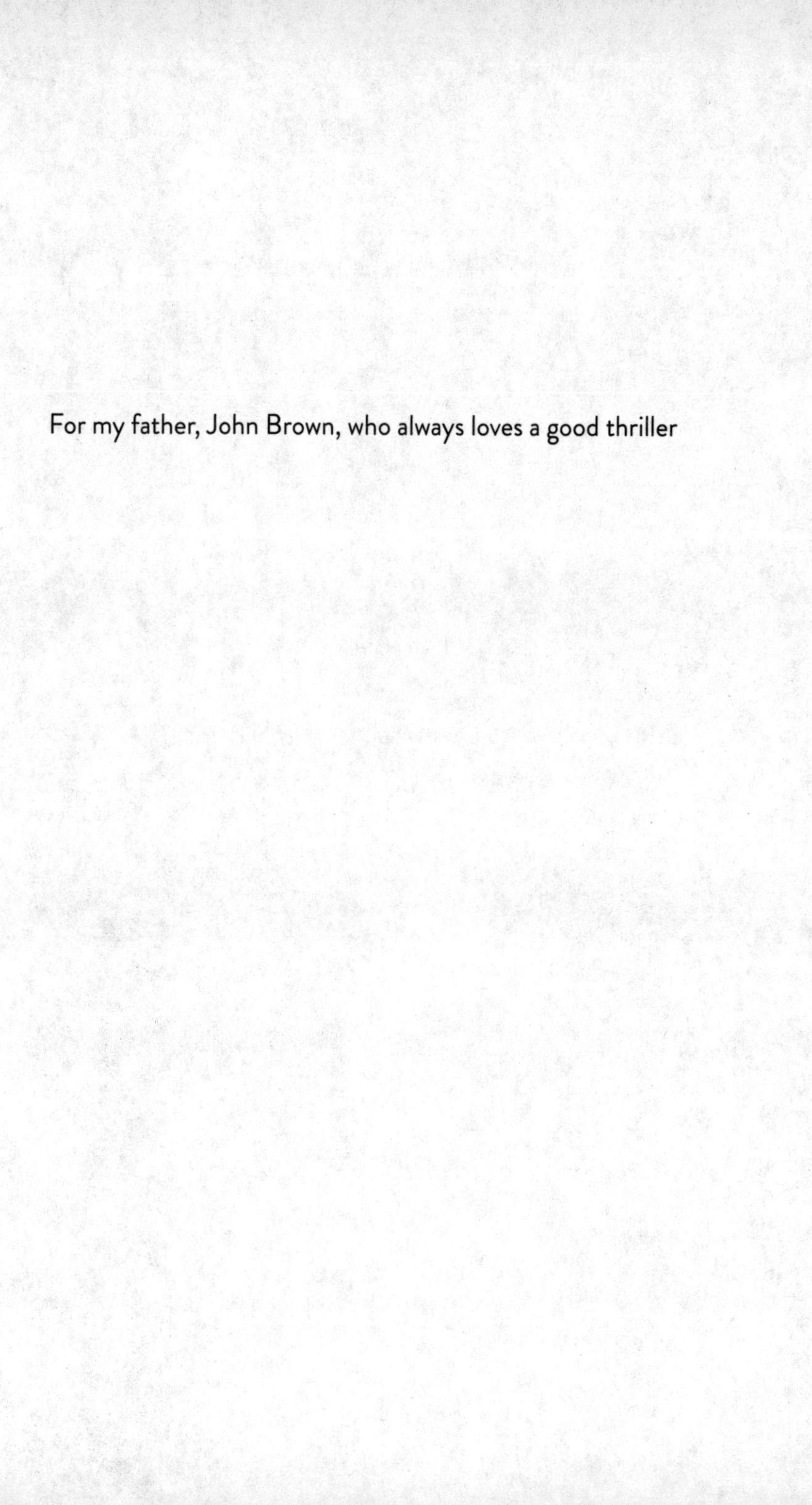

For my father, John Brown, who always loves a good thriller

ONE

CHEF BOYARDEE IS SMILING AT ME.

Put me in your pocket and walk out the door, his voice whispers in my ear—it's louder than the ringing I've been hearing the last day or so. *Then find a quiet place to smash me open with a rock and use your fingers to shovel this delicious and one-hundred-percent organic Beefaroni into your mouth until that burning pit in your stomach is plugged and you aren't going to die.*

Because I *will* die.

It's been almost three days since I've eaten, and I walked into the corner store without even trying to not look homeless, against my better judgment.

Judgment. Like that even exists anymore. I've been bathing in Starbucks bathroom sinks for eight months. What judgment could I possibly have left?

The cashier has been watching me with his noodle eyes since I walked in the door. Delicious noodle eyes.

I turn to glance at him over my shoulder and there he is. Still watching.

Not with eyes made of noodles—brains struggle when starved—but with narrowed, dark eyes like a shark. I haven't taken the Beefaroni yet, which is why he's *letting* me sit here staring at the can.

The can that's absolutely not organic. It also doesn't need to be bashed open with a rock because it's a pull tab, but my nutrition-deprived brain doesn't care about continuity.

It only cares that I get that Beefaroni into my stomach right now.

I can still feel the eyes of the cashier on my back. He's a white guy in his forties. It's probably his store, which is why he's staring so intently at someone who's attempting to cut into his profit margin.

Part of me wants to walk right up to him, pull the tab off, and shove as much food into my mouth as I can. To see if he even cares. Maybe he'd pity me and let me go.

But that's where I am right now. So desperate for food I'm willing to look like an absolute lunatic to get something in my stomach.

As if egging me on, my stomach rumbles. But not a normal rumble, because now the cramps that paralyzed me yesterday are back. I put the can down and brace myself against the metal shelf, waiting for the wave of pain to pass. Three days without food has been my limit since I left home eight months ago.

The door chime sounds, announcing more of an audience coming to see me looking desperate. I ignore it as the cramps slowly fade.

Then I take a deep breath and pick the can back up. I need this. And I don't care if the shop clerk is watching me; what's he going to do? Chase me down the street?

But he's talking to whoever came in. If they went right over to him, it was probably to buy cigarettes or vapes behind the counter. I can't hear what they're talking about, but the clerk is distracted enough.

So I slip the can into my pocket. I reach up and pull the other cans on the shelf forward so it doesn't look like one was taken.

Then I turn toward the front of the store, ready to make a quick, quiet exit.

Instead I stop in my tracks. Because there's a cop standing right at the end of the aisle, staring at me as though he's disappointed. My eyes flit over to the counter, where another cop is talking to the clerk, but they're both looking at me.

I'm so stupid.

I was so distracted by starvation, cramps, and overall desperation that I didn't even think to look for cops. Something I've been so good about.

And now, because of one little mistake, they're going to arrest me and send me back to my parents.

"I'll put it back," I say.

But the cop—a middle-aged white guy with a mustache—just says, "Wouldn't matter if you did."

"Please. I was hungry and didn't have any money."

His eyebrows drop as he sizes me up. "How old are you?"

Shit.

"Eighteen," I lie. What's another year and ten months?

"ID?"

I shake my head. It's in my backpack, which is stashed under a Starbucks dumpster two blocks away. The dumpster they started locking up at night to keep people like me from grabbing the unsold food.

"What's your name?" he asks. But I stay quiet. If I don't answer, they can't put me in some system. And they also can't send me home. I doubt my parents even told anyone I ran away, so it's not like my info will show up in their database, but if I *am* being arrested for shoplifting, at least I can hide my real name so I don't have a criminal record.

The cop sighs and takes out his handcuffs. As he walks slowly down the aisle toward me, I beg him not to do it. But it doesn't matter. This guy doesn't care who I am or what I've been through. To him, I did something illegal, and that means my whole fucking life should be ruined.

As he turns me around and puts the handcuffs on my wrists—a little too tight, if you ask me—I can't help but think this never would have happened if my parents loved me.

TWO

Eight Months Ago

THE DAY EVERYTHING CHANGES IS A BEAUTIFUL DAY. There's no reason for me to feel like my whole life is about to blow up. But I'm sure everyone feels like that before the moment their lives go off the rails.

The first shock comes when I see Dad's car in the driveway behind Mom's.

They're both home? At three thirty in the afternoon?

Maybe someone at church died. The last time this happened was my grandmother's funeral, but the thought causes an ache in my chest and little needle pricks at my eyes, so I ignore it and open the front door, putting my bag on the floor.

There's a stranger in our living room.

He's a broad-shouldered white man with dark blond hair and a thin beard that makes him look more creepy than handsome. He's wearing a baggy blue polo shirt with a gold-stitched cross and matching lettering below that says "Holy Re-Beginnings," which I fucking hate.

My mom and dad are sitting on opposite sides of the couch, and he's in a chair across from them. Neither of them look at me, but the creep-o gives me a smile. His teeth look yellow against his pale skin and blond beard.

"Hi," I say.

"Nice to meet you," the man says. "Why don't you have a seat?" He gestures to the space between my parents and immediately, warning bells start going off.

Who the hell is this man? And why am I supposed to sit between my parents, who won't even look at me, when I don't think we've ever sat down on that couch together at the same time once in my entire life?

Then it hits me. My parents look *ashamed*.

Divorce.

It's my first and immediate thought because my parents are *not* in love. They've never said it explicitly, but I know what subtext is. They don't love each other, like they don't love me.

I learned that last part in fifth grade. I won a prize for a short story competition at school. My story was about us finding a hidden treasure chest filled with pirates' gold in the local state park. When I came home and showed them the story and the twenty-five-dollar gift card to a local restaurant, my dad skimmed the story quickly.

Then he ripped it up and held it in front of me like a cartoon dad would brandish a rolled-up newspaper at the family dog that piddled on the floor.

"This is about greed," he scolded. "Greed is a sin." Then he snatched the gift card out of my hand and proceeded to cut it into pieces before throwing it and my story in the trash.

The whole time, my mother stood silently by.

If my dad had read the whole five-page, double-spaced manuscript, he would have found that at the end we decided not to spend the gold and donated it to a hospital to help people.

But now they're getting a divorce and, honestly, I feel a little giddy.

I have so many questions. What made them finally decide to do it? Whose idea was it? Who am I going to live with? Mom, obviously, because according to devout Christians, raising kids is women's work. Am I going to have a stepparent? Holy shit, is this creep in the polo and shitty beard my new step-Chad—er, dad?

I sit down, eager to see where this is going.

"My name is Garrett," Step-Chad says—Step-Garrett doesn't have the same ring. "I'm from Holy Re-Beginnings."

"What is a re-beginning?" I ask.

"A fresh start."

Yep, definitely divorce. Also, why not call it Holy Fresh Starts? Probably because that sounds like something Robin would say to Batman. Noted, Step-Chad. Please continue.

"A fresh start for who?" I ask. But again, I know it's my dad, because my mom would never stand up to him.

"For you," Step-Chad says.

Some dipshit on the imagination highway in my brain slams on the brakes and causes a million-thought pileup that quickly reaches a standstill because what does he mean, *for me*? I turn to look at my mother, then my father. But they both avoid my gaze.

"Sorry, is this some kind of . . . after-school program?" My brain won't say the words my heart knows.

"A camp!" Garrett says it like I'm supposed to be excited.

My first thought is conversion therapy—but that's not possible because I'm not out. My parents don't know I'm gay; not even my friends at school know I'm gay. But then my stomach seizes. Because one person *does* know.

"We've helped a lot of kids in your situation," he continues. He says *situation* like I'm stuck up to my neck in drying concrete, not attracted to other guys. "I was once in your place, too."

And he thinks he's cured. When I was eleven and I realized I was in love with Travis Lincoln because he talked to me in fourth-period science, I looked up camps like this. I was still worried about going to hell back then because I thought hell was real.

But thankfully I also found the Reddit threads that talked about people's experiences at those camps. And most important, how it didn't work. Regardless of what torture these people signed up for—or were sent to against their will—it didn't change who they were.

So I came out to the one person I trusted because I knew she was gay, too. It was a secret language we used to communicate through six years of church events and after-school Bible study.

There's no way she would out me, though. Even if we're not as close as we used to be.

Garrett seems to read my mind because he grins and says, "We've even helped one of your friends."

Oh, Frankie. *No.*

She came back from summer break refusing to talk to me. I thought she was pissed at me for not reaching out to her more after she told me she was going to her aunt's house in Maine for the summer.

She told me over a DM in June. It was the first time she'd mentioned going to her aunt's, and I was kind of pissed because we had so many plans. She had gotten her driver's license and she and her older sister were sharing a car. We were going to drive to DC and check out the queer bookstore and go to the Pride parade.

The realization hits that the DM may not have come from her. Especially if her parents sent her to this place. They must have taken her phone and seen the messages we shared, then sent me the aunt excuse.

We thought we were being so careful. Our fake social media profiles that we didn't use real names on, not even in our messages. We had code names, so how did her parents know it was me?

"Did she tell you?" I ask him, my voice shaking. I can't say the rest aloud because maybe I can still come back from this. So I clear my throat and try again. "What did she tell you?"

"I know what you're thinking," Garrett says with his righteous smile. Because he thinks he's better than me. He's been lying to himself for so long he thinks he's managed to find a way to change who he is by torturing it out of other people.

He continues, "She didn't rat you out. Frankie wants to *save* you. Save your immortal soul."

By torturing my earthly body.

I can't be mad at her. As much as I want to be, I know it's not her fault. She was brainwashed. But I thought she was stronger. She *seemed* so much stronger than me. More knowledgeable and filled with pride. The good pride, not the twisted, sinful, religious idea of pride.

I feel sick.

I can't let this happen. I'm not going with him. I have to get out of here.

But I can't run. I've read all about this online. It starts with him, Garrett, here alone in the house—he's the friendly, charismatic face who wants to take me without any fight or argument. But if I *do* fight, they have more people waiting in the van parked outside that I didn't notice because I was too distracted by my mom's and dad's cars in the driveway.

So I have to play along.

"Okay," I say. And it's not hard to cry because I'm terrified and so fucking angry. I turn to my parents, but neither of them will look at me. That shame on their faces is because of me. Because Frankie told this camp I was gay, too, and they told her parents, who told mine.

They're ashamed that I ruined their good Christian name.

My eyes burn and I choke back a sob. "I'll go with you. I've struggled with this for so long."

I'm not talking about being gay. It's *them* I've struggled with. This feeling that I'm supposed to love the people who are supposed to love me. But they don't. For so long I made excuses; I thought, eventually, if I didn't piss them off—if I pretended to agree with their unhinged thoughts on politics and humanity—they might be proud of me.

But they'll never be proud of me. Even if it were possible to fundamentally change who I am, they'll never love me. They didn't love me before—my creativity, my imagination, my *soul*—so why would they love the kid they had to pay thousands of dollars to cure of his queerness?

Garrett eases up and nods. "I'm so happy to hear you say that. And I know your parents are, too."

I nod and stand up. "So we go now, right?" I'm hoping the answer is no, but my eagerness throws him off. If he says yes, I have to run, as fast as I can. Leave everything and go.

But he doesn't say yes. Instead he holds up his hands, laughing. "Gosh, I just love your enthusiasm! You might want to pack a bag first. Just enough for a day or two of travel. We have a uniform while you're with us."

Without saying another word, I go back to the front door and grab my backpack. I make a show of unpacking my books and setting them on the floor, then head to my room.

Locking the door behind me, I fall to the ground. Now the sobs really hit and I bury my face in my elbow, trying to stifle them. But then I laugh. It's the hysterical laughter of absurdity and it catches me completely off guard.

Because I realize that if my parents had confronted me—if they had *looked* at me, said one thing out there while Garrett was trying to pitch this to me—I actually might have believed they love me. That they're making this choice because they think it's best for me. But they just sat there, looking ashamed.

Ashamed and embarrassed by their queer son. They're scared this is a ding on their heavenly scorecard. Like people who raise gay kids don't go to heaven.

Fuck that.

I can run.

So I wipe the tears from my cheeks and pack as many of my clothes as will fit in my backpack. Then I go to my secret stash of money that I'd been planning to use doing fun gay stuff over the summer with Frankie.

There's only a hundred and seventeen bucks, but it's enough to get me to a city. I'll take a cheap train or a bus and go to DC or Baltimore. They have shelters for kids like me who have to run from home.

There's still enough suspicion in my mind to look out the window for people waiting before I open it. I turn back one more time to look at my bedroom.

It feels like something I'm required to do. Like I'm taking a snapshot to remember it by. But I don't want to remember it. I don't need to. If Garrett brought a gun with him and put it to my head, demanding I tell him one good memory about this place, about my family, I don't know that I'd be able to.

"This," I whisper to myself. Leaving is the good memory I'll have.

I push out the screen. And I run.

THREE

I HOLD TIGHT TO THAT MEMORY OF LEAVING, WHEN everything felt possible. But now I'll be sent back.

This police station smells damp and chemically. As though it was recently mopped with dirty water that someone added a capful of lavender-scented bleach to. Only I've been handcuffed to a chair in the waiting area for over an hour and the smell hasn't changed, so I don't think it matters when the mopping happened; it just always smells like this. Perpetually un-Fabuloso.

I'm getting antsy and panicked. Like a trapped animal. When he put the cuffs on, Baldy-Cop made them tighter than they needed to be—my left wrist is starting to chafe.

And my stomach cramps are getting worse.

My ID is still in my bag under the Starbucks dumpster, but all they have to do is give me food and I'll tell them everything. Whatever they want in exchange for anything in the vending machine to my right.

I turn to stare at the Honey Bun teasing me from B7. My mouth is somehow dry and sticky at the same time as it struggles to produce saliva. My stomach grumbles again.

At least in juvie I'll get food.

When I left home, I underestimated how hard it would be to find food on my own. Before I got rid of my phone, I looked up a queer youth shelter and decided to get on a train to DC. I thought I could walk through the front doors and they'd find a place for me. That I'd have a newfound family of queer kids who had been through the same thing I had.

I didn't realize how *many* queer kids have already been through what I have. Or worse.

There was no room for me. The social worker called around to other shelters—even some in Baltimore, Philly, and New York—but everywhere was understaffed and they didn't have the room or the budget.

So the social worker told me the only option they had was to call Child Protective Services.

I knew what that meant. They'd call my parents and tell them where I was. Then they'd put me in foster care or a group home until my parents came to get me. I begged the social worker not to, but she tried to tell me they would be involved and looking after me, even at home.

They didn't understand what that meant. Private conversion therapy is still legal in West Virginia, and a parent has the right to send their child there if they think it's for the best. CPS wouldn't be able to stop that. There's also plenty of ways these companies get around the words *conversion therapy*.

So, like I did when Garrett showed up, I ran.

And no one chased me.

There were plenty of people who helped me survive. Other homeless people who had been at it longer gave me the best pointers they could, the biggest one being *Don't get arrested.* If that happened, I'd be in the system and I'd never be able to get a job, and it would affect my ability to get housing. I didn't tell them I was more worried about being sent home to my parents.

And here I am, waiting to be booked.

I'll need to survive whatever conversion therapy throws at me and then lie for two more years. I can do that.

But the thought makes me sick—and this time it isn't because I'm hungry.

Arrrrre you surrrre about thaaaaat? the strawberry Pop-Tarts in C4 ask me.

I turn away from them. Stare at the bulletin board on my left. It's plastered with paper printouts from the National Center for Missing & Exploited Children. They're all printed in color with the word *MISSING* at the top in dark red. Some of them aren't kids anymore. Their posters say they went missing when they were preteens, but that was years ago.

One of the posters catches my attention.

Because it's me.

I almost get up to take a closer look—completely forgetting I'm handcuffed to this chair—but my body won't let me. Maybe it's the starvation taking hold, but I'm stuck in place. My parents reported me missing. Maybe they feel bad or changed their minds. Maybe they really do want me.

And for a second, I imagine what it might be like to go home. To see my family again. If they are looking for me, maybe it means they *do* love me. Maybe, in my absence, they got a look at life without me, and that glimpse was enough to make them see past their bullshit religious hang-ups and realize they actually love their only child.

But whatever teeny bit of hope I may have dissolves instantly when I see the name on the poster.

Nathaniel Beaumont.

It's not me. It's some other kid who has been missing for almost ten years.

Below his name it says: *Nathaniel's photo is shown age-progressed to age 16.*

The picture of him was generated with a computer, but it looks like me. His brown hair is shorter because whoever the artist is—or maybe it's AI at this point—made it look like his hair had been cut and styled instead of grown out like mine. And the smile is off. It's the only thing that gives it away as a computer-generated image. Our noses are similar, though the bridge of mine is more prominent—something I hate about myself—and Nathaniel's ears stick out a bit like mine, too. Another thing I hate.

More than anything else, though, it's his eyes. They're the same gray-blue shade as mine. My dad's eyes, really.

Looking at the age-progressed picture gives me chills. It's like an alternate-reality me. From another world where with different parents I still had to run away from home and—

No. He didn't run away. According to the poster, he was six when he disappeared. Ten years missing in July.

Which means he had parents who wanted him. Lucky kid.

Is that sick? It's definitely sick. But if I were him—meaning if my parents were like his—and they found Nathaniel today, there's no way they'd care if he happened to be gay. His poor parents have probably spent every day for the last decade believing he was dead. Or maybe they spent those days hoping and praying he was alive and safe somewhere.

If they got the call that he'd been found, they would be so happy. They'd have their kid back. And Nate wouldn't be scared and alone anymore. He'd be safe with people who loved him.

I wish I could have that. A place where I can feel safe and not worry about where I'm going to find my next meal or where I'm going to sleep. I'm so tired of running.

Almost ten years is a long time to be missing, though. He wouldn't even be the same kid who disap—

A chill makes every hair on my body stand on end.

But before the thought seed can even root, I pluck it out. That would be too fucked up, even for me. I couldn't steal some missing kid's identity.

And there must be ways of verifying my story. DNA tests they'd give immediately to make sure I am who I say I am. Even though it's been nine years and so many months, I still feel like his parents would know if I was really their son.

"All right, your turn." I look up at the policewoman walking toward me. She's a short white woman with shoulder-length, curly red hair. She bends down with a key and unlocks the cuff that's tethered me to the chair for the past hour and a half. "Put out your right hand, please."

I do as she says, and she puts the cuff back on my right wrist, then motions for me to stand.

"Come this way." She turns and heads around the reception desk. I take one last look at Nathaniel's picture before following her.

Let's say I'm Nathaniel Beaumont. What does this woman do? Types my name into a system and sees that I've been missing for almost ten years. Then what?

Ahead of me, the woman reaches her desk and motions to the chair next to it. I sit.

"Right." The woman—her name tag reads "R. Walters"—sighs and turns her attention to me. "Name, hon?"

If I borrowed Nathaniel's name, just for a bit, maybe Nathaniel's parents wouldn't even have to meet me. If the cops took me to the hospital for the DNA test, or at least uncuffed me and left me out in the waiting area, I could make a run for it.

If I disappeared again, the police would know I wasn't Nathaniel at all. They'd realize I saw the missing poster, took his identity, and played them. They'd apologize, and the family—if they ever found out—could sue and they'd get a nice settlement.

Or am I lying to myself? Making myself feel better for what I already know I'm going to do? My choices are simple: Tell the truth and go home, followed by conversion therapy and torture. Or I tell this officer I'm Nathaniel Beaumont and maybe go to a hospital, uncuffed, while they verify my story. I need a moment to breathe. I need to not be fighting every damn day.

Think of something else. Anything else!

"Nathaniel," I say. Officer Walters types it in, then looks back at me for the last name. "Beaumont." I spell it for her, and she thanks me.

She opens her mouth to ask something else but stops. Her eyes dart around the screen and she clicks something.

She looks at the computer, then at me again.

She's very interested in me now. The boredom is completely gone from her face.

"Holy shit," she says under her breath.

Holy shit indeed.

FOUR

EVERYTHING AFTER THAT HAPPENS SO FAST I BARELY have a second to think.

First they uncuff me.

Then they put me in an interrogation room, where they don't interrogate me but instead give me water and doughnuts—apparently that cliché about cops is true. Of course I try to eat too quickly and throw it all up. Once my vomit is cleaned, I try again, taking small bites until the doughnut is gone, then reach for another.

After that, people come in to talk to me. A beautiful middle-aged Black woman with long, straight black hair pulled to the right side. She says her name is Detective Hall, and she has a man with her, a tall and skinny white guy with a salt-and-pepper crew cut wearing a nicely fitted suit. She introduces him as Supervisory Special Agent Grant.

FBI.

Grant looks as if he's about to say something but thinks better of it. The detective asks me question after question while Agent Grant watches from the doorway. She asks me my name again, where I'm from, where I've been, what I'm doing in DC.

I give her quick, concise lies—keeping track of them as I go along. I'm nervous at first, but then it starts to feel familiar. I used to lie to my friends and family all the time. If I went to a party, I'd tell my parents I was going to a church event. Then I would go there for an hour first, in case they asked anyone if I was there. I lied to church friends and school friends, and didn't tell them I was gay.

Until Frankie. She was the one person who saw who I really was, because she was lying, too. While it felt like we were the only two gay kids in our grade, we knew it wasn't true. But we also knew we had to lie. To keep up appearances so we weren't tormented incessantly.

Detective Hall asks follow-up questions that I avoid or try not to provide too much information on.

Where are your parents?

Where did you live?

Who did you live with?

How long have you been living on the street?

I don't want to give an address that could eventually be traced back to my real family and I can't just make one up. If it's not real, that's a dead giveaway. But if it *is* real, I'm making some random person a suspect in a child kidnapping. So I act overwhelmed and tell her I can't remember. When she presses me on it, which she does over and over and over, I finally say I won't speak anymore without a lawyer. She tells me I'm no longer under arrest, but even if that's true—which it's not—they could change their minds and tell a judge I *was* under arrest and chose not to remain silent.

Agent Grant watches, letting Detective Hall do all the questioning. Never once does he ask for clarification or more details. He stands in the open doorway, watching, and because he's so quiet, he's the one who scares me most. But then he leaves.

After that, two new officers take me to a hospital, but every time I try to ask what's happening, they pass the buck to someone else. The officer tasked with watching me in the emergency room says the doctor will explain. The doctor says the police will explain. The nurse says the doctor *or* the police will explain. All while they keep asking invasive questions and doing the tests they do to any missing kid who turns up out of the blue.

But the longer this goes on, the faster everything moves along. It's like a speeding train out of control, and I know the track ahead is out. At some point they're going to test the DNA in the blood sample the nurse took. Or they're going to catch me in a lie. Or they're going to find out the real Nathaniel Beaumont was found dead two weeks ago and they never got around to taking down that missing child alert.

This was a huge mistake. No resting tonight; I need to get out of here immediately.

Finally, a little after two in the afternoon, I'm shown to a room in the pediatric ward. Then things start to calm. Once I'm in the bed and the nurse comes to check my vitals—clipping a pulse oximeter onto my finger and checking my temperature—I realize I still don't have my clothes. They had me put them in a plastic bag and change into a gown and itchy, thin pants.

I ask the nurse where my clothes are, and she says she'll find out for me. When she leaves, I get up and poke my head out the door.

To my right is the nurses' station and elevator. The police officer babysitting me is sitting in a chair staring at his phone.

To my left are more rooms, a bathroom, and at the end of the hall is an exit sign.

My way out.

They still haven't come back to handcuff me, so I am assuming the results of the DNA test they're doing—or are planning on doing—haven't come back yet. As soon as the nurse is back with my clothes, I'll change and slip out as fast as I can.

My stomach growls again. Now that I've eaten something, the hunger pangs are worse. Like my stomach can remember the idea of fullness and now craves it.

Maybe the hospital will feed me before I run.

No. I can't risk staying here any longer than I need to. As soon as I have my clothes, I have to get out of here.

So I wait, and wait. The nurse comes back to check on me, and I remind her about my clothes. She says she's going to find out, again. Then tells me she's going to have some food brought up for me.

I'm craving the high-speed way that time was moving only an hour ago. Now I feel stuck. The bullet train to the end of the line has slowed, but not enough for me to jump off. And it's agony.

Finally, around four, Detective Hall appears in the doorway with a few others, including a doctor, a woman I haven't met yet, and Agent Grant.

And this is it. My blood test came back and they know I'm not Nathaniel Beaumont.

I sit up.

Detective Hall steps to the side of the door while Agent Grant stays outside.

The doctor comes in. I forget her name; she was the third new doctor to come say hello to me down in the ER when they were giving me checkups.

"Hi, Nate," she says, and it catches me off guard. They wouldn't be calling me Nate if they tested my blood and found out it didn't match Nathaniel Beaumont's family's. And she doesn't look like she's trying to catch me in a lie. She looks like she's trying to be kind. "I want to introduce you to someone. This is a pediatric psychologist, Dr. Zapata."

She motions to the woman behind her, who steps into the room.

Dr. Zapata is a short woman with fair skin and straight dark brown shoulder-length hair. She wears dark jeans, an untucked button-down, and a navy blazer. She has a friendly face but her expression stops short of a smile.

"Hi, Nate, it's nice to meet you."

They're still calling me Nate. And they have a psychologist. Which means maybe they think my lies were temporary insanity and they have the shrink here to talk me through it before cuffing me again. That's nice of them, at least.

I don't say anything, and in the silence there's a commotion in the hallway. Agent Grant steps away from the door and begins talking to someone. Two someones. There's a back-and-forth between them, and Detective Hall goes out to join them.

"What's going on?" I ask.

Dr. Zapata's lips drop to a straight line as her brow furrows. She opens her mouth, but the woman from the hallway shouts over whatever she was going to say.

"I don't give a shit, I want to see my son!"

Son.

Shit. No, no, *no.* They wouldn't have told this poor family I'm their son without confirming it, right? Like with scientific evidence that stands up in a court?

Another voice—a man—calls after her. "Val!"

The woman pushes Detective Hall aside, and behind her Agent Grant moves out of the way, looking like this is all getting away from him. When the woman glares at her, Dr. Zapata looks frustrated but steps aside.

She's a tall, skinny white woman with wavy brown hair wearing maroon scrubs and a long gray cardigan. And she has eyes the same shade as mine.

Nathaniel Beaumont's mother. And from the way she's looking at me, they definitely didn't tell her that I'm not Nathaniel.

FIVE

NATHANIEL'S MOM—THOUGH EVERYONE HAS BEEN CALL-ing me Nate, so maybe that's how his parents referred to him—looks as if she's seeing, well, someone pretending to be her son who's been missing for over nine years.

She stares at me from the doorway, mouth agape and tears welling in her eyes.

This is so fucked up. It never should have gotten this far. I was hoping they would try to confirm my identity before contacting Nate's parents. Then I'd have a chance to make a run for it before the blood test came back. Maybe in the middle of the night while the nurse on duty is tired and distracted. But here's Nate's family, expecting to see him and finding an imposter instead. Guilt churns my stomach.

I open my mouth to apologize, but I can't make my voice work.

"Nate" is all Nate's mother says. "Oh my . . ." She breaks into sobs and crosses the room so fast it takes my breath away.

Wait.

She called me Nate.

She can't seriously think I'm him? This isn't right. She squeezes me tight, sobbing, and I can't help it. I'm surprised to find that I'm crying, too.

Why am I crying? And why am I hugging her back so tightly? I don't even know this woman. Maybe being alone for the past eight months has gotten to me more than I thought it could. I don't even know when the last time I got a hug was. And if I think even harder, I don't remember *ever* being hugged by my mom or dad.

She lets go and holds me at arm's length. Tears spill from my eyes as sobs rack my body.

Nate's mom wipes away my tears with her thumbs and looks into my eyes. "It's okay, pumpkin. It's okay."

Movement draws my eyes to the doorway and I see a tall, portly man with salt-and-pepper hair, a dark mustache, and thick eyebrows. He has broad shoulders and a belly that sticks out against a blue shirt and dark suit.

This must be Nate's dad. He doesn't look at me the way his wife does. He's more guarded. Because in his heart he knows something isn't right about all this. Maybe he's the pessimist in their relationship. Or maybe he decided long ago that Nate was dead while his wife held on to hope.

Hope that I'm probably going to destroy.

Someone else steps around him. It's a young man, probably a few years older than me. But the family resemblance is there. He's tall and broad, like his father beside him, but he's lean like the mother, who still holds me tight. The young man—Nate's brother, I assume—wears a fashionable button-down tucked into slacks and gives me the clearest look of suspicion out of everyone in the family.

Dr. Zapata is talking quietly to the other doctor, Detective Hall, and Agent Grant. Nate's father still watches me. Finally Dr. Zapata turns back to us.

"We'll give you all some time together." Her eyes lock on me. "But Detective Hall and Agent Grant will have to talk with you some more after. I'll be here, too." She looks at Nate's parents, ignoring the brother. "The two of you are more than welcome to stay, but I would advise you to step outside in case there's anything—"

"Absolutely not," Nate's mom says. She grips my hand and looks into my eyes as she brushes my hair away from them. "We're not going anywhere."

"Okay." Dr. Zapata ushers everyone else outside and Nate's brother shuts the door behind her. Then he crosses his arms and leans against the wall, regarding me with what I can only imagine is suspicion.

Nate's mom sits down on the side of the bed. Her hands brush my cheeks, and she looks me up and down. "Oh, my baby. Are you okay? Did they hurt you?"

"Valencia." Nate's father says her name like a warning.

She sighs and shakes her head. "Sorry. Dr. Zapata says we shouldn't press you without her here. I just . . . oh!" She pulls me into a tight hug. "We've missed you so much. Are you . . . are you okay?"

Nate's dad steps forward and puts a gentle hand on Valencia Beaumont's shoulder. "Hon, you heard—"

"I don't care. This is our *son*, I'm going to ask him if he's okay as much as I damn well please."

Nate's dad steps back again and crosses his arms, matching the posture of his older son, who still hasn't said anything. When his dad looks at me, it's not with love, but more curiosity. It's a look that stops just short of saying, *I know you're not my son.* Nate's mom is the only one in this room who believes I'm really Nate. How long before they convince her of the truth? I don't know what to do or say, so I keep on doing what I've been doing.

Lie.

"I'm okay," I say. "A little confused." My eyes drift back to Nate's maybe-brother, who stares at me, stone-faced.

Beside him, Nate's dad scoffs. "I think that's going around today."

Valencia nods and grabs my hand. "We're going to sort everything out. Then we'll take you home."

"That's not him, Mom," the young man across the room says.

Mom. Obviously my intuition about him being Nate's brother was right. Like his intuition is about me. Nate's brother gestures toward me as though I'm a piece of trash he passed on the street—which, okay, valid. But my stomach clenches. He's right, and I need to tell them.

But before I can, Valencia turns to him and says his name in a scolding tone: "Easton!"

Easton Beaumont.

Something in his look motivates me, and before I even know what my brain is doing, I stare directly into his eyes and reply, "It's okay. He was always jealous of me."

Easton's eyebrows go up in surprise, then he tilts his head and the corner of his mouth slips into an almost-grin. His dad looks between the two of us, not sure what to say. But Valencia laughs and wipes a tear from her eye.

I don't know why I said that. Maybe because I was so sure they'd know I wasn't really Nate—and to be fair, his dad still doesn't seem convinced—that it felt like a challenge. And maybe now, after meeting this family, I'm jealous, too. Jealous for the life Nate had before he disappeared.

For the first time, I think of Nate and wonder what *did* happen to him.

The mood in the room lifts, and even Easton allows his grin to expand.

"So where the hell have you been?" Easton asks. It's almost as if he's reading my mind, and I get a chill.

Easton's dad holds up his hands. "No, we need to have the doctor and police in here if we're going to talk about this."

Easton snorts. "You *want* the cops in here?" His eyes drift over to me, and he grins in a conspiratorial way. "I'd hire a new lawyer if I were you."

Lawyer?

"I'm not his lawyer. I . . . ," Mr. Beaumont starts, but his voice drifts off. Was he about to say "I'm his father"? Or "I don't give a rat's ass what happens to this kid"? Instead, he shakes his head and says, "You don't need a lawyer anyway. Shoplifting is a misdemeanor at best, and since you were kidnapped, they aren't even pressing charges."

"Great, so I'm free to go?" I pretend to stand up—only half joking, honestly, because it would be wonderful if they let me leave.

Valencia puts a gentle hand against my upper arm. "Not yet. They're going to keep you overnight for observation. You're dehydrated and malnourished. But tomorrow you'll come home with us."

She says it like it's supposed to be a good thing, and maybe for

Nate Beaumont it would be. But I have to fight not to shake my head. I can't go home with these people. The DNA test is going to come back eventually. The Beaumonts probably gave a sample when they got to the hospital. Maybe it takes a few days to get the results back. It'll be even worse if they get a call that I'm not their son while I'm *living* with them. They're going to find out I'm not Nate eventually; it's better if it happens before I go home with them.

I have to run tonight.

Nate's father sighs and leans against the wall. "Easton comes home for summer break and we suddenly have two teen boys to feed. We're never getting that boat I want."

"Marcus," Valencia scolds him, but she does it with a smile. And thankfully now I know his name.

"Kidding," he says. Then he stares into the distance as if he's doing math in his head. "I can probably still get the boat."

"You don't need a boat," she says, her joking demeanor slowly dropping.

"I mean, no one *needs* a boat," I say, trying to defuse the thickening tension in the room. "They're just nice to have." I don't know anything about owning a boat, but it sounds nice.

Valencia laughs, clamping her hand over her mouth. Marcus grins and maybe even looks proud of me?

Again I'm reminded of how quickly everything has gotten out of hand. I'm pretending to be their son, and they expect me to go home with them.

How would it hurt them if I ran off again? To them, they finally have their son. Easton has his brother back.

I shouldn't care. These are strangers, and I'm pretending to be their kid because it was the only way I could think of to avoid being sent back to my own asshole parents, who were ready to ship me off to some camp to be tortured into a kid they still wouldn't love.

But stoking those bitter, ever-burning thoughts of my own family betraying me isn't enough, because Valencia's arms go around me again and it feels wonderful. It's enough to block any negative feelings I have about my real parents, and about these lies I'm telling this family, because this family is here, and they're willing to fight for me.

For a brief moment, my logic reminds me they're here to fight for *Nate*, not me, but I bat the thought away and just enjoy Valencia's embrace.

SIX

DR. ZAPATA SPENDS THE AFTERNOON TALKING WITH ME and Nate's parents—Easton is sent down to the cafeteria despite his objections. Detective Hall interjects with a few of her own questions when the conversation allows. She asks me about my kidnapping and where I've been, but I don't offer any real answers. I keep everything vague and dodge as many questions as I can without looking suspicious.

If anyone *is* suspicious, they have great poker faces. Even Marcus seems to be believing it all a little easier now. Agent Grant, on the other hand, remains stoic and unreadable.

Still, it doesn't hurt my case that Dr. Zapata says post-traumatic amnesia is common in kidnappings. At one point before asking some darker questions, she asks if Nate's parents would like to leave the room. Marcus looks as though he wants to, but Valencia says no and reaches for my hand.

Of course Dr. Zapata asks about sexual abuse, because why wouldn't you ask that of a kidnapping victim, but I make sure she knows there wasn't any. I'm okay with lying about who I am to get out of jail, but sexual abuse victims are rarely believed to begin with, and there's no way I'm contributing to that by lying about it myself.

Weird how my morals are so clear-cut on some things, but not others. Manipulating grieving families? Okay! Lying about sexual assault? Definitely not okay!

"I'm sorry, but how much longer do we need to talk about this?" I finally ask. It's all starting to hit me—exactly what I'm doing here—and I hate it. I hate how kind these two parents are; lying to them makes me feel awful. Maybe there was another way I could have avoided going to juvie, but I still can't figure it out. Not that it matters, because I'm already in too deep.

Dr. Zapata nods. "You're right, we should probably pause for the day."

Pause? How much more could there be? "No. I'd rather try and get it all done now so we can move on."

Dr. Zapata's eyes flick over to Nate's parents, then back to me. "Nate, your road to recovery is going to be a long one. You've been through immense trauma—not least of which is that you've lived on the streets for the past eight months."

I did tell them that part. But it was under the guise of me running away. I couldn't remember who or where I was running from, but I ran. It's close enough to the real story that it was easy to sell.

Valencia turns to me. "Dr. Zapata has her own practice when she's not doing consults for the hospital. We've asked that she be your psychologist."

"I'd like you to come see me at least once a week," she says. She must see that I'm about to argue, so she puts up her hands. "To start. We can add more days if you need. Or if you're adjusting to your home life okay, we can pare back."

At least the Beaumonts will have her to speak to when I disappear again. Maybe she can tell them it's part of my trauma and I'll be back one day.

"Okay," I say. I have zero intention of staying long enough to have even one session with Dr. Z.

Dr. Zapata thanks me, then tells my parents she'll call them tomorrow to set up my first appointment. She also mentions that it might be best if they go home for the night. "I understand you probably don't want to let him out of your sight again, but he should rest."

There's a fair amount of subtext in her words—maybe she discussed this when they first met, because Valencia doesn't argue with her.

"There's going to be an officer posted outside his room all night," Detective Hall says. "He'll be safe here."

"I don't need a police escort," I say, trying not to sound too anxious about the idea.

Agent Grant speaks from the corner; it's the first time he's said anything. "Until we know more about your kidnapping, we'll be keeping a close eye on you. Abductions like this are usually a single person. But with your amnesia"—he says it like he doesn't buy the excuse—"we don't know if it's one person or a bigger trafficking ring that might be looking for you. It's for your protection."

"You'll be okay, sweetie," Valencia says. Then she leans over me. I flinch slightly and she backs away, looking either sad or embarrassed. My cheeks burn. I didn't realize she was trying to kiss my forehead. No one's ever tried to do that before.

"Okay," I say, trying to move past the awkwardness. I'm not escaping from the hospital tonight. But I'm curious to know whether it's for my own protection or to make sure I'm not going to run off before they find out who I really am.

Nate's parents say goodbye to Dr. Zapata, and Detective Hall and Agent Grant go outside to talk with her some more. Valencia reaches into the bag she set on the ground and takes out a phone. She hands it over to me. "We activated a new line on one of Easton's old phones for you on the way here. Our numbers are all saved in there. If you need us, you can call or text at any time, okay?" She looks embarrassed for a second, then laughs. "And . . . I might text you good night. Or when we get home. Or from the car."

I can't help but laugh and it manages to dial down the remaining awkwardness to zero. I take the phone from her and the screen lights up. The wallpaper is a family photo of Marcus, Valencia, and Easton. They're standing on a dock, dressed in summer clothing, with the ocean behind them, all smiling as if they didn't survive a trauma together. My heart flutters, but I'm not sure if it's guilt again or the idea of being a part of a happy family.

"Thank you," I say.

"We'll be back tomorrow," Marcus says.

"We'll stop somewhere on the way home to pick up some new clothes for you," Valencia adds. She goes over to my plastic bag of clothes, which the nurse finally dropped off. "What size are you now?"

"Those pants are a little big," I say.

Valencia looks at the tag, then at me, and for a second looks like she's going to cry again, but she nods quickly.

She comes back and kisses me on the cheek before pulling me into another warm embrace. I still have to fight not to flinch. When she's done, Marcus even comes over to the bed and gives me a hug, albeit a slightly more reserved one.

Then they go out into the hallway, where they talk with Detective Hall and Agent Grant.

I get up, grab my IV bag off the hook by my bed, and walk over to the door.

Agent Grant is speaking. "—advise you to order a DNA test to confirm that he is really Nate."

"You took his blood," Valencia says. "You matched his blood type to us."

What?

"Mrs. Beaumont," Detective Hall says, "blood type doesn't—"

"You said that boy in there is B-positive. Nate was B-positive because I'm O and Marcus is B-positive. Go in there and ask him whatever questions you might have. Or *look* at him, for chrissake! He is our son. I don't need you taking his DNA and ours to file in some database."

"Val." Marcus's voice sounds calm and steady. "If it will put all this to rest—"

"No," she says. "It *is* put to rest. That's our son and we're taking him home tomorrow. What are you going to do if we don't submit to a DNA test? Claim he isn't ours? Put him in foster care? You have two parents here who have missed out on almost *ten years* with their child!"

Marcus says her name again in a hushed tone, but she keeps going. "Ten years he's been missing, and you all couldn't find him. And now one of *your* officers arrested him because he was starving and had nowhere to turn. If you do try to take him away, we *will* sue you once that *court-ordered* DNA test comes back a match."

I feel like this is all a huge bluff, but Valencia is certainly selling it. Agent Grant says "Very well" and wishes them both a good evening before his dress shoes echo away down the hall.

Detective Hall sighs and says, "This is Officer Rhodes. He'll be here until six p.m., then Officer Daniels will take over until six a.m. You have my card if you need anything in the meantime. And I'll see you both in the morning."

"Thank you, Detective," Marcus says. She doesn't respond, but her footsteps head the same way Agent Grant went.

Officer Rhodes says good night to Marcus and Valencia, and their footsteps are the last to go, the two of them whispering to each other in a low argument I can't make out.

I go back and lie down in the hospital bed, raising the back a bit more so I'm sitting upright. Based on what I overheard, the police didn't test my blood to make sure I was Nate. And considering what was said between the police and Nate's parents, it sounds like it's up to Marcus and Valencia.

At least for now.

Valencia said they were going to buy me new clothes. If I do go home with them, I could pack better than when I ran away from my parents. I could get a bigger duffel bag and fill it with my new clothes. And food—I can take canned food that they won't miss. Marcus made that joke about feeding two teens. They probably wouldn't notice if food was disappearing quickly.

The idea brings my guilt right back again. Valencia was so happy to see me, to see her *son*. The one she probably thought was dead and gone years ago.

The phone they gave me vibrates on the bed next to me and I see the text notification from "Mom" on the front screen.

I unlock it—no passcode yet—and open the messages.

We're so excited to bring you home tomorrow! Sleep well, pumpkin! We love you! 😊

My chest feels a little tight reading her message.

My mom—my *real* mom—never texted me things like that. Neither of my parents even said "I love you" or "Sleep well" before going to bed. Only "Night" or "Don't forget to brush your teeth."

Good night, I send back. Then I type out love you, too. But I don't hit send. Would it be a lie for Nate to say that so soon? Would he trust these people this quickly?

Or is it meaner to say it and then run off again?

I delete the words. But she still sends a message back:

That little emoji heart is enough to bring me back to reality. I have to make sure I get away with this. At least long enough to run.

My curiosity gets the better of me, so I search Nathaniel Beaumont's name. My stomach drops because not only are there news articles dating back to his disappearance almost ten years ago, but also newer podcasts and YouTube videos about it every few years—the most recent one was posted ten months ago.

One of the earlier news articles has footage of where he was allegedly last seen: on a blurry gas station security video, sitting in the back of a blue Honda Civic driven by a woman with brown hair wearing sunglasses. But several of the later videos talking about this footage say it's not Nate. The gas station attendant had seen a kid who matched Nate's description from the Amber Alert and called the police. They never caught up to the blue Honda, and the attendant didn't catch her license plate.

I go back and start at the beginning with one of the earliest articles that isn't hidden behind a paywall.

On the afternoon of July 7, Nate was in his yard playing with his older brother, Easton. Around one in the afternoon, Easton left to go over to his friend John's house, where he stayed until four p.m. Upon returning home, he learned from Valencia that Nate hadn't been in the yard when she woke from a nap. Marcus had been out grocery shopping and returned around two p.m., but Nate wasn't there then either.

It wasn't odd for both boys to go to a friend's house or the nearby park together, so their parents weren't alarmed to see neither boy in the yard. Easton said John asked him to come over and Nate didn't want to go so he stayed behind.

The Beaumonts' house sat on the eastern shore of the Chesapeake Bay. Search and rescue scouted the area for signs of him but found nothing.

That's when the gas station tip came in. It was several hours later, from a rest stop in Pennsylvania. Since the police were treating the case as an abduction and it was now possible Nate had crossed state lines, the FBI got involved.

Agent Grant.

I put my phone down as a nurse comes in with food and more of that sugary drink they keep forcing on me. It's supposed to help starving people, but honestly it's so disgusting I kind of lose my appetite.

But the nurse sits there and watches me drink the whole thing before taking the cup and leaving again. I look at the hospital food—a dry, cheeseless burger, a fruit cup, juice, and the saddest-looking iceberg lettuce salad I've ever seen.

I'd prefer the Beefaroni.

My stomach does a little grumble, letting me know I'm going to eat it all eventually, but yeah, maybe we should pace ourselves after that disgusting drink. So I go back to reading about Nate. But all the articles are the same after that. No new leads. No sightings, no suspects—at least none that the police were willing to disclose to the press.

How does a kid go missing without a trace?

SEVEN

MARCUS AND VALENCIA SHOW UP A LITTLE AFTER NINE the next morning. Just them. There are no cops, and Valencia says Easton stayed home to finish up one of his final essays for school—which he left early when he heard they found me.

Even after they arrive, it takes almost two hours for the nurses to finally discharge me. The Beaumonts give me a new T-shirt, jeans, socks, and underwear to change into and then walk me out to an expensive-looking gray Mercedes.

From there, they take me to get my hair cleaned up and to shop for more new clothes. Valencia picks out shirt after shirt, asking if I like them while Marcus looks bored or answers emails on his phone. Several times Valencia scolds him when she thinks I'm out of earshot, and he tells her he still needs to be accessible for work.

After that we go to an awkward lunch where Valencia tries her best to update me on all the things I've missed in the ten years since I disappeared.

Mainly it's about Easton. How smart Easton is, how he graduated fifth in his class before going to Columbia, how he plays baseball—one scary moment when he hit a fastball and the ball went right at the pitcher and knocked him out. But the pitcher was fine, just a concussion. And all about Easton's ex-girlfriend, Casey, who broke up with him before he left for college.

"But don't ask about her," she says. "I think he's still a little bruised over it."

Then we drive two hours from DC to a small town in Maryland—stopping off at a Walgreens to pick up a toothbrush and deodorant. Around three in the afternoon, we pull into the driveway of a massive three-story stone colonial.

The Beaumonts live in a sprawling suburban neighborhood where every house is surrounded by mature trees and a fence line marks the edge of each huge property. Behind every home on the Beaumonts' side of the street is the dark blue of the Chesapeake Bay.

I get out of the car and look up at the house. It's made of gray-brown stone and each of the windows has dark green decorative shutters. There's a small white portico above the front door with roman-style columns.

Valencia puts her arm around my shoulders and looks up at the house with me. "Does it look how you remember?"

Out of the corner of my eye, I see Marcus turn to me. This question feels like a trap. What if it's not even the house Nate grew up in? The articles I read didn't have a picture of the house, just of six-year-old Nate. My eyes drift to the bay beyond the garage. It probably is the same house, but it might be easier to stick to the post-traumatic amnesia thing.

So I shake my head. "Sorry."

Valencia still smiles. "It's okay. We repainted the shutters last year. And five years ago we had to replace the roof. Such a shame we had to get rid of the slate, but it was so damn expensive to maintain. And these asphalt tiles aren't bad-looking."

If Valencia feels bad about having asphalt instead of slate, she should see the house I grew up in, a two-bedroom rancher with a much smaller yard. My hometown didn't have neighborhoods like this one. It was mainly ranch subdivisions, townhomes, an extremely modest "downtown" area with row homes and apartments, and a smattering of new construction on the edge of town.

But my parents weren't a lawyer and a dentist—which I learned about Valencia while I was googling the family last night.

Valencia grabs a few of the shopping bags and I take the rest. Marcus heads for the door in the garage but Valencia scolds him, telling him we should go through the front door. He sighs and gives me a look I can't read. Maybe it says *I hate my wife* or maybe it says *Always with this carefully curated way of living* or maybe *I'm tired and need to do some work.* Either way, we follow her to the front door.

I take the time to look at the houses across the street and next door. The Beaumont house is a stone colonial, but the one across the street looks like a mid-century wet dream. The road is freshly paved and completely empty except for a maroon sedan parked a few houses down.

"Oh, wait!" Valencia stops me at the door, and I take one of the shopping bags from her, freeing her hand so she can reach into her back pocket. She takes out a lone key on a key ring and holds it out to me. "Try out your key."

I take it, looking at the sharp, newly cut edges of the metal. Then I put it into the front door lock. It turns easily, and I push open the door and walk into the house. Immediately a warning alarm chimes and Valencia heads over to a keypad on the wall and types in a code to turn it off.

"Easton?" Valencia calls out. "Honey, are you home?" No one answers so she shrugs. "He must be seeing some friends. We weren't sure how today was going to go so we told him to do his thing. Sweetie, did you talk to him?"

Marcus nods. "I texted him while we were shopping. He's hanging out with JT." Marcus shuts the front door and locks it.

My throat goes dry, and I have a few seconds of panic as I realize I'm trapped with these people. I put my hand into my pocket and feel the sharp teeth of the key, slipping it between my index and middle finger. Marcus steps around me and my heartbeat slows.

Valencia says something about JT and his mother, but I don't listen, instead focusing on the house.

The entryway is a large room with stairs in the middle that lead up to a landing with a big leaded glass window looking out over the backyard and the Chesapeake. Two smaller sets of stairs branch off to the left and right of the landing.

Beneath the left side of the stairs is a doorway that looks like it leads back to the kitchen, and on the opposite side is a closed door. To my immediate right is a large entryway into a living room with a stone fireplace. To the left is a dining room. There's a white tablecloth over the table and it's set for eight, with multiple utensils, plates, and glasses at each setting.

"We also repainted," Valencia says, looking around. The walls of the entryway are an extremely light—almost white—gray. The living room is darker gray, and the dining room is beige. "Do you remember how the dining room used to be that strange, almost robin's-egg blue?"

I shake my head. "Sorry."

Valencia's smile drops. "That's okay."

The look on her face feels like a knife stabbing me. I don't know why I feel like that. I shouldn't! These are strangers and they're not my real parents. Or maybe it's because if they were my real parents, they wouldn't be trying so hard.

Is it because Valencia cares?

"Sorry, everything is a little . . . murky," I say, trying to keep my cover.

"Is there anything you *do* remember?" Marcus finally asks. It's definitely a test this time. I can see it in his eyes.

So I pause, thinking for a long time and trying to run back some of what I read. Something I could use as a breadcrumb for them. If I can give them one little part of Nate's life, maybe they could fill in more information.

Then it clicks.

"I remember the bay," I say, pointing toward the back of the house. "Not what it looks like." I close my eyes and instead picture the time my parents rented a house in the mountains. Not for fun, of course, but because there was a revival with our church and four other local churches. It was late fall, so we didn't go swimming, but there was a lake in the neighborhood and we walked down to it one night. "But I remember the leaves in the trees and the way the orange at sunset would reflect off the water."

I open my eyes to see Valencia staring at me. There are tears in her eyes.

When I glance at Marcus, he's looking down at the floor.

Valencia takes a step forward and puts her hands on my cheeks, trying not to cry as she smiles up at me. She opens her mouth to speak but instead hugs me.

I guess it worked.

I put my arms around her, and she squeezes me tight. The heaviness in my chest loosens, like cured concrete cracking away from me. I don't like this feeling. Two thoughts at odds but fighting it out in my gut. On one side, there's a blaring alarm and a megaphone voice telling me it's wrong to be taking advantage of these people. But on the other is the empty pit of loneliness I've been feeling for months—and in all honesty, *years* before that—telling me to let them in. To let them treat me like the missing son they've been worried about for ten years.

I should be listening to that first voice. The alarms. But then the hug silences all that.

Valencia lets go first and I realize we've been hugging for longer than what's probably considered normal. My face burns with embarrassment and before I even know what I'm saying, I apologize again.

"For what?" Valencia asks with a look of concern.

I shrug.

"Let's get you settled," Marcus says. He seems a little less suspicious now and picks up some of the shopping bags, leading the way upstairs. Valencia grabs a bag and hands it to me, then takes the rest, and we follow Marcus up the stairs and to the left.

The second-floor hallway wraps around the entry like a U-shaped balcony. There's a large window looking out to the front yard and the roof of the portico. The door to the first room at the top of the stairs is shut. The next, which is open, leads into a blue-tiled bathroom.

The third door toward the front of the house is also open and Marcus walks in. It's clearly Nate's bedroom. Only it looks as if it hasn't been touched since he disappeared. The dresser is a dented, warm-colored wood. There's a stegosaurus-shaped rug in the center of the wood floor and little dinosaurs hang from the metal pull chains attached to the ceiling fan. The shelves are filled with old books a six-year-old would read. One thing stands out from the rest: a full-sized bed made of dark wood and a gray fabric headboard.

"This was the nicest grown-up bed we could find last night," Valencia says. "Your old one is down in the basement, but we know you wouldn't be able to fit into a toddler bed anymore. We were planning on buying you a new bed before . . ." She chews at her cheek, then shakes herself out of whatever sad nostalgia zone she veered into and returns to the present with a smile. She points to the mismatched dresser. "We can get you matching furniture, too. We just wanted to be sure you liked the new bed first. We didn't want to change *everything*, you know? But I was thinking it could use a fresh coat of paint! What do you think? Would you like to pick a color and—"

"Val." Marcus makes it seem like the two of them have already decided what should and shouldn't be spoken about, and maybe the lack of change to Nate's room—when so much in the house apparently has been updated—was one of the things they didn't want to discuss.

Valencia doesn't acknowledge Marcus's scolding and focuses on me. "We'll give you some time to get settled. Maybe you want to take a shower?" She walks over to one of the closed doors on either side of the dresser and opens it to the blue Jack and Jill bathroom that connects to Easton's bedroom on the other side.

I step in. It's more dated than the other trendy parts of the house. The walls and floor are the same soft blue tile, and the built-in bathtub matches. The pedestal sink and toilet are both white porcelain, but at least the toilet looks a little more modern.

"This should look the way you remember it," Valencia says. I can see Marcus give her an exasperated glance. "We were going to remodel when Easton went away to college, but things have been so busy we've been holding off."

There's a long, awkward few moments of silence before Marcus speaks.

"Come on, hon." He puts a gentle hand on her lower back. "Let's give the boy some space and let him get settled. I have some emails and calls to make and I'm sure you want to check in with the practice."

She doesn't look so sure she wants to do that but she nods. "We'll be downstairs if you need anything."

"Okay, thanks." They walk out the bathroom door, and I listen to their footsteps, trying to figure out how the house sounds as they move through it.

In my old house, I could tell where anyone was at any time. The kitchen floor would creak between the oven and the fridge. The living room floor groaned when I walked in front of the coffee table. The bathroom door stuck so you had to slam it closed or pull hard to open it. The hinges of the front door squeaked, and the dining room chandelier rattled no matter who walked past.

So far, here, the hardwood floors all creak.

I shut the hallway bathroom door—it closes silently—then go over to Easton's door and shut it as well. There's a lock on the hallway door, but not on my or Easton's bedroom doors.

A shower sounds amazing, so I turn on the water before realizing I don't have a towel. The two towels hanging on the rack are hand towels and there are no hooks on the doors, so I go into Nate's bedroom. The other door is an empty closet with two taped-up boxes on the floor and bare wire hangers.

I go out to the hallway and look past the entryway to Marcus and Valencia's bedroom. There's another, smaller door halfway down that side of the hall before a doorway with more stairs going up to the third floor.

"Honey!" Valencia calls up from downstairs. "There's towels in the linen closet next to our bedroom."

"Okay."

I go over to the skinnier door and grab a towel, then head back to the bathroom to shower.

I stay under the warm water long after I've scrubbed off all the dirt and grime that's accumulated on my body over the last God knows how many days—focusing on parts I might have missed in my paper towel baths in the Starbucks bathrooms.

I take the quiet time under the water to think about my next move. Obviously I need to get out of here before they find out I'm not their son. But the only thing that would get me in trouble is if they did a *real* blood test. Not one to check my blood type, but to check that I am Valencia and Marcus's kid. Something Valencia was fighting hard against last night.

I stay under the showerhead until the hot water starts to cool, then get out to dry off.

I hang my new shirts in the closet, then fold my jeans and pants and put them in the third drawer down in the dresser. In the top drawer I put my new underwear and socks. The undershirts and a couple of the graphic tees Valencia said looked cute go in the second drawer.

I put on one of the tees and a pair of jeans, then take a second to look around the room. Clearly Nate was into dinosaurs when he was a kid.

So was I.

The bookshelf has copies of Magic Tree House and Captain Underpants books as well as a few picture books.

I pull out one of the more well-worn Magic Tree House books. *Dinosaurs Before Dark*. I remember reading this one. I flip it open and on the title page is Nate's name, written in pencil in his blocky, childlike handwriting. I sit down on the bed and flip through the pages.

When I saw Nate's age-progressed picture and read about him, it felt like he was some nebulous being who didn't really exist. But being in his room—seeing the things that used to be his, where he slept—has changed this whole thing for me. I thought it would be easy. That I could get here, steal some of the Beaumonts' food and the clothes they bought me, and get out—though of course I need to figure out where *here* is. According to my phone, we're in a town on the eastern shore of Maryland called Webber's Landing.

I'll check the map later and figure out an escape route. But right now I feel like I should be doing something more—even though I know there's nothing I *can* do. The cops and FBI were on the case long before I even knew who Nate Beaumont was.

I can't stop thinking about him. Just a six-year-old kid who was kidnapped. Or possibly even murdered.

I take a deep breath and lie back on the bed. To distract myself I start to read the book. Slowly, memories of the first time I read it flash in my head. And all at once the day catches up with me. I put the book down and close my eyes. Within seconds I'm asleep.

EIGHT

WHEN I WAKE UP, THERE'S A BLANKET OVER ME AND THE sun has set. Panicking, I bolt upright, forgetting where I am.

But then it all comes back.

I'm Nate. And I'm in Nate's room in Nate's house with Nate's family.

Nate's family, who are talking downstairs. Their voices drift up through the hall, but I can't make out what they're saying. I reach for the phone Valencia gave me and there's two texts, both from her.

We're going to order pizza for dinner. Any toppings you want?

Then two hours later.

We didn't want to wake you but there are leftovers in the fridge if you wake up hungry. FYI the doors and windows on the first floor have an alarm, which we set every night. You can open your own but keep the rest closed. I'll see you in the morning! 😌🖤🖤🖤

She sent that one about an hour and a half ago. The doors and windows are locked and alarmed, and I don't have the code. My throat tightens. This is a huge house, but the longer I'm here the smaller it feels. Unlike the house I grew up in, the ceilings are high and there's lots of open space. But still the walls feel like they're closing in on me.

I set the phone down on the bedside table and carefully walk to the cracked-open bedroom door. I hear Marcus's voice from the kitchen. The chandelier in the entryway is off, but the sconces on either side of the stairwell window are on.

Across the hall, Valencia and Marcus's door is shut.

Another voice, this one male. It must be Easton.

As I step out into the hallway, the floorboard squeaks, and I put my weight down slowly to keep it quiet.

"—out of nowhere. Where has he been?"

"We don't know yet." Marcus again. "The shrink says he might not remember or he might not feel safe enough to tell us."

Whatever Easton says back is too quiet for me to hear.

"Watch it," Marcus says. "For now, we're going to see how he adjusts to living with us and go from there. All we can do is take it one day at a time."

"Or you can get a DNA test and be done with it."

My stomach turns. Easton isn't as sold on me being Nate as his parents are. Or at least as sold on it as Valencia. Marcus might be on the fence.

"Enough," Marcus says. "He's here. Just be cool, be nice, and we'll figure everything else out later."

There's a long pause, but then Easton speaks again. "What if I give my blood for them to compare DNA?" Marcus doesn't answer. "If Mom won't do it and doesn't want *you* to do it, what if I did? I'm nineteen. What's she going to do if it comes back that he's not my brother, disown me?" He could do that. In all honesty, he *should* do that. Anyone in their right mind *would.*

So why haven't they?

"Easton, I said let it be."

There's a long stretch of silence before Easton speaks again. "Denial is my favorite family trait. Nineteen years, still going strong." His voice is getting louder, and a shadow emerges from the kitchen doorway.

He's coming up here.

I turn and step quickly back into my bedroom.

Easton's footsteps reach the staircase, each step creaking beneath him.

I tiptoe back to my bed, trying not to make too much noise. He's at the landing now. I reach the bed as he ascends the side stairs to our hallway.

Easton's footsteps get closer, passing his bedroom. Then the bathroom.

He's headed here.

I get in the bed, throwing the blanket over me again and shutting my eyes. Blood pounds in my ears as I try to settle myself. He's suspicious of me as is; I can't have him knowing I was eavesdropping. He's the only one in this house who seems sure that I'm not who I say I am.

Easton comes to a stop outside my bedroom door.

I peer through my eyelashes and see his silhouette. He holds something in front of him. The door cracks open and squeaks on its hinges.

He enters my bedroom, walking carefully over to the side of the bed but not trying to hide his footsteps.

Easton puts whatever he's holding down on the bedside table.

I shut my eyes a little tighter and try to steady my breathing.

"Nate," he whispers. "You awake?"

I don't answer. Easton's body moves slightly, and he says my name—Nate's name—again, then takes something off the bedside table. There's a click.

The phone. I take a chance and open my eyes a little. He's crouching next to the bed, staring at my locked phone. Thank God I set up the passcode, because I can't remember if I cleared the history of my Beaumont search from last night. I close my eyes as he puts the phone back. Then he stands again, and after a few moments he turns and heads into the bathroom, shutting the door behind him.

I open my eyes to stare at the door, expecting him to open it again. But all I hear is the sound of running water from the sink.

There's a plate on the bedside table. A big slice of pizza with peppers, onions, and black olives on it. Did he bring that up to eat himself and leave it by mistake?

Easton continues getting ready for bed. Eventually I hear Marcus's footsteps on the stairs. They come to a stop at my bedroom and I close my eyes again. The door squeaks on its hinges as he pulls it shut, then crosses the hall to his bedroom.

In the shared bathroom, the water stops running and Easton's bedroom door opens and closes.

Then the house is silent.

I reach for the pizza. It's still warm.

And Easton definitely didn't bring it up for himself because I heard the buzz of an electric toothbrush and him spitting in the sink.

Which means he brought it up for me.

It wasn't him being a nice big brother, though. It was an excuse for him to check on what the stranger who conned his parents into taking him home with them was doing. And he did stare for a while.

Maybe it was part nice big brother, part curiosity.

And I am hungry.

I peel the onions off the pizza while I type Nate's name into the search bar on my phone, then click on the news and filter it by the newest articles. The last one is still from ten months ago. Which means no news outlets have picked up that "Nate" has been found.

Maybe that's a good thing.

Once all the onions are off the pizza, I wolf it down. I definitely want more, but I don't want to go downstairs in this strange house alone. I set the plate aside and log into my old email account, which I haven't checked in months. I check through the junk, deleting it, then my heart stops when I see Frankie's email address. And the subject.

I'm sorry.

I stare at it for almost a full minute, then open the email. The body doesn't say anything else. Because what *would* it say? Part of me wants to reply and tell her I forgive her. It's the one thing I take from Christianity—forgiveness. And I really do believe she didn't realize how bad it might get for me. Or maybe it was her only option.

But I still can't trust her. If she goes to my parents or tells them I'm accessible by email, they might figure out a way to find me. So I leave the email. For now.

Of course, that doesn't help me feel any more relaxed with these strangers in this strange home.

NINE

MY FIRST MORNING IN THE BEAUMONT HOUSE IS OVER-whelming. Marcus has already gone to work by the time I get up and go downstairs, where Valencia is waiting for me.

"Good morning!" She takes the pizza plate I brought down, putting it in the sink, and asks me how I want my eggs.

"Scrambled is fine, thank you."

She hands me a thick fan deck of paint samples to look at for my room and tells me to sit at the kitchen table while she cooks. I absentmindedly look through the colors but I still feel weird changing Nate's room.

"How did you sleep?" she asks.

"Fine." In truth I slept better than I thought I was going to. Maybe it was exhaustion catching up with me. Or maybe the past eight months have taught me to get sleep however I can, wherever I can, for as *long* as I can. Because who knows when the next time I'll get it will be?

"I've taken the rest of the week off," she says.

So she'll be here all day? That's not good.

"You don't have to do that. Really, I'm fine."

"I know how overwhelming all this is for you." She uses a spatula to put the eggs on a plate and walks it over to me. "You're in a strange house, to *you* we're strange people. I don't want you to feel alone."

I think I'd rather feel alone for a bit. Especially because if I'm alone, then I can get out of here.

The front door opens, and Valencia moves to the kitchen doorway. Her smile grows and she waves. "Honey, come in here. Your brother's up."

Easton enters the kitchen and looks right at me. I can't tell what he's thinking because his face is blank. He's dressed in shorts and a sweat-soaked T-shirt, so he must have gone for a run.

"Hey," he says.

"Hi."

Valencia goes back to the stovetop. "Do you want some breakfast?"

"Sure," Easton says. Then he goes over to the fridge and gets a bottle of water. He chugs it down, his Adam's apple bobbing, and stares at me from across the room. Just like last night, it's as if he's studying me, trying to find the flaw that proves I'm not who I say I am.

My heart is in my throat.

Once he finishes the water, he goes over to the sink and stops, staring into it. Then he looks back at me and smirks.

"You took the onions off."

Valencia turns to him. "What's that, hon?"

Easton reaches into the sink and takes out the plate. "The onions on the pizza. He took them off."

"I don't like onions," I say. But my heart is picking up speed. What if Nate was an onion fanatic? Maybe they got onions on their pizza *for*

Nate. I don't mind cooked onions in things like casseroles, but raw on a pizza is a definite no.

"Yeah," Easton says. "I know you don't. You never did."

I look at Valencia, who's staring at the plate with wide eyes, as if it's the last bit of proof she needed to know her son is home. Then she laughs.

"Some things never change," she says, and goes back to cooking Easton's eggs.

My heart starts to slow. Easton puts the plate back in the sink and refills his water bottle.

Fucking onion. Maybe Nate and I aren't that different after all.

Easton sits across from me at the kitchen table. He gives a resigned sigh and shakes his head. "Welcome home, Nate-o. Try not to get stolen again, please."

"Easton!" Valencia scolds him from across the room.

"It's fine, Mom, humor as a coping mechanism is very healthy."

"Well, maybe I'd rather not make a joke about the single most traumatic experience of our lives."

"The joke is me *making* the joke. It's funny *because* it's uncomfortable and something I shouldn't say out loud, and you making me explain it is removing all the humor. I've got a real good tight five on child kidnappings that I've been working on the past ten years."

Valencia looks exasperated as she walks a plate of fried eggs over to Easton. "Well, I'm not ready for it, so you're going to have to put your comedy routine on the back burner." She sets the plate in front of him and pats his shoulder.

She tells him they'll have to pack up his dorm at the end of the month and then asks about his finals. He tells her four of his teachers are letting him take the final online, one is passing him without taking the final since he already has a high average and aced the midterm, and another said there wasn't going to be a final but rather an essay, due next week.

He also starts explaining what his essay is about—something to do with the evolution of medicine from the twentieth century to today—but it all goes way over my head.

Easton is smart. *Really* smart. But not boring smart.

Finally, he jumps up and says he's going to shower. "Then I'm going to hang out with JT. There's a party tonight we might go to."

"I was thinking we'd have a family dinner tonight," Valencia says. "Gramma is coming over."

Gramma? Valencia's mother, maybe.

Easton looks disappointed. "Can I invite JT?"

Valencia deflates a little. "I think family might be enough."

"Because Gramma is a very low-key individual with a calm and soothing personality." But the way he says it makes me think Nate's gramma is not any of those things.

"You don't think introducing your brother to JT might be a little overwhelming, too?"

Easton smirks again. "Of course I do. But in a humorous way. And say it with me, family: humor is a . . ."

He conducts us with his hand as Valencia rolls her eyes and looks at me. I actually can't help but smile, so I say at the same time as Valencia: "Coping mechanism."

Is this how families usually act? You mean to tell me it's not all walking on eggshells and hiding in your bedroom until you're called to dinner?

"There we go." He throws his water bottle into a recycling bin under the counter. "And didn't even have to make a joke about kidnapping."

"Fine, JT can come. But try and keep him calm."

"Impossible," Easton calls over his shoulder, hitting his hand against the top of the doorway on his way out.

"Who's JT?" I ask.

"His friend." Valencia shakes her head. "His very, very . . . strange friend."

At least it's someone I don't need to watch how I act in front of. And with a grandparent in the mix, maybe I'll hear a few good stories to help me fake my way through this.

"Sounds like fun."

TEN

AROUND THREE IN THE AFTERNOON, I FINALLY HAVE some time alone again. Valencia helped me pick out a new color for Nate's room—something she kept pressing me on until I realized maybe it was something *she* wanted more than Nate would. We finally went with "Juniper Fog"—a gray-green sage that isn't too bright or too dark.

She decided to run out and pick up the paint, then go to the grocery store to grab a couple things for dinner. When I asked to stay behind, she was anxious, as though I wouldn't be here when she got back. But then she must have remembered the security system.

And thank God she did. She downloaded the app for me and showed me all the features. It sends notifications to all our phones whenever the doors or windows are opened. If the alarm goes off, it sends another notification.

That's going to be an issue when I try to run away. She, Marcus, and even Easton—unless he turned the notifications off—will get the alert that the front door opened. And of course they have a doorbell camera, too.

I have to assume all this was installed after Nate was abducted; Valencia would have been terrified someone was coming back for her other son. I'll have to figure out how to escape the house without setting off any alerts to the family. The last thing I need is to break a leg trying to leave through one of the unmonitored windows on the second floor.

Valencia showed me how to set the alarm and asked that I keep it on while she's gone.

But I have to figure out how to test the system. See what gets a reaction from them and whether they'll notice me leaving the house while they're at work. So ten minutes after she leaves, I turn it off and go out the back door.

Two alerts pop up moments apart. The first saying the alarm has been turned off. The second that the back door has been opened.

I wait for another notification. Marcus or Valencia asking if that was me.

Of course Valencia is first.

Is that you going outside?

I respond with a picture of the backyard and the Chesapeake, telling her it's too nice a day to stay inside and that I promise not to go any farther than the backyard. Though I'm sure that does nothing to make her feel better, since that's where Nate was when he disappeared.

Okay, she responds. I don't know how, but I can tell that's a nervous "okay"—like she is very much not okay. Guilt mixes with the food in my stomach. The longer I spend with Valencia, the more I realize how much Nate's disappearance messed her up. When I'm with her, I don't feel the same anxiety and fear I get when Marcus is around.

Valencia is genuinely thrilled to have her "son" home. Marcus, on the other hand, is suspicious and guarded.

I put the phone away and take in the fresh air. It's a warm May day, and the sun feels amazing on my skin. The Beaumonts have a little deck with a long table and grill on it.

A willow tree sits in the far right corner of the yard, growing high over the white waist-height iron fence that separates the Beaumonts' yard from the neighbor next door. But just before it is a white boathouse and a dock that extends out into the bay.

I walk down to the edge of the backyard, looking out at the bay. I'm not sure if this is the Chesapeake or an inlet, but it's beautiful. There's a small island—maybe the size of a football field—thirty yards out.

The boathouse is about the same size as the two-car garage attached to the house. But it looks newer. The sides are painted white, the roof the same asphalt tiles of the house. There's a navy double door and a few double-hung windows.

I step onto the dock. Water sloshes against the wood pilings, but the dock itself is a mix of metal and some composite material. I try opening the door a few times before giving up and peering into the windows. Inside I can see there's a large door that takes up most of the far wall facing the bay. But there's no boat.

Marcus mentioned wanting a boat, but I thought that was a joke. Why build a boathouse if you don't have a boat? And how rich are these people that they could spend money on such a ridiculous thing?

I walk along the dock, looking in the windows of the boathouse. In the middle there's what looks like a small workbench, almost like a kitchen island, but with no tools or boat materials on it. On the floor by the far wall is a large kerosene heater—probably for working on a boat in the winter.

I start walking back to the house. There are mulched plant beds along the deck that wrap around the house.

A dog barks and I turn, trying to find where it's coming from.

"Hi!"

There's a boy about my age in the yard next door. He has a friendly smile and curly strawberry-blond hair. He waves and starts walking across his backyard toward the fence. A white-haired golden retriever trots alongside him. I wave as I approach him.

"Hi, I'm Nate Beaumont." Might as well get used to introducing myself like that.

His face changes a little bit, his brow furrowing as he looks me up and down, but then he nods. "Yeah, I heard on the LISTSERV you were back." His dog plants its front feet on the top of the white fence and I put my hand out to it.

"LISTSERV?"

He chuckles and motions with his arm toward our houses. "The whole neighborhood has a Google group to gossip on. They used to use the town Facebook group but decided to make their own little side chats. Probably to talk shit about the Facebook group. My mom said Valencia sent out a blast last night telling everyone they found you."

"Great." Now the whole neighborhood can celebrate with Valencia that her missing son is back. I wonder what they'll say when I'm gone. Maybe they'll make a whole other offshoot of their Google group. The "Not the Beaumonts" group, where they can talk shit about the family who got conned by a sixteen-year-old.

The neighbor shrugs. "It's all everyone's been talking about because nothing else exciting happens around here, especially since the group didn't exist when you got kidnapped. Sorry, by the way. I probably shouldn't be saying any of this to you." But he doesn't stop talking. In fact, his teasing tone is a little too flippant. It's not offensive, though—maybe it would be if I were really Nate, but right now it feels like a refreshing change of pace compared to the awkwardness with Nate's parents. "You've been through this trauma and now I'm here telling you you're all over the neighborhood gossip group."

"I think it might be more ridiculous that I didn't realize I would be." The dog, finished with my pets, hops down and starts circling the yard with her nose to the grass.

The neighbor waves a dismissive hand. "Don't worry. As soon as summer hits it will go back to arguments between the lawn folks and the native-plant folks, and Mrs. Kenilworth body-shaming Mrs. Nowalk for sunbathing nude in her own fenced-in backyard. Also, it's an election year, so there's bound to be plenty of competing misinformation flying around."

"Oh great, I hope someone says I'm a Russian spy."

"Actually, I heard you were a thirty-year-old Slovakian serial killer with a rare form of dwarfism masquerading as a teenager."

"I'm that obvious, huh?"

"The accent gives it away. I'm shocked they even let you into the country." His smile grows and his eyes crinkle. There's a light smattering of freckles across his nose and cheeks. He puts out a hand. "I'm Miles, by the way." He points vaguely to the dog. "And that is Chardonnay. Yes, my mother named her, and she says it with a straight face, if you can fucking believe it."

I laugh and shake his hand. "Nate."

"Yeah, you said that. And I told you about the LISTSERV; remember, this all happened less than three minutes ago. Wow! Your old age must be catching up with you, Slovak."

My face burns because I remembered as soon as I said it that I already introduced myself. I was a little distracted by Miles being cute and how his dark brown eyes contrast sharply with his light hair.

I grin and blink at him a few times. "Well, this was a sufficiently embarrassing introduction. I think I should go back inside and try not to replay this over and over tonight while lying awake in bed."

Miles's face changes again. This time it looks sad, like maybe he doesn't want me to go yet. But then he nods. "It was nice meeting you. And don't worry, your secret's safe with me, Slovak."

I wave goodbye as my stomach does a little flip, but it's not a good one like I want it to be. This is yet another person I'm lying to. And lying to cute boys isn't the best way to start any new relationship, friendly or not.

I shut the back door behind me and go to the alarm app to reset it. But the keypad beeps in the front hall and I get a notification.

Sensor issue: FRONT DOOR. Bypass?

What does that mean? I walk out to the front hall and see the front door is open. My stomach drops and I look around the room.

Did someone come home? Maybe Valencia got too anxious about me being here alone. Or Easton and his friend came back early?

I open my mouth to call out but something in my gut stops me. What if it *isn't* someone from the family? I peer into the dining room, but it's empty. I listen for creaking upstairs. Easton or Valencia. Nothing.

Then I remember the front doorbell camera app on my phone. I open it up and see there's an error message there as well.

FRONT DOOR CAMERA OFFLINE

My hands are trembling. Something isn't right here. If it was someone coming home early, the camera wouldn't be offline. The only reason to disable the camera is if you don't want to be seen.

I walk to the front door, glancing back and forth between the dining room and living room, expecting some costumed psycho slasher to pop out from the doorway with a knife. But the house remains still.

At the top of the front stairs is the doorbell camera. I reach down and pick it up to look. There's space for six double-A batteries, but only three are still inside. I find one on the steps and look around for the others. One has rolled down the stairs and landed on the walkway. The other went to the right of the door into the mulch bed.

I replace the batteries and remount the doorbell while the power-up light above the camera lens circles in white. The way it's mounted, I need to flick a lever on the bottom to resecure it.

I open the doorbell camera app and look at the last video taken. It's from seven minutes ago. I click it and wait for it to load.

The clip is short. Only a few seconds of the front yard before the camera shifts and falls forward onto the concrete. I replay it, turning up the volume. Right before the camera falls, there's a loud click. I turn back to the doorbell and unlatch the lock on the bottom of it, and it makes a similar *snick* sound.

I play the video again, only this time I use my finger to play it frame by frame.

The camera shifts. Tilts. Falls. And then I see it.

It feels like I've fallen through ice into a frozen lake.

There are two fingers in the bottom right corner of the screen. At least, they look like fingers. They're pink and rounded, but only an inch or so was caught on the video. When I search the front step, I don't see anything that could possibly be confused for fingers. Nothing growing up from the mulch beside the door. No trick of the light.

Someone's here.

I spin quickly, expecting to see someone waiting behind me. But the doorway is empty.

What the hell do I do? Call the police? I can't do that; they'd show up and ask more questions, and right now I am *not* calm. My heart is beating so hard I don't think I've ever been this scared in my life. It's like my whole chest is pounding.

I step inside and listen to the silence of the house. Trying to hear anyone walking around. This is the creakiest fucking old house I've ever been in; I should be able to hear something!

But the silence is even worse.

Leaving the front door open, I head to the kitchen. Every nerve in my body is on edge and my hands are shaking, but I grab the biggest knife the Beaumonts have out of the knife block by the stove.

It's not until I'm back at the kitchen doorway that I realize all the other knives are accounted for. So that's good at least.

But what kind of serial killer doesn't bring their own knife?

I go upstairs first. Slowly.

To Nate's room.

The door is open how I left it—I think?—but that doesn't make me feel any better. The room doesn't look ransacked. In fact, it looks like it did when I left this morning.

But what if someone is hiding behind the door? I push it open a bit more.

Then I spring around the edge of it, knife raised.

No one there.

Nothing except the closed closet door. I reach for the handle but stop myself as all the nightmares of my childhood come back. The monsters in the closet. And the ones hiding under the bed.

I glance over my shoulder at the bed.

Is the stegosaurus rug out of place?

Quickly, I bend over and look under the bed, but there's nothing under there. So I pull open the closet door, thrusting the knife forward into the darkness.

The empty darkness.

And now I'm starting to feel ridiculous. But someone *was* here. They dismantled the doorbell camera and opened the front door. Maybe they opened the door expecting me to be inside. But I was out talking to Miles so they turned around and left.

I still check the bathroom and Easton's room. Both are empty. Across the hall, Valencia and Marcus's bedroom, too, is quiet and empty. Now I'm even more sure of it. Someone came in, expecting to find me here, alone. And when they didn't, they left.

"Nate?"

I startle and almost scream, but stop when I realize it's Valencia's voice coming from the front hall.

"Up here!" And still holding a knife in my hand. Shit!

Valencia charges into the front hall, looking up to the balcony. "Why is the front door open?"

I have to tell her the truth. Someone definitely broke in and left. We're out in the Maryland suburbs; there's no reason for a random burglar to show up in the middle of the day. And that would be way too much of a coincidence. It has to be someone involved in taking Nate.

But when I reach the stairs, I stop myself.

Valencia is already on high alert. She has been since Nate was taken and she locked down the house. If I tell her someone broke in, that will only make it worse. She might up security, or she might not leave me alone ever. She might demand I go to work with her or Marcus every day and I'll never get out of here.

She can't know.

And maybe the person who knows I'm not Nate knows that, too.

My hands are tied, and I can't tell the truth without risking my escape plan. And I still can't stay here forever.

"The doorbell fell off," I say. I lift the back of my shirt and carefully slide the knife into my waistband—oh, please don't cut my butt.

"The doorbell . . . ?" Valencia looks confused as I descend the stairs—carefully, so the knife doesn't slip.

"The camera. Check the app. The last video shows it falling off. The batteries came out and I was fixing it, but I thought it might need some tape to hold it on properly. I was checking the linen closet. I'm not sure where you keep tape."

Valencia stares at me like she doesn't believe me. Then she steps backward to look at the doorbell camera. She reaches over and I can see her trying to jostle it. "It's fine now."

"Maybe it wasn't set right whenever you last changed the batteries?" I suggest.

She nods but still looks concerned. "Please don't leave the door open again."

"I won't, sorry."

Valencia attempts a smile, but it doesn't feel genuine. "Can you help me bring in the groceries?"

"Of course, yeah." I back up in the direction of the kitchen. "I'll go through the garage if you want to close the front door."

She nods and closes it. I take out the knife and run back into the kitchen. I turn on the faucet and rinse it off—I mean, it was only against my underwear, which is clean, but the idea kind of skeeves me—then I put it back in the knife block and run to the garage door to help Valencia bring the groceries in. I try to put on a calm face, but my hands are still shaking, and it feels like I'm going to crawl out of my skin. This is all so damn overwhelming.

I thought I could do this; that it would be better than going to juvie. But instead this feels like a different kind of prison where I need to watch every single thing I say. And now I feel like someone is watching me.

As I reach for the garage door handle, my heart catches in my chest.

When I went outside, I used the back door that went to the deck. That door was unlocked the whole time.

But I know for a fact the front door was locked.

So whoever opened it had a key.

ELEVEN

AS I HELP UNPACK THE GROCERIES, VALENCIA ASKS WHAT I did while she was gone. I tell her about checking out the backyard and the boathouse and meeting Miles next door.

Her face lights up. "Oh, that's wonderful that the two of you got to catch up! Do you want to invite him over for dinner tonight? I mean, JT is coming, so I guess you could invite a friend, too."

Shit.

Of course Miles knew Nate. Which is why he looked at me that way.

Valencia catches the look on my face. "Oh."

"I . . . I didn't realize I had met him before."

She sighs and sets down the zucchini she was about to put in the fridge, then walks around the kitchen island and pulls me into another hug. I let my body relax so she can squeeze me tighter. It feels wonderful. Everything in my mind is telling me not to get too close to this woman. Not to let her touch me, because what's the point? I'm leaving soon. But the second she does, I can't help but give in. It's like when she hugs me, all those overwhelming feelings get obliterated into dust and released into the world, away from me. Is this what other kids get from real parents?

"I've decided I'm going to treat this whole thing like a traumatic brain injury," Valencia says. "At least until Dr. Zapata tells me it's not healthy. Or maybe it will be your brother who does that. You and Miles were great friends. The two of you were together all the time and, honestly, I think he took your disappearance almost as hard as we did."

That explains why he looked so hurt when I didn't recognize him. She lets me go and puts the last few groceries in the refrigerator, then motions for me to follow her out of the kitchen.

"Come on," she says.

I follow her up to my room and she opens the closet door. She pulls out one of the cardboard boxes and slides it over to the stegosaurus rug, then sits down beside it and rips away the tape keeping the box closed.

She pats the floor next to her and I sit cross-legged as she opens the box.

The first thing she pulls out is a framed picture of Nate and Easton. Nate is probably four years old and his hair is lighter. Easton's hair is almost black-brown and wet. He looks to be seven or so. Nate is wearing a Mickey Mouse T-shirt, while Easton has Ninja Turtles on his. Nate's eyes are closed as someone pours water over his head from a souvenir cup of some kind.

"This was when we were visiting your grandmother in Florida," Valencia says. "Marcus's mother—not mine, who you'll meet tonight. You probably don't remember his mother, so I should tell you she died a year after this picture was taken. Your grandfather on your dad's side died three years ago, and my dad died the year after you . . ." She tries to figure out what word she's going for. "Disappeared."

Why did she pause? Did she almost say *died* but had to correct herself so she didn't say it in front of me? Because she *told* herself Nate was dead for all those years?

"Sorry" is all I say.

"Don't be; they lived a good life and were kind and wonderful people. But this day—oof! This was when we went to Disney World, and it was almost a hundred degrees and humid as hell. Easton wanted to get on the Seven Dwarfs Mine Train ride and there were no FastPasses, so we were stuck waiting in line for two hours. I thought you were going to *kill* Easton. This was when your father decided to start pouring water on the two of you so you'd stop bickering."

She laughs at the memory, and I can't help but smile with her. She puts the picture on the bedside table and reaches for another item from the Nate box.

"Oh! It's Nanook!" It's a husky stuffed animal that looks very loved. Its right front leg has a tear in the seam with stuffing coming out and its tail looks like it was sewn back on more than once. "You got this on the boardwalk. I had a dental convention in Atlantic City, so your father drove you kids up for the weekend and we went to Wildwood one night. You wanted this dog so bad, but you had to do that game where you shoot water in the fake clown's mouth to blow up a balloon. Do you know that game?"

I decide that even post-kidnapping Nate would know that game, so I nod.

"Well, you felt bad about spraying water at the clown, so you didn't want to play it but wanted the stuffed animal. I think your dad paid forty bucks for this thing just to bypass the game. Meanwhile Easton gladly sprayed the clown and won two prizes. Your dad also named him Nanook, but I don't think we realized until after that it might be cultural appropriation since it's an Inuit word. If you want to keep him, I'd consider a name change."

She hands him off to me and I look at the fake blue eyes, trying to recall whether there was anything like either of these moments in my own childhood. My parents would never take me to Disney World. First, they didn't have the money, but they also believed Disney was trying to corrupt children, pulling them further away from God. I've never even seen a Disney movie.

We did go to the carnival that was set up annually in the field between the church and the firehouse. But I didn't get to play games. I'd work the church booth with my parents and collect donations or hand out prayer cards, cheap plastic rosaries, and small desk calendars with a picture of the church printed on them. Then they would let me spend the tickets we were "paid" with to go on some of the shoddily constructed rides.

And, yes, they had the water gun game.

Valencia pulls out every item in the box, explaining the stories behind them.

Nate's baby book with pictures of the day he was born, four-year-old Easton kissing his forehead in a posed manner for the camera, and the first few years of Nate's life. Class pictures from kindergarten and first grade. An old duck costume from the Mother Goose play he was in during first grade—"We thought you'd be taller than Easton, actually," she says, holding up the flip-flops with orange plastic webbed feet stapled to the thong. "We had to make these special for you because your feet were too big for the plastic duck shoes they bought."

Listening to Valencia talk about Nate gives me conflicting emotions that I don't know what to do with. On the one hand, I love listening to her talk about him. She does it with so much love and admiration, I can't help but feel that same love from her. On the other, it makes me feel strange and uncomfortable because my real parents aren't like this at all. They didn't take any pictures of me growing up, they didn't share fun stories—if they existed. My grandmother was the only person who ever showed me that family members could love each other.

It feels similar to all this.

And, yes, it's not real and I have to keep telling myself that. Because *I'm* not real. But sometimes—like when Valencia shows me the candid she took of Marcus cheering on Nate at peewee soccer—it *feels* real. I know it's not for me, but I wish it were.

For a second, I wish there were another world where I was born to the Beaumonts instead of to my parents. Even though Marcus was disappointed when he learned Nate didn't like playing soccer, they supported Nate in whatever he wanted to do.

But then I remind myself we aren't in that world, and Nate *is* real. And he was kidnapped. Or even killed. And the person who did that might have been here earlier today.

Valencia looks up from the award Nate got in first grade—best line leader—her eyes glassy. She reaches out and rubs my neck lovingly.

"I want you to know that I'm proud of you. I always will be, no matter what."

My breath catches in my throat, and I can't speak because my chest is so full. So I nod. I want to believe her, but something won't let me. It won't let me trust that this is the truth coming out of her mouth, because I *know* the truth.

Parents say they're proud of you and they always will be, because they're supposed to say that. But it's not true. That unconditional love everyone spouts off about *is* conditional. Conditional on how they want you to live your life according to their own rules and beliefs.

I can't help but wonder if six-year-old Nate ever did something that caused Valencia's unconditional love to waver. If he hadn't disappeared, would she even still feel this way about him?

She puts the award back in the box and glances at her watch. "I should get dinner started. Stay here and go through this stuff. See if there's anything you want to pack away, throw out, or keep. Put whatever you don't want to throw away in the box and we'll put it in the attic with Easton's stuff."

Then she kisses the top of my head and leaves.

I find another photo, this one loose at the bottom of the box. It's Valencia in front of a small office building with a sign that reads "Millbrook Dental Partners." Valencia holds Nate in her arms while Easton stands beside her with his tongue out.

I want to believe Valencia that the Beaumonts had this picture-perfect little family, but something is stopping me. Maybe it's my own trauma and, yeah, I should own that. It doesn't feel like it's that, though. My gut keeps telling me to run. That I can't trust her. Can't trust this family.

But I still can't help but *want* that feeling of being loved by someone who is supposed to love you. And no matter how often I tell myself this is all fake, that need is still there. Whispering for me to let my guard down.

I only wish I had that love before this all happened. Maybe I wouldn't be in this situation.

TWELVE

ONCE EASTON GETS HOME A FEW HOURS LATER, THE atmosphere of the house changes instantly. There are three voices downstairs—Easton, Valencia, and presumably JT. I've gone through a second box of Nate's stuff, which held more stuffed animals, pictures, a participation trophy for soccer, and a karate outfit and white belt with a blue stripe of tape on it.

I put everything back in the boxes because I'm not throwing away any of Nate's things, but also I might be able to use them later. If someone tells a story, I could come back up here and check the boxes to verify the truth.

When I get downstairs, Easton is drinking from a can of flavored seltzer, but his eyes lock right on me as if he heard me coming even over JT's loud, boisterous voice.

He nods at me, but JT keeps speaking—about farming, apparently? He's talking about crop yield and distribution rights to Valencia, who is doing her best to seem interested. I've only known her for two days, but even I can tell she's just being polite.

She also locks eyes with me, but unlike Easton, it's not in greeting; it's a *please help me* look.

JT turns and his eyes go wide. "It's Nate the Great and Missing!"

Valencia grimaces at the nickname as he walks around the island and puts out his hand with enough energy that I recognize he's looking for one of those hand slap/shake thingies straight guys do, where they hug after. So I take the lead and do it.

"Hi, nice to meet you."

"Nate, this is JT," Easton says.

"What does JT stand for?" I ask.

"Jerkoff Townie," Easton says before JT can answer. Without looking at him, JT snaps and points at Easton.

"Do not listen to him, little brother. He's just jelly that I can find purpose and drive in a small town. Real name is John Thomas, but I go by JT 'cause I don't want to walk around with a name that's slang for a dick."

"Which he is, anyway," Easton says.

"Hey!" JT doesn't take his eyes away from me but keeps pointing at Easton. "That's . . . actually true."

John. Yes, it's a common enough name, but is this the same John who the articles said Easton was with when Nate disappeared?

"Enough with the penis talk," Valencia says. "Please. I thought the two of you would have matured by now."

"Mrs. Bemo, I've always been very mature for my age." JT clears his throat, then reaches into his back pocket and takes out an orange inhaler. He puts it to his mouth and breathes in while he looks me up and down. But his gaze feels more like one of appraisal than judgment.

Easton glares. "Is that why you were suspended in sophomore year for throwing fart bombs in the hallway between lunches?"

JT caps the inhaler and turns back to Easton. "No, I was suspended for pulling the fire alarm; they never caught me for the fart bombs."

"That's right, I forgot."

"And the fire alarm thing was your idea, if I recall."

"Easton!" Valencia turns away from a pot of pasta she's stirring, her jaw dropping open. "Is that true?"

"It is true, Mrs. Bemo." JT leans against the island. "He's a total sociopath, look at him. You can see it in his eyes. He actually wanted to set the gym on fire. I was the one who suggested pulling the alarm instead."

"*That's* not true, but yes, fine, I did maybe float the idea that he should pull the fire alarm so we wouldn't have to take a chemistry test."

"And I never ratted him out either."

"No, you did not. Thank you, buddy." He holds out his hand for a fist bump, and JT hits it, then explodes it, making a noise with his mouth.

Valencia shakes her head. "You barely even needed to study for school. Every teacher was always so impressed by you. Even in elementary school. Remember Mrs. Duffy? She called me in for a parent-teacher conference because she thought you weren't paying attention. But every time she'd call on you, you'd know the answer."

"Why'd she want a parent-teacher conference, then?" I ask.

"She wanted to know what she could do to challenge him more. So she started making him special tests that were a little harder and gave him different homework than the other kids. She was such a wonderful teacher."

JT puts a finger up. "Actually, not all teachers were impressed. I distinctly remember Ms. Lockwood in seventh grade *hating* him."

Valencia shudders. "She was a nasty piece of work. I had to stop going to those parent-teacher conferences." She turns back and looks at me. "I sent your father instead, and he *hated* that woman."

"I'm sure the feeling was mutual," JT says. "She was probably a man-hater because she was allergic to *nuts*." He looks at Easton while he grabs his crotch. Easton gives him a disgusted glare and shoves him, telling him to shut up.

"That's not nice," Valencia says. "Also homophobic. JT, please don't say things like that in this house."

That catches me by surprise, and I feel my heart defrost even more toward Valencia.

She continues speaking to JT and it snaps me out of my thoughts. "But especially don't make jokes about the way people die."

"Sorry," JT says.

"I forgot all about that, honestly," Valencia says, picking up the pot of boiling water and dumping it into a colander in the sink.

"How did she die?" I ask. The door to the garage opens and closes.

Valencia looks ashamed. "We shouldn't be talking badly of the dead. She didn't hate Easton, and Marcus didn't *really* hate her."

"Hate who?" Marcus appears in the kitchen doorway.

"Yo, Mr. Bemo!"

"Ms. Lockwood," Easton says once Marcus gives JT a begrudging fist bump.

Marcus sneers. "Speak for yourself. I absolutely hated her."

"Enough!" Valencia's voice has gone completely cold and the melting ice on my heart seizes once more. She stops working on dinner and turns to everyone. "Just because she was strict and didn't like Easton doesn't mean she deserved to choke to death."

I wince. "She *choked* to death?"

"Anaphylaxis," Easton says. "She ate something in the teachers' lounge that had nuts in it and apparently didn't have an EpiPen on her."

Valencia says, "They didn't have a full-time nurse on staff, so when one of the other teachers ran to the office, it was locked, and they couldn't get the EpiPen in time. Marcus's firm did get her family a nice payout from the school, though."

Marcus pops a piece of green pepper into his mouth. "And we took a third of it, too."

"Capitalism!" JT holds up his hand for a high five and Marcus actually gives it.

Easton frowns at them and looks over at Valencia, who shakes her head.

"Okay, that's it, everyone out of the kitchen. Boys, go outside." Easton gives JT a light shove toward the back door, and I move to follow, but Valencia stops me. "Hold on, Nate."

She waits for the door to shut behind them, Easton giving me a better-you-than-me glance, then turns her attention to me.

"I made your first appointment with Dr. Zapata," she says. "It's next Tuesday afternoon. She has an office in Easton, so I'll take you to work with me in the morning and you can hang out in my office. And I'll give you a dental cleaning. I'm sure you need one."

"Sorry, you said an office in Easton?" The phrasing doesn't make sense to me because . . . well, Easton is a person. Valencia laughs and gives Marcus a knowing look; he returns it with a smirk like there's some kind of inside joke.

"Easton, Maryland," she says. "It's a town about twenty minutes away. When you were learning how to read you would point out every sign with Easton on it and say, 'Look, Easton, you live in two miles!'"

"And then we'd spend fifteen minutes trying to get the two of you to stop bickering," Marcus says, taking another green pepper and popping it into his mouth—but not before Valencia playfully slaps his hand.

"I think you only did it because you knew it pissed him off," Valencia says.

"Well, he should have gotten you to drive through Nathaniel, Maryland, more often," I say. But immediately my cheeks burn with embarrassment. I didn't mean to make the joke—the embarrassment isn't from it being a *bad* joke, which it is, but more because I feel like I don't have the right to joke with this family. I'm not their son. It feels disingenuous to be a part of their inside jokes.

But Valencia still guffaws and even Marcus snorts a laugh through his nose.

Their approval only makes me feel worse. Marcus tells Valencia he's going to get changed, and he attempts to snatch another green pepper, but Valencia catches his wrist and pulls it away instead. Marcus wraps his arm around her waist and kisses her neck.

I look away, but at the same time I'm fascinated. I feel like I'm doing an anthropological study on parental behavior. Is this how they're supposed to act?

As Marcus walks past, he pats me on the shoulder. "Good joke, kiddo."

Kiddo? Now there are two emotions at war in my chest. I still feel awkward for trying to joke with this family. But I can't help but feel a sense of pride as Marcus tells me my stupid joke was good.

My mother's voice sounds in my head: *Proverbs 16:5.* Her voice ends there because I know the verse by heart. Every June our pastor read it aloud as part of his condemnation of the gays. *Everyone who is proud in heart is an abomination to the Lord.*

Be assured, he will not go unpunished.

"Do you need help with anything?" I ask. If I find a way to be useful, maybe I can ignore these feelings. Shut off my brain.

"You okay?" Valencia asks. She looks at me with concern, which only makes me feel worse. I know she's not a mind reader, but there should still be some kind of hesitancy from her. I can see it with Marcus, and with Easton, so why doesn't she have that?

I nod and fake a smile. Pulling on the imaginary Nate mask I've worn since I got here. Trying to look the part.

"Okay." But Valencia doesn't buy it. Still, she nods toward the cabinets next to the fridge. "Grab some plates, napkins, and silverware and take it out to the table. There's gonna be six of us."

I do as she says, moving quickly so I can get out of the kitchen and onto the deck. Away from her eyes, which question every part of me while ignoring the seams between who I am and who Nate was.

THIRTEEN

WHILE VALENCIA FINISHES MAKING DINNER AND MAR-cus goes upstairs to change out of his work clothes, I stay on the deck with JT and Easton. Since I got here, I've seen Easton the least out of everyone in the Beaumont household. Is it because he feels awkward and doesn't know where to pick up with the brother he last saw ten years ago?

Or because he knows I'm not really Nate?

JT is in the middle of a story he seems to have been waiting all day to tell. Easton is listening intently, so I watch him. Trying to figure him out.

"What's your deal?" Easton turns to look at me.

Shit. How long was I staring at him? And how long did he realize I was staring at him? I shake my head. "Sorry. Thinking about Mom sending me to a shrink."

JT's hand goes right up for another high five. "Nate the Great taking care of his mental health."

I just stare at JT, leaving his hand in the air. How can someone be so obsessed with high fives?

"Up top!"

I don't break my gaze, daring him to realize how ridiculous he looks.

"It's not going to happen," Easton says, as if he can read my mind. "He'll keep it there until you do it, so you might as well humor him."

I lean back in the chair and side-eye JT. "How good *is* your upper-arm strength, JT?"

He leans forward, his arm steady in the air. "I hand-trim weed for a living. I can do this all day."

So *that's* the kind of farming he does. I take out my phone and start the timer, then place it face up on the table.

"Hello!" A woman's voice carries around the corner of the house.

Easton turns in that direction and then looks back at me. "Oh boy. Gramma Sharon is here. Can't wait for you to meet her."

A short, round white woman with a mess of curly gray hair waddles around the corner of the deck. In her hands she holds two pie plates covered in tinfoil. She looks to be in her late seventies or early eighties and is wearing a blue floral sundress.

"Easton, be a peach and take these inside for me," Gramma Sharon says, holding them out to him. He takes them and she turns her attention to me. Pursing her lips, she gives me a judgment-filled up-and-down. "Nate. Well, you're not how I remembered you."

I'm not sure if it's a joke or if she knows deep down that I'm not Nate. But before I can dig too much into what she said, she holds out a hand. I take it and steady her as she slowly moves up the steps onto the deck.

She stops and looks at JT, who is still staring into the distance with his hand up. She sighs. "You're exactly how I remember you." Then she waddles around him, swatting his hand down. I pick up my phone, shutting off the stopwatch.

Gramma Sharon lets out a loud groan as she takes off the orange leather purse slung across her body and lowers herself into one of the chairs. Then she reaches into the neck of her dress and pulls out a fan. I almost laugh because the image is so ridiculous. Was she . . . keeping that fan tucked away under her boobs?

"JT, go get me a glass of water. And have Marcus bring me out a drink."

"You got it, Gramma." He jumps up and goes inside. She shakes her head, then turns to look at me as she unfurls the fan.

"Well, sit down." She kicks out the chair I was sitting in, and I do as she says. While she fans herself with one hand, she reaches into the orange purse with the other and takes out a pad of paper and a deck of cards. "Do you know how to play gin rummy?"

"No."

She nods toward the phone in my hand. "Then look it up. I'm not going to teach you."

I'm not sure what I was expecting from Gramma Sharon, but this was not it. And I kind of like it? She's so much less intense than the Beaumonts. If someone told me she was JT's grandmother, I would have believed it instantly.

Putting her fan down, Gramma Sharon starts shuffling cards. "Go on. I'm not going easy on you just because you don't know how to play!"

I thought she was joking, honestly. But I look up how to play on my phone and she starts dealing. The back door opens and Marcus comes out with a glass of water and a small glass of brown liquor and ice.

"Good to see you, Sharon."

She says hello to Marcus and takes a sip of the alcohol. "What is this?"

"We're out of Jim Beam, so you get the good stuff."

She scrunches her nose. "If you say so." And takes another sip.

Marcus eyes up the cards and then turns to me and gives me the exact same better-you-than-me look Easton gave earlier—must be a family trait. Then he goes back into the house. Easton and JT haven't come back out yet and I'm getting the feeling no one really likes to be alone with Gramma Sharon.

"Age before beauty," she says, gesturing to me. I check my cards to see if I want the one on top of the discard pile. I don't, so I tell her to go ahead. She pulls the top card of the deck, then discards a jack. I have two jacks, so I take it.

"So? How've you been?" she asks. She pulls from the deck again and discards a two.

How've I been? She asks it like she hasn't seen Nate in a week, not nine-plus years. I look over the top of my cards at her, but she just fans herself, watching me expectantly. I have no clue how to even answer her, but for the first time, none of this feels like a trap?

And maybe that's why everyone else is in the house. They're scared of her because she doesn't seem like the kind of woman you can bullshit. That's why she's asking me such a flippant question.

So I give her a flippant answer: "Kidnapped. How 'bout you?" I take a card from the deck and put down a three.

The corner of her mouth quirks slightly, like she's impressed. Then she picks up the three and puts all her cards down. "Gin."

I look down and she has an ace, two, my three, and a four—all clubs—a jack, king, and queen—all spades—and three sixes.

"How?" I ask. "That was so fast!"

"Gin's a fast game, keep up." She writes down her total and tells me to show my hand. She writes my total in another column and gathers all the cards to hand over to me. "Shuffle and deal."

I do as she says.

"What was your kidnapper family like?" she asks. "I see they didn't feed you."

"No, that was all the time I spent starving while homeless," I say quickly. I might be trying for a gotcha moment, but Gramma Sharon doesn't even flinch.

"Well then, you get extra of my pies. I brought chocolate chiffon and key lime, so I hope you like both."

I do. Gramma Sharon makes me smile. There's something about her gruff, no-nonsense attitude I love. It reminds me of my own grandmother. My dad's mom.

My earliest memories are all of her. After I was born, she would watch me during the day while my parents worked. She wasn't like them at all. She had a Christian upbringing, even went to church with us on Sundays, but she was different.

She actually practiced what Christians preached. She was kind and generous. She didn't judge people, and she showed me more love than my parents ever did. She would walk me to the library, and if it was too hot or too cold to be outside, we would sit in the children's section, where she'd read me every book I brought her.

On nice days—usually in the fall or spring—she would let me

play on the playground while she read on one of the nearby benches. Her eyes went up to me every time I called out to her to watch me go down the slide or jump from the swing. She'd applaud her free hand against her thigh, asking me to do it again until I got bored and she could return to her book.

Then, when I was six and started going to school all day, she stopped watching me. I didn't find out until later it was because my mom thought she was ungodly. She disagreed with how Grammy practiced her religion and demanded that my father stop talking with her. Grammy also stopped going to our church.

I didn't even know she'd died until one day I came home from school in fifth grade and my parents were both home. My mom was in a black dress and my father in his suit. He was sitting quietly at the kitchen table and didn't even look up when I walked in.

When I asked what was wrong, my mother waved a dismissive hand and casually said, "Your father's mom died last week. The funeral was today. Go upstairs and get your homework done. I'll call you down when dinner is ready."

I went upstairs and cried silently in my room. That was the same year my dad ripped up the story I wrote. It was then that I started to realize something was wrong with my parents. They weren't like other people. They were hateful and full of self-righteous superiority.

The Beaumonts may not be self-righteous, but they're definitely cut from a different cloth than Gramma Sharon.

As I deal out the cards again, the back door opens and Valencia, Marcus, Easton, and JT emerge with drinks and small plates of appetizers.

Gramma Sharon talks with them as we trade cards back and forth. This hand lasts a little longer, but once again it's her who calls out "Gin!" first. While she shuffles the cards, Valencia talks about Easton and how he's doing in school.

"Yes, yes, yes," Gramma Sharon says. "He's very smart, we all know." She turns to him. "But tell me something exciting. You're living in New York City! Tell me about the fun things you're doing. Your brother survived being kidnapped by a psycho and living on the streets. Whatcha got, kiddo?"

"Mom, please." Valencia takes a big sip of her wine.

Easton glares and it startles me for an instant. But then he seems to realize he might be feeling a little resentment from Gramma Sharon's words and his face relaxes. He turns back to her with a shrug. "Not all of us can be so lucky."

I'm about to open my mouth to playfully scold him before I realize that, for a second, I forgot I'm pretending to be someone else. Like I'm in some bizarro world where I was born to a different family. I'm not Nate, and his family *didn't* get lucky.

"It's not about luck," Gramma Sharon says, discarding an ace. "It's about applying yourself. You're a small fish in a big pond now. You have to stand out. Stop trying to be so ordinary and get people to notice you."

"Easton is anything but ordinary," Valencia says. She smiles at him, and he returns a half-hearted one of his own.

Gramma Sharon's eyebrows go up in a manner that says she doesn't quite believe that, but she lets the subject drop as she asks Marcus how work is going instead.

* * *

The rest of dinner is much calmer as Gramma Sharon backs off of her pushy questions. Not that I minded them. She wasn't really pushing me much; she was pushing Easton. And maybe Easton deserves to be pushed. Valencia talks about him like he's a genius, but Gramma Sharon did have a point with the small fish in a big pond comment.

After dinner, Marcus and Valencia bring the dishes into the house as Gramma Sharon takes out her cards again.

"Now we play rummy," she says. "Look up that one."

"Isn't that what we were playing before?" I ask.

Gramma Sharon shakes her head. "We were playing *gin* rummy. Gin rummy is a two-player game. Rummy you can play with up to five."

So again, I look up the rules. Marcus and Valencia return with the pies and dessert plates. Gramma Sharon hands me the cards and tells me to deal while she cuts the pies.

"But don't deal in Easton," she says. "He cheats."

Across the table, Easton rolls his eyes.

"He was seven, Mom," Valencia says.

But Easton doesn't care. "It's fine, JT and I are going out soon anyway."

So I deal in Marcus and Valencia, leaving out JT and Easton. Gramma Sharon hands me a plate with two huge slices of pie on it, then asks everyone else what they want.

She was serious when she said she wanted me to eat pieces of both pies, and despite how full I am from dinner, I can't help but try both. They're delicious.

After dessert—and after Marcus wins one out of the four rummy games we play, while Gramma Sharon wins the rest—Easton and JT say they're going to a friend's house.

"Call us if you need a ride home," Valencia says.

"I'm not drinking, Mrs. B," JT says.

She gives him a skeptical look. "Smoking weed and driving is still driving under the influence, John Thomas."

"I promise I will never do that." He quickly adds, ". . . with Easton in the car." Then says good night and sprints off the deck and around the house, leaving only a scowl from Gramma Sharon in his wake.

Easton kisses Gramma Sharon on the cheek, then Valencia and Marcus, and says good night. Shortly after they leave, the sun sets, and Gramma Sharon stands and puts the remaining pie on a plate, telling Valencia to make sure I eat the rest.

"Nate." She hands me the empty pie plates. "Walk me out to my car."

My chest tightens and I look to Valencia and Marcus. They both seem to think this is normal, so maybe I don't need to be concerned yet.

I step off the deck and wait for her to say goodbye to Marcus and Valencia, then hold out a hand so I can help her down the steps. We walk quietly around the house. I expect her to turn to me and tell me she knows I'm full of shit. For police cars to come flying down the street, lights and sirens blaring as she pulls a badge out of that orange purse of hers and says she's a retired detective.

But when we reach her car, parked on the street, she opens the door and takes the pie plates from me. She places them in the back seat and nudges the door shut with her hip.

Then she gives me one more up-and-down look and puts her hands on both my cheeks and holds my gaze.

This is it. Here's where she looks into my soul and sees that I'm not Nate.

But she smiles and shakes her head. "It's good to see you again."

My mouth goes dry and I swallow. She pulls my head down to her and kisses my forehead. Then gets in the car.

"Stay out of trouble!" she yells before shutting the door.

Too late for that, Gramma Sharon. I'm stuck in place as she pulls a U-turn in the middle of the street and heads off into the night. I'm in plenty of trouble as it is.

You know what? Screw it. I've done the damage and taken Nate's identity. I don't want to think about the future when I'll have to run away again. For the moment, I just want to be here and enjoy this placeholder family.

Maybe I can make a *real* family like this in the future. As long as I stay out of jail and don't get caught. But for now, why shouldn't I accept the love Valencia, Marcus, Easton, and Gramma Sharon are willing to give?

There's a whispering voice in my head that tells me it's wrong, but the warmth in my chest is strong enough to shove it away. Push it off for now and be done with it.

Because I've been homeless for eight months and had shitty parents who thought torture was better than acceptance. I deserve a break, goddammit.

But standing out in front of the house, alone, I can't help but feel that familiar eyes-on-me feeling. I shiver as I look out at the other houses around us. Lights are on but I don't see anyone standing in any of the windows. Miles mentioned that Valencia told the neighborhood LISTSERV that I was back. Was that what made someone come to the house earlier? Maybe it was a neighbor who Valencia tasked with watering plants while they were away on vacation and they made a copy of the house key.

And if they were a neighbor, Nate might have trusted them. At school I was taught to never trust an adult who was asking a *child* for help. But maybe Nate wasn't. And when he was outside in his yard that day in July almost ten years ago, maybe a neighbor—someone he knew—showed up to ask him for help.

If they still live in the neighborhood, it means they kept on watching the family after Nate was gone.

My fear immediately shifts to anger. I want to know who would do this to the Beaumonts. This family who only seem to be trying their best.

And why break in? Why not kidnap me again or kill me right there?

Maybe because they can't for some reason. They got away with it before and now they're worried they can't. They knew they could break in, but for now, there's something protecting me. Something that's keeping them from doing to me whatever they did to Nate.

Maybe that something is this family? How much they're paying attention now?

As I walk back to the deck, the dog barks from the yard next door.

Miles is in his backyard with Chardonnay—seriously, is there a worse name for a dog?

I should do some damage control from earlier. Or maybe it'll cause more damage if I go over there. Still, I can't help myself. I don't want Miles to be mad at Nate for not remembering him. Even if it's a lie.

I've already told plenty of big lies. One more little one won't hurt, right?

FOURTEEN

MILES IS IN HIS BACKYARD WEARING A HEADLAMP. HE'S scanning the grass and using a pooper-scooper to pick up poop as Chardonnay watches him. Every time he finds a pile of her shit, she barks at him while he picks it up.

"Wouldn't it be better to do that during the day?" I call out.

Miles jumps and turns to me, holding out the pooper-scooper like a weapon. "Jesus." He puts the scooper down next to the tall plastic trash can he was carting around the yard and comes over to me.

"How long have you been watching me pick up piles of shit?"

"Long enough to know Chardonnay certainly doesn't like you doing it." Chardonnay jumps up again for pets, which I'm happy to provide.

"Yeah, well, Chardonnay doesn't like anything. Don't believe the hype, golden retrievers are assholes. She hates me, the mail carrier, the hot UPS guy, the ugly UPS guy, the neighbor's cat, and our lawn man—who is coming to mow tomorrow, which I forgot. Hence picking up dog shit by moonlight so he doesn't throw a hissy fit and charge my mom for cleaning his mower blades."

"Ah, it all makes sense now." But does it?

"Does it, though?" Miles asks. I can't help but laugh harder than I probably need to since I just thought the same thing.

"I did come over here to talk to you, though."

"Moi? How exciting. Have you come to teach me the traditional Slovakian dance of Odzemek?"

"How much do you know about Slovakia?"

"Only what I googled this afternoon to set up that bit."

"Well then, I'm here to tell you two things."

Miles closes his eyes and crosses his fingers. "Please be the dance."

"One, I'm not a Slovakian serial killer with dwarfism!"

"Dammit."

"Two. My mom told me we used to be friends. And I came out here to apologize." Miles grows serious now. "I . . . My doctor—therapist—said I have post-traumatic amnesia. Apparently I blocked out mostly everything from before eight months ago."

He looks at me as though he's studying a foreign language. "Right. And what, pray tell, happened eight months ago?"

I wish I could tell him the truth. I wish I could tell everyone the truth. Being Nate has been exhausting. The constant worry that I'm going to slip up and say something wrong.

"I escaped from whoever kidnapped me," I tell him, sticking with the lie. "I lived on the street until I was arrested for shoplifting in DC three days ago and they told me I had been missing for almost ten years."

Miles nods. "Ten years in July. And it's okay, by the way. When I saw you earlier, I thought . . . I don't know. I didn't think *amnesia*—little too soap opera, no offense."

"All offense taken. My life isn't your pop culture."

He snorts and narrows his eyes at me. "So listen, we were friends before. Want to be friends again?"

My chest starts to feel a little warm and fuzzy. I haven't had a friend in a while. "I'd like that."

He gestures back to the trash can behind him. "I have to finish cleaning up after Chardonnay, but want to come hang out?"

I didn't expect him to want to hang out immediately, but I definitely wouldn't mind getting out of the Beaumont house. But then I remember how Valencia freaked out because I explored the backyard and left a door open.

"My mom is a little . . . overprotective right now. I'll have to ask if she's okay with it."

"Understandable. You apparently got kidnapped and don't have any memory of anything before eight months ago!" It almost sounds like he's mocking me, and it makes me laugh. It's nice not to be treated like I'll break if someone says the wrong thing. He holds out his hand. "Give me your phone."

I hand it over, glad I closed out of any Nate-related searches I've done. He types something and hands it back. When I look at the screen, I see a text saying, Hi it's me. Here's my phone.

"Ask her if she'll let you walk next door to hang out with an old friend. If yes, text me. If no, text me."

I nod. "Wish me luck."

He picks up the pooper-scooper. "Shitloads of it."

"Ugh." But still I smile all the way back to the deck. Marcus has his arm over Valencia's shoulders and their wineglasses have been topped off, the bottle sitting on the table between them.

I decide not to wait it out and just ask. "I was talking to Miles, apologizing for not remembering him earlier. He asked if I could go over and hang out."

Valencia looks paler in the dim light of the deck. "Tonight?"

"Yeah."

She takes Marcus's arm off her shoulder, turning it into the light to read the gold-and-silver watch on his wrist.

"It's a little late," she says, letting Marcus's arm go. But I know from my phone it's only eight thirty.

Marcus puts his hand on her leg. "Hon. He'll be right next door. Let him see his friend."

Valencia still looks like she's sending me off to war. Or college.

"Be home by ten," she says quietly. Then pipes up, "Or sooner, if Miles's parents say so."

I tell her okay and go into the house to text Miles. I cut a piece of each pie and put it on a paper plate, wrapping it in plastic wrap. I pass Valencia and Marcus, telling them I'll be back by ten, and go around to the front of Miles's house.

He answers the door before I press the button on his doorbell camera.

I hold out the plate. "I brought you pie."

He gasps, taking the plate from me. "What a gracious guest." Chardonnay hops up on her hind legs, nostrils flaring as he holds the plate high out of her reach. He steps aside for me to enter. Miles's house is a little more modest than the Beaumonts'. The exterior is redbrick and it has a normal staircase instead of their grand staircase. But the rest of the layout is very similar. The dining room is to our left, and on our right is the living room, where his parents are sitting on the couch watching TV. They come over to join us.

Miles's mother is tall and thin with lightly tanned skin and beautiful wavy brown hair. His father has the same strawberry-blond hair as Miles; it's just as curly, but he keeps it cut shorter. He's also paler and covered in freckles like his son. They both greet me, shaking my hand.

Miles points to the pie. "So, first step in your reeducation process is . . . I'm type 1 diabetic, so I probably shouldn't eat these." He pulls up his shirt to show me a little plastic pod stuck to his lower abdomen. A blood glucose monitor.

"Oh." My cheeks flush. "I'm sorry."

But Miles's mom holds out her hand for the plate. "We're not, though. He gets that from his grandfather. We'll happily enjoy this and report back."

Miles puts his finger to his lips. "I'm going to guess chocolate tasting notes for this one . . ." He points to the chocolate chiffon pie, then drifts over the other. "And lime for this one."

Miles's dad peels off the plastic wrap and acts like Marcus smelling a glass of wine. "One has plum notes, and the answer may surprise you."

Christ, is being an adorable family in the water around here? Or maybe they're overcompensating. Where were Miles's parents earlier this afternoon while their son was distracting me? Too distrustful? Probably. But I didn't survive being homeless for eight months by being naive.

Miles takes me upstairs to his room. It's bigger than Nate's and doesn't have the Jack and Jill bath like Easton and I share. As he closes the door behind me, I scan the pictures and posters hung up around the room. What's visible of the walls is painted navy blue, and different-colored string lights hang from hooks screwed into the ceiling. Next to his bed is a collage of pictures—Miles with friends from school. Some other pictures on the wall above his dresser are black and white and look more artistic. One is a flower, one is graffiti on a brick wall, and another is unmistakably that island out in the bay behind our houses.

There's a professional-looking camera on his desk, next to a large flat-screen monitor hooked up to a laptop, which is closed.

I point to the pictures. "Did you take these?"

"Yeah." He crinkles his nose. "That was when I was figuring out how to use actual cameras instead of my phone. They suck."

"They do not." They're actually really good. But Miles picks up the camera on his desk and turns on the screen, standing beside me. He scrolls through some of his more recent pictures, and yeah, they do look a lot better. Professional.

They're pictures of a girl. She's posing in different areas—on the bench outside a supermarket, on a dock, at night under a streetlamp. All in the same emerald-green dress.

"Well, I still think the others are good, too," I say, then nod to the camera. "Is she your girlfriend?"

He snorts and side-eyes me. "Gurl."

I laugh, but the subtext is nonexistent.

"I mean, you're not *totally* wrong, because we did date for a week in fifth grade."

"So ex-girlfriend."

"To be fair, we never officially broke up. . . . Oh my fucking God, do I have a girlfriend?"

Again, I laugh and it feels *normal.* All this feels normal. Like maybe if I stop trying to *pretend* to be Nate so much, I can just be him. Or be myself with Nate's name. No one has seen Nate in almost ten years, so who's to say he isn't like me?

Miles puts the camera back on the desk next to a microphone plugged into the same dock the monitor is plugged into. Next to it is a pair of noise-canceling headphones. I point to the microphone.

"Do you livestream or something?"

"Or something." He shakes the mouse to wake up his computer, then unlocks it with a password. There's a program up with rows of different-colored bars stacked atop each other, and little sound waves across the length of the bars. "I run a highly unpopular true crime podcast. We average twenty listeners a month! That's down from thirty-five last year, but at least it's not zero."

A true crime podcast? I wonder if he ever did one on Nate.

"Cool," I say.

"It is!" he says, crossing his arms over his chest and leaning against the desk. "That's actually how I know you're not really Nate. So why don't you tell me who you really are, and why you're pretending to be him."

FIFTEEN

MY MOUTH HANGS OPEN AS I STARE AT MILES, UNSURE how to respond. I got too comfortable trying to be *me* and not Nate. My brain is totally blank.

Miles stares at me, waiting for me to say something.

So finally I say the one thing repeating over and over in my head: "How . . . how did you know?"

His eyes go wide and he flinches. "Wait. Seriously? I was right?"

Again, my mind goes blank. He was bluffing? Miles straightens up, staring right at me, studying my face.

"No," I say, trying to sound cool. "I'm kidding."

"Nice try. You're totally not Nate!" He's smiling but his eyes are still wide in shock, or maybe it's excitement. Like he really was bluffing but he caught me.

"Yes, I am." In the moment I don't know what's worse about Miles ratting me out: getting arrested and sent home, or destroying the Beaumonts' hope that their son is okay.

"Bullshit. I was right. Oh. My. God. I can't believe this." He starts to pace around the room with nervous excitement. "I had a hunch, but I had zero proof, and wanted to see if you'd dig the hole any deeper until I could *prove* you weren't him. I was going to make up memories about us as kids and see if you'd tell me you remembered them or not." He stops and runs over to his computer. "Oh shit, can I record this?"

"No!"

He glances over his shoulder. "You're in my house, and you know now that I'm recording, so you can choose to talk or not, but I'm definitely recording this."

I step around him and grab the microphone, ripping the jack out of the dock.

He holds up his hands. "Okay, hold on. That's a Sennheiser and it cost a hundred and fifty bucks, so why don't we put that down and we'll talk. No recording."

I place it on the dresser behind me. Away from any errant USB ports it might accidentally find its way into.

I nod at the computer screen. "It hasn't been recording this whole time?"

"Unfortunately for me, no. I have journalistic integrity, so I wouldn't record you without your consent." He crosses his arms again. "That being said, what you're doing is pretty messed up, so even if I did record you without your knowledge, I'm sure the Beaumonts wouldn't mind."

I sit down on his bed because the room seems to be spinning now. My heart beats hard enough in my chest that it feels like I can't breathe. I should have known Miles was bluffing. How would he be able to tell I'm not Nate after only speaking to me three times?

And how do I convince him not to tell the Beaumonts?

"What made you think I wasn't Nate to begin with?" I ask.

He shrugs. "You're not the first person to do this."

I'm not?

He turns around and types something into his computer, then steps away so I can look. I peer at the Wikipedia page of some guy with a French name. I'm not going to read the whole Wikipedia article, so I shake my head.

"He was a French serial impersonator," Miles says. "Somehow, he managed to convince the Spanish police, Interpol, the FBI, and this family he was a fifteen-year-old blond kid with blue eyes from Texas who disappeared three years earlier. Despite, you know, being French and in his mid-twenties with receding brown hair and brown eyes."

Okay, at least my eyes match Nate's. "How did he get away with it?"

"Well, he didn't." Miles scoffs. "Obviously, since I'm telling you his story. But they 'believed' it for probably the same reason you're getting away with it right now. The Spanish cops didn't want to deal with it, Interpol didn't want to deal with it. Neither did the FBI, or the Texas cops. I know *Law & Order* reruns tell us cops are good at their jobs, but let's be real. Inaction is the main job description of police in America. The Supreme Court even says they aren't required to protect people.

"Most crimes in America go unsolved. The highest clearance rate is fifty percent and that's for murder—and spoiler, murder is usually committed by someone close to the victim. A family member or friend. It's like a cheat code for solving murders. Pressure the people close to the vic until you find evidence, they mess up, or they confess."

Maybe eating the Beefaroni in front of the clerk and then running was the way to go after all.

"You know a lot of crime statistics." In fact, I feel like this isn't the first time he's said all this out loud. It feels rehearsed.

"Well, when your primary ADHD symptom is hyperfixation and your best friend disappears without a trace when you're six years old . . . yeah. You find hobbies."

Of course. Miles has spent the last ten years trying to figure out what happened to his best friend. And then I came along.

"So you were really bluffing?" I ask.

"Pressure people close to the victim until they mess up. You messed up, dude."

I put my face in my hands, trying to cool my burning skin. I'd been so goddamned careful up until now. Maybe I can convince him to give me a head start before he exposes me. Get away while I can.

"The amnesia was what pushed it over the edge for me," Miles says. "If we're being honest. Amnesia isn't usually contained to such a specific and convenient time period."

"The Beaumonts accepted it."

Miles nods. "Because they were desperate to believe it. Same with the cops. To them you're a nice little gold star for their clearance rate. Though if you *did* convince them, I'm not sure why they're still tailing you."

My heart seizes in my chest, and I look up at him. "What?"

He frowns. "You clearly aren't as used to this street as I am." He reaches into the top drawer of his dresser and pulls out a pair of binoculars. "Don't get excited, my window doesn't face anyone remotely attractive, so it's mainly for picnics on the dog beach." He lowers his voice as though talking to himself. "Lotta shirtless runners in the summertime."

He motions for me to follow him over to the window and pulls down one of the plastic blinds. I take the binoculars and he points down the street.

"See the car?"

The sedan is dark blue or black today, not maroon. But it's parked in the same place as the one I saw when I arrived. I thought it was one of the neighbors parked in front of their house, kind of like how Gramma Sharon parked in front of the Beaumonts'.

"How do you know it's a cop?"

"Chardonnay is a wonderful scouting companion," he says, like that should explain it. "I didn't recognize the car, so I took her out for a walk yesterday. It was a maroon car then. First I thought it might be a reporter, someone looking to do a story on your reappearance. I was hoping if they were famous enough, I'd get them to agree to be on my podcast if I gave them some information."

I give him a glare, but he returns it in kind.

"Send that high horse right to the glue factory, bitch."

Fair point. I look back at the car. There's someone sitting in it tonight.

"Anyway, it wasn't the media. Some skinny guy with a cop haircut. He was sitting there with the windows down. I could see his badge and the gun clipped to his hip."

So they're following me. Shit. I couldn't run even if the house wasn't securely locked down by apps and instant phone alerts. Maybe that's why someone's out there right now. Waiting to see me walking down the street with a backpack full of supplies and clean clothes. Which means even with a head start, I'm screwed.

"Wait." I turn back to him. "Older white guy?" He nods. "Gray hair, mustache?"

Miles shakes his head. "No, he was younger than that. You're talking about Grant, right?"

I flinch. "You know him?"

"Yeah, he lives in town. And he's the only reason *anything* got done when Nate disappeared. The local cops—again, inaction is the prime directive—weren't even going to issue an Amber Alert. They still said that forty-eight-hour bullshit. But I think Marcus knows someone who knew Grant and he got them to issue the alert. Then when the tip came through from Pennsylvania, he took over the case. Man, he's someone I'd love to do a podcast with. Probably has so many cool stories. But I'm too scared to ask him."

I get it. Grant *is* very intimidating.

"Anyway, he's retired now, so it wouldn't be him out there."

"He came to the hospital."

Miles is suddenly very interested. "What did he say?"

"Tried to convince Valencia to get a DNA test to be sure I'm who I say I am."

He tilts his head. "And she didn't want to?"

"My blood type matched, and she said that was enough."

"But she didn't want a DNA test to be sure? What about Marcus?"

"Both him and Easton said they should."

He starts to chew his lower lip as if he's figuring something out. "Then why would she be so adamant about not getting one?"

I shrug and look back at the car, wondering if whoever is in there can see us up here.

"Are you sure I can't record *any* of this?" Miles asks, his voice taking on a slightly whiny tone.

"No."

He snatches the binoculars out of my hands. "Hold on, can you go back to the beginning? How did this all happen? If I can't record it for my podcast, at least satisfy my own curiosity."

I look one more time at the cop in the unmarked car and sigh, then sit back down on Miles's bed and start from the beginning.

Miles lets me talk the entire time without interrupting. He sits across from me in his desk chair. I watch him carefully to make sure he isn't recording the conversation, but it isn't until halfway through the story that I realize he could have a camera hidden somewhere. Or maybe he's wearing a wire and this is all a trap.

But when I finish the story, no SWAT team runs in. There's no gotcha moment. Just Miles staring at me.

"Shit," he says.

"Yeah."

"Conversion therapy sucks. I mean, I've never been because I have parents who are, forgive me, not assholes."

"Noted."

"But I'm sorry that happened. And I'm sorry you had to run." He pauses as if he's mulling something over. "But why pretend to be Nate? Why not make up a name and a whole new story and be that person?"

Because the police would want more information, or they might put out a news report with my picture asking people if they knew who

I was. Then people from my hometown might see it and contact my parents. I'd be right back to where I was.

I decide not to get into it with Miles because I'm sure he has plenty of ideas on how to avoid that. Some other case where a kid showed up and became someone new.

So I go with the real answer. "I was desperate. And I hadn't eaten in almost three days, so I wasn't particularly in my right mind."

"Clearly."

"I thought it would be easy. I thought they'd take me to a hospital and do a DNA test and at some point I'd have a chance to run away before they even called the Beaumonts."

"But you forgot about your Fourth Amendment right."

"What right is that?"

"Protection from illegal search and seizure. They can't take things from your body without your permission or a warrant. The blood test was something the hospital did as part of your care, so I guess that was enough. If you'd turned out to have a different blood type, they probably wouldn't have contacted the Beaumonts."

"I didn't think things would get so out of hand."

Still, the muscles in my shoulders loosen. Telling someone, talking about it aloud, actually feels better. I feel less alone. I've been so lonely for so long. Then the Beaumonts made me feel wanted, though I knew it was fake. Temporary. But confessing everything to Miles feels . . . not. It feels genuine.

Confession is good for the soul after all.

"So what happens now?" I ask. "Do I get a head start, or are you going to rat me out right away?"

The look on his face says he hadn't thought about it. But as if catching himself, he turns stoic again and shrugs. "What if I didn't have to?"

"And why wouldn't you?" I don't trust the way he says it.

"Listen, I'm gonna be real with you—I've been trying to get the Beaumonts to agree to be interviewed for my podcast for years, and they've always very politely declined."

"You want me to convince them to do your podcast?"

"No, no. I can't possibly continue making the episode I want to after knowing you're an imposter."

Imposter. I hate the word, but it *is* apt.

He continues. "Look, at some point you're going to leave—with any luck, which admittedly has been on your side so far . . ."

If you say so.

"They're going to *know* you weren't really him. I assume you'd tell them the truth in a letter or something so they don't think they lost their son twice, right?" I nod. "Okay, so my podcast is going to be about you instead."

"So you're going to admit you knew I wasn't really me?"

His face pales and I can tell he hadn't thought that far ahead yet. "Oh, yeah. I guess I will. Shit." His so-called journalistic integrity won't let him lie. With a flick of his hand, he waves the idea aside. "I'll burn that bridge when I'm on it. What I want from you is some intel. You go over there and find out what you can for me, report back, and I'll keep your secret. At least then I can make a few episodes about Nate's disappearance before dropping the bombshell that I knew you weren't him. Maybe people will take pity on you. And me?" He doesn't sound sure, though.

"What intel are you expecting?"

Again, he bites his lip. I haven't known Miles that long, but it seems like he does that when he doesn't want to say what's on his mind. So I sit there and wait for him to spit it out.

"I assume you did some kind of research on the person you're pretending to be?"

"A little."

"And . . . you probably saw a few theories online. About what might have happened to Nate?"

"Serial killers, serial abductors, sex traffickers, aliens, time travel." I shrug, waiting for him to tell me which one he believes.

"Them."

"The Beaumonts?"

Miles nods. "I think they killed Nate."

SIXTEEN

THE BEAUMONTS KILLED NATE? THE IDEA MAKES ME FEEL like an elevator's safety cable has snapped. All my insides have jumped up to my throat and I'm in free fall.

How could they? And why? I shake my head. "They're a nice family. They're genuinely happy to have Nate back. I don't think people who killed their own son would invite more scrutiny."

"No, you're removing scrutiny. People have suspected Nate was murdered for almost ten years. Now that you're here, it's case closed. You said yourself that Valencia refused the DNA test. Why would she refuse to find out the truth after nearly a decade? That doesn't seem suspicious to you?"

Well, yeah, now that he mentions it. Still, I shake my head.

"Why would they kill him? They need a motive, right?"

Miles shrugs. "I mean, that's kinda the reason I'm asking you to do the investigation. Find out what might have made them snap. Hold on." He turns around and unlocks his computer again. He pulls up a document and waves me over.

It's a timeline of events from the day before the disappearance to the day after. Wow, Miles really *was* hyperfocusing on this. Every event has a time and date next to it.

"So, look, the night before, Valencia and Marcus have friends over for a dinner party. They sit outside on the deck until two a.m. drinking." He turns to me and lowers his voice. "My mom provided that intel. Their room is on that side of the house and she remembers looking at her phone at 2:03 a.m. when the noise woke her up. So the next day, Valencia apparently has a hangover and takes a nap. Marcus goes to town. The police checked his story, and there's security camera footage of him at the grocery store and the ice cream place picking up dessert for later. He gets home around two in the afternoon, notices Nate and Easton aren't home, but assumes they're out playing somewhere. Meanwhile Easton is at a friend's house from one until he comes home at four p.m. Marcus and Valencia say they were home the whole time, but they're the only two people who can confirm that."

Easton's friend. "I read an article that says Easton was with his friend John. Is that JT?"

"Yeah. The two of them are inseparable. Wherever JT goes, Easton follows. We were all in school together until they graduated last year, and Easton was only mildly popular because he hangs with JT. That stoner can make friends with a cantaloupe." Again he lowers his voice to a mutter. "Probably has."

So Easton left Nate to hang out with JT. Then there's a blank time between two and four when only the Beaumont parents were home.

"So you think the parents had something to do with it?"

"I don't *not* think it. But it's a theory. That's why I want your help. You're the closest to them. You can figure out what went on during that unaccounted-for time." He points to the two-hour period on his timeline.

"Do you really think Valencia and Marcus are the type of people who would kill someone?"

Miles puffs out his cheeks and blows the air between his lips before answering. "I don't want to cloud your investigation, but Marcus has a temper. Nate and I played peewee soccer together and Marcus yelled at him so hard for missing a goal that it made Nate cry and he quit playing."

Heat creeps up my neck to my ears and the tendons in my throat tighten. Maybe I'm relating too closely to Nate, but I've been on the other end of parental rage, too. I never played soccer, but there were plenty of times when my dad screamed at me for saying something he didn't like or being too antsy in church.

Marcus was supposed to be at work today, but he could have come home early, knocked off the camera, and used his key to go through the front door.

Especially if he got the notification that the alarm system was off.

Or it could have been Valencia.

"No." I back away from the computer. "I'm not getting into this investigation for you. If they really did kill their kid and I start looking into it, who's to say I'm not going to disappear next?"

"Then I'll tell them the truth." He stands to confront me with a steely gaze. "Maybe Valencia won't believe me, but I can easily call David Grant and say, 'Hey, I have a lead for you and would gladly trade it for you coming on my podcast.'"

My heart rate skyrockets. We're back to the beginning of this conversation. There really is no way out of this. I'm trapped with the Beaumonts; I'm trapped with Miles. But at least I know Miles won't kill me when I tell him no. Also, he was faking before, so maybe he's doing it again. And maybe it's my turn to do some bluffing.

So I shake my head. "Go ahead. If you think they killed Nate, maybe it's better I come clean and tell the police what really happened."

His face softens as his shoulders slump. "Dude, I was bluffing again. I'm not going to rat you out and send you back to your asshole parents. Or jail. Can you think about it? Please? I won't tell."

I stare at him; the steely, self-assured gaze he was giving me moments ago is gone and he seems genuine. Then my eyes flit to the computer. I'm still not sure I trust him. He's been investigating Nate's disappearance for so long, why would he give up so easily?

Miles seems to read my mind and holds out his pinky. "I promise to keep your secret either way. I mean, as long as you're not planning to rob them or do anything illegal."

I arch an eyebrow and he nods, realizing his mistake.

"Okay, anything *else* illegal."

Frankie was supposed to keep my secret, too. But what are my options?

I link my pinky with his. "Okay. Then yes, I'll think about it."

But I have no intention of thinking about it. In fact, now I need to figure out my escape plan so much sooner. Especially with the police watching the house. Another thought comes to me.

"Wait, was that cop out there this afternoon?" I ask. "When we first met?"

Miles shrugs. "I think so. I walked past him on the way home from school. Why?"

"I think someone broke into the house today." So, yeah, guess I'm trusting him. "When we were talking. I went back inside, and the front door was open and the doorbell camera was knocked off the house."

He becomes very interested again. "You think it was whoever killed Nate."

"What do *you* think?" I genuinely want to know. Because if it *was* the person who killed Nate, why didn't they try to kill me?

He nods and thinks for a second. "Yes. I get what you're asking about the cops, but no, they wouldn't break in. There's no reason."

"I was hoping they *saw* who broke in."

"But wouldn't they tell the Beaumonts if they saw someone shady around? And how do you ask without looking suspicious?" I can tell he's just speaking aloud to work through his thoughts, so I don't answer. Then he snaps his fingers. "They didn't come to the house after."

"No."

"So whoever it was didn't look suspicious to them." He widens his eyes at me. "Like someone who *lives* in the house?"

"Or a neighbor who knew the cop was there and when the coast would be clear." Cops have to pee or get lunch at some point, right? I don't know why I'm giving the Beaumonts the benefit of the doubt—I think I just don't want it to be true. "But if someone was going to break in, why not kill me?"

Again Miles thinks it over. "Maybe they know they can't yet. Cops outside, family on high alert. So they're toying with you. Whoever it is knows you're not Nate because they killed him. And they want you to know they're watching."

My mouth goes dry because, yes, that's what I was afraid of.

My phone alarm goes off, making me jump. Miles lets out a startled cry, then laughs. It's almost ten.

"I should get back home. Valencia is still anxious about me being away from the house." Another reason I don't think she could be responsible for Nate's disappearance. Miles nods and walks me out.

He follows me into the yard, past the viewing area of his own doorbell camera. I look over his shoulder to see the car is still there. The person inside still sitting in the driver's seat.

"Oh." Miles's eyes light up. "If you decide to help me out, I can help you get away."

My eyes drift over his shoulder to the cop car again. "How?"

"I have my driver's license. I'll borrow my mom's car—if you're ducked down in the back seat I can sneak you right by them."

"Wouldn't you get in trouble for helping me evade the police?"

He shrugs. "Not if you don't rat me out."

It would be the easiest way, sneaking out right under their noses. But Miles will only do it if I help him get information for his podcast. And I don't want my escape to be dependent on him deciding what I give him is good enough.

"Okay," I say. "I'll think about it."

"Listen. A tip while you're thinking it all over. Don't let them take your picture."

"Why?"

"Because right now all they have is that age-progressed picture of Nate they made with a computer. When you need to run again, they're going to go looking for you. And if the Beaumonts have a 4K picture of your smiling face, that's what they're going to put on the new posters. You won't be able to hide."

My stomach drops as I look back toward the house. "I'm already on their doorbell camera."

Miles shrugs. "Those things are shit usually. It only stores a few days of footage in the cloud. And the videos get compressed and they lower the bit rate to— Oh my God I sound like a complete lunatic nerd. Sorry. Point is, you'll be grainy, but you won't be exposed if they use that footage. Be careful of still photos."

I nod. "Thank you." I want to ask why he's helping me, but maybe he really does feel bad for me.

Miles looks uncomfortable for a second as he squeezes his eyes shut. "Don't make it weird, but . . . do you want a hug?"

I don't know how to answer that without making it weird, because I kind of think it already is. "How do I not make this weird?"

He sighs and shakes his hands in front of him like they're dirty. "Calling attention to the weirdness makes it weird, man!"

"You're asking if I want a hug with no context!"

Miles gestures to the space between us like it *is* the context. Then he lowers his voice as his eyes flit nervously around to make sure no one is nearby.

"Your parents tried to send you to conversion therapy, you've been homeless for eight months, and now you're trapped in a house with potential killers. I thought you might need a hug. I know *I* would need a hug. But getting one from said potential killers may not provide the emotional support a hug is supposed to, so . . ." He opens his arms wide. "You want it or not?"

I do. But *asking* like that definitely made it weird. Still, I remember the way Valencia's hug made me feel in the hospital—and consider how one from her in the future may not feel the same. So I step forward and let Miles wrap his arms around me and squeeze gently.

I rest my chin on his shoulder and squeeze him back.

Miles's warm body against mine. It does feel nice.

SEVENTEEN

AROUND MIDNIGHT, I GIVE UP TRYING TO SLEEP AND GO down to the kitchen. I put a kettle of water on the stove and light the burner, then grab a chamomile tea bag.

I can't stop thinking about Miles's investigation. I don't want to be a part of it, but what if he's right? If Valencia and Marcus are the only two without alibis, could they really have been responsible? Maybe Marcus got home and was hungover like Valencia, only he didn't get a nap. With Easton gone, Nate was bored and bothering his dad. Something happened and he snapped and pushed his son away.

It could have been an accident. Maybe Nate hit his head. Then Marcus hid the body. Or Valencia woke up and *helped* him. She might be trying to keep me here to help cover their tracks and replace the son she lost. Meanwhile Marcus is scared this will invite more scrutiny when the cops find out I'm not really Nate.

Add that to the fact that someone was here, in the house, earlier today. And it was most likely a threat. Or a warning. That they know I'm not Nate, and none of these alarms or locks are enough to keep me safe. And if I want to live, I should run now, while I still can.

I grab a mug from the cabinet and turn toward the kitchen island. Easton is standing in the doorway. I utter a startled cry and almost drop the mug in my hands. I didn't even hear him come in. The alarm was on when I went up to bed. He must have turned it off from his phone.

"You're still up?" he asks.

I nod. "I couldn't sleep."

He pulls out a chair from the island and plops down on it. "What did you do tonight?" he asks.

"Went over to Miles's house." And, you know, worried for hours about a killer watching me.

"He ask you to be on his podcast?" He says *podcast* like it's a dirty word, and when I look over at him, I can see he's sneering.

"He did. I told him I'd think about it."

"Don't bother. No one listens to it. He's trying to use you—he asked us all to do it multiple times. Nerd couldn't take a hint."

"I probably won't," I say. For a few moments Easton doesn't say anything else, but he looks as though he's still not sure he believes me. Then, out of nowhere, he speaks again.

"I want to say sorry," he says.

"You don't—"

"I do. I have to apologize for giving up on you." He looks over at me, his eyes glassy. The look on his face makes my heart seize. Like someone plunged their fist into my chest and squeezed the first soft, fragile thing they could find. If he were on a stage looking like this, even the people in the very back row would be able to see how upset he is. "I need to apologize for that day, too. Because we got in that stupid fucking argument when we were playing out there, and you said you were going to tell Dad. I went to JT's because I was scared he'd be pissed at me."

He looks so damn guilty, my heart hurts for him. He was just a kid, it's not fair for him to take on all that responsibility. "Easton, stop, it's not your fault."

"It *is*, though! I was supposed to be watching you but then we started arguing about I don't even remember what, and you ran off. I should have gone after you—but you remember how Dad was back then."

How he was? I don't, obviously, but Easton did say he was scared Marcus would be pissed off at him. And Miles mentioned the yelling at peewee soccer. Still, maybe Easton's dad is strict, but he doesn't seem abusive. At least not based on the way people act around him. Valencia was able to stand up to him, and he and Easton seem respectful and caring toward each other.

And Easton said, *Remember how Dad was back then.* Maybe Marcus turned over a new leaf once he lost a son. Or got better at hiding his temper.

"I didn't want him to freak out at me," Easton continues. "I remember that much. Maybe I punched you or tripped you or was picking on you, I don't know. But when I finally did get the courage to go home, I realized you weren't there. And you never told Dad about whatever we were fighting about."

Easton looks down at his hands again. His shoulders are slumped and he keeps avoiding my gaze, at though he's embarrassed or scared to even look at me.

"If it makes you feel any better," I say, "I don't remember any of that either."

I'm nervous he won't realize I'm joking, but he laughs. In fact, he laughs so hard he has to wipe a tear from his eye. Whatever tension is between us breaks and he finally looks at me.

"Yeah, well, I have more to apologize for than that day." He grows serious again. "I . . . gave up on you, Nate. At first it didn't make sense that you would disappear. I assumed you'd come home eventually, hungry for dinner. Then, when the cops were looking for you, I thought for sure they'd find you soon. And when they didn't, after a year or so, I . . ."

His voice breaks and he can't look at me again.

Shit. I really did mess up. Easton thought Nate was dead and had moved on. And now I'm here, and it may have disturbed his grieving process.

"I knew you were dead," he says. "After that much time I couldn't find a logical way that you could still be alive. I told myself you were dead, but Mom didn't believe that, so I kept my mouth shut about you around her. And of course she was acting . . ." He trails off, shaking his head. "We're not supposed to say 'crazy,' so I guess I'll say weird."

"Weird how?"

"Mental breakdown weird. Can't blame her—and I don't—" He adds it quickly, as if she might be listening and he doesn't want her to punish him. "It was scary. I mean, the whole incident was, but afterward *she* was scary."

"Scary and weird are all you're giving me. I'm going to need a bit more." Because I want to know *how* scary things got for him.

"Nah, it's stupid. I was a kid and you disappearing was the first time I realized that bad things could actually happen to us. So I was scared of Mom and Dad and what they might do. But again, I was just a stupid kid."

My heartbeat quickens. Even Easton—Marcus and Valencia's *real* son—was scared of them. Why? I need to know. But I don't want to push him or look like I'm desperately digging for information. I try to act nonchalant and shrug.

"I mean, I'm here, aren't I? So whatever you were thinking wasn't real. Doesn't mean you were stupid; you were scared."

He doesn't say anything, and I'm worried I missed my shot. I should have pushed harder to figure out why he was worried, and about what. But then he looks up at me.

"She—Mom—she . . ." He can't say it. Whatever it is that scared him so much as a kid, he can't even say it now. I should tell him it's okay, that he doesn't have to tell me. But I need to know. Because I need to know who in this house I can trust.

So I stare back at Easton, trying to telepathically tell him it's okay and he can tell me. And maybe it works, because he sighs and continues.

"She would say stuff—I don't even remember exactly what, but it was dark. Like if she ever found out you were really dead, she'd want to be dead, too. For all of us to be dead."

I swallow hard. Holy shit, that's dark. Poor Easton. For him to hear that as a kid must have been awful.

Easton waves a hand. "It's fine, though. I think Dad convinced her to go to therapy or something, and things got better."

"What about Dad?"

Easton shrugs. "I don't know. He never wanted to talk about any of it. Or maybe he wrote you off the quickest. As soon as you disappeared, he feared the worst." There's a long moment of silence before he looks at me again. "But I'm sorry I gave up on you. I shouldn't have."

That makes my heart swell. I know it can't possibly always be like this, but little moments like these must be what makes having a sibling wonderful. Even if I am lying to Easton, maybe I can put this in a box and save it—save how it feels to have someone on my side.

"Stop feeling guilty," I say. "None of this is your fault, and you definitely don't need to feel bad for thinking I was dead. I know how lucky I am. Most kids who disappear—especially for as long as I did—they don't get this happy ending. So give yourself a break."

He stares at me and his face changes. It's like he's an animal who has discovered something intriguing, stopping short of tilting his head like an inquisitive dog trying to hear something better.

"'Happy ending' is a strange way to say you got a second chance at a new life," he finally says.

He's right. I really shouldn't have said that. In all likelihood, despite the missing posters and age-progressed pictures, Nate is dead. I believe that even more after today. Which means there is no happy ending for this family.

"What is it?" Easton asks.

"I guess, yeah, it's not an ending so much as a continuation."

He nods. "A continuation. And I'll always be the guy whose

brother was abducted . . . or murdered by his parents. You'll always be the kid who was abducted."

"Murdered by his parents?" I act like it surprises me, but I'm also curious to know what he thinks about those rumors.

"Yeah, I've seen what people say online about us. I knew it wasn't true, but at least you can say you got to come back ten years later, right?" He grins again. "Back from the dead."

"You make it sound way cooler than it is."

There's a creak from the hallway outside the kitchen, followed by footsteps. Before he even enters the kitchen, I know it's Marcus because of the loud way he walks. He stops short in the doorway, looking at both of us.

"Couldn't sleep," I say, pointing to the kettle.

Easton points to himself. "Adult on break from school."

Marcus snorts and shakes his head, walking past us and grabbing a glass from the cabinet. "You can both stay up as late as you want. Your mother's the one who will make sure you're still out of bed by seven a.m." He fills the glass with water and says good night to us, calling back over his shoulder, "Don't forget to turn off the lights."

Once he's halfway up the stairs, Easton pushes himself up from the chair, then stops in the doorway. "Glad to have you back from the dead, little brother." He knocks against the wall and gives me a grin before leaving.

Behind me, the kettle starts to whistle. After I make my tea, I turn off all the lights—like Marcus oh so politely asked—and head up to my room.

* * *

I don't know what time it is when my alarm goes off, but it's dark outside. I reach over for the phone to silence it, still not understanding how it could be so loud.

But then Valencia screams my and Easton's names.

It's not my phone that's letting out that shrill sound.

It's the burglar alarm. Whoever broke in earlier is back.

EIGHTEEN

THE DOOR TO MY BEDROOM BURSTS OPEN AND VALENCIA is there, telling me to come with her. I don't think, just spring out of bed. Marcus is already downstairs, phone in hand. He's coughing as he runs to the front door. Easton is right behind him.

Valencia puts an arm around me and guides me down the stairs.

That's when I smell it.

Sulfuric and eggy. Gas.

It's not a burglar; it's a gas leak.

We rush outside. Easton and Marcus are already there; Marcus is talking into his cell phone, most likely to the alarm monitoring company, telling them to send the fire department.

Valencia corrals Easton and me toward the road, away from the house. She asks Marcus how far he thinks we should be, but Marcus holds up his index finger.

"Should we move one of the cars out of the garage?" Easton asks.

"No," says Valencia. "Stay here."

"If the house blows up, it's going to—"

"The house isn't going to blow up," Valencia says. But she sounds as if she might not be so sure.

Fire engine sirens sound in the distance as Marcus hangs up with the alarm company, but he immediately jumps back on to call the gas company to let them know there's a leak.

The fire trucks arrive, and Easton and I stand out of the way while Valencia talks to the firefighters and Marcus handles the gas company.

By now, lights have turned on in a few of the houses around us.

"What time is it?" I ask Easton.

He takes out his phone, which he must have been smart enough to grab when the alarm went off. "Two twenty-seven."

I turn to look at Miles's house and, sure enough, there's a light on.

The firefighters go inside our house with gas masks on. The one leading the way has a small yellow box with a flexible metal hose extending from the top of it that beeps when they reach the front door.

We all stand there, waiting in the flashing red lights. My stomach is in knots and my heart pounds as I picture the house exploding into a fireball at any second. Miles and his parents emerge from their house and walk down the front sidewalk toward us.

Marcus meets them and asks if they smell gas in their house, but they say no. Miles sidles up next to me.

"The LISTSERV is going to be abuzz," he whispers.

I groan because he's right. More people are standing outside their houses, wondering what's going on. It doesn't help that an ambulance has turned up now, too. And right behind that, a cop car, followed by another brown sedan. Which, if I were of legal betting age, I'd bet is the car that was watching us earlier. I turn to look down the road, and sure enough, the car that was parked a few houses down when I was out here with Miles is gone.

The EMTs approach us, and Valencia tells Easton and me to go with them. Easton attempts to argue, but Valencia—with the help of one of the EMTs—tells him it's to check his oxygen levels.

Easton and I head over to the ambulance, where they put pulse oximeters on our fingers while we sit on the back bumper. I look over at the cop cars again and the hairs on the back of my neck stand on end.

Agent Grant is there.

My mind goes to multiple places all at once. Miles said Grant lives nearby, but who called him? Or was that him in the sedan tonight? Miles also said he was retired, so he doesn't have the authority to investigate.

Unless the FBI thinks there's something bigger going on and he's been assigned to watch us. He's here to check up on me. And he's been watching me and the Beaumonts.

Once the EMTs say we're both fine, Marcus and Valencia each have their pulse ox read while I go back over to Miles, trying my best to ignore Agent Grant.

"Weird week, huh?" he asks, wiping sleep from his eyes. He's wearing a pair of green pajama pants and a black Orville Peck concert tee.

"Yes," I say with a sigh.

"Any chance you've thought any furth—"

"No," I interrupt him. Though it's not exactly true. I thought about it plenty before falling asleep a little over an hour ago. I just haven't made up my mind yet.

"No, you don't want to, or no, you haven't thought about it?" I glare at him and his hands go up. "Okay. Your decision, your timeline."

My eyes drift over to Agent Grant again. He's staring right at me. "How long did that imposter get away with it?" I ask.

Miles thinks for a second. "Five months, I think?"

Way too long. I'll be lucky to last five days if I keep drawing attention like this with an FBI agent in town.

The firefighters emerge from the house and take off their masks. They approach Marcus and Valencia—Agent Grant stands behind them, close enough to listen. I don't hear what they say over the sound of the fire truck's engine. Easton is close to them, though, and turns to me with his eyes wide.

"Seriously, Nate?" he says.

Agent Grant locks eyes with me.

"Uh-oh," Miles mumbles. "Girl, you might not have five months."

I ignore him and walk over to the Beaumonts. Valencia is giving me a sad look, while Marcus and Easton have matching scowls.

"You left the gas on after you made your tea," Easton says.

I did? No, I definitely remember turning it off when I poured the water. I shake my head. "No, no, I turned it off."

"When did you make tea?" Valencia asks.

"He was in the kitchen when I got home," Easton says.

"It was only slightly on," the fireman says. "You probably thought you turned it all the way off, but while it was enough for the flame to go out, the gas valve in the stove was still a little open. It was a slow leak, which would explain why it only now set off the alarms. Good job on getting those, by the way. Most people stop at carbon monoxide detectors."

"Can't be too careful," Valencia says. She was probably the one who insisted on the combination carbon monoxide and explosive gas monitors.

The fireman tells us to let the house air out for a bit but then we can go back inside. They drive away as Valencia and Marcus talk to the neighbors and tell them everything is fine. I last saw Agent Grant talking to one of the township officers, but when I look back, he and his car are gone.

Eventually we all go back inside. The four of us go around the first floor shutting and locking the windows before Valencia turns the alarm system back on.

I double-check that the window over the kitchen sink is locked and turn my attention to the stove. The kettle is still there. I turn on the same burner I was using to make my tea and turn it right back off.

The gas stops immediately.

I know I turned it off.

Didn't I? I was a little preoccupied thinking over my evening with Miles.

I try it again and this time the knob does stick before it's off all the way. There are footsteps heading to the kitchen. I shut off the knob all the way and take two large strides toward the door, almost running into Marcus.

He looks around the kitchen—his eyes going to the stove.

"Don't worry, I double-checked," I say. "They're all off."

"And I'm sure going forward you're going to triple-check them."

"Correct." I'm a little embarrassed. "Sorry. I really thought I turned it all the way off, but it must have stuck a little bit."

"No worries. We're all fine." He motions for me to leave the kitchen and shuts off the light behind me.

I say good night to everyone, apologizing again. But once I'm back in bed, I can't sleep. I can't believe I was so distracted by Miles, I forgot to turn off the stove all the way. Or maybe it was something Easton said to me.

I get up in the dark and walk over to the window that faces the front yard. I glance down the street.

The sedan is back. It's not the same one Grant was in, so maybe someone else has taken over. But it's there. Which means they're suspicious of me. If Agent Grant is out to prove I'm not Nate, they must have an idea of what really happened to him.

Miles wants me to help him get something he can turn into a podcast, then he'll help me escape. But what if Marcus or Valencia *is* responsible for Nate's death? If I can find some kind of evidence and present it to Agent Grant, he might let me go. He might even agree to give me a head start so he doesn't have to send me to my parents. Miles could use the same information to jump-start his podcast, and I escape into the night. Everyone is happy.

Except for Easton, who is left to find out his parents are murderers.

The idea keeps me up well into the early morning.

NINETEEN

I DON'T CARE IF AGENT GRANT HAS PEOPLE WATCHING the Beaumonts' street. I'm going to find my own way out of here before Miles has a chance to rat me out.

Because—despite the hug and the genuine way he seemed to care about me—I don't think I believe him. I don't believe he didn't have a recording device somewhere in that room last night, and I don't believe he's going to keep my secret despite what he said about solidarity. Not outing someone is queer solidarity; committing a crime to let a stranger continue to steal a missing-and-probably-dead-kid's identity is *not*.

So when Valencia says she's running out to pick up dry cleaning and check in on her dental practice, after setting the alarm and double-checking every door is locked, I search for a backpack. There's one—probably Easton's—in the front hall closet, but right beside it is a slightly larger duffel bag with ratty gym shoes in it—also probably Easton's.

I put the shoes in the backpack and take the duffel instead, then go straight to the pantry. There's plenty of canned goods, beans and tomatoes mainly, but I only take two cans of garbanzo beans and put them in the bag. I don't want to be too weighed down if I need to run.

There's also a box of protein bars, but there are only eight left, so I take three, hoping they won't be missed.

Before closing the pantry, I snatch a packet from the open Pop-Tarts box. It's an okay start. If it all goes at once, they might notice. I'll take a couple things every few days until I think I'm ready.

After that, I head up to my room and look at the clothes the Beaumonts bought me. It sucks that I don't have any of my own—my stashed backpack under the Starbucks dumpster is probably long gone by now—but I take two shirts, two pairs of underwear, three pairs of socks, and a pair of jeans, and put it all in the duffel bag, nestling the food between folded clothes to protect it.

Then I slide the bag under my bed, toward the headboard. I walk over to the door, imagining what the Beaumonts might notice if they peeked in. So far Valencia and Marcus haven't been snooping around, but a random bag under the bed might be suspicious. I can't see it from here, but being so exposed makes me nervous, so I grab it and put it in the closet on the top shelf. I push it back against the wall so it looks like any old bag.

"Where's Mom?"

I startle as I close the closet door, and there's Easton. I didn't even hear him come in.

"Running errands, and then she said she had to check on the office." I go over to the bed and lie down as casually as I can and take out my phone. I shouldn't have silenced it, because there's notifications that the alarm had been turned off and the front door opened and closed. When I look up at Easton, I have to force myself not to glance over at the closet.

He grins. "And she left you alone! I can't believe it."

"She said she knew you'd be home soon."

"Probably tracking my location, as usual." He seems bored by all this, but he makes a good point. Is she checking *my* location at all times? I knew I'd be leaving this phone here when I left, but didn't realize she'd be tracking my every outing until then.

"She watches our phones?"

Easton shrugs. "You were kidnapped. She's paranoid. I've found it's best to leave your phone behind sometimes if you want privacy." He takes his phone out of his pocket and puts it on Nate's old dresser. "Come with me. I want to show you something."

I get up, looking at his phone, and he nods.

"Leave it here with mine."

"Are we going somewhere?"

"Yes. And she never tracked us when we used to go there. Put on some shoes and let's go." He heads downstairs and I watch him for a moment before putting my phone on the dresser next to his. I slip my feet into the new shoes Valencia picked out and follow him.

He stops to wait for me in the mudroom between the kitchen and garage.

"I'm going to show you one of my tricks." He reaches up to the sensor stuck on the garage doorjamb. There's a small white piece of plastic on the jamb, and another larger one on the door itself. He peels up the smaller one slowly, and it instantly clicks over to the larger.

"Magnetized," he says, pulling open the door. The contact stays attached to the larger sensor. "No alarm notification. You can use that if you need to sneak out once I'm back at school."

Holy shit. My pulse quickens. Easton just showed me how to get out of here unnoticed. He leads me out to the garage, pressing the automatic opener. Mounted on the far wall are two kayaks. The aquamarine kayak in the top mount is a two-person, the red one below it is one-. He grabs one side of the aquamarine kayak and motions for me to get the other side. There are three paddles against the wall, and as we walk out of the garage, he grabs two of them.

I stare at the large garage door as we pass under it. "Mom and Dad don't have an app for the garage door opening?" I ask.

Easton shakes his head. "There was one they could use to open and close it, but the company went bankrupt and the app isn't supported anymore. They just use the openers in their cars."

He takes the lead once we're clear of the garage—using a PIN pad on the exterior of the door to close it—and walks down to the dock.

"Why isn't this thing kept in the boathouse?" I ask, pointing to it with my free hand as we pass it.

"An empty boathouse means Marcus can bug Valencia about getting a boat to fill it whenever he gets the chance," he says sarcastically, and the way he uses his parents' names instead of "Mom and Dad" makes my lips pull into a smirk.

He sets the kayak into the water, doing most of the work himself, then holds it steady.

"You get in first." He nods to the front seat. Nerves buzz in my stomach as I picture the kayak tipping over. But with Easton holding it for me I'm able to sit down without making a total ass of myself. He hands the paddles over for me to hold while he gets in the back and pushes us off the dock.

I hand one back and turn to watch him paddle, mimicking his movements.

"Now you row on the opposite side, so we go straight."

Straight ahead to the island in the bay. "We're going there?" I point to it.

"Yep."

It seems so far away, but as we paddle across the calm waters of the bay, I'm shocked by how quickly we're traveling. Water laps against the sides of the kayak. Easton's strokes are almost silent, while mine are clumsy and splash water onto my hands.

I breathe in the salty air and a light breeze skims the water. The knots in the muscles of my chest, stomach, and shoulders all loosen. I breathe deeply and it feels like the first breath I've taken in days. I don't think I ever realized how calming something like this could be. As we approach the island, I find myself wishing we could keep paddling around the bay.

But Easton beaches the kayak onto the shore and hops out. I follow, and he pulls the kayak up to a patch of tall grass. The edge of the island is dirt and rocks, not sand, and there's a little path leading into the trees.

The house on the shore looks so much smaller from here. Maybe the island is bigger than I originally thought from the reverse point of view.

"Come on."

Easton stands on the path heading into the woods. I look back to the house once more before following him.

"We used to come all the way out here?" I ask. He bends a sapling that's grown over the path out of the way, waiting until I pass to let it spring back.

"Yeah. I mean, I did all the work because you would always whine about getting tired halfway here." He gives me a knowing glance. "Thanks for almost pulling your weight this time."

"*Almost?*" My arms are already a little sore from paddling.

"Holy shit," Easton says ahead of me. I can't see his face, but I can hear that he's surprised. "I can't believe it's still here."

The path leads to a clearing with a large dead tree lying across the middle of it.

I step around him and focus on a little A-frame structure built against the tree. The top of it comes up to eye level, and it's made of broken tree branches and tied together with frayed twine. Dirty old blankets covered in dead leaves make up the "walls" of the fort. It's messy and structurally unsound. Obviously created by two kids who knew little to nothing about architecture and went with whatever stayed upright.

Easton steps aside and holds out his hands like he's showing off a new boat Marcus bought.

"Ta-da!"

"Yeah, looks . . . great." Honestly, it looks like something from a horror movie. Like a group of lost hikers would stumble upon this and then one of them would go into the woods to pee only to be decapitated by the lunatic who built the hut. There's a dirty green beach towel on the ground inside—acting as a rug, I guess.

"You helped me build this," Easton clarifies.

I nod because I don't know what else to do. Paddling over here helped with the never-ending anxiety and feeling of being trapped that comes with living at the Beaumonts', but now the guilt is back. I didn't help build this; Nate did. Easton thinks he's sharing a special moment with his little brother, but I'm just some random kid.

Easton crouches down, then crawls into the stick hut. He goes back as far as he can to the dead tree. He sits cross-legged and looks up at the structure with childlike eyes. Then he smiles at me and pats the beach towel in front of him.

I sit at the entrance to the hut. It's not big enough for both of us to sit in—at least, not without touching the musty blankets on the sides. Though maybe it was big enough when Nate was six and Easton was nine.

He grows serious and draws a line in the dirt next to him. "Can I tell you a secret?"

I want to say no. Keep your secret, Easton. I'm not worthy of a secret. Especially not since you spilled your heart out to me last night. Talking about all the guilt you've kept for so damn long, thinking Nate was dead.

"Is it a fun secret?" I ask, trying to lighten the mood. And maybe also hint that he can keep it to himself if he wants.

He frowns and turns his attention back to me. "What secrets *are* fun, Nate?"

Got me there, bitch. So far, none of the secrets in my life have been fun.

"Surprise party," I say as soon as the idea pops into my head.

He doesn't smile or laugh. Just stares at me for a few more seconds like he's trying to figure out if I'm joking or if I really think surprise parties are the only fun secrets to have.

"That day." He doesn't need to clarify which one. "I wasn't at JT's house like I told the police I was. I hid here."

Hiding? From what? Who? I don't know how to ask, and honestly I don't know why I want to so badly. But Miles's offer pops into my head. It's new information that he doesn't know. Would it be enough to get him to help me escape from this place?

"Why?"

"Because I thought Dad would be pissed at me. I still don't remember what we argued about, but I know I shoved you and you pushed me back and we kind of fought. And you said you were going to tell on me when he got home. So I got a kayak and paddled out here by myself. That's why you got kidnapped."

Jesus, this kid. How much guilt has he been carrying for the past ten years? I'd feel bad for Easton any day of the week for holding on to this secret for so long, but knowing that he's confessing it to me, thinking I'm Nate, makes it so much worse. And why the hell are Valencia and Marcus paying for my therapy but neglecting their actual son who *clearly* needs it?

"Stop saying shit like that," I say. He looks into my eyes and it seems like he's about to cry. His eyes aren't glassy, but his face is twisted in pain. "What happened to me isn't your fault."

He lets out a bark of a laugh and shakes his head. "You can say that all you want, but it doesn't make it any truer."

And it definitely doesn't help him feel less guilty.

"Why did you tell everyone you were at JT's instead of out here?" I ask.

He shrugs. "I was still scared I'd get in trouble with Dad. I was a kid, so I don't think I realized how serious it was. When Mom and Dad asked me where I'd been, I panicked and said at JT's because I didn't want to get in trouble for fighting with you, for going to the fort without you. And . . ." He stops and sighs, and when he speaks again it sounds like he can't even believe he's telling me this. "This is also our place. They knew we came out here, but they didn't know about the fort. They thought we were playing around on the island. We promised each other not to tell them, that it would be our secret place. I wanted to keep that promise."

And once the lie was out, he couldn't go back on it. Not even when the police came and started asking questions.

I know the feeling.

"Well, stop worrying about it at least. I'm here, right?" It's the one lie that I can't go back on, after all.

He laughs and looks back up at the structure, pushing at the sticks. "I think we need to expand. Or build an addition at the very least."

"Yeah," I say. "We should probably do that on a day when Mom isn't going to return to the house to find us both gone."

In reality, I don't want to mess with something he built with his brother. I'd never be able to forgive myself if I helped take this apart and put some other fort up instead. I imagine Easton paddling out here by himself after I'm gone and he's found out the truth. Crying as he destroys the fort and wondering if his real brother is alive or dead.

He nods. "Shit, you're right. Let's head back."

I stand and we walk back out to the kayak. If I do help Miles, he might be able to figure out what happened to Nate. I don't want to tell him about Easton, though, because he might say in his podcast that Easton's lie is the reason Nate was kidnapped. It doesn't matter either way, though. Nate would have disappeared regardless of whether Easton told them he was at JT's or the fort. So if I can protect him from Miles—and guarantee that Miles will leave him out of his podcast—maybe I can help him get closure another way.

Miles knows more about the case than I do, and he's obviously a great investigator, so maybe he'll have an idea of where I should start.

In exchange for his silence and help.

Because Easton has given me a good getaway plan. The police aren't watching the bay like they're watching the street.

Once I'm back up to my room, I text Miles.

Okay. Where do we start?

TWENTY

MY FIRST WEEKEND WITH THE BEAUMONTS, THEY TAKE me to the quaint main street of town. I expect people to stare—watching the family they all whispered about and the son everyone thought they had murdered—but no one even looks twice at us.

Saturday night, Easton goes out again with JT. He offers to bring me along in front of Valencia, who immediately blanches at the idea, then looks relieved when I say no thank you.

Instead, I invite Miles over and we hang out on the deck, where we're safe from Valencia or Marcus eavesdropping. I still don't want to tell him about Easton's lie. It's not important, and I kind of feel a bond with Easton now. Maybe he's trying to make up for lost time, but he's always checking in with me, asking how I'm doing, asking if I remember anything yet. And on more than one occasion, he's asked if there's anything he can do to help.

Thanks for making me feel even guiltier, Easton.

"Have you learned anything new?" Miles asks once we're sure we're alone. He still keeps his voice low.

I shake my head. "I haven't really had a chance to talk to either of them one-on-one. They want to do everything as a family." I'm acting annoyed, but in reality I'm more than okay with it. For one, it means whoever broke in the other day can't get me alone—yes, it obviously could be one of the family, but again, we're not alone so, yay, safety in numbers. And the supersecret menu item: I enjoy hanging out with the Beaumonts.

Miles nods. "Do you know what you're going to ask them?"

"What they remember about my disappearance. I start therapy on Tuesday, so I'm going to ask if they remember anything I should talk about."

"Hmm." He seems to be considering whether that will work.

"Well, give me some pointers, then. You're the true crime nut."

"Don't say it like that."

"Why not?"

He scoffs. "Because it sounds like I have a problem."

"I mean, you might. I don't know your life."

"Fair point. I prefer *aficionado*."

I can't help but laugh because this whole thing is ridiculous, if I'm being honest. I'm sitting on my fake parents' back deck talking with the only person who knows I'm not really Nate, planning an investigation that I have no idea where to start.

"Enough, get serious." Though I don't really want to. Miles joking with me makes this all feel a little like pretend. Like we're just two kids sitting on the deck playing some game and my life isn't in constant, imminent danger. Because Miles has to be scared, too, right? If he's seen with me enough, the killer might start watching him, too.

"I am serious. True crime aficionado until I decide if I want to become a private eye or investigative journalist."

"That's what you want to do with your life?"

He shrugs. "I mean, private investigator *sounds* like fun, but according to the internet it's ninety percent sitting in a car taking pictures of people walking in and out of motels. I don't think I can be trusted to keep myself entertained."

"What about a photographer?" I ask.

"That's just a hobby. I'm not actually good." I open my mouth to correct him but he holds a hand up to stop me. "My mom embarrasses me enough with the encouragement as it is."

"So I guess that leaves investigative journalism?"

He sighs, sounding wistful. "Also more interesting in theory. Especially because most journalism now is posting whatever pisses off enough people to get clicks. Maybe I should become a hit man. That's probably fun."

"You just became my prime suspect."

"Yes, children are always the prime suspects in another child's disappearance."

"What do you think happened? I mean really. You're the aficionado—"

"I prefer nut."

"Shut up. What do you think happened to him?"

Miles keeps his smile, but something changes in it. The humor dissolves, and sadness clouds his eyes as he shrugs. Then he sighs.

"In sixth grade they made us all do this book report. Like, they took us to the school library, almost no guidance on what we were supposed to write, just pick any book, read it, write a report on it. It was exciting for like three minutes because we were eleven-year-olds presented with free will for the first time."

I chuckle but don't tell him they did something similar at my school.

"I chose *The Face on the Milk Carton*. You heard of it?"

I shake my head.

"It starts a bit like your story, but back in the nineties, instead of a missing poster, they used to put kids' faces on milk cartons? Don't ask me why. Anyway, this girl finds out she was abducted when she was three and then abandoned with the people she grew up thinking were her parents. She ends up reconnecting with her birth family in the end. I kind of always hoped that's what happened to him. At least then he's not dead. He might be happy, even. Living his life, not realizing his real family is still out there. I know it's silly." He shrugs again.

"It's optimistic."

Miles nods. "That's because the truth is way worse. Because shit like that doesn't happen in real life."

"I dunno," I say. "I thought what I did never happened in real life, and then you went and told me about that French dude."

"Well, in that case, you better hope Nate shows up *after* you leave." A chill runs down my spine at the image of Nate knocking on the door. Valencia opening it to see him standing there. How much would we look alike? I try to push the thought away and focus on Miles.

"So do you think he's still out there?"

Now his smile is completely gone. "No. It's not realistic. Something happened to him and he's either dead or someone . . ." His voice trails off as he shakes his head, not wanting to acknowledge the truth of the matter. Because he's right; it's not a better outcome, and it is more realistic. Whatever the truth is, it's bad for Nate.

"Okay," I say. "What should I be looking for?"

"No clue, but that's why you're going to snoop. I feel like we won't know what we're looking for until we find it. And if we don't find anything, it's good news. It means maybe the Beaumonts really didn't have anything to do with it. If it's a stranger who came and kidnapped him, that would explain why the police and FBI weren't able to find any new clues."

"Valencia goes back to work Monday. I'll see if there's anything I can dig up while she's out."

He thinks for a moment and breaks into a grin. "You know . . . I could come help you. Oh my God, I've never skipped school before. You know what, that's all the motivation I need. I'm gonna ditch!"

"Whoa. A couple days with me and you're breaking the law. Maybe you *should* be on my suspect list."

Miles chuckles and stands. "Text me when the coast is clear on Monday."

I stand, too, and walk to the edge of the deck with him. He hops off into the grass and stops himself.

"So what do you want to be?"

His question comes out of nowhere and catches me fully off guard. "Sorry?"

"You asked if I wanted to be a PI in the future. What do you want to be?"

I don't want to answer that truthfully because it feels silly. So I lie. "I guess I just want to be myself again."

Miles narrows his eyes at me. "Okay. So who are you really?"

Is he asking my name? I'm definitely not giving him that. Miles is smart enough—even if I disappeared tomorrow, he'd be able to track me down eventually if I didn't change it. And I have no clue how much work changing my name would be without all my legal documentation.

So I shrug. "A queer homeless kid from West Virginia."

He frowns. "Still hiding, huh? Don't worry, I'll break you down eventually. *Nate.*" Then he says good night and I wait until he goes around the side of the house before I head into the kitchen.

Valencia and Marcus are speaking in hushed tones in the living room, so I close the door quietly behind me and tiptoe across the kitchen tile to the doorway.

". . . have to pay it back," Marcus says.

"Then we'll pay it back. We'll use the home equity line and pay it back."

"The rate is variable, Val."

I realize whatever they're talking about can't be all that interesting if it's about interest rates, so I'm about to turn back into the kitchen to grab another drink before heading upstairs, but Valencia's voice stops me.

"Can't you be happy our son is alive and well and back in our home?"

Marcus's voice gets a little louder, and I can hear some of the temper Easton mentioned. "That's not what this is about!"

"Do not raise your voice to me. And yes. It is, Marcus. That's exactly what all this is about. And I don't give a shit how much money we have to pay back. They can have it. At least we have him."

"We don't know—"

"I don't want to hear any more about how much fucking money we owe! We'll pay it. Do you understand me?"

A long silence stretches between them, and it gives me enough time to try to figure out what they're talking about. Obviously me, but what does money have to do with it? And who do they owe it to?

"I'm making myself a cocktail," Marcus says. His voice is lower now. Calmer. "Do you want one?"

Valencia answers with a huff. "I'm fine, thank you."

A shadow enters the living room doorway and I turn around and run for the back door. I pull it open quickly, then shut it loudly to make it sound like I just came in. I'm halfway across the kitchen when Marcus enters. He gives me a quick glance—it might look a little resentful?—then heads over to the fridge. He already has a crystal rocks glass in his hand, and he pulls open the freezer to put ice in it.

I go out into the living room and sit down on the couch next to Valencia. She smiles brightly, like she and her husband weren't arguing about money and my presence less than two minutes ago.

"Miles go home already?" she asks.

"He had some photography stuff to work on." I turn my attention to the TV. "What are you watching?"

"Some HBO show about space pirates." Her voice takes on a playful tone. "You're welcome to stay, but there's lots of sex, so you may not want to watch it with your parents."

Marcus enters and gives us a side-eye, which Valencia misses. Then he goes to the bar cart in the corner of the living room and picks up a bottle of gin. I'm honestly surprised the Beaumonts have their liquor out like this. My parents didn't drink, but I figured parents who did would keep stuff locked away so their kids wouldn't dip into it.

Marcus mixes his cocktail and reaches for one of the tools held in a stainless steel block. He pulls it out but stops, looking at it. It's sharp and looks like an ice pick. He's about to put it back but then puts it in his glass and uses it to stir the cocktail before placing it back on the cart.

"I think I'll skip the Space Sex Pirates, but thank you." I stand. "I'm tired anyway, so I think I'll go to bed."

"Painting tomorrow?" Valencia asks.

"Sounds good."

"Love you, honey," Valencia says. "Good night."

"Night," I say back.

Marcus doesn't say anything; he just sips his cocktail as he unpauses their show. Whatever they were arguing about, I'll have to see if we can find out what it is on Monday when Miles comes to help me snoop.

TWENTY-ONE

ON SUNDAY, MARCUS, EASTON, AND I MOVE NATE'S furniture into the middle of the room so we can paint. I'm glad I decided to put the duffel bag with the food in the closet instead of under my bed. I still feel bad changing Nate's room, but if he really is dead, it's not like he'll be using it. I'm still not sure how I'll feel once I get out of this situation. But maybe a fresh coat of paint will help them move on, or even sell the house, after they find out I'm not Nate.

Easton doesn't stick around to help paint, saying he's going to work on the essay he's turning in as a final instead. Marcus tapes off the molding around the room and instructs me to take off the outlet covers and switch plates. Valencia brings us a Bluetooth speaker and mentions that she's going to do some administrative work for her dental practice while we paint, saying that three of us painting the room would be too many cooks. But it's clear she's trying to force some "father-son" bonding.

Which is fine. Because it means I can figure out where Marcus lies on my hierarchy of suspects. So far, he's solidly at the top of the list. He had anger issues, he's a straight white male—which is usually the profile of psychopathic killers—and there was that whole argument about money last night.

Plus he's a lawyer. And a criminal defense lawyer at that. He's seen all the mistakes his clients have made.

So I broach the subject as we paint opposite sides of the room.

"Have you ever had a client who murdered someone?" I ask. Across the room, he pauses but doesn't look at me. Then he goes back to rolling the gray-green paint onto the wall.

"I've had clients who have been accused of murder."

"Did they do it?"

Again he pauses, and this time he turns. "I wouldn't be able to tell you if they told me they did. There's something called attorney-client privilege."

"But you're not telling me *who.* Just if it ever happened."

Marcus smirks. "I'm not a nobody in the criminal defense world."

Which means there's articles online. Especially if it was a murder trial. I make a mental note to tell Miles to do a deeper dive into Marcus's work life.

"Generically then, let's say you did defend a person who murdered someone. How do you usually get them out of trouble?"

He sighs and goes back to painting. "If they *did* it, I'd suggest they take the plea deal. Maryland doesn't have the death penalty anymore, but there are work-arounds—like if the crime was committed on federal land, it could still be tried as a capital case despite Maryland, Virginia, DC, and Delaware all abolishing the death penalty. Pennsylvania still has it, but the governor hasn't put anyone to death in years." He stops himself, probably realizing he's gotten into the weeds on jurisdictional law and capital punishment. Then adds, "So I would say, take the plea, do the time."

"What if they don't take the plea?"

"Then they need an alibi or alternative theory. Someone else to blame. But that only works if the evidence against them is flimsy, and in order to even pursue legal action for something like murder, you need a lot of solid evidence."

"Like a murder weapon?" I ask.

He nods, and as he continues painting and talking, he seems less guarded. "That would definitely help. But the body is the main crux. Without a body, you need physical evidence that a crime took place. Blood, body parts, video evidence or eyewitnesses. Otherwise you put someone in prison for a murder that never happened, and seven years later you find out the guy is innocent."

Maybe that's why no one has ever found Nate's body. Because his father knows the best way to not be found guilty of murder. Even if it was an accident. Like if he lost his temper one day and snapped. It all started with a reprimand, maybe grabbing Nate to swat him on his backside, and then he lost control.

"Nate?"

I turn to see him staring at the paint roller in his hand.

"You're not planning on killing anyone, right?" He dips the roller and, without looking at me, continues painting.

I give him a fake laugh. "I got caught shoplifting, what makes you think I can get away with murder?"

He stops painting and looks over his shoulder at me. "Never said I thought you'd get away with it."

He locks eyes with me for what seems like an eternity, and it makes the blood in my veins feel like ice water. It's like he's telling me that he knows I'm not Nate and he knows I won't get away with this. And that he knows I can't outsmart him. Then he grins like it was all a joke and goes back to painting.

It takes us two coats of paint and until four p.m. before we're moving the furniture back where it started. Easton helps us with that. Marcus and Easton go to move Nate's dresser back, but Marcus stops and picks up the remaining half-full paint can.

He holds it out to me. "Grab the rollers and put all this stuff in the garage with the other paint supplies." We've already thrown out the used cloth rollers, and he's taken the paintbrushes he edged the ceiling with down to the utility sink in the basement. I take the can, tarp, and unused rollers and head to the garage.

The paint supplies are on the middle rack of the wire shelf, next to Valencia's gardening stuff. But there isn't room for the paint can. I put the unused rollers on the shelf, place the tarp on top, and set the paint can on the floor of the garage, then shut off the light on my way out.

TWENTY-TWO

ON MONDAY MORNING, VALENCIA IS DEFINITELY ON edge. I know it's because she's anxious about going to work and leaving me home alone, but I'm not sure why. She knows the alarm app will tell her every door and window I open—she doesn't know Easton showed me how to bypass it. Maybe she's worried about me snooping?

Which, yes, Miles and I are absolutely going to do that as soon as the house is clear.

"What do you think you'll do today?" she asks, sipping her coffee as I eat a leftover bagel from Saturday.

"I was thinking about walking to the library," I say. "I looked it up; it's only a half mile away." I have no intention of going to the library today, but I want to test her reaction to me having some autonomy. It might come in useful when I *do* want to get out of here.

She sets the coffee mug down a little too hard but tries to play it off. For a moment it seems like she isn't going to say anything, but then she looks at me. "I'd like you to stay in the house."

"Why?"

"Because I'm asking you to?" She says it tentatively, like she's trying to be nice, but also hinting that she's doing more than *asking*.

"I'll have my phone on me. I'm not going to disappear."

Finally she snaps, and her voice goes full-on scoldy mom mode. "Well, disappearing isn't the worst thing that can happen to a person, Nate, and a phone won't protect you from that."

I flinch, and to her credit, Valencia looks embarrassed. But not enough to apologize or elaborate any further.

Easton enters the kitchen, dressed for the day. "Christ, Mom, cut the cord already." He goes over to the fridge and takes out a jar of peanut butter.

"I don't need it from you, too," she says. She sounds exasperated and turns her attention back to me. "Stay home. Please. I'll drive you to the library on our way home from your appointment with Dr. Zapata tomorrow. And I promise I will loosen the reins at some point. I'm just not ready to do it right now."

"Fine," I say under my breath. I want to understand why she's acting like this. Sure, she's anxious that the son she just got back might be taken from her again. But it feels possessive, not overprotective. I can't help but wonder what she knows about the real Nate's disappearance. Or maybe what she's suppressing. Easton gives me a pitying look as he scoops a spoonful of peanut butter.

"I hope you're eating something else," Valencia says. "And other people may want peanut butter, so I'd appreciate if you didn't eat it directly from the jar."

He shrugs. "Habit. I'm the only one who usually eats it. Nate, if you want peanut butter, you'll have to deal with my cooties." He turns back to Valencia. "Which, by the way, are the *same* cooties." He dips his empty spoon back into the Jif jar defiantly.

Marcus enters with his own empty coffee mug. He's dressed in a brown tweed suit, blue shirt, and navy-and-gold tie. He kisses Valencia on the cheek, then puts the mug in the kitchen sink. Valencia reminds him of the leftovers in the fridge and he grabs a Tupperware and asks Easton if he's ready to go.

He's going to the office with Marcus because he needs to have someone monitor him while he's taking one of his finals online. Easton's professor said he'd allow him to take the final remotely as long as he had a proctor who wasn't a family member, so one of Marcus's assistants is going to sit in a room and barely watch him take a test. Or at least sign a paper saying they did that.

"Did you remember to set the timer on the garden spigot?" Valencia asks Marcus.

He closes his eyes and shakes his head. "I forgot. I'll do it tonight when I get home."

"Can you do it now? It's supposed to get up to ninety today and I don't want all the hydrangeas to burn or get droopy."

He laughs. "You're the one who bought the overcomplicated timer. I can't figure the thing out in five minutes, and if we don't leave now, I'm going to be late for a meeting. The flowers will be fine for a few hours. I'm calling a car for Easton when he finishes his final, so when you get home, can you water the plants?" He turns to Easton.

"I was going to have you send me to JT's."

But before Valencia or Marcus can ask him to come here first, I speak up. "I can water them." It's actually perfect, because I can open the back door to let Miles in and Valencia will get the notification on her phone that the alarm is off. "I'm stuck here all day. Let me at least do something boring like watering the flowers."

"Thank you, Nate," Marcus says pointedly while looking at Valencia. "See, darling? You don't even need the timer."

"You know what, that's a great point. Maybe I'll show you how to fertilize them, too, before I leave."

"Wonderful," Marcus says. "Now that that's out of the way, Easton, grab your stuff. We gotta go."

Marcus gives me a polite goodbye and they head for the garage door. I stand to put my plate in the kitchen sink.

"I'll show you where the Miracid is for the hydrangeas. You add a scoop—"

"NATE!"

Marcus's voice booms from the garage, startling me. Even Valencia flinches, spilling her coffee on the counter.

She reaches out and grabs my hand, as if by instinct.

"Get out here! NOW!"

Valencia lets go quickly and rushes to the garage. Easton is standing inside the mudroom, shaking his head and smirking.

"Probably should have left it the original color," he murmurs as he looks at me.

Valencia gasps and I step around her to see the carnage in the garage. The motor finishes pulling up the garage door, letting the morning sun illuminate the crime scene.

The front of Marcus's black Mercedes is stained green.

No. It's Juniper Fog.

Whatever was left in the paint can I put away yesterday is splattered across the hood and drips down to a massive wet puddle in front of it. The paint can is on its side at the puddle's edge. The lid sits glued to the windshield with a layer of dried spatter. There's a half-moon-shaped dent in the hood where the edge of the can must have hit.

I shake my head. "How did this happen?"

Behind me Easton snorts. "Seriously?"

I glare at him over my shoulder. "I put it on the ground!"

"Then how the fuck did it get all over the hood of my car?" Marcus yells. A vein pulses at his temple and his face has gone red.

"Marcus." Valencia's voice is a warning.

"What?! Half of it's probably dried, I don't have time to go to the car wash, and it won't come off without detailing anyway." He walks over to the driver's side door, opens it, and reaches in to pull a lever. The hood pops and, carefully, he steps around the paint to reach under the hood and unlatch it. His hands come away green-gray as he lifts it up. And yes, the paint has seeped around the edges and into the engine compartment. It only goes down the sides, not touching anything important, but it's definitely there. Some of it pools around a raised edge, which is most likely there to keep water from getting into anything vital.

Marcus glares at me, shaking his head. He slams the hood again and some of the tacky, still-wet paint splatters onto his pants. He curses again, and Valencia tells him to calm down.

I step around her and point a shaky hand to the ground. "I swear I put it right there."

"You sure?" Easton asks. "Dad did tell you to put it with the paint stuff."

"Yes, I'm sure." I point to the wire rack behind Marcus. "Look, there wasn't enough room for the paint, so I put it on the ground."

The paint rollers aren't where I put them. I open my mouth to say so but Marcus interrupts me.

"You're right," he says. He points to the dent on the front of the car. "There wasn't enough room, which is why it fell off and landed here."

Someone must have moved it. Easton or Valencia. Or, shit, maybe Marcus himself did it and now he's embarrassed it fell over and he's looking to pass the buck. Someone clearly moved the paint rollers to put the can on the shelf but didn't realize it would tip over.

I shake my head. "No! I *swear* I put it on the ground."

Valencia puts a gentle hand on my shoulder. "Honey, it's okay if you put it on the shelf. No one is mad."

"The fuck we aren't!" Marcus yells, gesturing to his car. "*I'm* mad! Look at this mess." There's that short temper I've been hearing about.

"Yes, and you need to clean yourself up if you're going to get to work on time," Valencia says, stepping in front of me like a protective mama bear. But I'm still shaking. Marcus is acting like my own father now, and it makes my heart race with a familiar fear. My dad never hit me, but the threat was always there. Like when he'd get too mad and throw the kitchen chair into the living room or kick some nearby inanimate object, then wince in pain.

Marcus clenches his fists and shakes his head. Then he reaches into his pocket with a hand that doesn't have paint on it and tosses his keys. I duck, thinking he's throwing them at my face, but they go wide around me and Easton catches them.

"Easton, back the car out of the garage for me. Nate, you made the mess; get the hose and clean off whatever isn't dry."

"I didn't *make* the me—"

“I don’t care! Do it!” Marcus storms past us and into the house, cursing under his breath and looking down at the paint on his ugly suit.

Easton gets in the car and backs it out while Valencia puts an arm around me.

“I swear I put it on the ground,” I say. I don’t know why I care so damn much, but I need her to believe me.

She nods. “It’s okay. It’s just a car. And he’s been itching to buy a new one anyway; he’s waiting for bonus season.” She gently rubs my arms. “Go hose off what you can. He’ll take out all his anger on some scathing motion he’s gotta write and cool off by the time he gets home.”

Valencia is the only one who has treated me like Nate from the start, and even she isn’t saying she believes me. She keeps saying *it’s okay* and *no one is mad* but never *I believe you*. She never even offered up another theory like Marcus said a murder suspect needs. She just decided not to defend me altogether.

I swallow hard and try to ignore the tears blurring my vision as I walk out to the driveway. Easton watches me as I unravel the hose attached to the spigot on the side of the garage. I peel off the paint can lid and turn on the hose. Most of the paint starts to come off pretty easily, but the dried areas are stubborn, and no matter which setting on the hose nozzle I use, it isn’t enough to wash it off.

“So what did he do?” Easton asks.

“What do you mean?”

“To piss you off. Obviously he said something yesterday. When I was helping you move the furniture back, the energy was . . . odd. Now you plaster his car in paint—”

"I didn't do this."

His hands go up. "Sure. Fine. But he thinks you did, which means he thinks you had a reason to."

So Marcus set me up? He said the only way to get away with murder is an alternative theory, but there's no evidence for one here. He told me, in front of Easton, to take the paint downstairs to the garage. Specifically to put it with the other paint supplies. I put it on the floor, and it somehow ends up on the car, which is impossible.

Marcus returns wearing a new suit. Without saying anything to me, he gets in the car. Easton gives me an anxious look and climbs into the passenger seat after him. The door is barely shut before Marcus shifts into reverse and backs out.

I spray down the driveway, washing the paint water into the grass so it doesn't stain the asphalt—another thing for Marcus to freak out about when he gets back from work—and then put away the hose.

Valencia comes back out with her work bag and glances over at the paint on the garage floor.

"Can you do your best to clean all that up, too?" she asks. She tells me where some cleaning supplies are, and I nod.

"I swear I put it on the floor, not the shelf." Again, I don't know why I care so much that she believes me. But the look on her face—the one that says she feels sorry for me—tells me she doesn't believe me at all.

She reminds me to set the alarm when I go inside, then I clean up the garage floor.

While I mop, I keep replaying what Easton said. The energy in the room was weird after I asked Marcus about how to get away with murder. If Marcus had something to do with Nate's disappearance—he told me himself the best way to avoid a murder charge is for the police to not have a body—then he knows I'm onto him.

TWENTY-THREE

AFTER CLEANING THE GARAGE FLOOR, AND MYSELF, I text Miles to come over and then turn off the alarm to open the back door.

I expect a text from Valencia, but none comes as I water the hydrangeas on the side and front of the house—making sure to walk in front of the doorbell camera so she gets a notification.

Miles hops over the fence as I'm coiling up the hose.

"Ready to snoop?" he asks, his eyes a little gleeful.

"You sound way too excited to be invading your neighbors' privacy."

"Yeah, I keep telling myself if we find out they're murderers, it wipes my karmic slate clean. So let's try and get something good."

He marches around the house and I follow him, closing and locking the door behind us. I also set the alarm, because I want to know if someone tries to get in here again. If they really are watching, and they know I'm alone today, they might try. But at least I have Miles with me. If Valencia asks why I opened the door later, when Miles goes home, I'll tell her I was fertilizing the hydrangeas.

Maybe she'll be so grateful that I fertilized them, she'll change her mind about the paint being a destructive outburst.

"Where should we start?" I ask Miles.

"I'd say start in Valencia and Marcus's room."

"Fine, but I'm not going through their drawers like a pervert."

"Drawers are cliché," Miles says, climbing the stairs. "All the freaky stuff is in the closets. I mean, we'd know, right?"

His joke is stupid, but he's not wrong. I hid my go bag in the closet, after all.

We head into the large walk-in closet Marcus and Valencia share. All her stuff is on the right; all his on the left. Marcus's side also has a chest-height dresser with a watch box and small dish of cuff links, keys, change, and miscellaneous other items he probably tosses in after coming home from work.

Valencia's side has shoeboxes up on the top shelf. I take them down to look inside, but they're all her expensive shoes she probably only wears on special occasions.

"Oh-kay, Valencia," Miles says, taking out a pair of black leather heels with red bottoms. "Louboutin. Fancy." Then he scrunches up his face and puts the bottom of the heels against the bottom of his own shoes. "Not my size. Shame."

I snort at the image of Miles walking around in those shoes. "You would look ridiculous."

He points at me with the shoe. "But you're picturing it."

I huff in annoyance but my cheeks still burn. While he puts the shoes back, I turn to Marcus's side of the closet to hide my blushing from him.

Marcus has a shoebox on his top shelf, too, but it's a blue Cole Haan box. I reach up for it and it feels heavy, but the weight is sitting differently than a pair of shoes would. When I open it, my stomach drops.

"Holy shit."

Inside is a black handgun.

My hands start to shake as my pulse quickens. Even though this gun has a lock on the trigger, I hold the box like it's a bomb. There's too much potential energy there; it's like the gun *wants* to go off, and it doesn't care what it's pointing at.

Miles appears behind me and whistles. "Do you think they bought it before or after Nate disappeared?"

I tilt the box toward him. "You thinking murder weapon?"

But Miles shakes his head. "Too loud. Someone would have reported a gunshot. Trust me, every Fourth of July the LISTSERV is rife with 'gunshots or fireworks' emails. It's like, you all live in the suburbs, not downtown Baltimore, cool your tits, you know?"

Again I laugh. "But they do own a gun. That's something in the potential-murder column, right?"

"No. *My* parents have a shotgun in their closet and they're liberal hippies. If I had to guess, they bought it *after* Nate's disappearance. Everyone around here was freaking out after that. Alarm signs went up in yards, the LISTSERV started. Maybe that's why so many of them are worried about gunshots on a national holiday."

I place the lid on the box and put it back up where I found it, then we leave the room.

"What's upstairs?" Miles points to the stairs at the end of the hall, which go to the third floor.

"Valencia says it's a guest room, Marcus's office, and some storage."

"Office, eh?" Miles heads for the stairs and I follow.

The steps to the third floor are narrower than the open first-floor stairs, and they're carpeted with dingy, high-pile beige carpet.

The third floor has a small cedar closet, bathroom, and guest room—I have no problem checking the dresser drawers in the guest room, and they're empty anyway. We continue down the hall and there's another door to my left and one straight ahead. I open the one on the left first. It's Marcus's office.

Unlike the rest of the rooms on this floor, it looks like it's been renovated. There's a leather chair facing a desk and the walls on both sides of the room have been changed to bookshelves. Each shelf is filled with expensive-looking law books with dates on the spine; they go all the way back to 1994.

Marcus's desk looks expensive, too. The wood is dark and shiny, like it's been treated with some kind of wax. There's a computer monitor that's hooked up to a dock that Marcus can connect his laptop to. The chair is leather and tufted, and behind the desk are two windows looking out to the backyard.

I go around the desk and start pulling open drawers. In the top right there's only pens, pencils, Post-its, paper clips, highlighters, and little sticky tabs in a variety of colors. Miles pulls on the drawers on the left side of the desk, but they're locked.

"Hmm. If you were a key, where would you be?" he asks.

"Probably with all the other keys. Which means he's got it with him at work."

"You didn't happen to learn how to pick locks in your time living on the streets, did you?"

I tsk. "You know what, I skipped Lockpicking for the Homeless 101. I took How Not to Starve to Death, like a dummy."

But Miles's eyes light up like he realized something. "Wait, I have an idea." He runs out of the room, and I call after him, asking where he's going, but he doesn't answer. His footsteps go down the stairs to the second floor, but then I lose them.

I turn my attention back to the file drawer on the right side of the desk, which is also unlocked. But it looks like it's all house stuff. There's copies of the deed, some tax documents, and property insurance. There's also a folder on the boathouse, but when I flick through, it looks like invoices for the construction dating back a little over a year, but nothing interesting. I put it back and see the final folder is labeled "NATE LI-P/O."

I take it out and set it on the desktop. It's a bunch of letters from a life insurance company. The top letter is from August two years ago. It says that because of a judgment, they're paying out the life insurance the Beaumonts had on Nate.

"Holy shit."

It was a five-hundred-thousand-dollar policy. Besides the payout, there are invoices for the policy payment in full from fifteen years ago, when Nate was a year old. There's another document that looks like a petition Marcus filed with the court six years after Nate's disappearance to have him declared dead. And the approval from the judge.

Miles appears in the doorway, a small key in his hand. "This was in that tray of change on Marcus's dresser. Think it fits the desk?"

"Maybe, but I found something more important."

He walks around the desk and looks over the documents.

His eyes go wide when I point out how much the payout was. "Half a million! Shit."

"This is something, right?" I ask.

"It's definitely motive." Miles keeps looking over the papers as he talks. "Life insurance is one of the biggest reasons family members murder each other." He points to the court documents. "And they got paid out for it based on your disappearance. Look. Marcus even had to file an order with a judge to have you declared dead." He pauses. "He probably knows a judge who helped him push it through."

He sets down the papers and takes out his phone. I peer over his shoulder to see he's searching how long a person needs to be missing before life insurance pays out.

"Life insurance companies have to wait seven years before they pay out a missing person's life insurance. Unless a judge declares you legally dead beforehand, which, according to this, is hard to do."

I go back to the drawer and look for the Beaumonts' other policies. In the household folders I find more life insurance policies. Marcus's is for five million dollars. Valencia's is, too. Easton has one in his name for five hundred thousand dollars that dates to the same time as Nate's. I turn Valencia's around to show Miles. "Five million dollars. If Marcus killed Nate for the insurance money, why not kill her instead?"

Miles shrugs as he reads it over. "Maybe he didn't like Nate. It's entirely possible for a parent to choose their spouse over their kid."

The idea fills me with rage. Will my own parents collect life insurance on me in seven years? If I'm still around then, I'm definitely going back to prove I'm still alive and fuck it up for them. Though I doubt my parents even bought a life insurance policy for me.

"Is that weird?" I ask. "For parents to have life insurance on their kids?"

Miles finally turns his attention back to me and he looks unsure. "I mean, maybe not? For funeral expenses—but five hundred K is a pretty swanky funeral, if you ask me." He goes back to reading the insurance documents.

Five hundred thousand dollars really is a lot of money. Valencia and Marcus are both wealthy people with high-paying jobs, so would they really need half a million dollars so much that they'd kill their own son?

I pose the question to Miles.

"There's always a reason. Maybe Marcus has gambling debts. Or maybe they're leveraged out the ass and can't keep up? These old houses are expensive to maintain."

Valencia did say they had to have the roof redone. Maybe that and a few other big items hit and they couldn't keep up, so—

My heart seizes and goose bumps burst across my arms. "Wait, what date was that court order declaring Nate dead?"

Miles hums as he flips through documents. "August twenty-seventh, two years ago."

"Holy shit. Do you remember them building that boathouse?" I point out the window at it, then go back into the files for the boathouse invoices.

Miles catches on and his eyes go wide. "Yes. I think they finished it like a year ago?"

"After Nate was declared dead." I put the final invoice on the desk. And yes, the total costs almost half of Nate's five-hundred-grand policy.

Something changes on Miles's face. Uncertainty. "I think a boathouse is an extreme reason to kill your own kid. And they had to wait eight years for the payout."

"You said—"

"I was being flippant. Unless he's an absolute psychopath, I don't think that was the reason. Maybe it was the reason they filed the paperwork to have you officially declared dead, yes. But people don't buy *toys* with murder money, they pay off debts or mob bosses. Or politicians maybe. Plus, now that you're not dead, he's going to have to pay it all back."

If I thought I had chills before, they get even more intense now. "What?"

"I mean, they don't get to keep the money. You're alive, so the insurance company is going to come knocking for it. And they definitely won't accept it in installments."

The conversation I overheard on Saturday. I update Miles, telling him what I heard Valencia and Marcus discussing. "I didn't realize at the time that they were talking about life insurance, but it must be, right?"

"Definitely." He chews on his lip as he thinks something over. I ask him what it is, and he tilts his head. "It sounds like Valencia really thinks you're Nate. Or she's trying hard to keep up the delusion. Marcus was probably trying to convince her to finally do the DNA test."

"Why wouldn't he do it without her permission?"

"Because he can't just take your hair and prove you're not his kid. First off, DNA is flimsy and never exact. It's not like it is on TV, where you put it in a machine and it says it's a ninety-nine-percent match. You need samples from both parents, but maternal samples will give the highest markers.

"Those mail-order DNA kits, forensics, even paternity tests compare the child's DNA to the mother's first, *then* cross-reference the father's markers. You should really pay better attention in biology."

"Yeah, I'll make sure I get on that when I'm enrolled in school and not homeless." Miles laughs, and I feel a teeny bit of pride. "Okay, so he wants to test me so he can keep his pretty boathouse—without a boat, by the way."

"Well, you wouldn't buy a car without a garage!" he says with faux shock.

"You're so right." I flop down into Marcus's chair. "So he wants the test because he doesn't want to pay back the insurance money. And he's very sure that he won't have to pay if they do the test."

Miles nods, picking up on what I'm saying. "Because he knows the test will prove you're not Nate."

"Oh my God." Again my body tingles, only this time it's more from fear than shock. Miles asks me what's wrong. I tell him what happened this morning with the paint. And our conversation yesterday while painting Nate's room.

He has a thoughtful expression on his face that turns skeptical when he speaks. "You think he's trying to set you up so Valencia finally starts to wonder if you're not the real Nate? I mean, you're sure you put the paint on the ground, right?"

"Positive like a mitochondrial DNA test."

"Terrible example, but I understand the sentiment."

"So it's him. He killed Nate."

Miles holds up his hands. "Hold on. That's still a leap. It could just be that he knows you're an imposter and wants you out of his house."

"We have the insurance payouts, and he's not just trying to prove I'm not Nate, he's trying to make it look like I'm a psycho who throws paint on his expensive car."

Miles sighs. "He's also a criminal defense attorney who all but told you that without a body or some kind of compelling evidence, he can get away with murder."

He says it like he's telling me what he had for dinner last night.

"How can you be so calm about this? I'm the one who's stuck here. Can you at least *pretend* to be concerned?"

"I am! I swear, but . . ." He shakes his head as he looks over the documents, putting them back together in order and closing the folders. "It feels too easy. And, look, I know you're going to be pissed when I say this, but are you absolutely sure you put the paint on the ground?"

"Are you serious right now?" The whole point of Miles coming over today was for him to find evidence—evidence that is *in* his hands—and he suddenly becomes a skeptic?

"I don't want to jump the gun."

"You were the one who said you thought they killed him!"

Now Miles looks like he's the one who got caught in a lie. "I said . . . what . . . I thought would make an interesting story."

I stare at him, trying to figure out if he's joking or not—and, honestly, given the situation, even our queer-based gallows-humor-laugh-because-if-you-don't-you'll-cry coping mechanism isn't appropriate.

"Are you for real right now?" I ask. "You came here to—" But then a thought jumps out. "You only came here for your podcast. Something you can throw in around the midway point to either heighten the stakes or throw people off."

"That's not true. I do want to find out what really happened to Nate."

"This!" I pick up the papers on the desk and hold them up to him. "This is what happened!"

"Stop yelling at me."

"No! You told me to help you; I'm helping you."

"But you're also lying!"

One of the papers falls out of my hand but I don't bother picking it up. I thought—and I don't know why—but I thought Miles really did care about all this. Nate, me, maybe the Beaumonts. But he doesn't. He cares about his podcast with twenty listeners.

Once the silence between us goes on for too long, he shrugs. "I'm sorry. But . . . I'm not going to jump to conclusions based on everything we found here."

"You mean the stuff you snooped out with an imposter."

Miles has the decency not to lie and say that wasn't what he was thinking. "I'm sorry. I trust you, because you told me the truth. But I'm not sure how far that truth goes yet."

So he, like Valencia, probably doesn't even believe me about the paint. Or the gas leak, both of which I'm now convinced were Marcus.

"So because I'm lying about who I say I am, you ignore evidence."

Miles picks up the paper on the ground and takes the rest from me. "It's *circumstantial* evidence. If it was something tangible, he would have thrown it out or found a way to destroy it so it couldn't come back to him. This wasn't even in the locked drawer."

"Then what are we doing here?"

"Information gathering. Getting something the police don't have and tying their investigation and ours together."

I'm not sure why I thought this day would go any different. I already learned this lesson months ago: the only person you can rely on is yourself. Guess I needed a reminder.

Miles holds the key he found in Marcus's room. "Should we see if there's anything else?"

I shrug. "Go for it. I'm sure if you found Nate's severed head in there, you'd say it doesn't prove anything."

He ignores the jab and unlocks the top drawer, but it holds only a couple of phone chargers, batteries, and key chains without keys attached to them.

"Phone chargers!" Miles gasps. "Now it all makes sense!"

I shoot him an annoyed look and pull open the drawer beneath it. Maybe *that's* the one Marcus wanted to lock. You can't lock one without locking the other.

And yes. It's definitely the one he wanted to lock.

Inside is a blue glass pipe with a Philadelphia Flyers logo stenciled on it. It's a bowl to smoke weed out of. My laughter breaks the room's silence.

"So Marcus is a stoner," Miles says. "Surprising." He takes out a black glass jar and holds it out to me. Sure enough, when I open it up, there are four ziplock bags of dried bud. Each bag has the strain written on it in Sharpie—*Slapz*, *Green Line OG*, *Motorbreath #15*, and *Blue Zushi*. He even has a grinder and pipe cleaners.

But that's it. It's only his weed stash. The fact that Marcus Beaumont is apparently a stoner doesn't add suspicion. If anything, maybe being a stoner improved his "short temper." I've never smoked weed. Frankie and I were offered it at a party once and I was afraid I would get too honest and say something gay. Frankie, on the other hand, jumped right in. She was normal old Frankie but dialed down. Maybe it's the same for Marcus. All the edges get smoothed off and it's just calm Marcus who sits quietly, studying the room.

Miles hands the key over to me and I put everything back the way it was and lock up while he goes out to the storage room at the end of the hall. I poke my head in to find him looking at boxes of holiday decor and old clothes. When he realizes there's nothing else there, we go back downstairs—returning the key where Miles found it—and go to the kitchen.

"You're mad at me, aren't you?" Miles asks.

"For what? Saying I'm unreliable? Because I'm a liar who can't be trusted?"

"You *are* a liar, and yes."

I lied to the Beaumonts. It doesn't make me a *liar.* It's not like it's a habit. Right? Though I'm lying right now, aren't I? To myself, but still, it's a lie. Almost everything I've said to the Beaumonts has been untrue, so yes, I guess that does make me a liar.

Miles lets out a frustrated sigh. "Look, I have to live next to these people. You're getting out of here soon, never to look back. I have to walk out the door every morning and see Marcus and Valencia driving to work. I'm back there picking up Chardonnay turds while Marcus cuts the grass."

I can't help it; I snort.

Miles softens and shrugs. "If I'm going to call one of them Jeffrey Dahmer, I want to be sure about it. Okay? And it's not that I don't trust you—"

"Bullshit."

"You're a liar, what do you want?" He grins.

And again, I laugh. I *should* be mad at Miles. He doesn't believe me and calls me a liar. And this was all very clearly filler information for his podcast—though he was kind of upfront about that with me.

He *is* the only person who knows the real me, though. And he's now the second kid my age I've met who is out and queer. Though if my friendship with Frankie is anything to go by, I shouldn't trust him. And yet . . .

"So?" I ask, leaning against the island. "Still think it's all too simple?"

"I think we're on the right track, but we'll have to find something more substantial if we want to go to the police."

We. I have no intention of going to the police. Or helping Miles anymore. But he is right. Marcus has gotten away with it this long. He's several steps ahead of us. That also means I have a target on my back. He wants me out of their lives before he's out half a million dollars. Though Miles doesn't seem to care about that, because all he cares about is getting an interesting story for his podcast. But murder isn't always complicated, with dozens of suspects. He even said most murders are done by people close to the victim.

"Fine, so it's not enough to go to the police, but is it enough for you?"

He flinches. "What do you mean?"

"You said you'd help me get away if I got you stuff for your podcast. There's your compelling theory or whatever. You have plenty to start with; you can figure out the rest on your own. When do I get out of here?" As much as I want to rely only on myself, I need a way to get somewhere fast.

"Oh." He looks like he's not sure what to say. "I mean, do you know where you're going when you leave?"

"I'll get on a train and go . . . somewhere."

"You might not want to go to a train station nearby. It's easy for the police to go with a picture and ask if they've seen you. And do you have money?"

Shit. I don't. I've been so desperate to get out of this situation, I didn't even think about needing money to *buy* a train or bus ticket.

Miles takes the look on my face as confirmation. "I'll buy you a ticket, but we can't get you out of here until the weekend. I can tell my parents I'm going out with another friend and drive you somewhere a couple hours away. Maybe Virginia. Or Philly."

My heart sinks. So I'm stuck here for a few more days. With Marcus trying to expose who I really am.

TWENTY-FOUR

AS I SIT OUTSIDE DR. ZAPATA'S OFFICE WAITING TO BE picked up after my first session, I can't help but run my tongue against my teeth. My cleaning with Valencia this morning was much worse than I was anticipating. My teeth ache, especially the lower back molars, which Valencia said needed extra attention. I knew it would be bad, but not that it would be this painful after the fact. I guess that's what happens when you don't always get to brush your teeth while living on the street.

At least I didn't have any cavities. Not *yet*, is what Valencia said. There was a soft spot on a back molar that she marked to keep an eye on—zooming in on the X-ray and pointing it out to me. Probably why she dug around so hard back there. But somehow one of my teeth feels a little sharper, and I keep running my tongue over it.

I can still taste blood.

I check my phone again and there are no further updates from Valencia. After dropping me off, she sent a message that she had to run back to the office for an emergency and that Gramma Sharon would be picking me up instead.

But it's now a quarter past three and I'm starting to wonder if Gramma Sharon knows that. If I were a smarter person, I'd take this chance to make a run for it. I could disappear and hope they never find me again. But Miles is right; if I disappeared without telling the truth, it would gain more attention. Then I'll never be able to hide.

Plus, I have even less than I did when I was arrested.

So instead, I sit on the curb and continue to wait. About two minutes later, Gramma Sharon's red Fiat pulls into the lot. She rolls down the window as she comes to a stop in front of me.

"If you don't tell your mom I was late, we'll go get ice cream," she shouts.

Again, my tongue goes to my sore gums and molars. I roll my eyes, pretending to be put out, then say okay and climb in.

"Your mom said you wanted to go to the library, so we can stop there first."

"You don't have to do that," I say. I wasn't actually planning on going to the library. I just wanted to leave the house.

She waves a dismissive hand. "I'm looking for something to do, and I feel bad for you being locked up in the house all afternoon. We'll go to the library, you can check out some books, and then we'll stop for ice cream." Before I'm even buckled in, she shifts into drive and hits the gas. My stomach lurches and I grab on to the door handle.

She drives like a madwoman.

Gramma Sharon starts asking about my day, but I play it off, saying I sat in Valencia's office on the computer. Definitely not on my phone looking up more queer homeless shelters. She nods, unsurprised. "This is why I told your mom I'd take you out—so you're not moping around the house the rest of the afternoon. Forgive her; she's got temporary insanity, I fear."

"Afraid I'll disappear again."

"Precisely."

"And I'm sure she told you I threw paint on Mar—" I stop myself. I can't believe I slipped up in front of her and started saying Marcus's name instead of "Dad." She glances over at me expectantly, but my heart is racing in my chest.

Finally she nods. "On your dad's car. Yeah, she mentioned an accident. You threw it on?"

"No. It was an accident, I just don't know how it happened because I put the paint on the ground."

"Ghosts," Gramma Sharon says. And just like that, the conversation is over and she pulls into the library parking lot.

We walk in and she approaches the front desk, telling them I need a library card. They ask for proof of residency, and Gramma Sharon reaches into her bag to hand over an ID and gas bill, asking if that's good enough. She also says I'm her grandson and I'm staying with her for the summer and to make sure I don't have any restrictions on the card. She wants me to be able to check out whatever I want.

Again I think of my own grandmother, and how she used to bring me to the library on the days she watched me. And again I feel that deep pit of loss in my gut. The one that started the day I came home and found my parents dressed in black from her funeral. The funeral they didn't even bother bringing me to. Marcus and Valencia wouldn't do that. Though maybe that's only because they try so hard to look normal. Which is better: The family who shows you who they really are, or the ones who might be hiding the truth?

"Okay." Gramma Sharon breaks me from the thought—and good timing, because I can feel the sting of tears in the corners of my eyes. She hands over my library card. "Grab what you want and come find me when you're ready to go. I'll probably be kicking around the scary stuff."

I thank her and head in the opposite direction, toward the back of the library. The young adult section has beanbag chairs and a bench, so I opt for one of the beanbags and drop into it to stare at my phone. My first instinct is to go to Miles's social media.

Even after yesterday's waste of time, I couldn't stay angry at him. I mean, I *could*, but he's the only person I can really talk to about everything. So I created my own fake accounts but haven't posted yet. I followed him—and a few celebrities and influencers so it didn't look like a total weirdo account—and within minutes he texted me a screencap of my profile asking *IS THIS YOU?!*

It's not my old username, which I've abandoned. Instead, my new name is MitoDNAte—and, yes, I was absolutely trolling him. Also yes, it got the desired effect. He playfully called me a catty bitch—well, I'm 90 percent sure it was playful—and then he sent me a funny video.

There's a new one he must have sent during his lunch break. I open the post to watch the video, but out of the corner of my eye I see someone walking over to me. I look up, expecting it to be a librarian asking if I need help finding anything, but instead I see Agent Grant.

My mouth goes dry. This is it. They've finally figured it out and now he's coming to arrest me.

I lock the phone in my hands as he stops at the bench across from my beanbag chair. He gives me what I wouldn't call a friendly look.

Maybe something more like curiosity. Like I'm a brightly colored tropical bird that crapped on his freshly cleaned car.

"Are you following me?" I ask.

He gives me a wan smile and sits down on the bench, crossing his leg over his knee. "This is my local library. I was returning some books and saw you over here. Thought I would say hi. We never really got a chance to speak."

He's lying. The YA section is tucked away in the back of the library, with no real sight lines to it. Also there's a book drop outside.

What he means to say is we haven't had a chance to speak without Marcus and Valencia around.

"I don't think I should talk to you without a lawyer present."

His face doesn't change. "Why? Have you done something wrong?"

My stomach is in knots and sweat is gathering at the nape of my neck. Every word I say could get me into trouble. This is why they tell you to keep asking for a lawyer when you're arrested. Say nothing else but "I want a lawyer." Of course they ask you why an innocent person needs a lawyer, but that answer's simple. Because they want you to talk yourself into a corner. To make one mistake so they can get you whether you're innocent or not.

"It's not about doing something wrong," I say. "You're a cop, and there's that whole, anything I say can and will be used against me in a court of law."

"I'm retired."

"So this is an unofficial talk?"

He shrugs. "I came here to say hello. I'm a neighbor who just happened to be involved in your case when it was active."

"Then why did you say you wanted to talk to me without my parents here?"

His eyebrows jump slightly. "I didn't say that."

I replay in my head what he said to me and, shit, he's right. But I try to play it off like I didn't mess up. "Subtext."

"I did want to ask you if you've seen anyone strange around since coming home."

That gives me pause. Does that mean Grant doesn't suspect Marcus and Valencia in Nate's disappearance?

"Is that why you still have police sitting outside our house?"

He shakes his head, clearly unsurprised that I noticed the cop out there. "You were kidnapped, and your amnesia means you don't know who did it." And, yes, there's absolutely a note of skepticism in his voice. "We're worried someone might show up looking for you. It's for your protection."

"Then why are they down the street?"

The side of his mouth twists into a half smile. "Don't want you to feel like you're constantly under surveillance."

"But I am?"

This he doesn't answer. Instead he reaches into the breast pocket of his suit jacket and takes out a little white card. "I want you to take my card." He holds it out to me, his bony fingers steady.

"Thought you were retired."

"I am." He flicks his fingers to try and encourage me to take the card. I do. Under his name it says "Private Investigator." "But I help out from time to time. Especially on older cases that were still open when I retired."

"So why did they introduce you as a supervisory special agent?"

He shakes his head. "Habit?"

"You're a private eye now; who's paying you?"

"No one." He leans back and puts his arm across the top of the bench. "Do you have anything that keeps you up at night?" I don't answer. "I have a handful of unsolved cases that keep me up. Yours is one of them. So when the cop in DC saw my info on your report and called me, I showed up."

"I think you need a better hobby."

He gives a subtle laugh, air expelling from his nose. "Do you remember anything new yet?"

I shake my head. "Dr. Z says it's normal."

He nods slowly. "Can you do me a favor? If you *do* happen to . . . remember anything at all, give me a call?"

"Why?"

"Because if someone kidnapped you, they're still out there. And they might try to hurt someone else." He nods to the card still in my hand. "That's my cell. Day or night. Anything you might remember. Even about your . . . family members."

The air between us goes ice cold, or maybe that's my imagination, because a chill raises the little hairs on the back of my neck. The way he says *family members*. There's a hint of skepticism there. He knows I'm not Nate. I don't know how, but he does.

Maybe because he has some of his own suspicions about Nate's disappearance.

But then why hasn't he pressed the cops to get a DNA test to prove I'm not Nate? Now that I know he's retired and not *actively* involved in the case, he seems even more dangerous. Miles was probably right; the police were happy to scratch Nate off their open cases and move on. But since Grant is retired, he can look into things if they aren't feeling right to him.

"Can I ask you a question, then?" I try to keep my voice steady.

"Shoot."

"Why couldn't you find me?"

He stares at me for a few moments, his eyes icy and unmoving. "Because you disappeared without a trace. No security footage of strange cars or people in the area, and no one heard anything suspicious or saw anyone strange coming or going, even the neighbors outside working in their yards or having a cookout."

No one strange. Just the people who the neighbors would expect to see on a Saturday afternoon. I want to ask him if anyone mentioned seeing Marcus or Valencia after two p.m.—the time Marcus apparently returned from the grocery store—but I don't know how to ask that without raising suspicion. Yes, Grant may know—or think he knows—I'm lying, but I'm not going to confess that to him. Retired or not, if this is something that keeps him up at night, he's not going to bother protecting me.

"People don't disappear without a trace," I say.

He shakes his head. "No. Usually they don't." He stands and nods down at the card I'm still holding. "If you think of anything at all, call me."

I nod, even though I've already decided I'm never talking to him alone again. After he leaves, I wait a few minutes, trying to slow my heart rate, but I'm so anxious my hands are shaking. I run my fingers across the embossed business card. I need to get out of here. Still, I head over to the YA section and pick out three books at random—though one does pique my interest because the cover is an illustrated picture of a girl in a ridiculous hot dog costume. Then I find Gramma Sharon and tell her I'm ready to go.

I'm not at all in the mood for ice cream but I don't want Gramma Sharon to think anything is up, so I let her buy me a scoop of Purple Cow. After a couple spoonfuls I wince and say it hurts my teeth. Which, honestly, isn't a lie. Thanks, Valencia. She insisted on doing the cleaning herself despite being behind on patients. But at least I get to hang out with Gramma Sharon because of it.

"Listen," Gramma Sharon says, getting serious now. "How do you feel about me coming over to see you when you're home alone? I know your brother's there, but his friends'll all be coming home from school soon—save for that burnout JT. But maybe I can come by and see you when you don't have anything to do? We can go see a movie or play cards or go to the library. What do you think?"

I shouldn't feel like my heart is going to burst, yet here I am. This woman is a stranger to me, but my association with grandmothers and libraries has gotten the better of me. Having Gramma Sharon here has made me feel safe. Even Former Agent Grant's stalking and insinuation that he knows something is up gets pushed aside. Because I *do* want to spend time with her. So I answer her before the logical side of my brain can interject—the one that's trying to bust through the wall I put up.

"I think that sounds good to me."

But that wall breaks just a bit. Enough for the voice of that logic to whisper through the cracks how wrong this is. How I'm lying to this woman.

TWENTY-FIVE

AFTER GRAMMA SHARON DROPS ME OFF AT HOME, I text Miles and tell him to meet me in the backyard. He's already there when I get outside, Chardonnay sniffing along the ground behind him.

"Grant knows something is up," I say, holding out the card. Miles looks at it, running his finger across it.

"How do you know?"

"He followed me to the library today and cornered me."

Miles's eyes go wide. "Does he know you're not really Nate?"

"He didn't say explicitly but he definitely implied it. I think he also might have implied that he thinks there's more to Nate's disappearance than everyone is letting on."

Miles chews on his lip and hands the card back to me. "So he's investigating. Start from the beginning. Tell me everything."

I don't tell him everything because he doesn't need to know how my teeth hurt from the dentist or how I had to lie and deflect for an hour during therapy.

But when I get to the part where Grant sounded a little skeptical when talking about Nate's family, Miles flips out.

"Holy shit. He suspects Marcus and Valencia."

"What makes you say that?" I didn't make that connection; I assumed he knew I was lying and wanted to expose me.

"Because he doesn't think you're—no offense—smart enough to do all this on your own."

"'Kay, little hard to *not* be offended here."

"I mean he's overthinking it. He thinks Marcus and Valencia . . . I don't know, hired you? Found you somewhere and convinced you to pretend to be Nate."

"What about the life insurance money? If they hired me to be Nate, they'd have to pay the insurance company back."

Miles pinches the bridge of his nose like I'm annoying him. "Darling—" Oh. My stomach does a little flip at the way he calls me that. But I'm quick to remind myself it's just Miles being Miles and focus back on what he's saying. "Don't be a riff killer. When we're spitballing, we push the other theories aside because we don't know how true they are. You can't be stuck on one premise; you'll miss the others and might overlook what's really going on."

"Fine. Ignoring the insurance money, why would they hire me to be Nate?"

"Because then they don't have to be the suspected child murderers anymore. The police focused the investigation on Nate's parents for a long time. If you show up, the Beaumonts are in the clear. And sorry, Valencia, but refusing a DNA test definitely makes you look guilty."

But I still don't understand how Miles can think Grant made the leap that I was involved in their attempt to cover it up.

"If he thinks I'm a part of this, why wouldn't he come out and say it?"

"Better to put pressure on you when they weren't around. He started with that to get you freaking out, which—" He gestures to me like I'm wearing a shirt that says, "I'm freaking out because a retired cop cornered me in a library and all I got is this lousy T-shirt." "People who freak out make mistakes."

That's kind of how I got into this situation. Starving and freaking out, worried I was going to be sent home to my parents. And I made a mistake. One I need to finish.

"Okay, then we need to get me out of here," I say. "Now. If I disappear again, then maybe he can convince the cops to go back to investigating the Beaumonts. You said all that evidence is circumstantial. I could leave a note that says they hired me, whatever Grant needs to hear, and you can also give him the circumstantial evidence, and he can take it from there."

Miles holds out his hands. "Okay, let's take a breath. That's a terrible idea."

"No it's not. Look, I lied and said I was Nate to avoid going to jail or being sent home to my parents. Now, honestly, I don't care. I need to get out of here."

"Stop. Listen to me. If you disappear now, all this blows up. If you *lie*, the evidence you found so far will be thrown out in court because now you're the liar who said he was hired by the Beaumonts."

"I already am a liar!"

Miles lowers his voice as a hint that I should lower mine. "It's different! No jury is going to look at you, at what you've been through, and say you're a terrible person. Maybe you need to hear this because no one has ever said it to you before, but you're *not* a terrible person."

The pulse pounding in my ears slows and I replay what Miles said. Because it's not true. Even if it is only Marcus who's guilty, I've been lying to this whole family. And I don't care how desperate I was when I first told the lie. I could have come clean at any time. It's possible they might not even have sent me home.

I just didn't know what to do at the time.

"You made a mistake," Miles continues. "But if you run off now, you'll be making another one."

He's wrong. I shouldn't have even stayed this long. When I don't answer him, he reaches out and gently grabs my wrist. It's like an electric shock and breaks me from my thoughts. I look up at him, and his expression is one of pity.

"I know this is a shitty situation, but I promise I'm going to help you get out of this. For now, stay calm. And whatever you do, don't talk to Grant again." He smiles, trying to play it off as a joke.

I nod and take a deep breath, then tell him the lie he wants to hear. "You're right. Okay. I'm good now."

"You sure?"

"Yeah. Thanks for talking me down."

"Anytime." He nods over my shoulder. "You should probably water those hydrangeas again."

I turn to see that some of the hydrangea leaves have turned brown and droopy, which is strange considering it's ten degrees cooler today than it was yesterday. Sorry, Valencia, I don't have time to rescue your plants today. Miles and I say our goodbyes and I go back in the house.

Despite what Miles thinks, I'm not staying here anymore.

I race up to Nate's room and grab the duffel bag from the closet. It's a little after five. Valencia is going to be home within the next hour. Marcus won't get here until after six, and I have no idea where Easton is. Probably hanging out with JT.

I unzip the duffel and throw in my toothbrush and toothpaste. Then I grab one of the library books I checked out today and throw that in as well. I'll rip out one of the blank end pages for the note. And leave the book too, because the librarians might be able to track me down better than the cops.

"Nate?"

I freeze. Shit. Valencia is home. I look at my phone and, yes, there are notifications that the downstairs door was opened. My opportunity is gone. At least for now.

I'll use Easton's trick later tonight after everyone has gone to bed. Actually, that's a better idea anyhow because it will give me more of a head start. No one will realize I'm gone until the morning. I turn to put the duffel bag back in the closet.

Only the sweat on my hands causes the bag to slip. I try my best to catch it with my knee, but that topples it over. My clothes, food, toothbrush, and the library book spill out onto the floor, the cans making loud thuds as they fall out from between the folded clothes.

"Nate? Are you okay?" The floorboards creak as Valencia comes down the hallway. I scramble, trying to throw everything back in. My hands shake nervously and I almost drop another can before tossing it back in the duffel.

The bedroom door opens, and I freeze.

There's a look of confused humor on Valencia's face when she first enters the room. But that slowly drops when she takes in the scene. Me, with clothes and canned food, my toothbrush, and a duffel bag.

"What is this?" she asks. But the tone of her voice says she knows exactly what this is. She's just hoping she's wrong.

I don't have an excuse ready. My mind is completely blank. Now all my plans and preparation are for nothing. She's going to take the duffel bag and food and probably lock it up. It'll end up being more secure than the gun Marcus has in his fucking closet. So she can make sure I can't run. At least not prepared. I'll still find a way to get out of here.

Valencia shakes her head. Her eyes are glassy.

"What is all this, Nate?"

She wants to hear me say it. But I can't because she looks devastated. My own eyes start to burn and everything catches up with me. Before I know what's happening, my chest is aching with sobs.

I want to get out of here. And the most disturbing part of all this: I want to go *home*. How fucked up is that? I wouldn't let my parents send me to conversion therapy—maybe after all this I'd be able to stand up to them. Yell at them and tell them I'm not going. That they can try to send me there but I'll keep running away. I'll be good. I'll be quiet. They don't even have to know about my love life. When I get married to a man and adopt three amazing kids, they can continue to think I'm single. We won't talk about it.

Valencia wraps her arms around me, tight. I shake against her as tears drip from my face like a broken spigot. Her hug makes me feel safe, but that feeling is at odds with the confusion in my gut. She walked in on me very obviously with my queer homeless kid bug-out bag. She should be yelling at me. Calling me an ungrateful brat and locking me in my room.

Instead she gently rocks me back and forth on the floor while I cry. All the stress and anxiety of the last week has caught up with me at once.

After a few minutes, my sobs subside and the tears stop. Valencia gently smooths the back of my head and down my neck. When I've calmed down, she leans away from me but still keeps an arm around my shoulders.

"What's going on?" she asks. Her voice is calm, without an ounce of judgment or anger. "Did something happen at therapy?"

"No." I wipe at my face. "I . . ." What can I say? Their retired FBI agent neighbor knows I'm not her son and I freaked out? If she isn't mad now, she'd be furious then. And there's a deep, selfish part of me that doesn't want this moment between us to end.

Her comforting voice. The way she holds me like she doesn't know how to fix me but wants to protect me from everything that might be hurting me. Because that's how I feel right now.

The way she's looking at me, there's no way she could have hurt Nate. Because right now, if I told her Grant came to talk to me at the library and that's what freaked me out, she would probably drive to his house and burn it to the ground.

The thought makes me laugh.

"I don't know. I felt . . ." I can be honest about this at least. "Trapped. I got home and I felt so trapped and claustrophobic, and I needed to get out of here."

She picks up one of the protein bars from the floor. "We ran out of these over the weekend. So you've obviously been feeling trapped for some time now."

I nod. "I'm sorry."

"Come on." She pats my shoulder, then stands, groaning as her knees pop. "Sorry, I was starting to lose the feeling in my legs." She sits on the edge of the bed and gestures for me to sit next to her, so I do. Valencia reaches for my hand and clasps it between both of hers.

She takes a steadying breath as she stares into the distance and I brace myself.

This is when she should start yelling. But instead she turns to me and speaks calmly.

"I know that I can never understand what you went through over the last ten years."

Her words are supposed to make me feel better, but they don't. She's still talking about the lie. It's always the fucking lie.

But, as usual, instead of coming clean I let her continue.

"However, I can tell you what *I* went through."

Oh, please don't. But there's a lump in my throat that blocks the words.

"The worst part for me was not knowing. I woke up every day for months wondering if that was the day they would find you. Some days—and I'm not proud to say this—I wondered if we'd hear worse news. Then soon it became every other day. Or once a week. Eventually, I didn't think I'd ever hear anything again. But I never stopped thinking about you. Every night before bed I'd talk to you in my mind and tell you what was happening in our lives. And what I hoped was happening in yours. Pretending you were somewhere else, alive and happy and living your life." She gives a sad laugh and pats my hand. "Maybe that's not healthy, but you can ask your therapist about that."

I have no idea if it's a healthy coping mechanism or not, but I can't blame her either way. And now as I watch her speak, I believe it's impossible for her to do anything to hurt either of her children.

"Getting you back was the happiest day of my life since you were born." She reaches out to put a hand on my cheek. Meanwhile, the imaginary knife in my gut twists my intestines like a forkful of spaghetti.

Tell her tell her tell her. The words repeat in my head over and over, but I can't do it. Not after what she said.

"In college I read this quote by a woman named Bessie A. Stanley—of course, it's attributed to Emerson because why would we give a woman writer the credit? But anyway, I kind of took it to heart. I don't remember all of it, but I remember 'To leave the world a bit better, whether by a healthy child, a garden patch, or a redeemed social condition; to know even one life has breathed easier because you have lived.' She says it in the context of success, but I think it's more about why we're all here. And I know my purpose in this world has always been to be your mother. You and Easton both. Because nothing—*nothing*—makes me happier. I am so proud of you both, every day." She smiles, but tears spill down her cheeks. "I know I missed out on ten years, but even now I can see how you haven't changed. You're still the sweet, kind, and so damn *funny* kid you were ten years ago. You get that from my mom, by the way. Your dad and I are not funny."

I laugh. I can't help it, but I do. I take the time to wipe my own tears from my face and look away from her.

Valencia waves a hand at the duffel bag, clothes, and food still strewn across the floor. "I'm not going to pretend I understand what's going through your mind. But I want you to know that I love you. For always and always." She takes another breath. "And now I know you can take care of yourself. So I will *ask* you to please stay. Give us a chance to make you feel more welcome here."

She gets off the bed and starts packing up everything in the duffel bag again. I'm about to ask what she's doing, but she's already done and zipping it up by the time I get the nerve to say anything. Then she holds it out to me.

"You can keep your bag packed and ready to go." She looks like what's she's about to say next is going to hurt, but she steels herself and says it anyway. "And . . . if you decide you need to leave, I just ask that you tell me. You don't have to tell me where you're going. Though maybe you can . . . keep in contact. But if you can, if it's possible, I'd like you to try and stay?"

I stare at her, not understanding. She said how badly she wished for me to come back every day—shit, no, she said how badly she wished for *Nate* to come back every day. But here he is—at least as far as she knows—yet she's willing to let him go?

The duffel bag feels heavier when I take it. "Why?" is all I ask.

Her cheeks puff up as she lets out a big breath. "I guess I'm hoping you'll stay. But also because I mean it when I say I love you. I want you to be happy, and to feel safe. And considering you were on your own for eight months, I think you know better than us what makes you feel safe."

I stare at Valencia, trying to read her face. This has to be a trap, like as soon as I say I'm going to leave, she'll cackle like an evil witch and metal bars will slide down over every window, locking me here forever.

But that would require me *wanting* to leave. Because right now I don't. I can't, even. More than anything, right now I want Valencia to hug me again. It's wrong, and I know that. But I also know that my own parents have never said anything to me like what Valencia just said. They've never *trusted* me as completely as she's willing to do.

Yeah, what I did is messed up, and she's talking about another kid. But maybe I can pretend she isn't. Because for once in my life, someone has told me they're proud of me. That they love me and who I am. Has a week been enough for Valencia to see who I truly am and be proud of that person, or is it still the real Nate she's thinking about?

Honestly, fuck it. I don't care.

I put the duffel bag on the floor, then slide it under my bed with my foot. Valencia steps forward and pulls me into another hug. And it's a hug that really does make all the bad things in the world disappear.

Despite everything, when Valencia hugs me, I feel safe.

TWENTY-SIX

TRUE TO HER WORD, GRAMMA SHARON ARRIVES ON Wednesday morning right as Valencia and Marcus are leaving for work. Marcus is still acting awkward toward me because of the paint incident, but I don't care.

"What are you two doing today?" Valencia asks as she puts her lunch into a canvas tote.

"Thought we'd go drinking before noon and rob a bank around one," Gramma Sharon says with zero humor. "Sound good to you, kid?"

Valencia scoffs. "Well. Try not to get arrested." She comes over to the table and kisses me on top of my head before adding quietly, "Again." Which does make me laugh. She says goodbye and Gramma Sharon asks me what I really want to do, but I have no idea. I tell her I'm fine hanging around here.

"Bah!" She flicks a hand at me. "If I wanted to hang around a house, I'd do it at home, in my underwear, *alone*."

I snort, which makes her cackle.

The door leading to the garage opens again and Valencia is back. Her face has an ashen look that unsettles me.

"What's wrong?" Gramma Sharon asks.

Valencia takes a deep breath and sets her tote bag on the floor next to the door, then pulls out the chair next to me to sit down.

"I'm not mad," she starts—which, let's be honest, is a weird way to start a conversation.

Something else happened. It's my first thought, and my stomach twists into knots. It's her car that's had paint thrown on it this time. Or maybe it was keyed or the windows smashed in. Something Marcus could do while we were all asleep and still get away with it.

Something to frame me for.

Valencia reaches out and clasps my hand firmly. "Can you remember how much fertilizer you gave the hydrangeas?"

Zero. She forgot to tell me how much to use so I skipped it. But on Monday afternoon she asked if I fertilized them. She was already doubting me about Marcus's car, so I was stupid and said I did. I didn't want her to have another reason to be pissed or annoyed at me. So I lied.

And I do it again now. "However much the instructions said."

She nods. "Okay."

"Valencia, what is it?" Gramma Sharon asks.

She shakes her head but wipes a tear that spills over. "Nothing. It's not important. I think maybe the Miracid I bought was labeled wrong. Maybe it's extra-strength or . . ." She shrugs because she can't come up with a better excuse for whatever it is.

"What?" I ask.

"The hydrangeas are all burned," she says.

Burned? They looked fine yesterday. Droopy and they had some brown spots, but they weren't burned. I get up and go out the back door. Valencia calls after me, telling me it's okay and she's not mad. I walk, barefoot, around the house to look at the flowering bushes that line the side and front.

But I don't even think you could call them bushes anymore. The once purple-blue-pink flowers are brown and droopy. The leaves have fallen off into piles around the peeling stalks. Yesterday they looked a little peaked. Today, they're definitely dead.

"Oh." Gramma Sharon's voice is almost inaudible behind me where she and Valencia stand, watching my reaction. What is going on? Who keeps doing these things?

I spin to Valencia. "I swear I didn't do this!"

She looks at me with the most pitying look I've ever received—and I was homeless until last week. She has tears in her eyes that she keeps trying to wipe away.

"It's okay! I know. I'm sure it was a mistake with the fertilizer."

"No! I didn't fertilize them. I lied because of the whole paint thing! I didn't want you to be angry at me for not doing it so I lied and said I did but I didn't." The desperation in my voice must frighten her because she walks quickly to me and pulls me to her.

"It's okay! I'm not mad. And I believe you."

"Maybe blight, then," Gramma Sharon adds. But even she doesn't sound convinced.

But Valencia nods. "Probably that. It has been humid lately." It sounds like she's trying to convince herself. I have no idea what weather conditions cause blight but I'm pretty damn sure that's not what happened to Valencia's hydrangeas.

Both Valencia and now Gramma Sharon are doubting me. They

don't say it, but I know they don't believe the excuses they're coming up with. I didn't do this, yet the shame is still there, deep and painful in my gut, and it makes me want to run. Right now. Barefoot and all out until I can get far away from this place.

Because now that doubt is in their heads, and I'll never gain their trust again. But what's worst of all is I don't know why I care so much. These two are strangers. I'm lying to them. I shouldn't care—I should let them think whatever they want, and when I'm gone and they realize I was a fraud all along, they'll be happy to know their instincts weren't wrong.

I want to scream. Tell them both the truth. That someone else is doing all this.

But I still can't. Right now, they're both lying to themselves, coming up with any other explanation for why these things could be happening. As soon as they know the truth, they'll never believe me again. I mean, who would believe a word from someone who told a grieving family he was their missing kid?

Valencia leaves for work, still insisting she believes me and she'll replace the bushes. I go into the living room to sulk. But Gramma Sharon doesn't bother giving me the space. She follows me and plops down in the chair across from me.

"You know how I know you're telling the truth?" she asks, breaking the silence.

Wait. Is she for real? "How?"

"Because you didn't bother coming up with an excuse. You flat-out admitted you lied to her before—which, as far as lies go, kid, was about as appropriate as you can get when lying to your parents. I lied about doing chores when I was your age, too. My dad would find out and . . ." She puts her hands up like she's going to leave it at that. "He was a drunk. Probably get my taste for bourbon from him. Though I didn't know he was a drunk till I was older, which is also when I realized how much he lied. But he'd never admit he was wrong. When he said he was working late but came home smelling like cigarettes and booze, and my mother asked why there was a dent on the front bumper of the car, he'd lie and say someone hit him at the train station. 'Course, the yellow paint on the dent matched the yellow poles at the station parking lot."

Her eyes drift over to Marcus's bar cart. Shiny with mixing tools and bottles of liquor. And she shakes her head.

"Liars bury themselves in more lies because they know if they admit to one, they're admitting to them all." Gramma Sharon reaches over and nudges my knee. "So stop looking so damn guilty. They're plants. Plants die. Blight happens, or they're old."

"You really believe me?"

"I do."

I didn't think it was possible to love Gramma Sharon any more.

"Do you think Mom does?"

She thinks for a moment. "I do. But I think right now, she's upset and hasn't moved past that grief. They were old plants, and I think she put a little more of her emotions into planting and taking care of them than most people might. She planted those hydrangeas when she was about ready to pop with you. Sixteen years is a long time to take care of something."

Especially when she spent a good portion of those sixteen years taking care of the hydrangeas instead of Nate.

“Get your shoes on. I’m gonna pee, then let’s get out of here.” She stands and heads toward the bathroom. But when I go upstairs to get my shoes, a thought comes to me. I slip them on and race down the stairs and out to the garage.

Next to the wire rack full of tools and painting supplies is a wooden workbench with gardening equipment. And right on top, next to a rusty pair of gardening shears, is the box of Miracid. I pick it up and look closely.

It’s still sealed.

It wasn’t the fertilizer that killed the plants. So something else must have been dumped on them instead. Which means someone outside the house could have done it. Or at least someone who knew how to kill a bunch of sixteen-year-old hydrangeas.

TWENTY-SEVEN

GRAMMA SHARON AND I SPEND THE MORNING DRIVING around. Then she takes me to a Mexican place the next town over where we split crab nachos before walking around some of the kitschier stores that pull in most of their money during the summer months when tourists flock to the eastern shore.

It should feel like I have a babysitter, but Gramma Sharon doesn't treat me the way Marcus and Valencia do. Though Valencia has shifted slightly since finding me about to run off. As if she isn't constantly watching me like an overprotective mama bear.

And when she returns home from work it's like she never even discovered her hydrangeas were massacred. She asks Gramma Sharon to stay for dinner—"Like I'd leave and cook for myself?"—then comes to give me a hug, which I gladly accept.

"We good?" she asks.

I nod and she leaves it at that. I don't bother telling her about the unopened box of fertilizer.

"You see the weather this weekend?" Gramma Sharon asks as she sips bourbon after dinner. "Gonna be a beautiful one. We should have a family barbecue. How's Sunday?"

"We're going to Mexico this weekend," Marcus says from the kitchen sink, where he's washing dishes.

"Bullshit." Gramma Sharon turns her attention to me. "I doubt this one is allowed to leave the country. Do you even have a passport?"

Not in Nate's name and certainly not in my own.

"Then Sunday barbecue sounds great," Marcus says with barely contained sarcasm. "What are you bringing, Sharon?"

She snorts. "You can handle this one. Or have it catered. I don't care."

Marcus shoots a glance at Valencia behind Gramma Sharon's back that can only be interpreted as annoyance. He shuts off the water and dries his hands on a dish towel. "Well, we won't be having a *cookout* catered. But fine. We will provide food, service, drinks, and venue."

"Great," Gramma Sharon says, probably sensing the attitude in Marcus's voice and digging in to show he isn't bothering her. "Then, as usual, I'll provide the entertainment. Make Watergate salad, too!"

"There I'm drawing the line," he says.

"What's Watergate salad?" I ask.

"Something your grandmother brings every time we have a cookout," Marcus says, sounding disgusted. "And if you want it, Sharon, it's on you to make it."

"I made the pies last time!"

Marcus smirks as he sips his wine. "Aw shucks, no Watergate salad for Gramma Sharon."

"I'll make it for you, Gramma," I say, wrapping my arm around her shoulder.

"See?" She leans up and kisses me on the cheek. "My grandchildren care about me."

Marcus and Valencia laugh and Marcus looks over at me. "You look it up and then let me know how excited you are to make it. If *you* promise to help her eat it so we aren't stuck with the leftovers, I'll buy the ingredients for you."

"Deal," I say without hesitation.

Marcus's jaw drops and he speaks to me, again unprompted. "You didn't even look it up!"

"I trust Gramma's taste."

Valencia grimaces. "Oh, honey, that's a mistake."

Even Gramma Sharon laughs at that.

Just then, Easton enters the kitchen, wearing a different outfit than he had on earlier. This time he's in jeans and a button-down with the sleeves rolled up. "What's a mistake?"

"We're having a barbecue on Sunday," Marcus says. "Invite JT. Maybe if he's stoned enough we can pawn off some Watergate salad on him."

Outside, Chardonnay starts barking. Probably at Miles.

"Can I invite a friend, too?" I ask.

"Sure, honey," Valencia says with a smile. She doesn't ask who I want to bring because she knows the only person I know is Miles. Easton, though, gives me a confused look.

"What friends do you have?"

"Easton," Valencia warns.

Even Marcus lightly bats his arm with the back of his hand. "Knock it off."

Easton shrugs. "What? He's been missing for years and he spends most of his time now with Gramma."

"Miles," I say, nodding in the direction of his house.

"Then ask him what his stupid dog is barking at." Easton glances out the window.

"Probably lawn day tomorrow," I say, giving no other context. I tell them I'll be right back, and Valencia says okay without asking me where I'm going or telling me when to get home.

Almost like she trusts me.

I go out the back door and, sure enough, Miles is in his backyard, headlamp on, pooper-scooper in hand. Chardonnay barks and he quietly curses at her and tells her to knock it off. I watch for a few seconds before calling out.

"I really think that would be easier during the daytime."

Miles startles, then shakes the pooper-scooper in my direction. "Stop doing that!"

"Stop scooping up Chardonnay's poop at night and I will." Chardonnay hops up on the fence for pets while Miles walks over to me, head down so the light guides his way past any land mines. Once safely at the fence, he slides the headlamp to the top of his head so it's not pointed right at me.

"So I've been thinking about our last conversation." He glances over my shoulder toward the house to make sure no one is sitting on the deck, then when he sees the coast is clear, he bites his lip. He does that a lot when he's thinking. "I think maybe we should hold off a little longer before you make your grand escape."

Oh, right. I forgot I told him I needed to get out of here ASAP.

Talking with Valencia last night did calm me. Of course the hydrangea massacre brought my alert level back up again. But being out with Gramma Sharon helped bring it right back down. And I realized something while we were in one of those tchotchke shops looking at wooden ornaments and plastic knickknacks.

Whoever is doing all this isn't trying to hurt me. They're causing havoc and inconvenience. It's a game to them. Maybe it's someone trying to scare me off, or it really could be one awful coincidence after another. Am I being delusional? Maybe. Even Marcus is being less antagonistic despite everything. And Valencia genuinely seems to want to keep me safe. Like she's keeping her eye on me, but not smothering. Marcus wouldn't try to hurt me while she's being so protective.

Or maybe she told him about finding the duffel bag last night and now he's realizing it's a matter of time before I'm gone. Either way, it changes things—I don't feel like I'm in imminent danger anymore.

Like a truce. I'll leave a note saying I was never Nate so he doesn't need to pay back the life insurance payment, and he won't kill me to cover up his past murder. It's win-win! Until Miles finally gets the police involved to tell them what we found.

"No, I agree," I say. Miles looks surprised but doesn't ask me for information. "You were right, I was freaking out. If I left now it would be suspicious."

But I don't tell him about Valencia and how her protective nature feels like a drug I need more of. How I like spending time with Gramma Sharon. And, yes, even how I lay awake last night thinking about making this my real life.

I told you it was like a drug.

"I came out to ask if you'd like to come to a family barbecue this Sunday."

His eyebrows shoot up and he nods. "Okay, good idea. I show up and casually ask a few questions about life insurance. Gauge their reactions."

I laugh. "Sure. But I meant for fun."

Miles seems confused. "Pardon?"

"Not everything needs to be about the investigation. I mean, we can hang out. Take a break from the podcast."

Miles's confusion changes to surprise. "Oh. Ye—"

"Hey."

We both jump and Miles's headlamp slips back down to his forehead. As I step back, Easton holds up a hand, blocking the light from his eyes. Glass bottles and cans clank against each other in the blue recycling bin he holds with his other hand.

"What is this, a family trait or something?" Miles asks, putting his hand to his heart.

Easton squints as he looks at me. "Gramma Sharon is leaving, Mom says to go say good night."

"Okay, thanks." I turn back to Miles. "So? You in?"

"Yes. What should I bring? Other than fucking bells for the two of you to wear."

"Your appetite. I'll talk to you later."

I follow Easton but he leads me up the side of the house—past the hydrangeas—where Gramma Sharon is walking toward her car. He sets the recycling bin down at the curb next to the trash cans. JT's Jeep pulls up behind Gramma Sharon's car and he rolls down the window.

"Sharon! My life for you!"

She glares at the car as Easton hugs her goodbye, then climbs into the Jeep. JT does a three-point turn—narrowly missing Gramma Sharon's car—and speeds off.

Gramma Sharon turns to me. "I hope your friend is less obnoxious."

I assure her that he is and kiss her on the cheek. She climbs into the car, telling me she'll see me in the morning. I watch her pull into the driveway, then back out—much more gracefully than JT—and wave goodbye.

When I shut the front door behind me, the living room to my right is dark. I'm surprised. It's still early, and usually Valencia and Marcus watch TV before going up to bed. I hear movement from the kitchen.

Marcus appears in the kitchen doorway as I lock the front door.

"Nate, can you come in here a second?"

Something about his tone unsettles me. And I don't see or hear Valencia anywhere. My heart is pounding and I'm anxious as I walk across the center hall toward the kitchen. It sounds like I'm about to be scolded again. Maybe he went up to the third floor while I was out and noticed the weed was moved around. I thought I put the jar back the way I found it, but maybe not.

Marcus is sitting at the kitchen table when I enter. He motions to the chair across from him that's already pulled out. "Sit down."

My stomach twists. This is giving me flashbacks to my parents trying to send me away to camp.

I sit.

And Marcus pulls the gun from under the table.

TWENTY-EIGHT

HE PLACES THE GUN ON THE TABLE BETWEEN US AND doesn't say a thing. My heart is racing, and I think, *This is it.* He knows I'm not Nate and he's going to question me with a gun to my head. I'll tell him everything because at least then I can confront him about the games he's been playing.

But then I notice the trigger lock is still on.

I stare at the gun, then finally look into Marcus's eyes.

"You went into our closet," he says. Shit. How did he know? What did I miss when I put everything back? Marcus bends over and picks up the cardboard box the gun was stashed in from under the table.

Under the recessed lights of the kitchen, I can see the layer of dust on top of it. And the handprints on it. There's more on the side where I pulled it down. He must have been in there changing and saw the handprints. Of course.

"I'm sorry," I say.

He stares at me, and the longer he stares, the more ashamed I feel.

"Your mom and I give you and Easton a lot of privacy. We *respect* your privacy and expect the same from you both."

I nod. Somehow this scolding feels worse than anything my parents ever did. Usually with them it was only yelling. Marcus's calmness is what's so unsettling. It's kind of like Valencia last night. He *should* be yelling but he's so damn composed it's freaking me out. Especially because I've seen his short temper in action with the paint. And how pissed off he was about the gas being left on.

I don't know what to say, and the silence between us is making me feel even more uncomfortable.

"It's normal," I finally land on. "Having trust issues after everything that happened. I mean, Dr. Z says it is." Yes, falling back on my therapy is a great excuse. Use trauma as a shield and everyone will feel bad and shy away from scolding me for breaking rules and being an asshole. I wonder if that can work with admitting I'm not Nate.

"And that's why we're talking about this," Marcus says. "We understand that, but we have rules in this house—and we've been following them on our end. Your mother didn't know about your go bag until she saw you with it."

So she did tell him.

"All we're asking is that you respect our privacy on your end, too."

I nod while I anxiously pull at my fingers under the table. "I'm sorry. I won't go into your room again without permission." I'm kind of banking on the hope that he doesn't know I also went into his office.

He nods and looks down at the gun again. "We bought it after you disappeared."

That's something I notice about Marcus and Valencia. They both keep saying I disappeared, not that I was kidnapped. Easton is more up-front about it, like he doesn't think it's awkward to talk about.

Maybe because he understands it's best to confront things head-on while Valencia and Marcus are more cautious around my supposed traumas.

"We installed the alarm then, too," Marcus adds. "Your mother got paranoid and became overprotective of Easton. We all went to family therapy a couple of times—it was when Easton was a teen and he wanted to be able to go out and do normal things that teens do. Your mom was scared to let him go to dances, after-school events, hang out with his friends. Eventually she found ways to deal with her anxiety, but I can see the patterns repeating."

Patterns? What kind of things did she do to Easton to keep him home? And would she go as far as creating trouble—gas leaks, paint vandalism, killing her plants—to keep me trapped in the house? But that would fly right in the face of her saying she understood about my go bag.

"I get that all this is new and scary for you, but I still think respecting our privacy is healthy, and Dr. Zapata would agree. But feel free to let me know if she has other thoughts."

"Okay. And I'm sorry again."

He picks up the gun and holds it in his hand, staring at it. "When Easton was fourteen, I took him to the range and taught him how to use this safely. I should probably do the same with you."

Is this some father-son bonding moment? Are we supposed to go to the gun range and shoot a few targets and talk about girls?

I shake my head. "No, thank you. I'm a little freaked out by guns."

He places it back in the shoebox and puts the lid on. "That's how you get not freaked out. By learning how to safely use it." With that, he says he's going to go to bed. He stands and walks behind me, then stops at the doorway.

"Listen," he says. "Your mom's trying. Earlier I mentioned the repeating patterns, but she *is* trying. So be patient with her, okay?"

"Yeah. Okay."

He pauses and thinks for a moment. "With me, too. I know you don't remember my parents, but they weren't as . . ." He grins. "Direct as Gramma Sharon."

I laugh. "Is anyone?"

"No." He comes back and puts a hand on my shoulder, squeezing gently, like he's trying to tell me something. Maybe a warning? But then he kisses the top of my head. "Night, kiddo."

"Good night."

I listen to his footsteps go up the stairs to their bedroom.

TWENTY-NINE

MARCUS DECIDES THAT THE BEST WAY TO SPEND OUR Saturday morning is to have Valencia shop for the barbecue while he takes Easton and me to a gun range. Father-son bonding over guns? It's very heteronormative and I already hate it.

My real parents never had a gun. And knowing this one is even in the house—with someone who may have killed the real Nate—terrifies me. In fact, this whole trip feels more and more like an intimidation tactic.

When we arrive at the gun range, Easton presents the person behind the counter with his ID—I don't need one since I'm a minor and Marcus is responsible for me—and chooses a handgun to rent. They charge him for a box of bullets, then hand over ear protection and a target, and tell him he can go to the range, where someone will meet him to go over the rules.

Marcus tells them we're hanging back because he's going to show me how to properly handle a weapon first. Then he puts a locked box on the counter and the guy behind it watches as he unlocks it, then shows him the gun inside—the one I found in a Cole Haan shoebox even though this box exists somewhere—and that it's not loaded.

The guy reminds him not to load it outside the shooting area and

Marcus nods and buys a second box of bullets and a target. I take the orange plastic ear protection the clerk hands over and Marcus leads me to a seating area where another man is cleaning a big, terrifying rifle.

"Don't worry," Marcus says. "I'm not the hunting type, so you don't have to worry about those."

I must have shown my thoughts on my face. "I don't really like guns period."

"Well, you shouldn't," he says as he unlocks the handgun's trigger. "Guns are dangerous. We only have this one because it helped your mother feel safer."

"How bad was she? When I was abducted, I mean." I want to see how Marcus reacts to my question. Because he should look at me skeptically if he knows I'm not really Nate. Right?

But he doesn't even flinch as he sets the trigger lock down on the table between us. "How bad do you think? She's your mother and you disappeared. She could only hope for the best for so long before she had to fear the worst." His eyes drop to the gun in his hand. He pulls the top back and clicks something with his fingers. Then he pulls it forward and the top of the weapon slides off.

He looks at it, then at the rest of the disassembled gun in his hand, and blows into it before putting the top back on. It's like a nervous tic. Something he's doing to distract himself from what he's saying because he's uncomfortable.

"What about you?" I ask. "Didn't you have the same hope?"

He stops and looks at me. Hesitates. Then his shoulders slump. "Of course I did."

I stare at him as he stares back. I don't break eye contact, no matter how awkward it feels. I want him to break first. To stutter or say something he might regret later. Something, *anything*, that might prove he was a part of this. Or that he at least knows for a fact I'm not Nate. Because he knows Nate is dead.

And he does look away first. He puts the gun down, gently, on the tabletop.

"Nate," he says, still avoiding my eyes. "I did hope. But my experience in life is different. I see how this stuff goes all the time, and usually after a certain point, things get hopeless."

"But not for our family," I say, pushing him.

He finally looks up at me, surprised. Then he smiles. He puts his elbow on the table and rests his chin on his palm, shaking his head at me.

"Yeah, bud," he says. "I guess for us it was different." He sighs, and if I weren't suspicious about his involvement in his own son's death—if there weren't a gun on the table between us like a threat—this could be a nice father-son bonding moment. Or maybe it's another side effect of Valencia making me feel so loved. I might be looking for a way to excuse my suspicions about Marcus.

"Listen." Marcus leans back, crossing his arms. "I'm sorry I got so mad about the car." The car we drove here that looks exactly how it did before someone framed me for spilling paint on it. "It's just stuff. I'm happy you're back, kiddo. And I'm sorry I let my temper get the best of me."

Maybe he senses that I'm about to ask him if that means he believes me, because he returns his attention to the weapon.

"Okay. This is called the slide." He picks up the gun and pulls the top back and turns the chamber in my direction so I can see there isn't a bullet in there waiting for me. "First rule, always assume the gun is loaded. You pull the slide to check."

He picks up the empty clip from the table and puts it in the handle.

"Then you check the clip." He clicks something on the side and the clip slides out. Then he puts it all back together and places it on the table. "Now you try it."

I pick up the gun and again it feels heavy in my hand. I try to pull the top back, but Marcus puts his hand on top of mine.

"Not there, you'll pinch your fingers." He moves my hand and adjusts my grip. I pull back the slide and look again in the empty chamber. Part of me half expected a bullet to be in there. Like this was all a trick and he was setting me up.

I press the little button on the side of the handle and the clip slides out, clattering to the table. Marcus grabs it but tells me good, then holds out his hand. I give the gun back.

"Second rule is the safety. So remember, to start, always assume the gun is loaded." He tilts it over and points to a lever on the side of the weapon. "This is the safety."

He flicks it and a red dot appears under it.

"Red means dead. It means the safety is off. So you should always assume the safety is off. But if you see the red dot, you know for *sure* it's off. Repeat what I just said."

"Red means dead."

He nods. "Red means dead." Then he locks the safety into place again. He stands. "Come on, I'll have the range teach you how to stand and shoot. They'll do it better than I would."

I follow him out the door to the range, putting on my ear protection. But despite what Marcus said to me before showing me the gun, I can't shake the thought that this whole exercise is a threat.

A warning that if I step out of line . . .

Red means dead.

I half listen to the bearded guy talking about gun range etiquette—"Don't point the gun at anyone" being such an obvious rule that I really don't think you should have to say it, but here we are.

Then he takes me to a little cubby next to Easton, who is shooting slowly and methodically. Gun Range Guy shows me how to load the gun, how to clip my target on the reel, and how to send it back. He moves it close for me—about twenty feet away—and in the next lane over, I see Easton's is all the way at the back of the range in front of a massive mound of sand meant to catch the bullets.

The guy shouts loud enough that I can hear him through my ear protection and over the muffled sounds of gunshots.

It's overwhelming, so I nod, and when he tells me to give it a shot—pun intended?—I hold up the gun. His hands wrap around mine and he manipulates my fingers into the correct position, telling me if I pulled the trigger like that, the top of the gun might pinch the skin between my thumb and forefinger. I shiver and he tells me to go ahead.

I pull the trigger, but nothing happens. The man reaches out and tells me good job for keeping the safety on. I try again.

The gun jumps in my hand in a way I'm not prepared for, and for a second I'm worried I'll drop it. It's so powerful it makes my heart race and my hands tingle. I put it down and shake my head.

I don't want to do this. I hate guns.

Marcus leans down and yells next to my ear protection, "It's okay. It's a lot at first, but you'll get used to it."

I don't want to get used to it. But Marcus picks up the gun and holds it out to me again.

I hold it tighter, square up, and squeeze the trigger. This time the bullet hits the target. Or at least the paper. It puts a large hole in the bottom right corner of the sheet. But the terrifying part is the target doesn't even flutter with the impact. The bullet rips through and continues into the sand pile.

There are still eight bullets left in the clip, so I aim for the center of the target and pull the trigger a few quick times. Again, the guy from the range corrects me and tells me to adjust between each shot.

Adrenaline is coursing through my veins. I feel like I'm back at the convenience store, getting caught for shoplifting. My old life and my new one blending into some adrenaline-fueled nightmare.

By the time I empty the clip, my heart rate seems to have regulated. Marcus has me reload the gun and tells me to shoot the target.

It takes seven more shots, but I hit the bull's-eye. Marcus cheers and claps me on the shoulder, and I can't help but feel a little bit proud.

THIRTY

WHEN WE PULL INTO THE GARAGE, VALENCIA IS WORKing at the little wooden table where her gardening supplies are. She waves to us with gloved hands and a bright smile.

"How was shooting paper targets?" she asks.

"Nowhere near as fun as the real thing," Marcus says. He says it in a joking tone, but all I can think is he really means it.

Valencia rolls her eyes playfully before giving him a kiss. "Well, now that you've gotten your testosterone workout in, you can all help me in the garden." There are several new hydrangea plants, only a foot high, in cardboard trays on the garage floor.

Marcus frowns. "Sorry, gotta do some motion writing upstairs."

Or he's going to smoke a bowl to help him come down.

She frowns and turns her attention to Easton, who puts up his hands. "JT is picking me up in ten minutes."

"I'll help," I say before she can scold him. "I mean, I guess it's my own fault the old ones died to begin with, right?"

Valencia turns to me with a look of surprise. Then she reaches for the box of Miracid on the top of her workbench. She holds it out to me, showing me it's still unopened.

"You lied about fertilizing them. But I think Gramma Sharon was right. It was a blight, and that's no one's fault."

She believes me. I have no clue why I feel so relieved, but I am. Maybe because a blight would mean the plants weren't killed maliciously.

She tosses the box on the workbench again and smiles. "I planted the hydrangeas when I was pregnant with you. It's only right that we do it together this time."

Valencia hands me a pair of gardening gloves and tells me to grab a shovel. She leads me out to the garden, where large paper bags have already been filled with the branches of the dead hydrangeas. She tells me she cut them all away, but we still have to dig up the roots.

"Did we ever do this before?" I ask. I move aside some of the mulch and start digging around the hydrangea stump. "The gardening, I mean."

She laughs. "No. I never even cared about the garden until you were gone. The reason I planted the hydrangeas in the first place was because they're low maintenance. Water them on hot days and fertilize them and they're usually good. When you were gone, I started looking into new garden beds and bought some books." She nods toward the backyard. "I even had raised beds and a nice vegetable garden back there for a few years."

But now the yard is only grass.

"What happened?"

"Asshole squirrels," she says with hatred. "Those little shits would see my tomatoes, days away from ripening, and take a single bite out of every damn one. I'd be lucky to get one tomato a year, if that. So it was either kill 'em all or get rid of the raised beds." She shrugs, disappointed.

“So you got into gardening, and Dad got into boating?” I motion toward the boathouse.

Valencia smiles. “Well, he was always into boating. When we lived in DC—you were just a toddler then—we would all come down here on long weekends. Once, he rented a sailboat and had the captain *attempt* to teach us how to sail. You and Easton weren’t nearly as interested as he was, and we ended up having to end the cruise early. The next time he went alone, and I took you boys to a movie.”

“But he still put in the boathouse.”

Valencia nods. “He’s waiting on the perfect boat to put in there. But not a sailboat. That won’t fit.”

I think about asking how much it cost. I know the answer because I’ve seen the invoice upstairs. It was almost half of Nate’s life insurance policy. Which means there was plenty left over to buy a boat—I think? But now that they have to pay back the money, maybe that’s changed.

Something in the dirt catches my eye. It looks like a root—small, thin, and brown with dirt—but it’s harder than a root would be. I pick it up. Maybe it’s a broken piece of rock?

I throw it into the grass behind me and dig a little deeper.

But my shovel catches on something. This time it’s fabric.

Old, dirty, and shredded. Maybe it’s burlap that Valencia put down for the garden and forgot about?

I try to pull it out but it’s lodged under the dirt, so I dig around it, following the fabric until it stops. I pull a little more and it starts to come out. It’s not burlap, but maybe cotton.

Something rattles around inside as it unfurls.

And out tumbles a mess of dirty bones.

THIRTY-ONE

"EUGH!" I JUMP BACK, DROPPING THE CLOTH AND shovel. Valencia startles and looks back at me. Then at the piece of fabric that's covering the bones. I point. "Dead. There's bones, a skull, something dead."

Valencia reaches out and pulls up the cloth. And there it is. The bones are smaller than my brain originally recognized. All I saw were the eye sockets and teeth of whatever animal it was and my brain panicked.

But now I feel ridiculous, because it's obviously some rodent. Maybe a squirrel that a cat killed, then buried? Do cats bury their food to save for later? I've heard horror stories about people waking up with dead presents from their cat on the front porch or on a pillow.

"Aw. It's one of your guinea pigs."

"*One* of?"

"Yeah. You had a guinea pig phase when you were in kindergarten. Your teacher, Ms. Rafkin, brought one in as a class pet and you wanted one so bad. I wonder if this is Frank. Or was it Murray?"

My skin crawls looking down at the bones of one of Nate's first pets. "Murray?"

"I think Murray was your second. Frank was first, because that was also the class pet's name. And then I think after Murray died we let you get one more, but I forget his name. After the third we stopped getting them for you. I thought those things would have lived a little longer, but apparently they only live five to seven years, and who knows how long the pet store had them before we came in."

"They all died?"

"Peacefully in their sleep like old guinea pigs do. But honestly I probably should have let you learn that lesson once and called it a day."

"I guess every kid learns that sometime."

My pet was a little turtle my dad bought me on my sixth birthday. Looking back, I think it was because he and my mom might have forgotten my birthday that year. I remember my dad coming home from work and him and my mom talking quietly before he had to go back out for "something from the store." He came back with a green plastic water tray with a little island in the middle and a turtle sitting on top.

I got lectured about keeping his habitat clean, how to feed him, and a number of other things.

Kept him alive for a few months, too. But then one day when I was at school, he escaped from his shallow green prison, and the next time I saw him he was dead behind the couch.

From there I got another lecture on responsibility and eventually, from Mom, I learned that animals have no souls, which means they don't get into heaven. That was when I started thinking this religion thing was a little suspect. Why wouldn't innocent creatures get into heaven? Adam and Eve were supposed to be in paradise until they ate the apple and realized they were naked—something that I learned in seventh grade was a metaphor and there was never a literal apple. But animals were "pre-apple," and they weren't aware they were naked all the time, so why wouldn't they always have a place in heaven?

Asking those questions only got me more lectures, and once I started looking into it all myself, I turned to the dark side: agnosticism.

I wonder how Nate was raised on the subject.

"Are we religious?" I ask.

Valencia stutters a moment, then says, "We . . . Not really, I guess, is the short answer. Marcus was raised Catholic, I was raised Presbyterian, but we never took you boys to service. Gramma Sharon doesn't really do church anymore either. Why? Do . . . you want to go to church?" She asks it like she doesn't want the answer.

"No," I say, maybe a little too quickly.

"Did you go to church before? With the . . ." She doesn't say *people who took you* but I know it's there. She shakes her head. "Sorry. I shouldn't ask—"

For some reason I decide to answer her. Interrupting before she can finish her apology.

"I think so," I say. "I know guinea pigs don't go to heaven."

"Bullshit."

I turn to her, and she seems annoyed. Then she softens when she realizes I might believe in heaven—which I don't even know if I do. If there is one, though, I definitely won't get in because I'm lying to a family whose son has most likely been murdered. And, yes, I'm trying to solve his murder, but even my motivation for that is selfish.

She puts a gentle hand on my upper arm. "I mean it's bullshit that your pets wouldn't be in heaven. I don't know what I believe, honestly. Some days I think life is random and meaningless, other days—like the day we got the call that you'd been found—" That actually breaks my heart. She's so sincere, and I can't look at her while she says the next part. "Those days I believe maybe there is something out there. And if there is, and it involves the afterlife, why wouldn't the people, and animals, you love be there with you?"

The sincerity in her voice comforts me. My real parents were always quick to talk about people who *wouldn't* be in heaven, but for Valencia, it's an open place for all our loved ones.

And that does sound nice.

My mind allows that thought for exactly three seconds before clouding over with suspicion. Because someone here knows I'm not Nate. If they killed him, they know I'm faking it, so they're manipulating me. They're dumping paint on cars, and killing flowers, and leaving the gas on so I look careless. Framing me for small things to raise suspicion.

Or they're sincere, and maybe Easton moved the paint and didn't want to get yelled at. And maybe I was careless and left the gas on a teensy bit. And maybe the flowers really were blighted. Then I'm being a complete dick for no reason. But I don't let myself think that for long because that's how I'll end up dead.

"Well, if there is an afterlife, I hope you're all cool with me bringing guinea pigs around all the time."

"Of course. It was Marcus who hated them anyway. But if it is paradise, I'm sure he'll have worked through whatever rodent revulsion he has."

The red flags are up in an instant. Marcus again.

She laughs but avoids looking at me, instead turning her attention back to the remains of Nate's *three* beloved dead guinea pigs. If guinea pigs are supposed to live five to seven years, it is strange that Nate lost three of them. If he was in kindergarten when he got the first one, he was five, then he disappeared when he was six, so he had three dead guinea pigs in a year. Dead pets. Sure, that's not suspicious at all. But also, why doesn't Valencia think so? If she did, she wouldn't be telling me all this.

It reminds me again why I'm here. I've gotten too comfortable with Valencia and forgotten that something bad happened to the real Nate. And now there are dead animals to add to that.

Maybe the guinea pig deaths were payback. A way for Marcus to get rid of the rodents he hated and take something his son loved as punishment for making him angry. Physical abuse could be reported. But guinea pigs dying in their sleep . . .

Definitely something a psychopath would do. And he'd know how to get away with it. Just like he'd know how to get away with murdering a person.

THIRTY-TWO

THE MORNING OF THE BARBECUE I GO DOWNSTAIRS TO find Valencia making pasta salad. She smiles at me and walks over to the fridge, taking out two tubs of Cool Whip and placing them on the island in front of me.

"Oh. I think I'm good with cereal for breakfast, but thanks?"

She laughs. "You told Gramma you'd make her Watergate salad. Better get to work so it can chill before this afternoon."

Okay, but I didn't think a salad would have *Cool Whip* in it. Valencia goes over to a lemon-printed tin and pulls off the top. She flicks through the recipes inside and takes out a handwritten note card.

Gramma Sharon's Watergate Salad is written at the top—there are even little cartoon skulls and crossbones drawn around it. Valencia tells me the drawings were Easton's addition. I read over the recipe:

Two tubs of Cool Whip
One large can crushed pineapple (undrained)
One bag miniature marshmallows
¾ cup crushed pecans
Two packs pistachio instant pudding mix
Step one: Mix everything in a bowl and chill. Step two: Serve.

"The word *salad* is doing a *lot* of heavy lifting here," I say.

Valencia laughs and for a second it almost sounds like Gramma Sharon's cackle, and I can't help but smile. As she's getting out the rest of the ingredients, Marcus enters the kitchen. He frowns instantly, as if he knows what I'm working on.

"We can't have soda in the house, but sure, let's make a marshmallow salad," he says.

"If my mother wants to destroy her teeth, that's on her."

"Your son said he'd help her eat it," Marcus reminds her.

"I'm regretting that statement now," I say. Valencia and Marcus laugh.

"You don't have to eat it, honey," Valencia says. "I'm sending the leftovers home with her anyway."

"No. A promise is a promise." And I get to work on the . . . salad. After completing step one, it doesn't look any better. Maybe it will after it chills.

But a little before two p.m., when everyone is supposed to show up, I take it out of the fridge and it still looks like a green, mushy mess of Cool Whip, marshmallows, and pecans. I give it a stir for good measure as Easton reaches over my shoulder for the jar of Jif peanut butter on the second shelf.

"Disgusting," he says with a smirk. He grabs a spoon and takes a giant glob of peanut butter before putting the lid back on and the jar in the fridge.

"You invited JT, right?" I ask.

"Yeah." He tries to talk around the peanut butter, then licks his lips before continuing. "I'll tell him to smoke a little more before he arrives."

"Good idea."

The doorbell rings and I put the spoon back into the massive bowl of Watergate salad. "I'll get it."

Honestly, I'm hoping it's Gramma Sharon so she can see the mess I made and tell me, *No, no, that's not it, Valencia must have given you the wrong recipe.* Or maybe it's all a bit! A practical joke the whole family is playing on me because Nate had it at some school event and made Gramma Sharon make it and everyone hates it.

I pull open the door and it's Miles instead. He holds out a bag of tortilla chips.

"My mom told me I had to bring something." I take the bag from him and step aside for him to come in.

"Tortilla chips are my favorite," I say. Though that's not entirely true because Takis exist. I just don't know what else to say. Valencia comes out to the front hall to greet Miles but then her face drops. "I completely forgot to ask your parents if there's anything special we should make you." So she must know he's diabetic.

"Nope! As long as I keep an eye on my blood sugar, I'm an omnivore. And a voracious one at that."

"We'll see how you like Watergate salad." Easton emerges from the kitchen, the peanut butter spoon probably left in the kitchen sink. The doorbell rings again and I open it.

"Hello, family!" Gramma Sharon enters with a canvas tote bag she hands over to me. "I brought corn from the farmers market."

"Thought you weren't going to bring anything, Mom," Valencia says, reaching out to take the tote from me.

She shrugs. "I knew you wouldn't have corn on the cob and I wanted some. Who's this?" She turns to look at Miles with suspicion.

"Miles." He holds out his hand and Gramma Sharon takes it. "Nate and I were friends in a past life."

"Happy to have you, Miles."

Valencia asks Gramma Sharon what she'd like to drink and directs Miles and me out to the deck, where there's a cooler of seltzer.

I take him outside—past the Watergate salad on the kitchen island that he eyes hesitantly. Marcus is already at the grill with a black apron on. He greets Miles in an over-the-top friendly way, as though Valencia coached him on how to react to Nate's old friend coming over. A few moments later Easton comes out to put down cornhole boards.

I pull Miles away so we aren't in earshot of anyone. "Did you know Nate had guinea pigs?"

Miles thinks for a second. "We were in separate kindergarten classes, and I vaguely remember his class having a pet guinea pig. Don't worry, I wasn't resentful, and it's not the reason I asked my parents for a pet for years and am now cursed with the *un*-cuddliest golden retriever named Chardonnay."

"Well, I found three guinea pig carcasses buried in the garden yesterday." I point in the direction of the freshly planted hydrangeas.

He grimaces. "You think someone killed Nate's guinea pigs?"

I shrug. "Valencia says they all died in their sleep. Didn't think it was suspicious."

"Could be poison. Do you trust her?"

Maybe I shouldn't, but I really do. That doesn't mean she's right. She could *think* they died in their sleep. "She said Marcus hated them."

“That bodes well for my Marcus suspect murder wall.” He points to the side of his skull. “In my brain, I mean. I don’t want to look like a lunatic myself.”

“Nate!” Gramma Sharon calls out from the deck. “Bring your friend over and play cards with me.”

“Hope you’re ready to get your ass handed to you.”

“Don’t threaten me with a good time.”

His innuendo makes me look at his butt and my cheeks heat—the face ones, I mean. We walk up to the deck, and I pull out a chair and sit across from Gramma Sharon. Miles takes one to my left at the head of the table.

“Miles.” Valencia comes out from the kitchen with Gramma Sharon’s drink—bourbon. “Can I get you a drink?”

Miles tells her a seltzer is fine, and Valencia walks over with one of each flavor. Miles takes the lemon.

Gramma Sharon lifts up her heart-shaped sunglasses with a smile. “I saw the Watergate salad. It looks great, kid.”

I grimace. “If you say so.”

“Don’t wimp out on me now!” she says with a laugh.

Easton leans against the railing behind me. “At least now you have a friend who can help you finish it.”

“What is Watergate salad?” Miles asks nervously.

Gramma Sharon turns to Marcus. “Go bring out the salad.”

Marcus shakes his head but goes inside and several minutes later reemerges with the giant bowl of Watergate salad in one hand and a red plastic tray of raw burgers and hot dogs in the other. He sets the bowl on the table in front of us.

"Bon appétit," he says with a grin. Gramma Sharon reaches out for three paper plates on the other side of the table.

"Oh!" Miles gives a wide, fake, but polite smile. "That looks like a *lot* of sugar."

"Sure is!" Gramma Sharon says.

"I'm diabetic and that will probably kill me. So unfortunately, I'm gonna have to pass."

Gramma Sharon gives a sad tsk and turns back to me. "Guess we'll have to share his portion."

Yay.

I grab two spoons—because spoons are probably going to be best for this mess—and pass one across the table to Gramma Sharon.

Gramma Sharon scoops up a massive dollop of the marshmallow salad and plops it heavily on each plate, handing one over to me.

Miles watches as I scoop up some salad, giving me a look that says even if it wouldn't put him in a diabetic coma, he'd skip it. Gramma Sharon isn't turned off at all and takes a massive spoonful, smiling at me as she does.

"It's a Beaumont Bee-Bee-Cue!"

Miles and I turn to see JT coming around the corner with a Super Soaker in hand. He shoots it right at Easton's chest. Easton flinches, then touches the liquid spot on his shirt and brings it up to his nose.

"Dude, is this tequila?"

"John Thomas!" Valencia scolds.

Meanwhile, Marcus yells from the grill, "Hey, now the party can start." Again, there's a tinge of sarcasm there but he manages to make me laugh. Marcus puts down the meat and crosses the backyard to greet JT—and to confiscate the liquor-filled Super Soaker for his own enjoyment, squirting some into his mouth. He gives Valencia a sly grin as she continues to scold JT about bringing liquor to their house while he's underage. JT insists his own parents don't mind and it was a gift for Marcus and Valencia.

CRUNCH.

I turn at the sound of Gramma Sharon taking her first bite of Watergate salad, surprised at how crunchy the pecans still are after sitting in the Cool Whip for so long.

"Mmm!" Gramma Sharon is just as surprised because her eyes go wide. But that *mmm* wasn't like a *mmm, this is delicious* mmm. It was one of shock. She drops her plastic spoon, and it flops into the remaining mountain of Watergate salad.

Her jaw moves and her eyes widen as she makes another "MMM!" sound, this one scared and urgent.

"Gramma?" I say.

She reaches for a napkin and puts it to her mouth.

A light pink foamy mess of marshmallows, Cool Whip, pineapple, and pecans flows out.

"Oh my God."

Miles looks on in shock as the flood of Watergate salad pouring out of Gramma Sharon's mouth turns bloodred. She whimpers as she pushes out the rest of the bloody mess with her tongue. It lands on the napkin trembling in her hand and more blood flows from her open mouth.

So much blood.

She looks across the table at me, her eyes wide.

"Isth gwath!" she says with another bubble of blood.

"Mom?" Valencia sounds horrified.

Miles jumps up to grab more napkins and Gramma Sharon doesn't have to repeat herself because I understand her perfectly. Everyone surrounds the table, wondering what's happening, panicking at all the blood.

But I'm looking at the plate of Watergate salad in front of me.

And the thick shards of glass mixed in with marshmallows and pineapple.

THIRTY-THREE

I WATCH AS WATER DISSOLVES THE MINI MARSHMAL-lows in the colander over the sink. What doesn't dissolve is the pecans, pineapple, and glass.

So much glass.

Glass that wasn't there when I was mixing up the ingredients a few hours ago. I pick up a piece and hold it to the light. There are no marks or labels to give me a hint of its origin. It could be a drinking glass, wineglass, window glass. I have no clue where it could have come from.

"I take it back," Miles says, gazing down at the pecans, pineapple, and glass in the colander. "I love diabetes. It's my favorite thing in the world now."

"You think this is funny?" I snap. He holds up his hands in defense.

"I don't. And I think you know me well enough by now that that question is being asked in bad faith, so I'm going to assume this is you freaking out."

He assumes correctly. "Sorry," I say.

Marcus and Valencia drove Gramma Sharon to the hospital, leaving all the food and supplies for the barbecue. So Miles and I cleaned up what we could and put it in the fridge. But I wanted to see how much glass was in the Watergate salad. Turns out, it's a lot.

When I look at the glassware in the cabinets, it's all accounted for.

"Where did it come from?" I ask. Honestly, I think I'm still in shock. The paint, the flowers, the gas—all that could be logicked away if I tried hard enough, but not this. This was deliberate.

Miles goes over to the recycling and pulls out the rinsed can of crushed pineapple, turning it around in his hand and looking inside. "No chance it was a factory error?"

I look back down at the glass in the sink. It's not possible. I could pick up all the glass and put it in the can and it would probably overflow. I don't even think there'd be enough space for the pineapple.

When I tell Miles that, he drops the can back into the recycling bin. "I don't want to state the obvious, but Marcus was alone with the salad."

He's right. He brought it out to us. And he said I had to eat it if I was making it for Gramma Sharon. Then I remember Gramma Sharon's glass of bourbon that I dumped in the sink.

"Valencia was, too. Why hurt her mother, though?" I ask. "If I'm the target, why put glass in something they knew she would eat?"

"Because whoever it is isn't trying to hurt you. They're trying to expose you. If they . . . you know—" He looks around the empty kitchen, probably making sure Easton and JT haven't ventured inside. Miles makes a cutting action at his throat. "—Nate, and they're trying to keep the life insurance money, they'd probably want to expose you as quick as possible. And if it's a psychopath we're dealing with, yeah, they wouldn't care who got hurt along the way. Least of all their mother-in-law."

The doorbells rings, and Miles and I share a look.

"Were you expecting anyone else?" he asks.

I shake my head and go to the front door, Miles following closely behind. I don't realize until I'm already opening the door that I could have checked the doorbell camera app instead, but it's too late now.

There, standing on the front porch, is retired Agent Grant. He's still in a suit. And still has that grim look on his face.

I freeze. I don't know what to even say. Mainly because I have no clue what he's doing here. But the timing is certainly odd, what with the sink full of Watergate glass salad in the kitchen behind us.

"Hi," I finally manage. "Can we help you?"

"Nate." But again he says the name with suspicion. "Are your parents home?"

"No."

"Where are they?" he asks.

"They had to run out."

"Where?"

All the alarms in my head are telling me not to answer. "What do you need, Agent Grant?"

He finally gives up the act and his eyes flit over to Miles, then back to me. "I have a friend who's a nurse at Shore Medical. Said your parents brought your grandmother in with some pretty substantial injuries."

"Uh." Miles steps forward. "Not to be mouthy, but doesn't that violate HIPAA laws?"

"Not when she didn't tell me what the substantial injuries are. Just that she came in. I decided I'd check to see if everything was okay here. Since I'm close with the family."

"Then why weren't you at the barbecue?" I ask. When he doesn't answer, I finally try to end the conversation. "She ate canned pineapple tainted with something from the factory. She hurt her mouth."

He nods slowly.

"Anything else?" I ask.

"Is there?" Agent Grant replies.

Miles puts up his hand. "Actually, I have something. Forgive me for being so forward, but would you be open to coming on my podcast?" Agent Grant's eyes flick from Miles to over my shoulder. I turn and see Easton walking out from the kitchen. He looks pissed. Miles continues. "I think you'd be an iconic guest."

"What are you doing here?" Easton asks.

"I heard about your grandmother. I wanted to make sure everything is okay."

"Then go to the hospital, where she is." Easton steps in front of me, blocking my view of Agent Grant. He turns to Miles. "And Miles, I think you should go home, too."

"Right. Okay." He turns back to Agent Grant. "So the podcast."

"Now, Miles."

He nods and steps around Agent Grant. "Well, you know where I live. So . . . see you later, Nate."

Once Miles is gone, Easton asks Agent Grant, "Anything else?" He holds out his card, but Easton doesn't take it. "We've got one somewhere. Thanks." Then he closes the door in his face. He turns his attention back to me, shaking his head. "Hate that guy."

"Why?"

He walks back to the kitchen and I follow. "Who do you think started all the rumors about Mom and Dad being the ones who hurt you?"

I freeze in the doorway. "Seriously?"

Easton nods. "Guy's a dick. He's pissed off he isn't good at his job, so he makes shit up to make his suspects anxious. I don't have proof, but he asked a lot of questions when you went missing that came back around once people started blaming Mom and Dad."

Maybe Grant *does* make things up. Like that nurse thing seemed kind of fake. I doubt a nurse would tell him someone was admitted to the hospital, because Miles is right, even without specifics about the injury it would probably be a HIPAA violation. He might have been outside and seen Marcus and Valencia drive past with Gramma Sharon in the back seat, a bloody dish towel to her mouth.

Easton peers into the sink. "Speaking of blame. I gotta ask." He narrows his eyes at me. "You didn't do it on purpose, right?"

"No." I open the cabinets. "Look, the glasses are all here."

He points to an empty spot, and I shake my head and open the dishwasher to show him where the dirty glass is.

"Could have come from somewhere else." He goes into the fridge and gets out the jar of peanut butter.

My voice is verging on shrill. "I didn't put glass in the Watergate salad! I was going to eat it, too!"

"Okay, so you didn't do it," he says. "I was half joking, but happy to know you're not a total psycho." I watch him grab a spoon and take another huge glob of peanut butter from the jar.

"So what do you think?" I ask. "Where did the glass come from?"

He shrugs. "The factory. Maybe a light broke over the conveyor belt where they chopped up your pineapples or whipped the Cool Whip and you didn't notice when you were mixing it." His eyes go wide and he laughs. "Dad's gonna sue the shit out of them."

"It wasn't the factory, Easton. I poured out all the ingredients myself, and I didn't see any glass."

He stares at me, looking nervous. "So then who did it?"

"Who do you think?" I ask. I don't mean to sound accusatory, but I genuinely want to know. Easton shakes his head.

"Mom and Dad would never do that."

Before we can say anything else, the door out to the garage opens and I turn to see Valencia and Marcus. She looks worried and exhausted; his expression is almost unreadable.

Easton goes over to them and Valencia hugs him. "Is Gramma okay?"

Valencia nods and I feel a tiny bit of relief. Then she comes over and gives me a hug and a kiss on the cheek, too.

"She has some deep lacerations in her mouth," Marcus says. "A couple stitches on the tongue, cauterized the gums. She'll need to stick to a liquid diet for a few weeks. And they're keeping her overnight for observation to make sure she didn't accidentally swallow any. But she should make a full recovery."

He stares at me while he speaks, and I stare right back. It's like we're daring one another to tell the truth. Right here in front of everyone.

"Easton, go upstairs," Marcus says.

He shakes his head. "No, I can—"

"Now." Marcus's temper returns. Easton gives me an apologetic look. I nod to him, and he licks his spoon clean, drops it in the sink, and leaves the kitchen.

"How did the glass get in there, Nate?" he asks.

"Marcus." Valencia sounds like they've talked about this in the car and agreed not to bring it up yet. He holds up a hand to silence her.

"How did shards of glass get in the food you knew your grandmother would be eating?"

"You forget I had a plate of it, too."

"And yet you didn't eat it."

"I didn't get a chance to. JT showed up and—"

"HOW. DID THE GLASS. GET IN THE SALAD?"

"Why don't *you* tell *me*!" I yell right back.

He opens his mouth to scream back, but Valencia puts up her hands and stands between us.

"Enough! Marcus, you know damn well that glass probably ended up in the can of pineapples."

"Bullshit!" he says, throwing his arms up.

"I'm on his side, actually," I say to Valencia. "It *is* bullshit because *someone* put it there." I don't know which one of them did it, but I really don't want to believe Valencia would hurt her own mother. Especially someone as kind as Gramma Sharon.

Marcus blinks and gives us an incredulous look. "You think *I* did this?"

"You brought the salad out."

"You *made* it."

"Stop it!" Valencia yells. "Marcus, do you honestly think our son is capable of doing such a thing?"

"Yes!"

When he says it, Valencia looks as if he slapped her. "I mean, maybe he doesn't realize he's doing it. It could be some . . . I don't know, fugue state he goes into. Maybe that's what happened with the gas, and the paint, and now the glass. I've had clients where that happens. It's a trauma response."

"I'm not crazy!" I say.

Valencia turns to me and puts her hands on my cheeks. "No one is saying you are. But, Marcus, if this were a trauma response, would you still hold it against him?"

"I didn't do it!"

"Stop it, Nate!" Marcus yells. "It couldn't have been anyone else because I would never hurt Sharon."

"Neither would I!"

"Enough!" Valencia yells. "I don't want to hear another goddamned word out of either of you. Nate, Marcus didn't do this. What reason would he have?" I want to respond, but I can't. Not without exposing myself. And across the kitchen, the look on Marcus's face seems to dare me to tell the truth.

"And Marcus. Other attorneys in your firm have represented people who bit into whole *knives* in sandwiches. So maybe it's not that far-fetched to think a few glass jars broke on a conveyor belt in a factory." She reaches for the colander in the sink and rattles the glass around to show Marcus how much was in it. "Instead of arguing, you can call the company on Monday and give them the info on the can in that recycling bin and threaten to sue the shit out of them. Watch how quick their lawyers want to settle and then you'll see this was all a horrible accident caused by neglect. And not your son."

Marcus clearly isn't sold on the idea but he doesn't say anything else.

When neither of us speaks, Valencia claps her hands. "Great. Now both of you go somewhere else."

I go up to my room. This was way too close. I had planned to take a small amount of salad and swallow it whole, worried it would taste gross. I could have died. And maybe Marcus would be okay with that.

Then he'd keep his life insurance *and* sue the canned pineapple company for wrongful death.

I take out my phone and text Miles.

We need to go to Agent Grant. Give him everything we have and see what he wants to do next. Maybe he's got more evidence we don't have that can help fill in the blanks.

The answer is almost instantaneous.

Are you sure?

Am I? No. But do you have any other ideas?

This time there's a long pause between texts.

Then Miles responds. I guess not. Okay. It's time to come clean.

THIRTY-FOUR

ON MONDAY AFTERNOON, VALENCIA TAKES ME OVER TO Gramma Sharon's house to visit her. My stomach is in knots the whole drive. I'm worried she's going to hate me—or be afraid of me. I've tried to keep Marcus and Valencia at arm's length during my stay with them, but I wasn't able to do that with Gramma Sharon.

Miles and I have already decided to tell Agent Grant the truth. But I said I wanted to see her first.

Before we tell him, I want her to know who I really am.

Maybe that's the other reason I'm so nervous. Not only does she probably think it's my fault her mouth has been shredded, but she's going to find out I'm not her grandson.

Valencia leads me up Gramma Sharon's front steps and the door swings open before we even reach it.

Gramma Sharon gives a weak smile that makes her flinch in pain, then steps aside and welcomes us in silently.

"How you feeling, Mom?" Valencia asks. Gramma Sharon gives her a thumbs-up, but it's shaky. When she sees how I'm looking at it, she drops her hand and pulls me into a hug. Instead of a kiss, she gently nuzzles her cheek against my shoulder, and I might cry.

But she snaps her fingers in front of my face, then wiggles her index finger back and forth in a "no" gesture.

No crying, I'm fine, her face tells me.

"I'm sorry." I can barely get the words out.

Again she snaps her fingers and gives me the no gesture. Only this time her face says, *It wasn't your fault.*

That's not true. Sure, I didn't put the glass in the Watergate salad, but someone else did because of me. She just doesn't realize it yet.

I look over to Valencia, who is watching the exchange with a sad smile. Valencia isn't someone I want to tell the truth to yet. There are too many unknowns. Miles was quick to remind me that we didn't have any evidence against her, but if we're suspecting Marcus, we should suspect her, too. He also said women are more likely to poison food to hurt someone than men. And of course, in true Miles fashion, he also pointed out that men murder more often than women overall and the statistic sounds misogynistic.

"Okay," I say. "Want to play cards?"

She claps me on the shoulder and nods, then leads us into the kitchen and sits at the table.

"Want me to make you some tea, Mom?" Valencia asks.

But Gramma Sharon waves her hand and points to the chair next to her. *No, stop fussing over me and sit down.*

There's already a stack of well-worn cards on the table that she picks up and starts shuffling. Valencia tells her about the pineapple can theory and how Marcus is going to threaten to sue them. Gramma Sharon looks bored and uninterested but continues shuffling the cards.

We play a couple hands while Valencia tries to keep the conversation going with only me and her talking as Gramma Sharon gestures or somehow emotes using only her eyes. The whole time the knot in my gut continues to twist.

It feels like what I imagine coming out would feel like. If I got to choose, I mean. I never planned on coming out to my parents. I already knew what their reaction would be—proven by the events leading to the mess I'm in right now. But my plan was to go off to college, be myself, and if they ever asked if I was seeing a girl, I'd say no and leave it at that. They could ask more questions if they wanted, but I figured they would ignore it, not wanting to know the truth.

Maybe coming out to Frankie should have been scarier, but she came out to me first, so I felt no stress at all. Miles was also different because he had already figured out I wasn't Nate. Being gay was the less dangerous secret.

That might be the easier way to do all this. Come out as gay to Gramma Sharon, and while I'm at it, throw in "By the way, I'm not Nate either."

The thought makes me more nervous. And Valencia is still here. I was hoping for some alone time with Gramma Sharon when I asked to visit her, but Valencia said she was going to move her afternoon appointments so she could come with me. And now that she's here, I don't know how to get Gramma Sharon alone.

Soon enough, the afternoon is gone, and Valencia is saying it's time for us to get home. She checks that Gramma Sharon is okay with her dinner—warm bone broth and a protein shake—then we head for the front door.

I don't want to leave, though. And an idea comes to me.

"Can I stay here tonight?" I ask. Then I turn to Gramma Sharon.

"To make sure you're okay. I feel like you shouldn't be alone." But it also keeps me out of the house. Last night I slept with my hamper against the bedroom door and all the lights on. If someone is stepping up their game to violence, I know it's a matter of time before they outright attack me.

She gives me a kind half smile. Then gently shoves me toward the door. Valencia laughs. "You should know Gramma Sharon prides herself on her independence. I'll bring you by tomorrow— Oh, you have therapy tomorrow. What about Wednesday? I'll drop you off on my way to work and you can spend the day here?"

Gramma Sharon nods and, again, hugs me and does the cheek nuzzle against my shoulder. Okay, so Wednesday we'll be alone, and I can tell her the truth. And then I'll call Agent Grant and maybe he can even meet us here, away from the house.

I just have to avoid Marcus until then.

THIRTY-FIVE

MILES OPENS HIS FRONT DOOR AND USHERS ME IN—I shout a quick hello to his parents in the kitchen—then we head up to his room, where he has to push Chardonnay out with his foot and close the door quickly behind her.

"So. How'd it go?" he asks once we're in the quiet safety of his room.

"I didn't do it." He slumps and I drop down on his bed. "Valencia was there the whole time. Like she wouldn't even go pee or anything."

"So do we call Grant and tell him the truth? Gramma Sharon'll find out pretty quick then."

The muscles in my chest tighten. I can't do that to her. How messed up would that be? Finding out her own daughter or son-in-law was responsible for not only poisoning her with glass but probably killing her grandson?

Oh, and also, the kid you thought was your grandson is a big gay imposter.

And for the first time, a new future fantasy comes to me. In it, Marcus is the one who killed Nate, but Valencia helped cover it up. Gramma Sharon is heartbroken when they're taken to prison, but she adopts me. I end up being Easton's brother anyway. We're one—little—happy family.

"I know it's stupid," I say. "But I want to tell her first."

Miles sighs and plops down next to me. We both stare up at the ceiling.

"It's not stupid," he says. Then quickly adds, "I mean, continuing to live in a house with someone who is obviously out to get you isn't displaying Mensa-level intellect."

I snort.

"But I get wanting to tell her yourself."

When I turn, he's looking at me and his face says yes, he absolutely understands. Probably because he's been through something a little similar with his own parents.

"What was it like when you came out?" I ask.

He shrugs and shakes his head. "Not nearly as horrific as I imagined, but I'm lucky. I mean, I obviously don't have to tell you."

"Especially because it wasn't a choice and resulted in me being homeless and now living with at least one psychopath."

"Right. Like, you should write a memoir after this is all done." He puts his hands up in the air like he's framing a theater marquee: "*COME OUT ALREADY: IT CAN'T GET MUCH WORSE THAN MINE.*"

I fall into a fit of laughter that makes Miles giggle along with me.

"There's a colon there, by the way," he says. "Like the second part is a subtitle."

"Yeah, I got that, thanks."

Once we stop laughing, he continues. "I thought it would be . . . I don't know. Scarier? And it was at first, before I said anything. The lead-up, I mean. Every day after I made the decision I would sit down at dinner, knowing I was going to say it and how. But I couldn't. Day after day after day."

"For how long?"

"About two years."

"Two *years*?" I sit up on my elbows, looking down at him.

"Yup. And after all that worrying and hand-wringing and, like, a ridiculous number of script changes, none of it even mattered. You've met my parents. How could I even think they wouldn't still love me?"

He's right. The limited times I've interacted with Miles's parents, they seem like the kind of people who are written as cute background characters in a silly TV show. The parents of the quirky best friend who show up only to help solve problems or have a funny misunderstanding with the main character's messy parents.

"How'd you finally do it?"

"Oh my God." He rolls over onto his side to face me, resting his head on his hand. "It's so anticlimactic, you ready?"

"Born ready. Disappoint me."

"So we're having dinner, right—lasagna—"

"Nice."

"And my mom and dad are talking about work or whatever, I don't know, I wasn't paying attention, and my mom turns to me and goes, 'Miles, what's new in your life?' And before I could convince myself otherwise, I yelled, 'I'M GAY!'"

I laugh again. "And what did they say?"

"Nothing at first. Then my dad puts down his fork and stares at me across the dinner table and goes, 'Your mother asked what was *new*.'"

"So they'd already assumed."

"Please. I asked Santa for an Elsa doll when I was five. They knew."

I feel a blend of jealousy and happiness for Miles. "Did you get it?"

With a smirk, he rolls off the bed and goes over to his open closet and bends down to sift through piles of old clothes, boxes of photo paper, books, and toys. Then emerges with a wrinkled stuffed Elsa doll.

"And you kept her!" I say, taking it as he hands her over to me.

"Of course. I was fucking ob*sessed* with *Frozen*. I think my dad took me to see it three times in theaters. Shame the second one sucked."

"You know I've never seen it?"

"What!"

"I've heard people singing the songs and everything, but I wasn't allowed to watch Disney movies."

"Stop talking." Miles gets up and goes to his computer. "We're watching *Frozen*." I grin and don't even bother to tell him we don't have to. Because I kind of want to. I came over here with the idea we'd be talking about Nate and the Beaumonts, and now . . . maybe all I want to do is watch an animated musical about ice magic.

The Disney logo appears on the monitor and Miles hops onto the bed next to me.

That's when it hits me. I'm in a cute boy's room, watching a movie on his bed. His *twin* bed. So our arms are touching. Legs, too. Little connected parts of our bodies, buzzing with potential energy.

Miles turns to me. "Sorry. I hijacked the night, didn't I? Did you want to keep talking about the coming out stuff? Because we can."

"No!" I might have said it a little too fast, and my cheeks heat. "I mean, I like this. Not thinking about all the other stuff."

He grins and my stomach flutters. "Good."

THIRTY-SIX

EASTON COMES TO PICK ME UP FROM THERAPY ON TUES-day since Gramma Sharon is still on pain meds. I'm hoping that when I see her tomorrow morning she'll be able to talk. I want her to be able to respond to me when I tell her the truth. Whether she wants to tell me off, scream, cry, or—as my ideal fantasy goes—tell me she doesn't give a shit and that she still loves me.

Yes, it's a reach. But hearing her say that would be worth the wait. And Marcus has been avoiding me anyway.

Easton looks at me skeptically as I hop into the car, tilting his head. "Doesn't look like it shrunk."

"That only happens after several sessions," I say. "How was your cleaning?" It was Easton's turn to go to Valencia this afternoon, hence him having custody of her car.

He grins his perfect white teeth at me. "Still no cavities."

"Does Mom dig violently around in your gums or is that only saved for her homeless children?"

"No, she lets Hillary do my cleanings. I think her doing yours herself was a Nate special." He shifts into drive and pulls slowly into traffic. "Mom told me Dad's picking her up from work and they won't be home till later, so I said we'd go somewhere for dinner. Where you want to go?"

That actually sounds great. I can relax a little and not be in a constant state of fear back at the house. Hanging out with Miles last night was such a relief. I tell Easton he can pick, and twenty minutes later he pulls into the restaurant Gramma Sharon took me on our first lunch date. It's still early for dinner—only a little after five—so the restaurant is slow and the only other diners are people well past retirement age.

We're seated in a booth facing the street, which is clogged with rush hour traffic. Easton and I casually talk about our days while looking over the menu. When the server comes to us—a short-haired brunette Easton's age or a little older—we order, and she takes our menus.

"I've been meaning to ask," Easton says. "You and Miles have been hanging out a lot lately."

"Not a question, but yeah. Mom said he and I used to be friends back in the day, so I'm trying to rekindle that."

He nods. "You decide if you're going to talk on his podcast?"

"I said I'd think about it." But something about the way Easton asked makes me feel like he knows more than he's letting on. So I add, "But I don't think I will."

He nods, but it's like he isn't sure he believes me. "He started this whole thing sometime last summer. Came over one day to ask me if I'd come on his podcast and talk about the day you disappeared."

"I assume you said no."

"Of course. I hate that true crime shit. Because he wants to make it about him. He wants to be the special person who finds the one crumb of evidence overlooked by the police. He doesn't care whose trauma he's exploiting, just that he gets to be the one to present it."

I shake my head. "He's not like that."

"How do you know? You only met him a couple weeks ago. Unless you remember something from before?" He looks at me with what I can only say is suspicion. So I turn away from him and shake my head.

"No. But he doesn't seem so bad."

Easton leans across the table. "Don't trust him, Nate. He's going to hurt you. He asked me, Mom, and Dad all to record something. And now he wants the former FBI agent who was in charge of your case to come on and talk about us?"

"It's not about you all, it's about me. And him, too. We were friends before I disappeared. You said he's exploiting your trauma, but you forget he knew me, too. Maybe he's working through his own shit."

Easton's jaw tightens as he stares at me. "You already talked to him, didn't you? Recorded something."

"No."

"Why don't I believe you?"

Probably because I'm not selling it all that well. While it's true I haven't recorded anything, I *have* been helping Miles investigate.

When I don't answer, he shakes his head. "I was hoping he wouldn't get you involved, but I guess that was stupid of me."

"I was already involved in it," I remind him. "It's my life, too."

He laughs, but part of him is obviously annoyed. Maybe disappointed. "Yeah, I guess that's true."

When our food arrives, we eat in silence. Easton checks his phone several times, texting someone, but I don't bother to ask who.

When we finish, the server drops off our bill. Easton hands over his card without looking at her. She brings it back promptly, he signs for it, and we go back out to the car.

He pulls onto the road, but not in the direction of the house.

"Do you want ice cream?" he asks. The ice cream place is straight ahead, and he points with his index finger but doesn't take his hands off the nine-and-three position on the steering wheel. "I'm in the mood for ice cream."

"Sure." I want to mention we could have gotten ice cream at the restaurant when the server asked if we wanted dessert, but I assume he likes the ice cream at this place.

He pulls into the parking lot, and we get out to stand in the long line of people waiting to be served. We still don't talk, and this whole evening has turned a little awkward. I want to ask him what he wants from me. If all he needs to hear is *I won't go on Miles's podcast*, sure, I'll say it. Because I won't. He's doing his podcast with or without me, and I've already decided to be long gone by the time he does it.

But even that has started to get to me. Will it be nice not having to worry about Marcus trying to poison me with glass? Absolutely. But I've kind of started to feel close to Easton and Valencia. The only thing that could change my feelings toward her is knowing she was involved in Nate's disappearance, too.

When we reach the front of the line, Easton orders a vanilla cone and I order their non-trademarked version of an Oreo Blizzard.

As we exit, I start toward some seats on the right side of the shop, but Easton stops me, pointing to the left. "There's a few seats over here."

There's one table, and it's empty. But that's because the dumpsters are a few feet away. And they stink.

"There's places over there that *aren't* near the dumpster," I say.

"Yeah, but this side is quieter. Breathe through your mouth." When they call out Easton's name, he goes and grabs the ice cream, then sits across from me.

Finally he changes the subject, telling me about school and how he did on his finals—aced every class. He also asks about my therapy because he's interested in possibly going into psychology.

"I'm fascinated by how our brains work," he says. "Like, do you know what the *DSM* is?"

I shake my head, trying to enjoy the ice cream without breathing in the garbage smell. The shift from him scolding me about the podcast to talking about school is sudden and a little awkward. But maybe it's how Easton wants to say he's ready to move on.

"*Diagnostic and Statistical Manual of Mental Disorders.* Basically every mental disorder is listed in there. It wasn't even published as the *DSM* until the fifties, and even then it was antiquated. Like they said homosexuality was a sociopathic tendency. And then they didn't take it out until the seventies."

I almost choke on my ice cream.

"You good?"

"Brain freeze," I lie, trying to play it off. Is he sharing trivia or is he purposely telling me about the history of gay psychology?

He gives me a second before continuing. "It's wild to me because this manual—which everyone is supposed to refer to for diagnostic support—is from studies of people who have already been diagnosed.

Which, what if someone's diagnosis is wrong? We don't actually *know* what's going on in someone's head or why people are the way they are; we're guessing based on the knowledge we have. Like they used to give women hysterectomies as a treatment for hysteria. And then decades later they're like, 'Oops, our bad, we shouldn't have done that.'"

Easton's ice cream cone is melting; he's barely even touched it.

"So are you thinking you want to go into psychology because you want to figure out how brains work?"

He shakes his head. "I know how they work. I think it's interesting that people will go talk to someone else about their problems instead of fixing them themselves."

Oh. "Therapy *is* people fixing themselves. You talk to your therapist about your issues and they give you tools to help figure them out when you're on your own." I've actually enjoyed talking to Dr. Zapata. Sure, it's only been a couple sessions. But it's still nice to talk to someone.

"But what if they give you the wrong tool? Or diagnosis? And I don't mean by mistake; I mean, what if they choose to make you worse?"

"Why would they want to do that?"

He stares at me for a second, then shrugs. "To rip you off and overcharge your insurance company, I guess?" He licks his ice cream to keep it from melting onto his hands and stares off at the dumpster.

"Well, that's not my therapist," I say.

"Sure." He takes out his phone and checks it. "Want to hang out with me and JT tonight?"

"Because this has been a blast. I can walk home from here if you want to go."

He sighs.

"I'm sorry if I've been a dick tonight. I'm . . ." He shrugs.

"Feeling some trauma from when I disappeared?"

Easton laughs and the energy between us shifts. "Yeah, that's it. Come hang out with me and JT. You need a night out of the house anyway."

He doesn't know I was at Miles's house last night, so it would really be two nights in a row out of the house. And if all goes to plan, I should be home free tomorrow afternoon. Well, as home free as a homeless imposter can be. Plus, Easton is clearly trying to make up for being a dick. "Okay."

"Well, we're late, so let's go." He gets up and throws away his ice cream cone without even having eaten much of it. I take another spoonful of mine before throwing it away.

He stops me as we get to the car. "Listen. Valencia is going to be tracking your phone, and I don't want her freaking out and calling us home right away. Where we're going, she'll think I'm getting you high or something. Do you trust me?"

"You want me to turn off my phone?"

"No, because then she'll worry about the tracking being off. Put it on do not disturb and hand it over."

This feels like one of those moments we talk about at Thanksgiving dinner when we're in our late twenties. Confessing the troublemaking we got into as kids now that we're old enough not to be scared of our parents. Of course, I won't be here when Easton is in his late twenties.

I put my phone in his outstretched hand, and he takes out his own, showing me that he's stacking them together. Then he walks over to the dumpster, drops down onto his hands and knees, and puts them underneath.

"Seriously?" I ask. But I'm feeling a sense of camaraderie, as if Easton and I are more alike than I thought.

"It's Tuesday night, so the trash men aren't coming. And who would look under there anyway?"

I can't help but smile because he's right. It's the perfect place to hide your stuff. I should know; all the documentation identifying the real me was hidden under a Starbucks dumpster in DC. Probably in a landfill now. That's a problem for future me to figure out.

We get back in the car and Easton heads up the main road out of town.

He drives straight for a few more miles before he turns off onto a rocky dirt road. The road isn't well maintained but it's heavily used. It slopes upward through thick trees on both sides.

"Where are we?" I ask.

"I guess you wouldn't remember coming up here, huh?" he says. "There's a little lookout at the top of the hill that overlooks the bay. Dad would take us up here to watch fireworks on the Fourth."

Eventually the trees clear and the road opens up onto a dirt lot in the middle of a grass clearing.

JT's Jeep is up ahead, parked under a tall cedar tree.

He's sitting on the back of a park bench that faces out to the bay. The sun is setting and the sky is bright pink and orange. There are thunderclouds to the south that flash with lightning, but they're a ways off over more tree-ridden hills. It's beautiful, and I know Nate would definitely remember this.

As we pull to a stop, JT turns around. He immediately brightens when he recognizes the car and waves animatedly. Easton parks and we get out.

"What's up, Beaumont Bros!" JT puts something in his pocket and gets up to greet us. He walks over to Easton and they do a dap, but when he approaches me, he stops with his arms out. "You a hugger? I'm a hugger, but your brother hates physical contact in all manners and means."

I didn't know that. He hugged me, so maybe he's okay with family. I open my arms and smile politely. "Bring it in, JT."

"Less-go!" He wraps his arms around me and even lifts me off the ground. He smells very strongly of weed, and when the hug is over, he reaches into his pocket and takes out a small black object. He puts it to his mouth and lets out a puff of smoke.

A vape. So this is his weed smoking spot. Well, maybe *everywhere* is a weed smoking spot for JT.

"I thought you had asthma?" I say, remembering the inhaler he had when I first met him.

He nods and pulls it out, taking a hit. "That's what this is for." But he still coughs as he re-caps it. He holds up the black vape to me. "This vaporizes the flower, so it's healthier for my lungs."

Easton scoffs. "That is not true."

"Sure it is!" JT insists, but Easton is right. There's no way it's true. "So what brings you boys up here on this beautiful evening?" Thunder rumbles in the distance.

I thought we were invited. I give Easton a questioning look, but he grins at me and shrugs.

"Just wanted to see you," Easton says. He follows as JT returns to the bench but doesn't sit down. Instead he walks over to the edge of the hill and uses his shoe to move a large, craggy rock.

The hill has a sharp, steep drop-off. I glance down and see several large rocks and boulders jutting out of the cliff face down a couple-hundred-foot drop. Then there's only the bay.

"Well, I love the company."

I sit next to JT, because being too close to the edge of the cliff is making my legs tingle. Even Easton being that close to it makes me anxious. I'm about to say something, but he steps away and stands next to the bench.

"Hey, JT," he says.

"'Sup, baby?" JT pulls on his vape again, then holds it out to me as he coughs. I shake my head politely.

"Did you ever get asked to be on Miles Modine's podcast?"

Oh, here we go. Easton pretended to come up here to chill with JT, but really he wants to keep mocking me.

JT blows out smoke and coughs. "Who is Miles Modine?"

"Our next door neighbor. He was at the barbecue on Sunday."

"Oh shit, how's your gramma?"

"She'll live. But Miles is big into true crime. He and Nate have been working on something about his disappearance. I've overheard them talking about it a few times, actually."

Overheard. My face starts to tingle. Easton locks eyes with me and the annoyed look he gives me fills me with shame.

"But it's weird," Easton says. "Because he's not my real brother."

My jaw hangs open and the world has frozen around me. I don't feel the wind on my skin, the warmth of the setting sun; I don't hear the birds or the thunder in the distance.

Only Easton repeating over and over in an endless loop that I'm not his brother.

JT turns to me and scoffs. "What?"

"Tell him, Nate," Easton says. "Or whatever the hell your name is. Tell him the truth."

JT takes another rip of his vape, but he seems to think this is all a joke we're playing on him. And maybe that's all it is. Easton could be bluffing. Miles was at first, though I panicked and gave myself up. I won't do it again, though.

So I fake a laugh and say, "He's pissed off at me because Miles said he was doing a podcast about the disappearance and I was thinking about helping him."

"You're right, I am pissed," Easton says. "Because you showed up here, pretending to be my dead little brother, and now you want to go on some podcast to lie and say, what? You have amnesia?"

"I remember some things," I say. "Just not *everything*." I hope he doesn't ask me what I do remember, because I'm kind of limited to the things Miles and the Beaumonts have already told me.

Easton's eyes go wide but . . . he doesn't look like himself. And the longer he looks at me, the more I'm starting to worry he isn't bluffing.

How could he have found out, though? Maybe he did buy a DNA test online and test my saliva or hair. We share a bathroom. He might have been able to get something there.

If that's true, I don't know what I'm going to do.

I try one last-ditch effort to call his bluff. "Why do you think I'm not your brother?" I need to see if there's an easy way to disprove whatever flimsy evidence he might have.

"Because my brother is dead."

JT is getting bored with whatever's happening here. He puffs on his vape, letting out smoke as he speaks. "Listen, whatever is going on between y'all, it's harshing my buzz. So if you could maybe take it elsewhere—" He coughs again and takes out his inhaler.

"Sorry, JT," Easton says. "I need you to prove a point."

JT shakes his head but breathes in from the inhaler. "Sure."

Again, the way Easton looks at me gives me chills. "I'm . . . not dead," I say.

"*You're* not. Nate, on the other hand, very much is."

My mouth is dry and my heart is starting to race. "Okay. So if that's true, how do you know?"

"Because I'm the one who killed him."

THIRTY-SEVEN

I STARE AT EASTON, WAITING FOR THE PUNCH LINE. Because that's all this is, right? He's joking. Easton was the one who came to me and admitted that he'd *thought* I was dead.

Nate.

He told me he'd thought *Nate* was dead.

Because he gave up on him and blamed himself.

"This isn't funny," I say.

JT points to me but doesn't look over. "Yeah, I'm with Nate."

"I'm telling you," Easton says, his voice calm and collected. "That's not Nate. It's some other kid who is pretending to be him. And I think it's time he tells us why."

"Sure," JT says. "Go ahead, Nate, tell him why you're not you." JT clearly doesn't believe Easton either.

"I don't know what he's talking about." I'm still trying to figure out where this is coming from. Easton has to have some weird ulterior motive here. There's no way he killed Nate; he was ten years old when Nate disappeared.

Easton heads back to the cliff edge and looks out to the water below.

"Fine," he says. "I guess I'll tell my side of the story first."

He's so calm and it's really starting to scare me. It's a warm night but I feel cold. My legs are shaking.

This can't be true. He's got to be lying, trying to get me to crack because he has a hunch I'm not Nate.

"What about the onions?" I ask.

JT groans. "I'm so fucking confused."

Easton isn't, though. He looks over at me like he can't believe how stupid I am. "The *onions*? I made that up. And Mom is such a desperate fucking loser she pretended to remember. I mean, sure, Nate probably hated onions, but they're vegetables. What kid likes vegetables?"

"I like veggies," JT says.

"You're starting to believe me now, aren't you?" Easton asks me, ignoring JT.

I shake my head. "Listen, I know you're pissed off at me, but I don't get why you would—"

"I am," Easton says. His voice is low and calm. "I worked so *fucking* hard to plan out what would happen if they ever found Nate's body, but then *you* came along to ruin it. And now you and that talentless nobody next door are trying to dig around. I heard you the other night. *Not everything needs to be about the investigation.* Now tell me. Which investigation would that be?"

I don't know what to say because this is worse than being caught for pretending to be Nate. Easton finding out I've been investigating his family is a whole other horrific twist.

I still don't fully believe him, though. This is just him taking out his frustration on me, it has to be. Easton was a kid when Nate disappeared. He knows people think his family was involved in Nate's disappearance, and now he learns the person he thought was his brother isn't really his brother *and* he's been investigating his family.

"So why wouldn't you just tell everyone I'm not Nate, then?" I ask.

"Because I'm not trying to get caught. I had someone to blame, I had a *plan*. If I expose you, the rest of us are under scrutiny. I tried to tell Dad—*my* dad—to end this the day you came home, but he wouldn't go for it because he was worried about my mom having another fucking mental breakdown. But at first even he didn't fall for your shit."

The conversation I overheard the first day at the Beaumont house. Easton was trying to get Marcus to do a DNA test on me.

"But now, because you've been here for weeks and have been doing your own little investigation, we'll look complicit if I tell the cops you're a fake. Who in their right minds would let a stranger pretending to be their kid into their home? Someone who doesn't want to be blamed for that kid's disappearance, maybe?"

JT's weed must be giving him some clarity because he's looking at me as though I'm a puzzle he's trying to figure out.

"And now," Easton says, "it will look like we're the ones who found you and got you to do all this. My mom fought to make sure you weren't going to be DNA tested because she was so deluded that she didn't want the truth to burst her bubble. Or . . . depending on how the cops see it, she didn't want the police to prove that you aren't her son. Why do you think she'd do that?"

Wait. Is he saying Valencia is involved?

Okay, let's say Easton did kill Nate—he was ten years old. He could have done it by accident and maybe they didn't want Easton to go to prison so they helped him cover it up.

Shit.

"Wait." JT holds up his hands in a time-out gesture. "I need everyone to be real for a second. This is a bit, right?"

Easton shakes his head. "It's not a bit, John Thomas."

JT finally looks up at Easton. "You killed your brother?" Easton nods. JT sticks a thumb in my direction. "And this guy is an imposter your parents hired?"

Easton shakes his head. "No. This is an idiot who decided to bust his way into our family, pretending to be Nate. And now we're going to find out why."

JT stands up and shakes his head. "I'm way too high for this."

"Thought you might be," Easton says.

I can't do anything but sit here and tremble. Being exposed is so much worse than I imagined. Probably because I really thought Easton was a nice big brother.

Is it possible he's still bluffing?

"So you *killed* Nate?" JT asks. "Why?"

"Because I wanted to," Easton says. His voice gives me another chill. And now I don't think he's lying. "At first, I was only curious to see if I could. But once I started, I realized I *wanted* to." He turns away from us.

"Dude." JT's voice is low and serious. "I lied for you."

Lied?

"You did," Easton says. "Thank you for that, by the way. Having an alibi definitely helped take suspicion off me, though to be fair the suspicion was barely there to begin with." Of course. Easton wasn't home because he was at JT's. At least, that's what the articles said. And JT confirmed Easton's story because he thought he was being a good friend.

JT shakes his head. "You said you were at the playground and you didn't want to get in trouble for not watching him." He's finally putting together that he helped his best friend get away with murder. He turns to me and gives me a look I don't recognize. Maybe it's a *can you believe this?* look, or a *we need to run* look. And no I can't, but yes we need to.

I stand up.

And now I can see over JT's shoulder.

Easton has turned back around to face us. And he's grinning.

In his left hand, he has the craggy rock he was nudging with his foot.

"Look out!"

But it's too late.

Easton bashes the rock into the back of JT's skull before the words even leave my mouth. It lands with a sickening, wet thud and JT drops to the ground. His eyes roll back and his legs and arms start to spasm as blood pools around his shaking head.

I put my hands over my mouth. I want to scream but I can't. Thunder rumbles again in the distance, but it's louder now. I step back as Easton straddles JT. He smiles up at me as he raises the rock above his head.

He keeps his eyes on me, but when he brings the rock down on JT's head again he still hits his target.

JT's skull caves inward and his spasms stop.

Easton stands, tossing the rock over the edge of the cliff. My legs give out and I drop to my knees. My shaking hands are still covering my mouth like they're the only thing that's keeping my screams in. But I can't speak.

I can't make a sound.

Easton says something but I don't hear it. I can't look away from JT's body. His eyes are open and blood spills from his nose and ears. He's dead. Easton killed him. Which means Easton absolutely killed Nate. He killed Nate, told his parents and the police he was with JT—who corroborated the story like a good friend because, like me, he never imagined Easton capable of murder.

Easton steps forward, standing over me. He has a few speckles of blood on his chin and jaw.

"So," he says, checking his hands for blood before putting them on his hips. "Do you believe me now?"

THIRTY-EIGHT

THIS CAN'T POSSIBLY BE HAPPENING. BUT THE LONGER I look at JT's dead body, the realer it becomes. How could I miss this? How has *everyone* missed that Easton Beaumont is a complete psychopath? There are always red flags raised on people like him. There's a pattern. Like being a mean kid or hurting animals.

Nate's guinea pigs.

I look up at him. "You killed Nate's pets, didn't you?"

He looks shocked. At first he seems scandalized I would think he'd hurt an animal, but then he says, "Wow, you aren't as stupid as you look."

"And your teacher with the anaphylactic shock?"

"That was more of a happy accident. I snatched the EpiPen from her bag. She's the one who ate something with nuts in it."

Blood pounds in my ears. It was Easton this whole time. He opened the door and disabled the doorbell—probably to toy with me. He was there when Marcus told me to put the paint away, and waited until everyone was asleep to go back down and throw it on the car. He did the same when the gas was left on. The hydrangeas. And he was in the kitchen alone when Miles showed up; that's when he put the glass in the Watergate salad.

Not everything needs to be about the investigation. That's what he overheard a few nights before the party. He always knew I wasn't Nate, and maybe for a while he was okay with me pretending. But that all changed when he heard me talking with Miles.

Valencia had sent him to get me, and to put the recycling bin out for pickup. He must have taken the glass out of it that night. That's the glass he put in the Watergate salad.

Maybe to keep me from talking. Maybe to put more suspicion on me. Everything escalating slowly, and the whole time I thought it was Marcus.

"How many people have you killed?" My hands are trembling. All I want to do is run, but I can't move. Paralyzed by terror. It's like Easton is a wild animal, and I don't want to make any sudden movements to set him off.

He grins. "Wouldn't you like to know?"

I'm not sure I would. Because now I know he killed Nate and JT and also had something to do with his teacher's death. He didn't even care if his grandmother died, which means he's definitely going to kill me.

I have no idea why it took me this long to realize it. Or why I'm not running. I stand, slowly, so as not to startle him.

"Don't run," he says. He knows exactly what I'm about to do. But I have no other choice, so I bolt in the direction of the car.

I shouldn't look back. I should run, as fast as I can.

But I do look back, and he's there. Running after me. He has something in his hand—I can't make it out but I think it might be a knife.

I turn toward the trees, hoping I can lose him if I duck into the forest.

His hands clasp onto my shoulder and he pushes me. I run right into a tree, knocking the wind out of myself.

Easton pushes my head against the bark.

Something sharp stabs me in the back of the neck and I scream.

"Shut up!" He pushes me again, hard. Tears blur my vision, and sobs try to rack my body but I can't catch my breath. Easton pulls whatever is stabbing me out of my neck and I cry out. "I said shut up."

He holds it in front of me. It's not a knife; it's a syringe.

"What is that?" I ask. "Did you poison me?"

He huffs. "Stop being so goddamned dramatic." He loosens his grip on my hair but keeps me pinned against the tree. "It's something that will knock you out *if* I use it." He changes his grip to show me the needle, and though he did stab me with it, he didn't inject whatever is inside. "I stole it from Mom's office today. You'd think she'd be less trusting given the things she's been through, but she left me alone in there for the better part of an hour."

If he's telling the truth, it's some kind of drug to put people out if they're getting serious dental work done.

"I'm not going to kill *you*. That would look strange, my best friend and my brother having accidents on the same night, don't you think?"

I don't answer.

"So I'm going to let you go," he says. "But if you try to run again, I'll catch up with you and stick this in your throat." He looks at the needle in his hand. "And, honestly, I can't be sure I have the dosage right, so it might kill you anyway. Then I'll have to leave you up here with a needle sticking out of your arm, and when they finally do a DNA test, everyone will think you're a junkie who came up here to get high with JT, who fell off a cliff. Or maybe you pushed him."

Easton pushes me hard against the tree. "I have contingencies for my contingencies. So don't run." He waits until I nod, then lets me go. I put my hand up to my neck where he stabbed me, and a little bead of blood smears against my fingers.

"Relax," he says, putting a plastic cover on the tip of the needle. Then adds with a grin, "It's just a little prick." He walks back to the top of the clearing and stands over JT's body, gazing down at it. "You have as much to lose as I do, by the way."

"How?" I try to keep my eyes on Easton, but JT's dead, blank stare keeps drawing me back to him.

"You've got a cushy life here. I assume the homeless thing is true, right?" He looks back at me. "You had to be pretty desperate to plan this whole farce. Unless . . . is your real family a bunch of immoral con artists, too?"

"No. I was homeless." I have no intention of telling him I'm gay. If he really is killing people for fun, he doesn't need another reason to hate me.

"Which means you ran away. Or were kicked out." He points at me with a thin finger. "Gay. Which explains you and Miles hanging out all the time. Is he your boyfriend?"

No. He might hurt Miles. Especially now that he knows we've been investigating his family. Our conclusion may have been wrong, but with a little more research we might have figured it out. I shake my head. "He's one of Nate's friends. I'm trying to look as much like him as I can."

Easton stares at me like he's trying to figure out if I'm lying. Then maybe he realizes there's more important things to think about, because he looks back at JT.

"Well, listen," he says. "You've been playing your game for a few weeks—"

"This isn't a game."

He frowns. "It isn't? Are you sure about that? Because I'm pretty sure I'm winning."

Easton *has* been playing a game. And I might have only just learned that I've been a part of it, but he's right. I'm losing. He walks over to the bench, where JT's vape dropped after Easton hit him.

Tears stream down my face and I wipe them away. "You're sick. What's your plan when people find his body?"

Easton bends over and uses his own shirt to wipe the vape off, then, still holding it in his T-shirt-wrapped hand, puts it back into JT's hand, closing his fingers around it. Then he reaches into JT's pockets and takes the orange inhaler, tucking it into the back pocket of his own jeans.

"JT used to go up there to get stoned, Officer," he says in a sad voice.

He puts his hands under JT's body and pushes it toward the cliff.

"Stop!" I yell.

He ignores me and pushes again, JT's limbs flopping over the side.

"We went to see him, but he was smoking, and I didn't want my little brother around that. So we left and went to get ice cream."

The ice cream shop where our phones are. And where he paid with a card. Even if there aren't security cameras at the ice cream stand, he has a paper trail. Contingencies for his contingencies.

"I guess he lost his balance and fell." He pushes again and the rest of JT slides over the side and out of sight. Easton looks down after the body.

"What about the rock you bludgeoned him with? Your fingerprints are all over it and so is his blood." His blood is also soaking into the ground as we speak.

"And now it's submerged in the bay." He points down the cliff. "And looks like rain." The thunder rumbles again like it's agreeing with him. "So even if it stopped somewhere on the ground down there and they want to dust every rock for prints, the prints they *do* find will be garbage. The rain will wash away or dilute most of the blood up here. And our cell phones will never even ping off that tower over there." He points in the distance, where, against the thunderclouds, a red light flashes atop a metal tower. He planned *all* of this.

Easton takes a few steps toward me.

"Honestly, I'm not worried. I learned a lot when I killed Nate—primarily, how dumb cops are. Murderers are found because they make mistakes. *I* don't make mistakes."

Criminals are also found because their own hubris convinces them they don't mess up. I'm sure there have been plenty of murderers whose only slipup was thinking they didn't make mistakes.

"I had a plan for Nate," Easton continues. "I thought out every possible angle. But I was a kid back then, and I didn't take into consideration that even smart adults are more stupid than I was. Did you know the local cops didn't even contact the FBI and ask for help? They didn't get involved until a friend of Dad's put him in contact with Grant."

My face burns with embarrassment. I don't know how I missed any of this. He fooled me.

"Once the FBI was involved, they got the resources to search the bay but found nothing."

There it is. If I can direct the police to Nate's body, I can come clean and tell them what I've been doing, and that Easton was the murderer.

"What did you do with it?"

Easton smiles and shakes his head. "Nice try. No, we aren't going to worry about Nate's body anymore because Nate's here!" He brushes my shoulders off. "Alive and well and on thc road to recovery. For now. See, I'm going to let you keep up this charade because I feel like we're all in too deep now. You can stay and pretend to be Nate. But you're not going to be talking with Miles anymore. No more investigation. No stupid fucking podcast. And when you do finally leave, I want you to leave a note explaining you weren't Nate."

I nod. "I was going to do that anyway."

"Sure you were. What, after finding out who really killed my brother? Or were you hoping that finding his killer would help Mommy and Daddy not be mad at you for manipulating them?"

I don't say anything.

Rain starts to fall in small drops.

Easton looks back toward the edge of the cliff. "Guess Dad's going to have to find someone else to buy weed from," Easton says. Then he heads for the car. "Come on. We need to pick up our phones. And there's something else I want to go over with you."

He walks to the car and I follow him. Because I don't know what else to do. Easton has thought so far ahead for so long. And now I'm trapped.

THIRTY-NINE

EASTON PULLS INTO THE ICE CREAM SHOP LOT AND parks in the same spot we parked in earlier. He cuts the engine and turns to me.

"What you did—pretending to be Nate—was selfish and manipulative."

I don't say anything. I feel a little numb. I can't stop thinking of JT's body lying there. Or how his family is going to think he was clumsy and fell. I've known for weeks that I was being selfish and manipulative, but now I feel worse because Marcus and Valencia didn't kill Nate. And they have no idea their son is a psychopath.

He continues. "But I don't think you're a bad person."

"No, not like you."

He snorts. "I mean, there's no such thing as good people and bad people. *Good* and *bad* are words made up by idiots looking for meaning in their life. Society was built by religions telling us that we have to be good to get into heaven. But that's all bullshit. There's no God, no afterlife. We're all animals walking around on two legs. When I killed Nate, he died, and that's it. But what I'm saying is I don't want *you* to grow a conscience after all this."

He stares at me, that same chilling, unblinking glare he's been giving me since he let me see the real Easton.

"What do you mean?" I ask when the silence between us grows uncomfortable. The rain starts to patter loudly on the car.

"You might still want to be a 'good person.' But I'm telling you there's no such thing. I'm doing you a favor. Know that."

I scoff. "How so?"

"Because usually I don't leave people alive when they see the real me and not the mask I wear every day to fool them. But I'm letting you live because I admire the game you're playing." He grins. "And, honestly, it's the most fun I've had in years."

Christ, he really is a psychopath. I've been panicked and terrified for weeks—all of it rising to a crescendo tonight. But for him, the past few weeks have been *fun*. My stomach turns at the thought, probably curdling the ice cream.

"So you can keep your little game going until you leave. But I'm telling you, do not grow a conscience. Because if you do . . ." He switches over to a fake nervous voice. "We were having ice cream and he started yelling at me because I told him Miles was using him for his podcast. After that he ran off. I don't know where he went, but now that you mention it, maybe he *did* run back up to the cliff to smoke with JT. Oh no. You mean he's not my brother? Detective, do you think he could have been smoking with JT and accidentally said something he wasn't supposed to?" He goes back to his normal voice. "I don't need to be that obvious, but you get the point."

The chill spreading across my body almost makes me shudder, but I try to hide it. I don't want him to see how he's getting to me. He'll frame me for JT's murder. And if I'm the liar here—without proof that Easton really did kill Nate and JT—then that also gives me a motive.

Tears blur my vision, and I look away from him, trying to hide it. "Why did you kill him?"

"Because I had to prove a point to you. You wouldn't have believed me if I just told you I killed Nate."

He *did* tell me and I didn't believe him. Not until he killed JT. Until he let me see his real self. The anger and hatred in his eyes.

"He was your friend," I say, my throat tightening around the words.

"He was a tool. And I mean that in both ways. Yes, he was a loser and a stoner. But he helped me blend in. If you go too long without friends, people think you're antisocial. JT was too stupid to ever realize who I truly am. Even when I slipped up around him, he made it a joke. And with him, I didn't need to try to impress people at school. He'd do it all on his own, because he had to be the center of attention. And that took the focus off me. People weren't thinking, *Who is that weird guy hanging out with JT?* They were thinking, *Easton is so lucky to be friends with someone like JT.* But high school's over. He's outlived his usefulness."

"So you killed him?"

"To prove a point. Yes."

"You're insane."

He shrugs. "Or I'm like everyone else. Except I'm not afraid to live the life I want."

"And that's why you killed Nate? Because you wanted to be the only child?"

Easton grabs the steering wheel and his knuckles crack. "Stop. Looking. For a reason. I told you there is no *meaning* in life. There's no

God, there's no greater power. If there were, I wouldn't have gotten away with it."

Maybe you still won't. I would never say that out loud to Easton, though.

"I killed Nate because I wanted to." He unbuckles his seat belt and turns to me. I don't want to look at him, but I can't help it. "If you really want the truth, yes, I hated him. He was a whiny, spoiled little brat who got everything he wanted. Toys, stuffed animals, disgusting fucking rodents that he could keep in a cage, everything. He knew all he had to do was cry and whine and beat our parents down until they got tired, and he'd get what he wanted. Do you know what I wanted?"

My jaw hangs open. "You killed him because you *wanted* something and your parents wouldn't buy it for you?"

Easton laughs. "What I wanted they couldn't buy me. All I wanted that day was to see what would happen if I strangled him. I wanted to see how long it would take for him to die, and I was curious what I would do after. What everyone would do. I was obsessed with it. I fantasized about it for months leading up to it, wondering if I could snap his neck or if he would be able to fight back. So that's why I killed him. Because it was time I got something that *I* wanted."

I feel like I'm going to throw up. This can't be real. How could a ten-year-old think things like that?

"You look like you need a second to gather your thoughts," Easton says. "I'll go grab our phones. Then you need to figure out how you're going to pull your shit together before we go home."

He gets out and I take several panicked breaths. I could run. Right now I could run and hide from him. He wouldn't be able to catch up and drug me if he's halfway across the parking lot before he even realizes I'm running. I don't know where I'd go, but anywhere is better than here.

With a psychopath. A murderer.

A murderer who started killing when he was ten.

I stop panicking as something else becomes clear. Easton was *ten* years old. Yes, it's physically possible for a ten-year-old to kill a six-year-old. But how would a ten-year-old hide the body?

Unless someone helped him.

Outside the car, Easton reaches under the dumpster for our phones.

Maybe Marcus isn't totally innocent after all. If he already lost one kid, he would absolutely protect his only living son. Easton *was* talking to Marcus about me the night I arrived. He was telling him to do a DNA test on me to prove I wasn't Nate. And Marcus wasn't fighting him on it.

Easton opens the door, and I wipe the tears from my face. He hands me my damp phone and I see a text from Valencia.

"She wants to know where we are. Tell her we were getting ice cream, but we're coming home because it started to rain."

I do as he says, and he pulls out of the parking lot. A couple minutes later I get a smiley face emoji back from Valencia.

When Easton pulls into the garage, he shuts off the car and turns to me again. "Okay. I need you to get your shit together now. Put your mask back on and be Nate. If they suspect something and you fuck it up, I'm going to kill you. Got it?"

Every hair on my body stands upright and I shiver. He says it so quickly and casually, which is how I know he's telling the truth.

"And if you tell them what you know," he continues, "I will kill you. I don't show people the real me, but I showed you. Because I know you're like me, too."

Rage tightens the muscles in my throat while guilt pulls at my stomach. "I'm nothing like you."

"No, you just lied to a grieving family and told them you were their long-lost dead son. There's nothing psychotic about that at all."

"I didn't *kill* anyone."

"Not physically. Though it is your fault JT is dead. I wouldn't have killed him if it wasn't for you showing up here and fucking everything up."

That's not true. I feel like it was always Easton's plan to kill JT eventually. Things worked out this way because he wanted an excuse. And, yes, maybe giving him the excuse makes it somewhat my fault, but that's not guilt I'm taking on. Easton is a murderer. Not me.

"And you need to tell Miles to knock it off with his podcast. In fact, I think it's best if you end your relationship with him now. Whatever it is. Because if you don't, I'll kill him, too."

I'm sitting, but it still feels like the ground has dropped out from under me. My chest gets tight and it feels like I can't breathe.

"It would be easy. I could offer to go on his podcast and meet him where I killed JT. Then frame you for it. Or . . ." He pauses for dramatic effect. "I can use my original plan from back when he kept pestering me to be on his podcast. Burn his house down with him and his family trapped inside."

Like the gas leak. Would he find a way to frame me for that, too?

"So we understand each other?" Easton asks. "You keep playing your little game. I'll keep playing mine. Then, when the time is right, you leave."

Or he kills me.

"Got it."

"Put on your good person face." He smiles like it's so simple.

I take a deep breath and try to do the same.

Easton's mask cracks again. "Do better."

It's acting. I have to go back to before I knew the truth, and be that version of Nate. I can do that. I've been acting like him for weeks.

I settle my face. It's not a smile, but my eyes are a little more open and I have—what I imagine is—a look of calm. Easton eyes me, and he seems impressed.

"Good enough."

He gets out, and I follow him into the house.

FORTY

MILES HAS TEXTED ME SEVERAL TIMES SINCE LAST NIGHT, asking if I want to hang out or "plot," which is his euphemism for both planning my escape and looking for more evidence to prove Marcus killed Nate.

But Easton has been home all day, lurking around the house as if he thinks I'm going to call the police. So I ignore the texts for as long as I can, but when I haven't answered by the time he gets out of school, Miles gets more persistent. I finally text him back while Easton is distracted by a phone call.

Let's talk tonight, is all I say. His reply is instantaneous.

That sounds super ominous, Deborah, what's going on? But I don't answer.

Valencia comes home from work first and I put on my pretend happy face. It only falters when Easton comes down to the kitchen.

Valencia looks over at him and points. "How did you eat a *whole* jar of peanut butter? I just bought it on Saturday." Her face drops. "What's wrong?"

When Easton looks up, his eyes are red and glassy. "I got a call from JT's mom."

Shit. They found him. My own legs feel a little weak. I walk right over to the kitchen table—trying to get some distance from Easton and Valencia. I don't want her to see my face if I can't keep it detached from what really happened last night.

She walks around and puts her arm around her son. "Honey, what is it?"

"He fell," he says, his voice breaking. "He was up at the overlook smoking."

Valencia gasps. She puts her hands to her mouth.

"They found him this morning. He must have slipped when it started to rain and fell over the cliff."

"Oh my God, honey." Valencia wraps her arms around him.

It's a sweet moment. But it's all fake, and it's chilling to see. And I finally understand how he's gotten away with this for so long. He's perfected this fake Easton he's been playing. Like the night he apologized for "giving up on me." I really believed him then, and his mom really believes him now.

"Can I borrow the car?" he asks. "A few of us are getting together for a sort of memorial because his parents are doing a private funeral."

Probably because they can't have an open casket since you bashed their son's head in.

"Of course, sweetie." She hands him the keys and he leaves, telling her he'll be home a little late.

With Easton gone to show his fake mourning, it means I can go over to Miles's and tell him . . . I don't know what yet. I can't tell him the truth about Easton. That would put him and his parents in danger. Unless I have real proof, to everyone else, I'll just be the liar who took Nate's identity.

I also have to figure out how to tell him I'm not going to help him with his podcast anymore, and just hope he won't tell anyone the truth about me. He said before that he wouldn't, but that could change if he gets pissed.

Halfway through Valencia and me making dinner, Marcus comes home. He kisses her hello, and she tells him about JT. He seems genuinely shocked, but I can't help but wonder if that's where Easton learned it from. I still can't shake the feeling that Easton couldn't have acted alone. And if Marcus *is* shocked, it might be because he's scared his son is killing again.

After dinner I text Miles to meet me at the fence.

Chardonnay is the first one out the door in a bolt of white. She doesn't even pay any attention to me before running into the yard and peeing. Then sniffing along the ground.

Miles gives her a quick glance as he walks over to me.

"Hi! No, I really mean that. Hi. I'm Miles, I live next door, remember?"

Even with all the horror over the past twenty-four hours, he manages to make me smile. Something I didn't think was possible right now. But that only serves to create more dread in my gut. Because I need to distance myself from him.

I really don't want to do that.

"So why have you been ignoring me?" he asks, crossing his arms. "Or are we going to pretend I'm being needy when you don't respond to me in nineteen hours even though I know you're over here." He's making a joke, but there's something in his voice that betrays his hurt.

"I wasn't ignoring you." That's a lie so I try again. "I mean, not on purpose."

"But you were ignoring me."

"I take it back. You're needy."

He grins but shakes his head like he's calling me on my bullshit. "What's going on, Nate?"

Hearing him call me Nate makes my stomach roll. I should have told him my real name. I'd like him to know my real name. He knows the real me, obviously. Because he can tell something is wrong.

But I can't tell him. Even though I want to ask him what to do. I want to know how to outsmart someone like Easton, who has always thought so far ahead. How do we find the mistakes he made and tell the police?

This is dangerous enough as it is. If Easton is lurking around here—only pretending to have gone to some memorial for JT—he might think I'm telling Miles about him. I glance around the yard. Across the street.

In the corner of Miles's yard, Chardonnay has her nose to the ground, sniffing something.

Miles follows my gaze and yells over at her. "Chardonnay! Whatever it is, leave it!" He turns his attention back to me. "Seriously, what's up? Are you sick or something?"

"No."

"'Cause you look sick. No offense."

"I'm starting to think you don't know what 'no offense' means."

"I don't. No offense?" He says it like he really doesn't know what it means but he's trying to make it work. It makes me laugh and he grins back at me. And I get that warm, buzzy feeling in my gut again. The one that whispers how I wish Miles and I had gotten to meet in other circumstances. In an alternate universe where I don't have heartless parents who try to send me away to be tortured and brainwashed, one where I'm not an imposter with a psychopathic brother. Where instead of investigating a murder, we'd get to go to a school dance. A universe where we kiss.

But alternate universes are a sci-fi trope, and I'm stuck in a horror movie.

So I push the warm fuzzies away and steel myself. "We should stop the investigation. After Gramma Sharon I realized it's not worth it."

"Wait, what?"

"It's too dangerous. I'm going to be gone soon, so let's stop all this shit and move on."

"Hold on. Go back—*how* is it not worth it? Chardonnay!" He shouts at her this time, as she's still farther down by the corner of the fence, either licking or chewing grass there. She still ignores him.

"Because we can't prove what really happened to Nate."

"If you're freaking out because Gramma Sharon ate glass, you know someone *put it there*. Which means someone in that house knows what really happened to him."

Yeah, I do. And so does Nate's brother. And possibly one of his parents who helped him cover it up.

"Maybe I don't want to end up like him, too."

Miles nods as if he understands where I'm coming from. "Okay, yes, this is scarier than it was before, but don't you realize that means we're onto something? I'm not asking you to put yourself in harm's way. Did Grant say something after I left? If he knows about you, why don't we tell him the truth? Maybe he can help protect you."

He might be able to protect me, but I'm not sure how he could protect Miles and his family. Again I feel eyes on the back of my head, but I don't look this time.

"I don't need protection because this is over." I say it with as much authority as I can muster, so he knows it's for real.

"So that's it? It's over?"

"Yeah."

"Then I won't help you when you decide to run away."

"I don't need your help."

Saying that makes me feel sick because I really do. And seeing the hurt on Miles's face makes it worse. Immediately he catches himself and his gaze drops to the ground. Then he uses Chardonnay as a distraction.

"Chardonnay! Knock it off!" Miles walks over to her, pulling her by her collar. She grunts as he pulls her away from whatever she was licking, then snatches it off the ground. It's trash of some kind, but she tries to jump up as he walks back over to me with it in his hand.

He spins it around and I see it's a large jar of peanut butter. Of course Chardonnay would go for that.

"Where did you even get this?" Miles asks. "We're a Trader Joe's family."

I see the label and my heart goes right to my throat. It's Jif. The brand Easton eats by the spoonful.

"No," I whisper.

Valencia scolded him about going through a whole jar in four days. But he didn't eat the whole jar.

I snatch it from Miles's hands and he gives a half-hearted "Hey!" I look inside but the jar has been practically licked clean. The sides are clear all the way to the bottom, where only a little remains.

Chardonnay jumps up on the fence, her nose slathered in peanut butter.

FORTY-ONE

"YOU NEED TO GET HER TO A VET!"

Miles shakes his head. "It's fine, that brand doesn't use the artificial sweetener. Even if they did, she'd probably still be fine. She ate an entire jalapeño plant, peppers and all, when she was a puppy. And then had, like, a perfectly formed shit. She's practically a garbage disposal. Don't worry about it."

"No, you don't understand. This was poisoned!" I point to the jar. "You have to get her to a vet and pump her stomach!"

He looks at the jar, his eyes wide with horror. "How do you know?"

"It doesn't matter! You need to get her help now."

"You're freaking me out."

"Miles!" I give him the most pleading look I can, and it works, because he finally nods and says okay in a shaky voice. Chardonnay groans as he picks her up and runs into the house. He yells for his mom as the door shuts behind him.

And I'm left in the backyard with the empty jar of peanut butter.

Easton's newest threat.

I spend the night in my room, waiting for Easton to come home. When his door to our shared bathroom opens, I pull mine open as well.

"What did you do to Chardonnay?"

He stares at me before walking over to the sink and grabbing his toothbrush. "Excuse me?"

"Miles's dog. You threw your jar of peanut butter into her yard today. What was in it?" I checked the trash cans but didn't find anything that might be poison, but he could have used something else. And I haven't heard from Miles yet. I've also been too afraid to ask.

Easton stops mid-toothpasting the bristles on his brush. Then he grins and it's like I've stepped into a trap he set long ago. "If she found a peanut butter jar, I'd go out on a limb and say . . . peanut butter."

He stares at me as he puts his toothbrush in his mouth and turns it on. The low buzz of the electric motor fills the silence.

"I know you put something in there to hurt her. As a threat." I stare him down, unblinking, refusing to give in. I try to muster enough courage to sound unafraid. "I'm not scared of you. And if you're going to keep attacking people, our deal is off. I'll tell everyone the truth."

He just continues to brush his teeth, looking bored.

When the toothbrush stops automatically, he spits in the sink, cups some water into his hand, and rinses his mouth as he runs the brush under the water, then puts it back on the charger, looking down at the running water.

Then he lunges at me.

I step back but his hands go right to my throat.

He squeezes tightly as my mouth opens. "Don't make a sound or I'll kill you."

When I speak, it comes out as a whisper because I'm scared he'll actually do it. "How will you explain that away?"

But he doesn't look scared at all. "You forget you're not really my brother. I'll make it look like you attacked me." His hands tighten around my throat and my heartbeat starts to pound in my head. "Stop acting like you have the upper hand here. All I have to do is tell someone the truth and you're a court-ordered DNA test away from being sent to jail as a fraud."

"And I'll tell them you're a psychopath."

"What proof do you have?" he asks. "It's the word of a serial liar against mine. An affluent, handsome white boy with a lawyer daddy, bright future in medicine, and no criminal record. You're homeless trash. I will *always* win, because I am smarter than you. I'm stronger than you. And nothing in this fucking world scares me. Can you say the same?"

Oh God, he's right. I'll never be able to prove he did it. And he does always seem to be ahead of me.

When I don't answer he steps back, dropping his hands from my neck.

Without another word he turns and goes into his bedroom. I shut the door to my room, but there's no lock. I take the hamper Valencia bought me and put it in front of the door. It won't block him from coming into my bedroom, but it might make enough noise that someone will hear if he pushes it too quickly.

My phone lights up with a text from Miles.

Backyard. NOW.

I go downstairs, where Marcus is watching TV. Valencia has

fallen asleep in his lap, and he gently plays with her hair. I tell him I'm going to run over and talk with Miles, but I'll be right back. Marcus looks at his phone and sees it's almost ten thirty, but he just tells me not to be too long.

Miles is already standing by his fence when I walk out the back door. His arms are crossed, and he looks pale in the dim light of the deck. I turn to look up at Easton's bedroom. The windows are dark, but I imagine him staring down at us with a grin.

Miles opens his mouth, but I shake my head and hold a finger to my lips. I nod toward his house. He walks along the fence with me and then leads me to his front door. Chardonnay doesn't greet us when we enter; the house is quiet. We walk slowly up to his room and he shuts the door.

He turns and points a finger right at my chest. "Do you want to tell me why my parents just spent seven hundred dollars to induce vomiting only to find out Chardonnay ingested *peanut butter*?"

"Did they find any crushed-up pills or poison or anything like that?"

"They found her food, lettuce leaves my mom gave her that she swallowed whole, grass, and peanut butter. That's it. There was no poison! But hey, we finally found something she doesn't like—activated charcoal."

Relief washes over me. I breathe out slowly and sit on the edge of Miles's bed.

"Nate, what the fuck is going on?"

My eyes well up with tears but I don't know if they're from fear, frustration, relief, or because I need to tell him the truth now and it's going to put him in danger. A sudden and horrifying thought comes to me.

"What did you tell your parents?" I ask.

"I made something up. Told them I thought I saw her swallow something and I had no clue what it was but that she was acting weird. Then when you made me look like a complete lunatic, I had to say I was confused."

"She's okay, though?"

Miles sits down on the bed next to me. "Yes. I mean, they're keeping her overnight for observation—and to bleed us for more money, no doubt—but she'll be fine. Tell me what's going on."

I sigh and more tears spill from my eyes. You'd think I'd be cried out by now, but apparently I'm great at hydration. I know Easton threw the jar of peanut butter over the fence, but he was playing with me. Saying he's watching me. He probably watched me coming over here, entertained by how his game pieces are interacting—which means Miles *needs* to know the truth. Because he's part of this game, too.

"Easton killed Nate."

FORTY-TWO

ONCE I FINISH TELLING MILES EVERYTHING, HE SITS silently, a look of horror on his face. He'd heard about JT's death—apparently JT has a younger brother who is in Miles's class and word spread pretty quickly. But he thought it was an accident like everyone else did.

"We have to tell the police," Miles says.

"They won't believe us. All it will do is show that I'm a fraud and can't be trusted."

"We have to do *something*! Dude, I knew there was something off about him. But I thought he was traumatized from losing his brother, I didn't think he was a complete psychopath."

"Well, he is. And he threatened you and your family. I didn't want to tell you because I was scared he'd hurt you all."

Miles shakes his head. "He'd do it anyway." Then he grabs my hand and squeezes it. "I'm glad you told me. At least now I can keep a better eye out. But we do need to tell someone. Maybe if we get you out of town first, I can go to the police. I'll tell them it's a hunch."

"Without proof, they're going to have to investigate on their own. And Easton will know you said something. He'll figure it out."

"But he can't make a move on us while the police are watching him."

"He's patient. He'll wait years if he has to."

"Shit." Miles jumps up and starts pacing the room, chewing his lip. It makes me smile because I know he's thinking. So I watch him. "We have to find something on him. He was ten, he couldn't have gotten away with it so easily. So let's start there. He's ten, he kills his brother. Then what?"

"He has to hide the body. The police never found it, so it's gotta be somewhere."

"He wasn't old enough to drive, and it would've looked mighty suspicious if he was pulling his brother's dead body down the street in a wagon." Miles snaps his fingers. "The bay! He must have tied him to a cinder block or filled his pockets with rocks and thrown him out there."

"Didn't they do a search when they thought he drowned?"

He nods. "You're right, they did. They were out there for days." Miles plops down in his desk chair. "He had to have had help. If you thought it was Marcus before, my money is on him."

I bite my lip so I don't smile. We're talking dark stuff, but Miles agreeing with me gives me a slight sense of validation. "So where would Marcus take a body? You're the true crime aficionado—"

"Nut." Miles smirks at me and I can't help but smile back.

"Right. So if an adult did help him and they knew they had to hide a body, what did they do?"

"Bury it somewhere. But bodies turn up eventually. Property development or animals dig them up. Sometimes weather will do it."

And if a body hasn't been found yet, we aren't going to stumble upon it now. We don't even know *where* Easton killed Nate. He could have walked up to where he killed JT and thrown him over the cliff. But then they *found* JT's body. Sure, his Jeep being parked up there probably helped, but they would eventually have found Nate there sometime over the past ten years.

Easton said that was where Marcus used to take them to watch fireworks, so maybe Marcus would have been smart enough not to take the body there.

But if Marcus hid the body, it means we'll never find it. He's a criminal defense attorney; he knows how important a body is to a case.

So instead I try to think like Easton. He's always several steps ahead . . . and he wouldn't *want* Marcus's help. He'd want to do it alone. Not want—he *would* do it alone. Because he thinks he's so much smarter than everyone else. It would be something he'd want to keep from his family, to prove how much better he is than them.

His own secret.

I gasp.

My whole body tingles, starting with my cheeks as the blood rushes to them, then slowly out to my extremities. He would absolutely do it on his own. But Easton would also have a plan. He said he fantasized about it for months.

"What?" Miles asks.

He didn't kill Nate at the house because even Easton knows his limitations. He told the police he was with JT, and his parents believed him because he wasn't home.

"The island," I finally say.

Easton got his brother to paddle out to the island in a kayak. To their fort. He killed him there and left the body. The secret fort even his parents didn't know about. And then, ten years later, when he was playing a new game, he decided to take me out there and show it to me. To show me he knows I'm not his bother. To flaunt how smart he is by showing me exactly where he hid the real Nate's body.

Because every psychopath's biggest mistake is thinking they're so much smarter than everyone else.

FORTY-THREE

I'M SHOWERED AND DRESSED BY THE TIME VALENCIA gets down to the kitchen the following morning.

"Oh, good, you ready to go?" she asks, putting her empty coffee mug in the sink.

Easton isn't far behind her, and he watches me suspiciously over her shoulder as I say yes. I'm absolutely ready to get out of this house and away from him.

"Where are you going?" he asks.

"Gramma Sharon's."

"Why do you want to hang out with her all day?" Easton asks. He tries to keep his tone teasing, brotherly, but underneath I know he's digging for information.

So I use the teasing brotherly tone right back at him. "Better than hanging around here doing nothing." I turn my attention back to Valencia. "And I feel bad for her being by herself all day."

"Well, you have fun with that," Easton says, heading toward the kitchen doorway. "I'm going out for a run." Once the front door opens and closes, I tell Valencia I have to grab something upstairs.

"Okay, but be quick, I have to get on the road," she calls after me. Marcus is coming down the left-side stairs while I'm heading up the right. I say good morning to him and he mumbles it back.

When I get to my room, I take out the duffel bag in the closet and set it on top of the dresser. I take out the clothes and put them in the drawers. What Miles and I are planning today feels final. Whatever happens, by the end of the day, the Beaumonts are going to know the truth.

But it probably won't come from me. If anything, it's going to come from Agent Grant or the police. They'll know I'm not the real Nate. And they'll know Easton is the one who killed him.

But I want Marcus and Valencia to know at least one true thing from me.

When I get down to the kitchen, duffel bag in hand, I walk over to the pantry and take out the food I had been hoarding for my escape. I put it all back, one thing at a time. I can feel Marcus's and Valencia's eyes on me, but neither of them speaks.

When the food is back, I turn to them and hold up the empty duffel bag.

"I wanted you to know I don't need this anymore."

Valencia is the one who asks, "Why?"

"Because I don't need to run." Wait, that's not true. And I said I wanted to tell them something true. So I change it. "I mean, I don't *want* to run. This place feels more like a home than . . . anywhere else I can remember. And I love you." Hell, even Marcus, now that I know Easton alone is responsible for Nate's death.

Valencia walks around the island with tears in her eyes and pulls me into a hug. I know it's weird to have all these conflicting feelings, but I don't care anymore. Valencia and Marcus aren't bad parents; not like mine. Which was probably how I was so blind to Easton's psychotic nature. I trusted him instead of his parents. But raising a bad person doesn't make *them* bad. If anything, they were victims in this, too. And if Miles and I are successful today, they're going to find that out and lose another child. Then they'll only have each other left.

I want them to know, even when they find out I'm not Nate, that I appreciated them. I also want Gramma Sharon to know that.

When Valencia lets me go, even Marcus hugs me.

"I'm taking Nate to my mom's for the day; could you pick him up on your way home? I have appointments until six."

Marcus says he will, and Valencia and I leave.

After taking me to Gramma Sharon's, Valencia comes in quickly to say hi to her and bye to me. Then she gives us both kisses on the cheek and leaves. When she's gone, Gramma Sharon breaks out the deck of cards.

She doesn't speak to me, and I know how much her mouth hurts right now, but she still tries to give me a smile.

My phone vibrates with a text from Miles.

On my way. ETA five minutes.

I have five minutes to say what should probably take closer to a few hours. But we don't have a few hours. And I can't wait any longer for her to be able to speak.

So I put my hand out and stop Gramma Sharon from shuffling the cards.

"I have to tell you something," I say.

She looks at me, her jaw relaxed and her lips slightly parted. I can see a few of the stitches in her mouth.

Five minutes. And I need her to not call the police or text Valencia. If she does, it might ruin everything.

"I don't know how to say this so I'm just going to say it."

Gramma Sharon lets out a low grunt that I take to mean *go on.*

"I'm . . . not Nate. I lied when I was arrested. I'm a gay kid from West Virginia who ran away from home when his parents tried to send him to conversion therapy."

Sharon's expression doesn't change.

"I'm sorry," I say. "I never meant for things to get so out of control. I thought the police would do a DNA test and prove I'm not Nate before they even let Valencia and Marcus know. But then they showed up at the hospital and everything went so off the rails. I know it's no excuse, but also . . . it was nice. Having a family who cared about me. Having people who actually . . ." I can't say the word because it feels so foreign to me.

Sharon clasps my hands tightly. Her eyes are glassy. She gives me a slow nod.

Continue.

"I wanted you to know the truth. Before everyone else finds out, I wanted to tell you because . . . I wish I had a gramma who was like you. I mean, I did once. And you reminded me why she was so special. She might be the only person who ever loved me."

Sharon takes her hand away and smacks my arm hard.

"Ow!"

She looks mad now. "Mmm!" She points to herself.

Me.

And that's all I need to lose my composure. Tears spill down my cheeks and she pulls me into a hug, swaying back and forth as she holds me and lets me cry. She probably has so many questions and so many things to say—I mean, this *is* Gramma Sharon we're talking about. But she can't, so she holds me.

Soon a car horn bleats out front. She turns her head toward the front of the house and then looks back at me questioningly.

"I have to go do something." I can't get into the whole Easton thing right now. Not without proof. But she needed to know the truth about me. Because if I do find something, it won't be long before that secret is out, too.

I stand and pull back the curtain to see Miles sitting in his car out front. I hold up a finger, telling him I'll be out in a minute.

When I turn back to Gramma Sharon, she claps her hands together and then holds them out, palms up.

Where are you going? What's going on?

"I have to fix something. Or it's going to make it all worse." Miles texts me and I start a text back to tell him I'll be right out.

Gramma Sharon snatches the phone out of my hand. I reach for it back, but she shakes her head. She walks over to her bag on the kitchen counter and takes out her own. Then she hands it over to me. She holds a backward peace sign up to me and makes an *mmm* sound. V.

Valencia.

She can track my phone's location. I nod and put Gramma Sharon's in my pocket.

Miles honks again and she growls and looks in his direction. Then she holds my face in her hands, looking up at me. And it's still there. The love I've always felt from her.

I hug her. Then she holds up my phone lock screen. I give her my password and she types out something quickly. Gramma Sharon's phone dings in my hand—because hers is never on silent.

It's a text from me. I knew.

Of course she did.

She's Gramma Sharon.

Another honk from outside, this one longer. Gramma Sharon takes an annoyed breath through her nose and shoves me toward the door. I kiss her on the cheek, then run out to Miles.

As I shut the door, Gramma Sharon's phone dings again.

"Jesus," Miles says. "Put that thing on silent."

I do. It's another text from "Nate Beaumont."

Be careful. I love you, kid.

I love you, too, I send back.

FORTY-FOUR

WHEN WE GET BACK TO OUR BLOCK, THE UNMARKED CAR is gone. "Where did he go?" I ask Miles. He shrugs as he pulls into his driveway.

"I heard a bunch of sirens on the way over to Sharon's, so maybe something happened in town? Kinda lucky, though, right?"

It doesn't feel lucky. Something in my gut tells me it feels ominous. Like there's something coming. They've been there every day, but now they're not?

Miles grips my arm. "Nate's grandmom wouldn't have told anyone yet, right?"

"No." I know she wouldn't. But for whatever reason, the cop isn't there, so I'm taking it as a sign that we need to do this now.

We walk to the Beaumonts' garage and open the door with the PIN pad. Miles helps me get the kayak and carry it around the side of the house toward the dock, where we set it down. Then I run back for two shovels and shut the garage door again.

With any luck, when Easton gets back from his run, he won't go in the garage and notice the kayak is missing.

"At least shovels can double as paddles," Miles says.

We put the kayak in the water, and I hold it steady as he climbs in the front. I get in the back as he holds the shovels. Then we push off.

We paddle in silence, trying to move quickly. It's harder because the shovels are so much heavier than the plastic-and-steel paddles. But when we reach the island—sweaty and out of breath—we hop out and pull the kayak into the woods so no one can see it from the shore.

Right now, the only thing we have going for us is the element of surprise. Easton doesn't know we have any idea where he maybe hid the body.

No, *probably* hid the body.

I lead the way through the woods to the downed tree. The little fort is there, still looking neglected.

"Where do you think he buried him?" Miles asks. He looks across the clearing, trying to figure out where to start digging.

"Probably right here." I point at the fort and pull up the old towel Easton put down as the rug. Then I push the makeshift A-line roof so the sticks tumble aside.

I stick the shovel into the ground and start digging. It's not even ten minutes before Miles hits something hard and we both freeze.

"Oh God. We're really about to find a dead body, aren't we?" he asks.

I dig around his shovel and we use the tip of it to rake dirt away. And uncover a large rock.

Shit.

"Oh, thank God," Miles says.

"We're *looking* for the body."

"Right, but I think I was expecting it to take a little longer and was hoping to better prepare myself."

"Well, get to work on that," I say. Then I shake my head. "He couldn't have buried him here. Look how big this rock is. He would have had to take it out to bury Nate here." What we've dug up of the rock takes up almost a quarter of the fort.

We change locations and start digging separate holes to try to cover more area in less time.

I just hope I'm not wrong about all this.

FORTY-FIVE

BY ONE IN THE AFTERNOON, NEITHER OF US HAS FOUND Nate's burial spot, and I'm starting to doubt we ever will. Miles and I have both gone quiet, exhausted and borderline dehydrated. Our only saving grace is that the sky is gloomy and overcast, with rain in the forecast for this evening.

Miles is taking a break, leaning on his shovel and looking at the blisters on his hands.

"Maybe he buried Nate a little farther into the island?" he offers.

I shake my head. "He brought me *here*. He was definitely flaunting his crime in front of me."

Miles doesn't seem all that convinced; he continues trying to reason with me. "Let's go over the timeline."

His shovel falls to the ground with a clang. He approaches me, holding up a blistered finger.

"Marcus leaves around noon to go to the grocery store. Within twenty minutes or so, Valencia goes upstairs to take a nap." He holds up another finger. "They call the police around four p.m. If Easton brought Nate out here, he had a three-ish-hour window to kill him and hide the body."

"Right," I say, still digging, refusing to give up.

"We've been out here for three hours, and look how far we've gotten." He gestures to the holes around us. He's dug two in addition to the one we started together. I've moved on to my third, which is right at the entrance to the clearing. My hands burn with blisters of my own, several of which have popped and are now turning crusty with pus.

"What if the tree fell on the grave?" He gestures toward the fallen tree.

But I shake my head and pull up another shovelful of dirt. "They built the fort around the tree, so it was like that when they found this place."

Miles holds out a hand. "Stop digging for a second and listen to me." I do as he says, looking into his pitying eyes. "The police have ways of doing this faster. Cadaver-sniffing dogs, radar, sometimes even psychic mediums."

"He's here. He has to be!"

Unless Marcus or Valencia really did help Easton hide the body, and we'll never be able to convince the police of the truth. I'll be the liar who stole their missing kid's identity.

Miles frowns. He doesn't look frustrated or annoyed, just sad. Like he knows it's all hopeless and thinks I haven't already realized that he might be right. But then he flinches, as if struck by a thought.

"How did Easton get the shovel out here?" he asks. "Wouldn't Nate think it was weird?"

"He'd have a story prepared. Like he was expanding the fort or something." Miles looks disappointed. I wince as another blister pops, this one sloughing off a layer of skin.

"Let me see." Miles steps forward and takes my hand. He curses when he sees the blisters, then snatches the shovel away. "Okay, enough. We need to regroup, figure out our next steps, and wrap these blisters."

I sigh. "Fine." If Easton doesn't notice us paddling back from the island, we might be able to come back out here to keep looking.

Miles still holds my hand in his. Then he looks up at me, again with that spark of an idea. "Wouldn't Easton have had blisters on his hands? If a ten-year-old was out here digging for around three hours, wouldn't he be messed up like we are? And wouldn't his parents ask him why? Even if he said he was playing tug-of-war with JT, the police would wonder about it, right?"

Shit. He is right. "Which means he didn't bury him out here."

Hopeless. This was all hopeless.

"I'm sorry," Miles says. "I should have thought of it before."

"Yeah, well, I didn't think I'd get the blisters to begin with. Otherwise I would have brought gloves." Which maybe Easton was smart enough to do. But even if he was, I'm not willing to bring it up to Miles because I do want to stop. I'm tired. My hands hurt. I was hoping I could outsmart Easton, but I can't.

No one can.

"Come on," Miles says. "Let's head back and maybe get something to eat. Figure out our next steps." He picks up the shovels and I stare at the ruins of the fort. The branches, the towel, the blankets, the fallen tree.

I wonder how old the tree is. It's almost as wide as I am tall, though I guess since it's lying horizontally, this is how tall it is now. I follow the thick, rugged bark into the woods where the roots of the tree have been ripped up from the ground.

"Nate?" Miles still uses his name to call after me.

But I don't turn around because now I'm wondering if maybe Easton didn't want to be bothered burying his brother. I walk toward the bottom of the uprooted tree. The ground divots where the tree once grew. Grass and ivy spill over the top of the hole into the ground.

As I move around the roots, I see the basin of broken earth. At the bottom is a tattered blue sneaker.

And there he is. The body is small and withered with time. The T-shirt and shorts Nate wore when he died are dirty and threadbare.

"What is it?" Miles joins me, but before he can look, I turn away from Nate's body and stop him. Nate was his best friend, and only a few hours ago he was saying he wasn't prepared to find the body. Shit. He's also been trying to get me to give up on this. He might have even felt relieved not to find it.

"No," I say. "Don't."

"Did you . . ." Something changes on his face. Panic or fear.

I nod. The boy I've been pretending to be for the past few weeks. His life cut short by his heartless, psychotic brother.

"No." Miles pushes me out of the way. I call after him but he stops short at the roots of the tree.

Miles falls to his knees. I leap forward to catch him, worried he'll fall into the open grave that Easton was so sure no one would find that he didn't bother to cover it. But Miles leans back on his heels instead.

His body shudders under my grip and at first I think he's laughing. Like the ridiculousness of this day has caught up with him. But then the silence-shattering sob he releases sounds like a dying animal. It sets my skin on fire and my heart rate quickens. I don't know what to do so I let him cry.

He falls into me, reaching for my arms to pull them around him. He tries to speak through his sobs and he looks at me with wide, horrified eyes. His face wet with fat tears.

"It's really h-him," he manages before falling into another round of sobs. It hurts, watching him realize this. That his friend, after all these years, really is dead. Not only that he's dead and has been, but that his brother murdered him and left him here to literally rot.

Because, yes, everyone who knew Nate may have believed he was dead, but this is the proof. Now it's all real. Miles spent the last ten years hypothesizing and maybe even fantasizing. Finding ways for his best friend to still be alive. But he's not.

He's been here all along. A short row across the bay.

As suddenly as Miles started crying, he stops, wiping his cheeks violently and steeling his face.

"Come on," he says. "Let's go back."

He gets to his feet and goes back to the fort to grab our shovels. "Are you okay?" I ask.

"I'm fine," he says in a way that means he absolutely isn't. "But I want to get this over with."

I follow him out to the kayak and he places it at the edge of the water, climbing in the front without looking back. I push it into the bay and climb in the rear as he hands my shovel back to me. He doesn't speak the whole way to the Beaumonts' dock and I'm afraid to ask him again if he's okay.

He definitely isn't. I honestly have no clue what to do.

When we reach the dock, Miles stands quickly and the kayak rocks as he jumps onto the dock. I cry out, but Miles is already halfway to the backyard when he drops to his knees and throws up in the bay. I toss the shovels on the dock and jump up to follow him. I remember to pull the kayak up so it doesn't float away. But when I reach Miles, he's sobbing again.

There's nothing I can say to make him feel better, so I sit down next to him and rub his back.

His sobs continue but they grow quieter. Soon, it's just sniffles. And when he speaks, I startle at the sudden sound.

"We used to play house." He sniffs and wipes at his nose. "When we were little, in daycare together. It was innocent stuff—we pretended to have kids and played with this Fisher-Price kitchen set. And then sometimes we'd play *The Wizard of Oz*." He laughs and turns to me. "He found this pair of sparkly pink jellies that fit him in one of the toy boxes and he said they were the ruby slippers. So he was Dorothy and I was Toto. Which, by the way, kinda fucked that I had to be the *dog*. I would have totally killed it as Tin Man."

"Not Scarecrow?" I try with a smile.

He shakes his head. "I'm too smart for Scarecrow."

"Oh, so you're heartless."

"Clearly." His voice sounds snotty and sad.

"Well, I think that's all kind of adorable."

Miles points back at me. "Big Scarecrow energy." We laugh but it doesn't feel like our hearts are totally in it. His smirk drops and he suddenly looks lost. "He's really dead."

The boy he played house with. The boy he probably loved. Even at that age, they saw something in each other. Kindred spirits who played house and knew they could play *The Wizard of Oz* together without judgment. Nate knew he could wear a pair of pink jellies and his friend wouldn't make fun of him.

And maybe it *was* love. Because even kids that age know what love is. Sure, it was different from the warmth I feel when I look at Miles—the attraction when I want to run my fingers through his strawberry-blond hair, how I want to kiss his tearstained, freckled cheeks—but almost there. Undiscovered. And now something that won't ever be discovered because Nate is gone.

There's a part of me that might be a little jealous Nate and Miles got to share that even for a short time. Because that was never my experience. Even at that age I knew to hide those tiny slivers of who I really was. After being scolded by my father or teased by other boys, I knew what was considered effeminate, and I learned quickly how to bury it.

I've been pretending to be someone else a lot longer than a few weeks.

I don't want to do that anymore.

"I lied to you before," I say.

"Yeah, no shit, *Nate*." He says it teasingly but I shake my head so he knows I'm not joking.

"The other night you asked what I wanted to be. When I'm older, what I wanted to do with my life. I said I wanted to be myself again. And I guess it's not entirely a lie, but I mean I want to do something better with my life. When I ran away, I went to a couple of queer youth shelters but got turned away. They were understaffed and didn't have the room. I want to become a social worker so I can help kids like me. Or like you and Nate. People who need love and support because they don't get it anywhere else. I'm not excusing what I did, lying, but if there were more people out there who could show that, I might not be here."

Miles watches me. "But then you wouldn't be here."

I nod. I wouldn't have found Nate. Honestly, finding his body might not be enough to get Easton arrested, but maybe it's at least enough to jump-start the investigation.

"We should get the police out there," I say.

"Yeah." Miles reaches into his pocket and takes out a small white rectangle. He hands it to me. Agent Grant's business card. "Make the call."

He's right. We should call Grant first, tell him everything and see what we should do. Because we have to make sure we do this right. Easton is always a few steps ahead of us, but for now, we have the jump.

I dial the number, and he picks up on the third ring.

"Agent Grant, this is Nathaniel Beaumont. I need to speak with you."

FORTY-SIX

THE DOORBELL RINGS JUST AFTER FOUR. AND NOT A moment too soon. We haven't seen Easton, and the longer we waited, the more anxious Miles and I both got that he'd come back from wherever he's been all day only for Grant to show up right after.

When I open the door, Agent Grant gives me a blank look, his hands tucked into his jeans pockets. The sport coat he's wearing is pulled back to expose the gun clipped to his belt. He gives me a nod in greeting, then his eyes flit over to Miles. I step aside to let him in.

"Nate. Neighbor kid."

"Miles. And again, would love to have you on the podcast when . . ." He stops talking and glances nervously over to me. "Sorry. You know what? I think I'll wait, um . . ." He points to the living room behind him. "Over here."

He leaves us and Grant turns to me. "What's this about, Nate?"

I don't tell him right away that he doesn't need to call me that. Instead, I shut the door behind him.

"Can I get you something to drink?" I ask. "Water, seltzer? The Beaumonts have wine, and I'm sure they won't mind if you want something stronger." And maybe I will join him because who cares with all the laws I've already broken?

"Nate."

I sigh. "Come into the kitchen."

I motion for him to follow me. I didn't realize until we were already back on dry land that we should have taken a picture of Nate's body, but honestly, all they have to do is go over and look, so I'm not that worried.

Grant takes a seat at the table and I sit across from him.

"So, first off, I have to tell you the truth," I say.

His brow furrows, but he remains stoic. It's like he either doesn't want to show emotion or he isn't curious enough yet.

"I'm not Nate Beaumont."

It's not that I was expecting immediate relief, but I don't feel any different at all. After lying for several weeks, I would have thought there'd be a little weight off my chest, but instead I feel like I'm panicking. Probably because Easton is still out there. It makes me nervous, not knowing where he is.

"Okay." Agent Grant nods slowly. He doesn't seem shocked.

"Nate's dead."

Again, he's not surprised.

"Easton Beaumont is the one who killed him."

Finally a reaction. Agent Grant flinches and his eyebrows twitch upward, but only a little. He's probably an excellent poker player.

"Easton." It's almost a question. As if he was expecting me to say a different name.

"Yes."

"And you know this how?"

"He told me. After he killed his friend John Thomas in front of me. He bashed JT's head in with a rock, then threw the body over the edge of a cliff. They found him the next day and thought it was an accident."

Grant leans forward, putting up a hand to stop me. He takes a small notebook out of his back pocket and starts writing something. "So Easton killed his friend in front of you. Why didn't you call the police?"

"Because he said if I told anyone, he'd kill me. He knew I wasn't Nate, obviously, and he's the one who put glass in the food Gramma Sharon ate. He also turned on the gas, knowing the alarm would go off, and he burned Valencia's hydrangeas and threw paint on Marcus's car and made it seem like I did it."

"What time was this? When he killed his friend."

I try to remember. "I think around seven? Maybe seven thirty."

He writes it down. "Okay. And Easton told you he killed his brother?"

"Yes. He strangled him to death in the fort they built together out on the island in the bay." I thumb over my shoulder in the direction of the back door. "Miles and I went out and found the body today."

"Instead of calling the police, you and your friend went out there alone to find a crime scene?"

"Look, if all you're going to do is crime-shame me, we can skip to the end where I say, 'I know, I never should have lied to begin with, and I regret every decision I made along the way.' But you need to get the police to find Easton right now, before he can cover it up any more than he already has."

He stares at me with what I imagine is equal parts skepticism and curiosity. "Why did you call me? You should have called the police."

"Because I don't trust them to take me seriously. They fucked up Nate's investigation from the beginning, right?" He doesn't say anything, but the look on his face tells me he agrees. "And I think you believe me. Don't you? That's why you've been following me around and trying to get me alone without the family. You knew I wasn't Nate."

He purses his lips and closes his notebook. "I suspected. Honestly, I thought the parents hired you. You're sure Easton acted alone?"

So Grant does think Valencia and Marcus were involved in some way.

"I mean, it's not outside the realm of possibility that they knew, but I really don't think so." At least that's my hope. That Valencia had no clue. That even Marcus was in the dark.

Agent Grant leans back in the chair. He stretches his neck with a pop, then sighs. "So why have you been pretending to be Nate?"

"Seriously? That's not important right now! Easton is a psychopath and a murderer."

"It is important because I knew you weren't Nate when I met you. Your story didn't make sense—post-traumatic amnesia doesn't present the way you say yours does. Even your Dr. Zapata said she thought you were hiding something. She thought you weren't comfortable talking about whatever happened to you. But I've been doing this awhile and I could tell it was because you were making stuff up. So why steal this kid's identity?"

I tell him the quick version. That I ran away from my ultraconservative religious parents, was living on the street, and I didn't want to go to jail.

"I never thought it would get so out of hand. I figured I could sneak out of the hospital before you all called the Beaumonts. I thought you'd at least have to do a DNA test."

"Your 'parents' wouldn't allow it. And we can't take DNA and test it without a court order. So if you and your parents both say you recognize each other, we're likely to take your word for it—and the Department of Human Services has been woefully underfunded for years, so one less kid in foster care is good for them."

"You don't have to talk to me about underfunded social services. I already figured that out when I was homeless and couldn't find a place to live. So what are you going to do about Easton?"

"We need to call the police first. They'll send someone out to find the body. We'll have to tell Marcus and Valencia the truth, because we might need them to help bring in Easton. That's the only way—"

I don't hear what else he says, because Easton doesn't need to be brought in.

He's standing in the doorway to the kitchen.

I didn't even hear him come home. I didn't hear a door open or close.

Has he been here this whole time? I try to think of where he could have been hiding.

Agent Grant stops speaking and follows my gaze. But Easton is quicker.

I don't even get a scream out before I see the small utility knife in his hand.

"No!"

It's too late. Easton drives it into Agent Grant's neck in two quick, violent stabs.

Blood shoots out in a thick stream and lands on the kitchen island with a splatter. Another jet shoots out before Agent Grant's shaky hand goes up, trying to stop the bleeding. He reaches for his gun, but Easton moves again, this time grabbing his arm and shoving it away.

Miles is in the living room.

"Miles! Run!" I scream.

Agent Grant falls to the ground and more blood spills out in a quickly expanding pool. His face goes pale. Easton steps over him.

And finally I realize I have to run, too.

I leap up, but my shoe lands in the blood spreading out around Agent Grant and I lose my balance. I catch myself on the chair, managing to stay upright, then run for the back door.

This is it. He's going to kill me!

"Nate!" Easton's voice is so loud in the quietness of the kitchen. I unlock the door and turn to see where he is. But he hasn't moved.

Because he has Agent Grant's gun in his hand.

"Remember how good a shot I am?" he asks with a grin.

I do remember. His target at the shooting range was way better than mine. He flicks the gun in the direction of the chair I was just sitting in.

"Sit back down. We need to have a discussion before Mom gets home."

I glance back down at Agent Grant. He's dead. His hand has fallen away from his neck, and whatever blood is still spilling out of him is doing so slowly. His brown eyes stare into the distance.

Oh God. There's so much blood on the floor.

And I haven't heard Miles in the house. No door opening, no running.

"Miles!" I call out.

"HEY!" Easton snaps me out of my daze. "Sit."

I do as he says. My body tense and hands shaking. My heart beats like it's trying to tell me to *run!* Easton pulls out the chair Agent Grant was using and sits, being careful not to get his shoes in the blood on the floor. He places the butt of the gun on the table so the business end is leveled at me. His finger on the trigger.

"That's the second person I've had to kill because you couldn't keep your fucking mouth shut."

Second person. JT was the first, which means Miles is still alive.

"Where's Miles?"

"He'll live. If you're good."

"What did you do to him?" I'll never forgive myself if Miles dies because of me. And his death *would* be my fault. I'm the one who got him involved in this. And Agent Grant, too. Why didn't I call the police?

"He's taking a nap, stop worrying about him. So you found my brother, huh?"

"Yeah." I try my best to sound tough. Like I'm not about to piss myself in terror. "Guess you weren't so smart after all." Though I'm bluffing, hoping he doesn't realize I haven't called the police. Because, yeah, I was worried they'd screw up or wouldn't investigate before Easton could clean up the body. But maybe I should have called Grant and then them.

Easton scoffs. "Oh, don't act smug. It wasn't hard. The fucking *police* were supposed to find him, but they didn't even bother searching over there. Can you believe it? I even left the kayak out!"

Wait, he *wanted* to get caught? Why?

"Anyway, we're almost through here, but I have to be honest with you, Nate."

"Stop calling me that."

"You wanted to be him. Now I have to kill you like I killed him. But what really pisses me off is . . . I was kind of hoping you'd be better than him. When you showed up here, telling everyone you were Nate, I looked at you—the way you lied, the way you manipulated everyone—you were so fucking good at it. I mean, I thought *I* was good."

That makes me sick. "I'm nothing like you." But is that true?

Easton laughs. "You absolutely are. You—"

He stops and his eyes go wide as the garage door opener starts running on the other side of the wall.

"Oh shit," he says, sounding bored. He puts the gun down on the table. "Mommy's home. What are we going to do about this mess?"

He still has the knife in his other hand, but if I run now—out to the garage and into the car—if I can make it, I might be able to keep him from killing me.

I push the chair away and bolt for the door. But I can sense he's behind me because of the way the air shifts.

Something sharp hits my neck and my entire body jolts with the shock.

He's stabbed me, too.

I'll bleed out like Agent Grant. My legs go wobbly and I fall to the floor. I have to stop the bleeding. Oh God, I don't want to die.

I put my hand up to my throat, but it's dry. My hand shakes as I pull it away. There's no blood.

But the world around me is swimming. If I'm not bleeding, then what's happening?

I fall to the ground and even though my head hits the tile of the kitchen hard, I don't feel it. The edges of my vision start to darken, and I see Easton standing over me with the hypodermic needle in his hands. He says something, but it sounds so far away.

The last thing I see is him putting the needle into a vial and pulling out the plunger, refilling the syringe.

Then nothing.

FORTY-SEVEN

EVERYTHING IS STILL DARK WHEN I WAKE UP. BUT I'M only half-awake. My head pounds and my mouth is dry. My face is wet, and I know there are tears falling from my eyes, but I don't know where I am. It's quiet.

I can't move my arms. My legs either. Or if I can, they feel like they weigh a million pounds.

Where am I? How did I get here? I try to remember what happened, but I feel drunk. Woozy and numb.

I groan, and though I can't make out words, I hear something. Someone talking.

Easton.

Then blinding light hits me, feeling like a sharp spike through my forehead. Everything is still a little blurry, but I can see Easton. He's standing in front of me, saying something. Maybe he's saying, "How you feeling?" I mumble something that sounds like "hurts." He nods and says something I can't understand. It's hot, and sweat drips down my back.

My hands are taped to the arms of a chair. I look around and we're someplace familiar, but it's not the house. The walls and floor are wood and everything smells new.

The boathouse. We're in the boathouse. The shutters are closed over the windows, so I can't see outside. I have no clue what time it is.

There are three more people in the room with me other than Easton. They're all taped to chairs, too. Two of them have Valencia's tote bags over their heads. One doesn't—the boy directly in front of me. His eyes are closed, but he has tape over his mouth. There's more duct tape around his forehead, securing him to the headrest of a high-backed lounge chair.

Miles.

I try to say his name, but my throat feels like I swallowed a pint glass of razor blades.

Or maybe some Watergate salad.

My head is still pounding. Easton is talking, but I can't understand what he's saying. I close my eyes against the bright lights in the boathouse. My head falls forward and I drift off to sleep again.

A sharp smack brings me hurtling back to reality. I cry out and open my eyes. Easton is staring at me; he looks angry. He smacks me again, hard. Then again. I bite my cheek and the taste of blood spills across my tongue.

"Stop!"

"You gonna fucking stay awake?" *SLAP!*

"Yes!" My voice is hoarse, my throat dry. "Water."

"God, you're so whiny." He walks over to the workbench to my right and grabs a glass, then fills it with water from a gallon jug. While he's doing that, I notice a roll of duct tape on the counter. And a gun right beside it. Farther along is a bottle of what I think is vodka, and some kind of holder with metal tools sticking out of it, but I don't focus on that because directly next to it is a red plastic gas canister. Across from me, behind Miles, the kerosene heater is blazing red, which explains why it's so hot. But not why it's on in the middle of May. My eyes flit back to the gas canister, and I wonder if it's full of kerosene for the heater.

Easton puts the glass of water to my lips. I drink quickly. Most of it spills down my chin, and my throat still burns with every gulp, but I feel better already.

He takes the glass away and I turn to see Miles is still asleep. The other two no longer have their heads covered. Marcus and Valencia look like they're in the same dazed and confused state that I was moments ago. Valencia is to my left, and she's facing Marcus, who is on my right. Miles is in front of me. Easton positioned us so that we're looking directly at the person in front of us, but we can still see each other.

I have enough clarity to feel a twinge of guilt—Marcus and Valencia are restrained like Miles and me. Which means they were innocent all along. My own history clouded my judgment so badly I couldn't help but suspect these surrogate parents. And now we're all going to die. I try to pull at the duct tape around my wrists, but it only serves to rip out the arm hairs beneath it.

Valencia tries to say something, but her voice breaks.

"What's that, Mom?" Easton asks.

"What's happening?"

"Oh." He frowns. "Well, sadly, it looks like our family is coming to an end. It's funny; I was kind of hoping you'd all live long enough to get dementia so I could see how much I could get away with telling you.

Then, when you had lucid moments, the nurses in the home would think it was your demented ramblings." He chuckles.

Valencia groans and her head slumps over again.

Easton clenches his jaw and walks to the workbench, where he grabs something made of orange plastic. JT's inhaler. He goes back to Valencia and holds her head up by her chin. Her eyes flutter as she looks at him.

"I need you to breathe in, Mom," he says. "It'll counteract the sedative." He pushes down on the inhaler, but Valencia doesn't breathe in. He slaps her. "Wake up! Breathe!" He pushes again, and this time she breathes in through her mouth.

Her eyes open and she leans back in her chair, looking around in a dazed way.

"Where . . . why are . . . ?"

"One more," Easton says, holding out the inhaler.

"What is it?" she asks.

"Bronchodilator. I gave you a sedative, so you're bound to feel a little groggy. But now I'm bored, and I need everyone awake and aware."

Valencia looks at the inhaler like she doesn't believe the correlation, but then puts her lips on it. Easton presses the inhaler, and she breathes in. Easton then moves over to Marcus, who's drooling on his own shirt.

"Now, Dad got a good amount. Who knew his tolerance was so high? Must be all the THC you been doing, Pops!" He holds up Marcus's head and puts the inhaler to his mouth. "Pretend it's a bowl! The good shit. Breathe in."

Marcus does, and his eyes open almost instantly. Then he coughs.

"Yeah!" Easton laughs. "See? Good shit." He caps the inhaler and tosses it over his shoulder. It clatters to the ground somewhere in the boathouse.

"Easton?" Marcus says. He pulls at his restraints, and the chair he's in creaks. "What's going on?"

"Well." Easton puts his hands on his hips and turns to me. "Nate. Do you want to start or should I?"

FORTY-EIGHT

ALL EYES IN THE ROOM ARE ON ME. EXCEPT FOR MILES, whose eyes are still closed. Easton leans back against the counter, his arms crossed. He gives me a few seconds, then says, "Well? Tell them, Nate. Tell them the truth."

"Easton," Valencia says. "Untie us now. Whatever this game is, it's not funny."

"This *game*? Christ, Mom. You're really that deluded?" She opens her mouth to answer but Easton holds out a hand to stop her. He keeps his eyes on me. "Tell them how you've been lying to them."

"Easton."

"Mom! Shut. Up. Nate, tell them."

I swallow hard. My head continues to pound, but I start pulling up from the arm of the chair, trying to create some space between the wood and my skin.

"I'm not Nate," I say.

"What was that?" Easton steps forward, cupping a hand around his ear. "Speak up for everyone—they're still a little woozy, so you need to use your big boy voice."

"Easton, sweetie—"

"STOP TALKING, MOM!" Easton reaches back and grabs the

roll of duct tape on the workbench. "Or I swear to God I'll tape your mouth shut and those will be the last words you ever say."

Tears run down her face, and she opens her mouth one more time but doesn't speak. Easton turns his attention back to me.

"Tell them."

I look over at them. Valencia's eyes are closed, her cheeks wet. But Marcus is looking at me, resolute. He knows what I'm going to say. He might have heard it the first time, but he also probably knew before I said it.

"I'm not Nate," I say, a little louder this time. "I lied. When I got arrested, I saw his face on the missing poster and we looked alike, so I told the police I was him so I wouldn't get in trouble."

Valencia shakes her head but doesn't open her eyes. "I think everyone is a little confused—"

"No, Mom, you're the only one who is confused," Easton says. "Look at him." She doesn't open her eyes, so Easton marches over and turns her head roughly. "Open your eyes and look at him."

His voice is so calm it's terrifying.

Valencia slowly opens her eyes and two more tears stream down her cheeks.

"Tell her again," Easton says.

"I'm not Nate. Nate's dead."

Valencia's eyes snap closed again, but this time she starts to sob. Easton finally lets her go and her chin drops to her chest, her hair hiding her face. Marcus looks up at the ceiling, his own eyes glassy.

"That's right," Easton says. "Nate is dead. This isn't your son; he's an imposter. And sorry, dude, but a pretty shitty one, too. The retired FBI agent saw right through your lies within seconds. It's my delusional mother's fault we're *all* in this mess."

He turns back to Valencia, who's still crying.

"Mom, seriously. What the fuck? The empty nest hit you hard, huh? You let this complete stranger move into our house, sleep in your son's room. And when weird shit starts happening around the house—a gas leak, car vandalism, those ugly flower bushes, glass in that disgusting mess Grams calls food—did you even *once* think it could be him?" He sticks a thumb over his shoulder at Marcus. "Dad did. So what was your issue?"

"Honey, what's going on?" Valencia looks up at him. "Why are you doing this?"

Easton lets out an exasperated sigh as he realizes she's not going to answer his question. Then he points the roll of duct tape at me and Miles. "Because of these two."

He walks over to the workbench and puts the duct tape back down. Again I try to twist my hands and wrists. Out of the corner of my eye, I can see Marcus trying the same.

"This *imposter* showed up pretending to be Nate." Easton reaches for a metal stand that looks familiar, though I can't place where I've seen it before. Or the tools it holds. He takes something long, slender, and metallic out of the holder. "I was going to let this stupid game of his go on for as long as he wanted. To be quite frank, I was looking forward to the moment it all blew up in his face."

He comes back to us. I try to see what he grabbed from the workbench, but he's holding it in a way that it's hidden from my view.

"I figured," he continues, "the longer it goes on, the more it's going to hurt. After you pay for his college, his wedding—and what if he had fucking kids? Kids who call you Nanny and Pop-Pop. Then one Thanksgiving, the FBI raids the family dinner." He smiles with morbid delight. "The possibilities were incredible."

He comes to a stop in front of me. Then he crouches down so he can look up into my eyes.

"But you had to poke around to try and expose me, didn't you."

"Yeah," I say, trying to keep my voice steady. Easton is toying with us, and I don't want him to know how terrified I really am. But I'm toying with him back, because the longer he talks, the better the chances of Marcus or me getting out of our restraints and stopping him.

Easton stands and looks at his parents. I try again to pull at the tape, but my arms won't budge. I twist my wrists and hands desperately, trying to create some kind of weak spot in the bonds. Sweat slides down the side of my face to my neck.

"I knew, obviously," Easton says. "Remember when you called me, Mom? You said I had to leave school early because they finally found Nate? And what did I say?"

Valencia doesn't answer. Easton flicks his wrist and metal flashes in the light from the boathouse rafters. And I finally recognize what he's holding, and where he grabbed it from. It's from the bar cart in the living room. He puts the thin, steel ice pick to her neck.

"What did I tell you, Mom? When you called and said they found Nate, what did I tell you?"

Valencia swallows, then takes a deep breath. "You said Nate was dead."

"I did. Now how do you think I knew that?"

Again, she doesn't answer. Even with an ice pick pressed against the pulsing artery of her throat, she won't say the truth aloud.

"Nothing?" Easton asks. "No guesses?" He turns to Marcus. "What about you, Pops? Any guesses how I'd know my baby brother was long dead?"

Sweat beads at Marcus's forehead, and he doesn't answer. I twist harder in the chair, but there are too many layers of duct tape wrapped around my wrists. It's impossible to get any leverage.

Easton turns back to me and I freeze. "Fine. I did make you go first, so while we're on the subject of telling the truth." He sighs and does his best to look sincere. "Mommy. I killed Nate."

Valencia's head falls forward again and she shakes with more silent sobs.

"I killed him out there." He points the ice pick in the direction of the island in the bay. "He's been there the whole time. So close."

Valencia still doesn't look up at her son.

Sweat slides down the underside of my arm and my wrist starts to move. My heart leaps in my chest, and while Easton's distracted, I try to twist more. The sweat is making the tape tacky against my skin. If he keeps doing this emotional torture thing, I might be able to get out. But I need more of a plan than that.

I look around me. Trying to find a weapon. Something to use against him.

The gun on the workbench. Marcus's gun.

No. It's not Marcus's because his has that trigger lock that neither Easton nor I know the combination to. So it must be Agent Grant's.

But I need to get my arms *and* both my legs untied to reach it. There's no way I'll be able to do that without Easton noticing.

But I have to try.

"Did you hear me, Mom? You finally have your answer! After all this time, he's been right out there."

She still doesn't look up.

Easton turns to Marcus. "Right, Dad?"

I stop moving and look up at Marcus. His eyes are red and wide.

"Tell her." Easton nods toward Valencia.

"What are you talking about?" I ask.

"Come on, Dad. It was your idea to take him out to the fort. I was ten years old, I couldn't move a body all by myself." Easton spins around to grin at me. "Who do you think helped me?"

FORTY-NINE

VALENCIA FINALLY LOOKS UP, HER FACE WET WITH SWEAT and tears. Marcus's eyes are wide and he shakes his head, but he looks terrified. Like he got caught in a lie.

"Marcus?" It's all Valencia can say.

"No," Marcus says. "He's lying, don't believe him."

"Oh, come on, Dad, we're all being honest today. Tell your wife the truth."

"You helped him?" I ask.

Despite thinking this myself, it still feels like a shock. I really hoped Easton might have done it himself. He's so sure and calculated, it felt obvious that he was the only one who could do all this. I didn't want it to be true that one of his parents knew. But Marcus helped him all along. And he's been lying about it.

"Stop!" Marcus says. "Valencia, you know I would never hurt our children."

"No, Dad, you didn't hurt him. *I* did. You just sat there and cried and said I'd ruined my future and how could I be so stupid. Then you slapped me and said you'd help me hide him so no one would ever find out."

"Stop it!" Marcus screams.

But Easton's voice remains calm and cool. "Then you helped me row him out to the island."

"Shut up! Stop it! Stop it stop it *stop it*!"

"Oh, Marcus." Valencia sounds heartbroken.

"And then I told JT the story you made up so the police would know I had an alibi. The one you coached me to tell—you were a way better coach at that than you were at soccer, by the way."

"You're a fucking liar!" Marcus screams.

But I'm not sure who to believe. Easton isn't the kind of person who would give credit to someone if he did it himself. He'd relish how smart he is, and how capable.

Easton tsks and shakes his head. He stands over Marcus, looking down at him. "You know, Dad, I was really hoping this would bring us all closer together. That the truth would set us free and all that bullshit. But I guess not."

"You're a liar! Don't believe him, Valencia. It's not true." Marcus's eyes are almost as red as his face, and he looks like he's about to cry.

"Do you believe him, Mom?" Easton turns his attention back to her.

Valencia looks at Marcus with fear and confusion, her face wet with tears and sweat.

"I would never," he says quietly. A sob racks his body. "I would never hurt our boys. Please believe me," he pleads. Tears slide down his face. "I missed him, too. So, so much." His face contorts in agony as he sobs.

"Marcus," Valencia says.

Snot drips from his nose as he looks up at his wife.

"Well." Easton sighs.

Then he jams the ice pick into Marcus's left side. I cry out in shock. Valencia screams as Marcus gasps. Easton holds the ice pick there.

"I was hoping to send you on to the next world with a clear conscience, but . . ." He pulls out the ice pick and blood trickles down Marcus's side.

Marcus coughs up more blood as he looks to Valencia. "I . . . never . . ." He shakes his head.

"No!" Valencia cries. "NO!"

Marcus mumbles something else, then slumps forward, more blood spilling from his mouth as he lets out one final shallow breath. Valencia sobs, and my own eyes burn with tears. Marcus wasn't my dad, but it still feels like Easton jammed the ice pick into my own heart. Maybe that pain in my chest is for Valencia, because I shouldn't feel heartbroken for Marcus if he helped Easton.

But I don't even know if that's true. And maybe that's why this feels so awful.

"Shame." Easton walks back to the workbench and wipes the blood from the ice pick with a kitchen towel. "How about you, Mom? Do you at least feel a little better knowing the truth?"

Valencia is still staring at Marcus's body. She shakes her head.

"Well, sorry about that," Easton says. "But I thought you should know before you die that your husband has been lying to you for years."

She finally turns to him. Tears slide down her cheeks, but she's calm. "No, he hasn't."

Easton's eyebrows jump up in surprise. "What?"

"You're lying. He didn't help you."

"You can't be that delusional."

"I'm not." She turns to face me. And there's something in that look. Like she's telling me she hasn't been delusional about anything. Goose bumps rise across my sweaty arms.

"I missed Nate. Every day I missed my baby." Across the room, Easton grumbles something under his breath. Valencia looks back at Marcus. "He felt the same way I did. That's how I know he's telling the truth."

"You believe him over me?" If my vision weren't swimmy from the tears in my eyes, I'd think Easton actually looks surprised.

Valencia stares at her son with a look so frigid, it almost chills my burning skin. "He was my husband. I always put the two of you before him, just like he put you both before me. But I've known him way longer than I've known you. I *thought* I knew you. I grew you inside me for nine months, and when you were born, I thought, *This is my baby and I will always love him.* I knew I'd never feel a connection like that again. And I was right. You and me, we have something special."

Easton seems as confused as I am. Is she . . . saying she knew he was a killer?

"When you tell me you killed Nate, I believe you. Because I know what you are capable of." She doesn't look away from him. "Maybe it was denial, but I hoped I was wrong. I saw it when you were little. Those warning signs. How you didn't seem to be afraid of anything, and how when one of us was upset you were bored or disconnected. You didn't seem to be able to love the way we all did. I wanted so badly to believe you were okay, and then one day you were. I thought it was a phase, and you had grown out of it. And I held on to that hope, like I held on to the hope that my youngest boy wasn't dead."

My eyes dart between Easton and Valencia. She's so calm, while Easton looks genuinely scared for the first time. He's also distracted. I return to twisting my arms, trying hard to get my hands free, because with Marcus dead, it means the rest of us are next.

I glance back at the red gasoline container. My guess is that's the finale.

"You knew Marcus only as your father," Valencia continues. "I knew him as a husband and a father, and my best friend." Tears spill down her cheeks. "I know what he's capable of. And I know what *you're* capable of." She shakes her head. "He didn't help you, did he, sweetie? You did it all by yourself."

Easton stares at her for a few moments and I stop moving. Finally, he smiles that proud, terrifyingly toothy grin.

"I did," he says.

"So why lie, honey?" Valencia asks. "If this is how it ends, why lie?"

He laughs. "I wanted him to die thinking you hated him. Thinking that you believed he lied to you, and you would never forgive him."

Valencia puts her head back, looking up at the ceiling. More tears fall. "What happened to you?"

"Nothing *happened* to me." He takes several quick strides toward her.

He puts his hands down on her arms and looks into her eyes. "You said it yourself, you could see me all along. Until you couldn't. That's because I *saw* how you looked at me. That fear in your eyes, even though you were supposed to love me."

"I *do* love you."

"Bullshit. You were terrified of me."

"Every parent is terrified of their kids. We're scared every fucking second of every day that you're going to get hurt or sick or hate us or stop talking to us when you grow up."

I can't help but wonder if she also worried that he'd turn into a serial killer.

"It's different with people like me," Easton says. "Because I knew if I didn't hide who I was, you'd know."

She nods. "I would."

My right hand is moving more. I glance down to see that the sweat dripping down my arm has caused the duct tape to slip. It's almost halfway down my hand.

"And then you showed up."

I turn and Easton is looking at me. He points the ice pick in my direction and walks over. "You came in, and I genuinely thought, Wow. Here's someone who's just as bad as me."

"I'm nothing like you." Maybe if I say it enough, I might actually believe it.

"No?" He snorts. "You told this poor woman you were her dead son. You lied, and I watched you do it. It was so fucking easy for you. Like it was for me. Nate was a stupid little brat who could barely handle the slightest inconvenience, but you . . . you were interesting."

Easton gives me a genuine smile. But as quickly as it appears, it drops away again and his eyes cloud. He takes a step toward me, pointing at my chest with the ice pick.

"Then you had to go snooping around," he says. He turns back to Valencia. "If it wasn't for him trying so hard to find Nate's body with this nosy bitch"—he points to Miles, who still shows no sign of consciousness—"I would have killed him after making him write a note admitting that he was a fraud, and everyone could have gone back to normal." He's lying again. Just minutes ago he said he wanted my lies to continue for years to see how long they would play out for maximum devastation. Or was that the lie? Maybe Valencia catching him out about Marcus has shaken the control he thought he had over this situation.

So I try to do my part as well.

"You didn't get away with anything yet," I say. "What's your plan after you kill us? You stabbed Marcus. You think no one is going to think you killed us all?"

"Yes." He says it so confidently, it gives me chills. "Because I already planned it out."

He shakes his head as he walks back to Marcus's body. "It was always supposed to be him. I set it up so *he* was the suspect. Mom was asleep upstairs; Dad was at the store. I told the police I was at JT's. And I told them I was scared of Dad, so I stayed there. I don't know what he said to them, but they didn't even go out and check the island for a body. Sure, they had divers search the bay, but I sat and watched them—they boated around it; divers went into the water. No one thought to get off the boat and check the island."

When Easton looks at me again, he seems like he still can't believe it. "If half the serial killers out there are dealing with idiot cops like this, I bet there are so many people who get away with it! I *wanted* Nate's body to be found."

He spins and looks at Valencia.

"And, yes, Mother, I did do it myself. And, honestly, I'm fucking proud of me."

Even knowing who Easton is, I'm still shocked that he thought all this at ten years old. And he probably had contingency plans all along.

"I never wanted a missing brother; I wanted a *murdered* brother. And Dad was supposed to be the one to do it."

"Why a murdered brother? And why frame Marcus?" I ask.

He scowls at me. "I already told you why I killed him. He was annoying and I wanted to see if I could. And someone had to get caught in order for me to enjoy my freedom. Our family would be under the most scrutiny, so I knew it had to be Marcus."

"Not Valencia?" I suggest, as if I'm part of the planning. Easton turns back to his mother like I needed him to, and I work on the duct tape straps again.

"I guess I could have blamed you, Mother," he says. "Women can do anything men can do, so why wouldn't a mom kill her son? That was my own internalized misogyny, and I'll work on that." His tone makes it clear he absolutely will not.

"But why Marcus specifically?" I try again. Easton spins toward me, and I stop wriggling my arms. "Daddy didn't show you enough love?"

He scoffs. "What are you trying to do?"

"I want to understand where you're coming from," I say. My voice almost trembles because I'm walking a fine line between pushing him to keep talking and straight-up pissing him off. "You say you killed Nate because you wanted to, but there has to be a reason you tried to frame your dad. Did Santa not bring you a special toy for Christmas?"

Easton stares at me. Once the silence gets too uncomfortable, I try again.

"Maybe he didn't take you to enough baseball games? Or you saw that he loved Nate more than you and you couldn't take it. So you killed Nate and tried to frame Marcus for the murder."

Easton takes two slow steps, then crouches in front of me. "What else do you think? Keep going, maybe you're almost there."

But something in the way he says it makes me think I'm not even close. I swallow hard and try to think of my own dad. "Maybe you were proud of something and tried to show it to him and he ignored you? Was that it? Not shown enough attention."

"No," he says. "But now we know *your* issues, Mr. Projection."

My face burns with embarrassment. Even when I'm trying to play games with Easton, he outsmarts me. Finally, he stands and walks over to Marcus's body.

"I knew when the cops found Nate's body they'd want a suspect. I was trying to keep it simple, and Dad was the obvious choice." He lifts his leg and plants his foot against his father's chest.

"So a random stranger wouldn't work?" I say, still trying to distract him. To keep him talking while I slowly twist my arm to loosen the tape. I know Easton thinks he's better than everyone else. He's telling us all this so we *see* how smart and capable he is. He's bragging the way serial killers taunt police, and I have to keep him going. Because that's his only weakness. His pride.

And pride is a sin, after all.

Easton shrugs. "If they went with a random stranger I wouldn't have cared. But they didn't. They said Nate was missing and went with the kidnapping route because some bored gas station attendant in Pennsylvania said he might have seen a kid who looked like Nate. It's okay, though. Because now I get to rewrite the story the way it should have been told from the beginning." He pushes Marcus's body with his foot so the front legs of the chair lift from the floor. "You're some shitty homeless kid Dad saw on his lunch break one day. He knows that I suspect him of killing my little brother, so he pays you to pretend to be him. Then he brings us all here to try and kill us in a tragic fire—one you tried to start in our home a couple weeks ago by leaving the gas on."

Oh my God. He *has* been planning this all along. All that nonsense about wanting to see how long he could let my lies go on was the lie.

"I escape, the sole survivor, and they find Nate's real body along with Mom, Dad, and the imposter he hired. Case closed, end of story. Finally." He pushes hard and Marcus's body topples backward with a thud. Valencia whimpers next to me. Why didn't he mention Miles? "Then it's just me and Gramma left. Until I get bored and, I don't know, push her down a flight of stairs or some shit. I haven't figured it out yet, but I'll know when I do."

"You're proud of yourself," I say.

Easton shakes his head. "No. I'm just ready to fucking be done with this."

Next to him, Miles groans.

"Oh!" Easton turns his attention to him. "Our special guest is finally waking up." Easton bends down and taps his face lightly.

Miles's eyes flutter and then go wide. He tries to speak, but his head is strapped to his chair and his mouth is taped. He barely even moves a centimeter.

"You woke up just in time. We were talking about your boyfriend here." He nods in my direction and Miles's eyes go to me. He says something beneath the tape that sounds like my name. *Nate's* name.

I pull hard on my wrist. The wet duct tape rips out every hair on the back of my hand; it's excruciating, but I keep pulling. It's down to my knuckles now. Almost there. Almost free.

But Easton turns back to me.

He shakes his head. "Listen, I don't want to sound maudlin here. But you felt like more of a brother to me than Nate ever did. I never felt like I had anything in common with Nate, but you—watching you lie, how easy it was—I thought you were someone I'd be able to show the real me to."

That's not true. I don't hurt people. Although, that isn't exactly accurate. I look over at Valencia, then I focus on Marcus's body. And Miles. They're all here because of me.

I shake my head. They're not here because of me. They're here because of Easton. Because Easton *wants* to hurt them. And that's the difference between the two of us.

"No," I say. "I lie because I have to. Because the other option isn't safe for me." And yes, this has moved beyond my experience with the Beaumonts. Because that's *why* I'm so good at lying, like he said. I lied to my real parents because look what happened when they found out the truth. I *needed* to lie to survive.

I stare him directly in the eye.

"You lie because you like it. Because you want people to hurt. I lie because . . . sometimes it's the only option I have. I don't want to hurt anyone." I look back at Valencia. "You have to believe me, I never thought it would get this far. I thought I could run away again before the police figured out I was lying, before they even told you they found me." I focus on Easton again. "I got good at lying because I knew it was the only way my real parents would love me. And when they found out, they tried to change me. But that's the difference between you and me. I care about the people I'm lying to. Because I love them, and all I wanted was for them to love me."

Easton looks bored, because he has no idea how to relate to what I'm saying.

"You don't care about love," I say. "You can't feel it for other people and you can't feel it when other people love you. You have no one to love. Because you don't want it."

His face changes slowly, the corner of his mouth drawing up into a smirk.

"You know, that's a great point." He backs away. "I figured that out pretty early, actually. Watching cartoons and hearing stories about love, I didn't understand it. I don't care about people. I don't even *like* people. But you do."

He turns his attention to Miles. "You have people who you love."

No.

"So while we're on the subject . . ." He kneels in front of Miles, whose eyes go wide with terror. "Let's see how our guest feels about your love."

FIFTY

"LEAVE HIM ALONE!" I YELL. BUT I KNOW IT'S USELESS. He's never going to listen to me. So I pull at my restraints, trying to yank my hands free.

Easton reaches out and runs the ice pick down Miles's cheek.

"Remember when I said I was thinking about getting into psychology?" he asks me.

I'm not even half listening because I'm trying so hard to get out of the tape. I don't care if Easton sees anymore, but his back is to me while he focuses on Miles.

"I told you about how quickly, and sometimes slowly, the world of psychology changes. I did my final paper in my psych course on antiquated treatments in the psychological field. Less than seventy years ago, you know what they used as a treatment for insanity? They would lobotomize people." He turns to me and grins again. "Hey! Also for homosexuality! Fun fact, huh?"

He stands and takes a few steps back. The tape sticks tight around my knuckles as I try to pull my hand free.

"Now, for the first lobotomies, what they'd do is drill holes into the skull at certain points of the frontal cortex. . . ." He points to several spots on his own skull using the ice pick. "Then they'd inject ethanol into the holes to burn away all those pesky little synapses that gave people their personalities, thoughts, feelings—basically everything that makes you a 'functional' human." He uses rabbit-ear quotes around the word *functional.*

"The problem with that is it's messy. You've got all the bone dust and flesh and blood to deal with. And then the ethanol might accidentally burn away some motor skills and what have you. So they found a new way."

Easton holds out his right fist in demonstration. In his left hand he holds up the ice pick.

"What they'd do is, they'd slip the end of a thin metal spike—" He drops his hands slightly to look at us. "It looked like an ice pick but wasn't one. These were real doctors, so they had their own tools, but for all intents and purposes, it's an ice pick."

He holds his hands back up and I freeze. No longer pulling at my restraints as I realize what he's telling me. My heart starts to race.

"So they take the ice pick and slide it right in . . ." He slips the ice pick between his fingers slowly. "Around the eyeball, into the socket. Then they'd go up . . ." He slides the ice pick and it slips out between his index and middle fingers. "To the underside of the skull. And they'd take a little hammer . . ."

Easton takes his left hand away from the ice pick and turns it into a fist.

"And tap!"

He uses his fist like the hammer and gives the base of the ice pick a tap. He clicks with his tongue as the edge of the pick slips farther between his fingers. Then he pulls it out with a flourish.

"And there you have it! No surgery, no blood or bone dust. And a nice little desensitized homosexual with no more desires, fears, worries, or real purpose in life. Or a desensitized woman, because that's who psychologists chose to mutilate back then. Women and homosexuals. Which . . ."

He gestures at the three of us and laughs.

No. He can't possibly be thinking about doing that.

No no no no no.

"Easton." Valencia's voice shakes. Across from me, Miles screams against the tape covering his mouth.

"Don't worry, Mom. I'm killing you and Fake Nate." He focuses on Miles. "But you, I just want to see what happens. Lobotomies went out of vogue in the fifties because people said they were 'inhumane.'" Again, the fucking bunny air quotes. "But I'm curious to see what it does. I think it could really change your life."

"No!" I scream. I pull my arms as hard as I can, straining every goddamned muscle in my body until my shoulder cramps.

"Yes." Easton walks across the boathouse and grabs one of the chairs that he brought down from the deck and puts it in front of Miles. "Let's see what the history of medicine can still do in the present, shall we?"

"Stop!" I yell. "He has nothing to do with this!"

Easton turns to me as he walks to the workbench and picks up a bottle of vodka. "Of course he does. You two started the investigation—which, by the way, I assume means he knew you weren't Nate or that you told him. You really shouldn't have done that. Then you'd have been right. He would have nothing to do with this. But as it stands . . ."

"Don't do this, Easton, please!" Valencia says.

He uncaps the vodka bottle and pours it over the ice pick and his hands. "Even if I didn't want to, he knows way too much. I can't let him go." He shrugs and looks back at Miles. "So think of it this way: You get to live. You just won't be able to talk or tell anyone what you know. You'll go off to a nice medical center to live, and when it's time for me to do my clinicals, I'll come visit you and see how you're doing."

Miles screams and screams under the tape. Tears stream down his face.

"None of that," Easton says. He leans forward, reaching up to hold Miles's head steady against the back of the chair. "Now, I don't have a little hammer, so I think we're just going to have to push harder than normal. You'd better hold still. I've never done this before." He gives a rueful chuckle. "To be completely honest, I'm a bit nervous."

Valencia is yelling at him to stop. I'm yelling at him to stop. Miles is squeezing his eyes shut and screaming behind his tape.

"This isn't helpful, family!" Easton yells over us. I'm thrashing in the chair, trying to get loose to do something. Anything!

Easton reaches down with the thumb and forefinger on his right hand and pulls Miles's eyelid open. He fights against him, and Easton sighs and leans back.

"Listen, you can fight all you want, but if you keep this up, I can always just stab you in the eye and pluck it out. Do you want that?"

As if to show he isn't bluffing, he grabs Miles's head and positions the ice pick against his cheek.

Miles cries and finally opens his eye.

"That's better. You might feel a little pinch."

Easton uses his thumb to push up Miles's brow.

And Miles screams.

FIFTY-ONE

THIS IS ALL A NIGHTMARE. EVERY SECOND OF IT, FROM the moment my parents found out I was gay until now. I need to wake up.

It doesn't matter how much my muscles ache or how raw my throat feels as I beg Easton to stop. This can't be real. It can't possibly be happening.

But it is.

As Easton narrates what he's doing, I try not to listen. I pull at my restraints with all the strength I have. The tape has left a tacky mess on my hands, but my knuckles have disappeared under it.

I yank hard, and my right hand is free.

But my fingers are so sweaty that when I go to find a place to tear the tape around my left hand, I can't get a good grip.

Valencia keeps crying, begging Easton not to do this. And I still can't get my other hand free. I look around, trying to find something I can use. But there's nothing within reach.

Then I remember the house key Valencia gave me. I reach into the fifth pocket of my jeans, and there it is on its key ring. I rake the teeth against the duct tape securing my hand to the chair, watching the back of Easton's head as I saw away. Easton made his speech sound like this would all be quick and easy, so I have no idea how much time

I have. But the fear in Miles's muffled screams is my barometer. As long as he's screaming, it means it's not too late.

The tape starts to shred so I saw harder and harder, trying to keep my movements as slight as possible so Easton doesn't notice.

The tape rips, and it's enough to pull myself free if I keep moving my hand, so I focus the key on my legs. His taping wasn't as secure here—only wrapping around twice. I cut it easily, and by the time I'm scraping at my left leg, my left hand is free.

I look up to see Valencia watching me as she yells over and over at Easton to stop, trying to be as distracting as possible. It seems to be working.

Easton turns to her and I freeze. "Mom. Please shut up!" He takes another breath and returns to what he's doing as Miles tries in vain to speak through the tape covering his mouth.

The tape on my leg rips and I jump up.

I expect Easton to turn, see me, and run right at me. But when I'm halfway to the workbench I glance back, and he's still focused on Miles. His back is to me.

And to the gun on the counter.

I snatch the gun up, making sure the safety is off like Marcus showed me, and aim it at Easton's back. I should shoot him right now and end this.

But he has an ice pick pressing against my friend's skull.

One slip and he could blind him in that eye. Or kill him.

"Easton, stop!" I yell.

His head spins to look at the empty chair behind him. Then slowly he turns to see me with the gun.

My hands are shaking and my muscles still ache with the strain of trying to get loose from the duct tape. But I hold the butt of the gun to steady it, and I know my aim is good enough. From this close, I can shoot him. But not until Miles is safe.

"Stop what you're doing and back away, now," I say.

He grins and stands slowly. I keep my eyes locked on his. But he takes a step toward me, clutching the ice pick.

"Don't move!"

He tilts his head. "Did you check that the gun is loaded?"

Despite the immense heat in the boathouse—even Easton has started to sweat—a chill creeps down my spine.

I didn't.

And Easton knows that. He nods.

"Because what was Dad's first rule?"

Always assume the gun is loaded. But Easton doesn't wait for me to answer.

"So ask yourself"—Easton takes another step toward me—"why I would leave a loaded gun lying around, when I didn't plan on using it?"

I can't think of a reason through the panicked alarms sounding in my head. Is this another one of his games? One of his lies?

The safety is off. Red means dead.

But is it loaded? He's right. I didn't check because I assumed. Like Marcus told me to.

Easton lunges at me, the ice pick arcing over his head.

I pull the trigger.

FIFTY-TWO

THE GUNSHOT IS DEAFENING. THE BULLET HITS EASTON mid-lunge and he goes flying backward.

He was bluffing. It *was* loaded.

Blood spatters Miles and Valencia in little droplets.

Valencia cries out as Easton hits the floor hard, knocking over the chair I was tied to.

I stand there, staring at his body. My ears ringing.

I shot him.

Valencia's voice drifts through the ringing and the brain fog of shock. Calling my name over and over.

Nate's name.

I turn to her.

"Untie us!"

Right. I run to Miles first.

"Are you okay?" He gives a grunt beneath the duct tape. His eye is bleeding—a line of red down to the duct tape that follows the curve of his chin—but it focuses right on me, so he should be okay.

The ice pick is on the ground, near Easton. He's face down, and blood smears across the floor where he landed. But he isn't moving.

I stand and step over him, watching closely for movement. But he's still. And I don't think he's breathing. I snatch up the ice pick and jump back over him to Miles. Using the ice pick, I carefully poke a hole in the duct tape around his forehead, then rip it wider. I leave it there for him to take care of when he's free, because I know it's going to rip out hair.

I do the same with his mouth, and he takes several gasping breaths, thanking me. Then I cut his arms and legs free and let him pull the remaining tape around his head and mouth as I go to Valencia.

"Are you okay?" I ask as I take care not to accidentally stab her leg with the ice pick.

She nods. Then she opens her mouth to say something else, but Miles screams.

I turn and my blood runs cold. Easton is getting to his feet. His hand is pressed against his shoulder, blood spilling through his fingers from the bullet wound beneath. He glares at me, hunched and wincing as he breathes sharply between clenched teeth. For the first time, I see the real Easton. Before, when he killed JT, I thought I was seeing the real him. But he still had part of that person-mask he wears up. This is the terrifying, *real* monster that's been hiding all along.

He lunges at me.

I raise the ice pick at him, but he grabs my arm.

The gun. Where did I put the gun?

It's on the floor, behind Miles's chair. Too far to reach, but at least Easton doesn't have it. He tackles me to the ground, slamming my arm against the floor, trying to get me to drop the ice pick. But I hold on for dear life.

Then I see the bullet hole in Easton's right shoulder.

Blood drips from it in a slow stream.

Without stopping to think, I reach up and shove my finger into it. He screams in agony and punches me in the face. My vision trembles, and the taste of blood fills my mouth again before I feel another wallop from his fist.

The ice pick clatters to the ground. Easton reaches for it, but Valencia's leg kicks his hand away, then the ice pick. It slides across the room.

Easton pushes off from me, cursing at his mother as he scrambles for it. I pull at his shirt, trying to keep him from going after the weapon. He spins and tries to punch me again, but I roll away. I pull his arm with me, and he rolls on top of me, his knees on either side of my chest. He grabs my head with both his hands and slams it hard against the floor.

I scream and reach once more for the bullet wound, but he slaps my hand away and bangs my head down again.

Everything is blurry.

He stands and I reach for his ankle, but he kicks me away.

Easton slowly limps over to the ice pick; whatever adrenaline that was fueling him seems to be wearing off. I try to scramble to my feet. But the whole room lurches around me, as if we're on a boat instead of in a boathouse. My head pounds as I spit out blood.

Behind me, Valencia and Miles are shouting, but their words don't register.

All I can focus on is Easton. Walking toward the ice pick.

I lunge toward him as he bends down for it. I leap onto his back, wrapping my legs around his sides, and try to pull him over. He uses the momentum to move back toward the other wall where the workbench is. Then he spins, losing his balance, and I fall back onto the countertop.

My back knocks into something and it falls to the ground.

The smell of gasoline fills the room.

The gas canister. It's on the ground, and the yellow spout has fallen off. Gas glugs out slowly onto the floor behind me.

I kick away the can and stand upright as Easton lunges toward me, the ice pick raised high above his head.

He screams loudly as he brings it down. I try to duck but it's too late. The point pierces my skin with a sharp, hot burst of agony as Easton buries it in my chest all the way to the hilt, then pulls it out in a quick movement. I almost fall to my knees but brace myself against the countertop.

Easton drives the ice pick into me again, but it hits the back of my shoulder. I feel a horrific scraping shudder in my body.

I scream again and tackle Easton to the ground.

His hand comes away from the ice pick, but it's lodged in my shoulder. Blood pours out of the wound in my chest, half an inch below my clavicle. And maybe only inches from my heart.

I hope.

We're covered in blood and sweat. Easton reaches up and wraps his hands around my throat. He squeezes hard, and the ragged breaths I had been heaving immediately stop while the pounding in my head grows heavier.

I reach for his hands, clawing at them, drawing more blood. Trying to stop him. Trying to breathe. But he's too strong.

"Looks like you die the same way I killed Nate," Easton says through clenched teeth.

My chest burns, aching to take a breath, as I fight back. I reach for Easton's eyes, but he bites down hard on my left hand. I open my mouth, trying to scream as his teeth sink deeper, but his hands keep the scream trapped in my throat.

I try to pull my hand away from him, but the ice pick in my shoulder cuts into another muscle, sending out a fresh burst of pain. Instinctively, I reach up with my right hand and rip it out. More horrific pain.

But this is my only chance.

I aim for his face, watching his eyes go wide as blood spills from his mouth.

The ice pick hits him in the cheek, right below the eye. The tip scrapes down over Easton's cheekbone and exits through the skin under his jaw. He howls with pain, and I rip my hand back from him. His grip around my throat is gone, and I suck in a deep, burning breath laced with the smell of gasoline.

I scramble away from him, hacking and gasping. The ice pick is still in my hands. Easton keeps screaming slurred obscenities at me as he holds a hand against the blood spilling from his jaw.

Behind him, Valencia is screaming, too. She's standing by the door to the dock, and so is Miles. He must have gotten her free during the scuffle between me and Easton. But both of them are shouting something I can barely hear over the pounding in my head. Valencia is pointing as Miles tries to pull her away, toward the door.

I manage to slow my gasps for breath long enough to focus on where she's pointing.

The river of gasoline moving across the floor.

And where it ends.

That's when I recognize one word through the rush of blood in my head.

"Fire!"

The gasoline reaches the kerosene heater. And now I know why Easton had it lit. His plan at the end of the day was to fill the boathouse with gasoline and let it burn to the ground. Because without even touching the heater, the gas ignites.

FIFTY-THREE

WHATEVER GASOLINE WAS LEFT IN THE CANISTER explodes immediately. It bursts from the seams in the handle and sprays a wall of fire across the room, separating Easton and me. He stumbles out of the way. It's spreading.

There's plenty of water below the boathouse, but the steel ring on the removable floor panel on my side of the room is covered in burning fuel. The one on Easton's side is untouched, but a wall of flame blocks him from reaching it. He's trapped.

But so am I. I spin around, trying to find a free path or place where the flames aren't so high so I can jump to Valencia and Miles, who are by the door. But the fire is too strong.

Valencia yells something at me, but I don't hear it over the roar of the flames.

Easton leers at me, then starts walking along the wall of spreading fire, trying to find a place to jump over. But it's too high. And the flames are too hot.

We're both going to die here.

Black smoke fills the boathouse rafters, and it makes my already raw throat burn even more.

Valencia moves closer. "Fire extinguisher! Workbench!" She points.

I open the cabinet under the workbench and there it is—a small white fire extinguisher for putting out engine fires.

I pull the pin and spray the flames separating her and me. Aiming at the floor.

Once there's a spot large enough for me to jump through, she waves me over. I leap to her side, and she pulls me tight against her, squeezing. It hurts so bad, but I can't help but wrap my arms around her, too. Then I pull her back toward the door, but she stops.

"Mom!" Easton calls out. He holds a hand against his jaw where the ice pick exited his chin, and he sounds like a slurring drunk. "Mom, please!"

Valencia looks at me. Then takes the fire extinguisher.

"No!" I say, reaching for it.

But she doesn't listen to me. She walks over to him. Behind me, Miles is pulling at my arm, trying to get me out of the boathouse. But I have to stop Valencia. She can't let Easton go. He'll kill us all.

I run over to her, but she puts her hand out to stop me.

"Please," Easton yells between coughs. "Please don't let me die, Mommy."

He's so full of shit. He's faking it so he can kill her once she saves him. But of course she's going to save him. He's her only living son.

Her only *real* living son.

"You can't do this!" I tell her. "He'll kill us! You know he will."

"He's my son." She gives me a sad look. Tears streak through the soot on her cheeks.

Then she turns back to Easton.

"Marcus and I wanted children because we wanted to know that when we died, we were leaving something better in the world behind us. With all my heart, I love you. Despite everything, I *still* love you."

She sets down the fire extinguisher.

"But you're dangerous. Not just to us, but to everyone. I don't think you're capable of leaving the world better than when you came into it."

"Mom!" Easton finally looks shocked.

Valencia shakes her head. "I'll love you for always, my baby."

"Mommy! PLEASE!" Tears spill down Easton's bloody, quickly reddening face. If I didn't know better, I would think he's scared. But Easton doesn't know what fear is. Even now, I don't think he knows.

"I'm sorry." Valencia draws the gun she tucked into the top of her jeans.

"No!" He reaches over the fire for the weapon.

But Valencia pulls the trigger, and the bullet hits Easton right in the eye and exits the back of his head. He falls to his knees, then falls forward into the fire. Valencia drops the gun, putting her hands to her face as she lets out a heartbreaking scream.

I try to pull her away. And for a second, I'm worried she's about to stay. That after learning that her missing son has been dead, watching her only living son kill her husband, then having to shoot that son herself, she might not be able to find a way to go on.

But finally she does move. And lets me lead her out of the inferno.

FIFTY-FOUR

THE FRESH AIR FEELS AMAZING ON MY BURNING SKIN. I breathe deeply but immediately start coughing again and I collapse onto the grass of the backyard.

Miles runs over and hugs me. I groan as pain racks my entire body. He sobs against me and I hold him, whispering quiet apologies over and over. But I don't think I'll ever be able to tell him how sorry I really am for getting him wrapped up in all this.

I let Miles go and turn to see Valencia crouched down at the edge of the yard with her hands over her mouth and nose. She's watching the boathouse burn as the fire spreads up through the roof.

"I don't have my phone," Miles says. "To call the police. Or fire department."

"Someone will call," I say, too tired to get up and go into the house to find our phones. Miles's parents have probably been wondering where he's been all day. They'll look out and see the burning boathouse eventually. Then they'll call. Or one of the other neighbors will.

I look over at Valencia. She's sitting on the ground, leaning against her heels, almost as if she's praying.

"I'll be right back," I tell Miles. He nods as I stand and walk over to Valencia.

I crouch next to her. She's not crying anymore, but her eyes are glassy in the firelight.

"I'm sorry," I say. "I know there's nothing I can do, and sorry isn't enough. But I needed to—"

"I chipped your tooth," she says, interrupting me.

Is she talking about Nate? Was this something that happened to him? Some cute story maybe that she remembers about him? And she still thinks I'm Nate because having to shoot her own son has made her final tether to reality snap?

But then she turns to me, and she seems lucid. "When I did your cleaning the other week. I chipped your tooth."

"Oh," I say. What is she trying to tell me? A dental mishap is nothing compared to telling a lie—several lies—that destroyed an entire family. "That's okay."

She frowns. "When Nate was four, I gave him trail mix that had dried cherries in it, and one of them had a pit. He bit down on it, and it shattered one of his baby teeth. He needed oral surgery—minor—but there was some scarring there. On one of the back molars that was below the gumline."

Oh.

"So when you were in for your cleaning, I chipped a part of your tooth off, so it would look like Nate's. I thought if anyone demanded proof, I could show them the chip and Nate's old X-rays. They wouldn't be able to check your other teeth because Nate's X-rays were baby teeth. But they'd see the chip out of your adult tooth."

That's why it hurt so bad after she cleaned them. I thought it was because I hadn't been to the dentist in over a year.

But that would mean . . .

"You knew I wasn't Nate." For those keeping track, my record is now oh-and-*six* for people who actually believed I was Nate.

She looks like she doesn't know the answer to that. But then she says, "I was willing to do anything to believe you were him. I knew he was dead . . . I think from the moment Marcus woke me up and told me he was missing, I felt it in my gut. But I told myself it was nerves. That we'd find him pretty quickly, maybe playing with one of the other kids in the neighborhood. But it stayed with me. Every day." She puts a fist to her solar plexus. "I felt it, every day. Then I got the call about you. And it was like . . . a splinter had finally been removed. But I knew you weren't Nate the second I looked at you.

"And the splinter came back. But this time it wasn't a splinter; it was like a knife. I knew you weren't him, but I *wanted* you to be him so badly." She takes a deep, shuddering breath. "So I told myself you were. And then I told everyone else you were. And I felt better."

Valencia reaches out and grasps my hand.

"I did everything I could to force myself to believe that you were Nate. The more time I spent with you, though, the more I realized you weren't him. But I also learned that I didn't care."

A sob escapes my throat, and it shocks me so much I clamp my free hand over my mouth.

"I know you're not my son," she continues. "But you remind me of him. He was funny. Effortlessly. And there were moments after we brought you home when I saw that in you, too. You'd say something, but as soon as you said it you'd shut down, as if you were scared someone would notice you. The real you. And every time that happened, I wanted to hug you and tell you it was okay to be yourself. It felt like a second chance. You made it so easy to love you. I think even Marcus realized that, too."

And now I can't hold in the sobs. She reaches over and hugs me, and again, it hurts, but this time I squeeze back.

Valencia is what a mother *should* be. What my own mom should have been. She even had unconditional love for Easton despite what he just put her through. And I can't imagine how terrible it must feel to kill your own son, but even that was a mercy. Burning alive would have been horrific for Easton. I'd never say it to her, but he deserved it after everything he did.

I don't need to feel any kind of love for Easton. He wasn't my real brother, and he was a shitty brother to the real Nate. But Valencia still loved him.

Once I get myself together and stop crying, I sit back. The sirens of fire engines echo in the distance. They'll be here soon. And they're going to want the truth. Especially since the truth also now involves a murdered retired FBI agent.

"Do you think they'll arrest me when we tell them who I really am?" I ask.

Valencia shakes her head. "Not after everything we've been through. They'll have plenty of terrible shit they need to sort out."

I don't know if I should even say it, but I want her to know how much I appreciate her. "You were a great mom to me. So I wanted to say thank you, Valencia. I felt more love from you and Marcus than I ever felt from my own parents." Which is really saying something since I considered both of them to be murderers at multiple points in our relationship.

She smiles and wipes a tear from my cheek with her thumb. "Well, they're shitty parents for not realizing how wonderful their son is."

I laugh because she doesn't mean that. I'm a liar. Easton said a lot of fucked-up things, but that part was true.

She looks back at the boathouse.

"What if we kept lying?" she says.

At first, I don't understand, but then I connect the dots. But she can't really be serious. She isn't asking me to keep saying I'm Nate. How would we explain any of this? Including Agent Grant.

"What do you mean?" I ask.

"Not about Easton," she says. "JT's and Agent Grant's families need to know the truth. But about you. Your parents— Knowing you'd be going back to people like that . . ." Her eyes cloud with anger as she shakes her head.

"So I . . . keep being Nate?"

"That part's already covered," she says. "People will be focused on Easton now."

Would we be able to get away with that? Maybe for a bit, but with all the murder and mayhem now, a judge would definitely sign an order to have our DNA tested.

Or maybe Valencia is right. Maybe all the Easton stuff is a way to let me keep hiding in plain sight.

The sirens are getting closer. Lights flash down the street where the road curves.

Miles gives me a questioning look.

I turn back to Valencia. "We need to get our stories straight."

EPILOGUE

Okay. I'm done.

I HIT SEND ON THE TEXT MESSAGE AND ROLL OFF MY BED. As I head out the back door, Valencia calls to me and I stop. She pokes her head through the kitchen doorway.

"Still feeling up to . . ." She pauses. Tentative, as though she doesn't want to say what she's asking, and who could blame her? She finally seems to settle on something and says, "This afternoon?"

"As long as you are."

She sighs and it sounds like she isn't, but still she nods. "Now or never, and never really isn't an option."

True. "I'm going to talk to Miles and then we can go."

She gives me a loving smile and I head out to the fence where he's already waiting for me, pulling anxiously at his fingers.

"So?" he asks before I even reach him. "Did you hate it? Do you hate me?"

I laugh and something twists in my stomach at the thought. Because I don't think I could ever hate him.

"I did not and I do not."

In fact, listening to his voice for seven hours has made me realize how much I missed him over the past few weeks. Even after our house was no longer an active crime scene, Miles said we all shouldn't be seen together until the cops stopped coming around. And we definitely couldn't text anything about what happened, in case they figured out our lies somehow and subpoenaed our phone records.

"You're saying that to be polite." He says it like he's joking, but I can see in his face he thinks I really might be. So I shake my head.

"I promise you I'm not. I mean, I did hate listening to myself." The interview he did with me was the only time I've really seen him since everything with Easton went down. But the interview for his podcast was fake. And so was the story we told.

Creating the lies that followed the fire was harder than actually selling them. Probably because Easton didn't have a chance to cover his tracks this time around. He'd left Agent Grant's body in the kitchen. Easton had planned on framing me as the psychopath, leaving no one alive to counter his version of events. Unfortunately for him, Valencia, Miles, and I all told the same general story.

Miles told the police he was planning a true crime podcast about my kidnapping and had showed up to interview me when everything went down. We told them that Easton confessed to killing JT, so his family knows the truth. We used that as the reason I contacted Agent Grant. They did ask why Easton would kill Grant in front of me but not kill me and Miles right then and there. We said it was because he planned to frame me for the murders, leaving himself as the only survivor.

From there, Valencia sold most of it. She confessed all the warning signs she ignored in Easton as a child. And how he learned to mask them as he got older. She also used Nate's disappearance as an example of how he didn't respond the way most kids would to such a situation.

But for the police investigating the deaths of Agent Grant, JT, and now Marcus Beaumont, that seemed to be enough. They stuck around for a few weeks, returning on several occasions to ask us follow-up questions—with our lawyers present—and then, last week, the case was closed.

That was it.

It almost felt too easy, but then Miles reminded us of how the police work. For them, it was a numbers game. They had an open case, a dead suspect, and three eyewitnesses who gave the same story. Even if the story was batshit, it meant they could close the case and be done with it. Then put a tally mark in their imaginary case-closed column. And it could become an interesting story for them to tell at parties: the psycho kid who tried to kill his family. And let's be honest—without us telling them what to believe, they wouldn't be able to do it on their own.

Who could blame them? Is it easier to believe that a ten-year-old killed his little brother, got away with it, and almost ten years later, a queer homeless kid stole his brother's identity? Or is it easier to believe that one kid with psychopathic tendencies snapped and killed a few people after his missing brother returned, upending the life he'd had for the last ten years?

I know which was easier for the police.

"No one likes their own voice," Miles says. "But you promise you didn't hate it?"

"Yes. Why are you so worried?" I know my relationship with

Miles is new, but he isn't the type to be modest or even feign modesty to get a compliment.

He bites his lip and shrugs. "I don't know. I guess because . . . I might be having some second thoughts."

"On?"

"Releasing the episodes. I'm not sure I want to."

Okay, that actually surprises me. I scramble, trying to figure out the logic. "You spent all those hours recording and editing. Why let it go to waste?"

"Because it's not real?" He looks at me and I can see it again. The shell-shocked way he looked weeks ago, after we were free of the boathouse. "I still have nightmares. All the things he did, what he tried to do to me—I think about it all the time."

I reach over the fence and take his hand, because I know what he means. I think about it, too. So does Valencia. The constant thoughts of *What if the gun wasn't loaded? What if he didn't want to brag about killing Nate to his parents and killed us all instead of gloating? What if I didn't have the house key in my pocket or couldn't get free?*

But none of that is helpful because the gun *was* loaded. We did get free, and Easton's own pride really was his downfall.

The verse from Proverbs echoes in my mind: *Be assured, he will not go unpunished.*

"Do you want to know what helps me when I start to freak out about all that?" I ask him. He doesn't answer but gives me a curious look that tells me to go on. "How lucky I am to still be here. And yes, like your podcast, there are parts of my life that aren't real. But the important parts are. Valencia loves me, and that's nice to have."

Miles looks . . . almost impressed? And when he smiles at me, it's genuine. "Well, that settles it. I'm deleting the episodes."

I flinch, and my jaw hangs open as I try to understand him. "Wait, why?"

He takes my other hand and pulls me closer to the fence. "Because you're right. The important parts are real, like Valencia and . . . also you."

"Obviously that's not true."

"It is." He stares at me, and it takes me a second to realize what he's saying. "I know you came here as Nate and . . . well, yeah, technically you're still Nate."

"My real name—"

"Doesn't matter anymore. You said the important parts are real, but what's the point in telling the story if it's not all true?"

"That's some strong journalistic integrity you got there."

"I know, I should get a Pulitzer. Too bad no one will ever know." He looks down. "Except me, because I know who you are. Who you really are, Nate. And I'm glad you're here."

His eyes meet mine. Maybe I am happy I'm here, too. Miles leans forward and I meet him. Our lips touch, gently at first, like we both aren't sure if we should be doing this. But then it's like our bodies have been wanting this our whole lives. And Miles is the first boy I've ever kissed, so yes. For me, I *have* been wanting this my whole life.

His hands go to my cheek and my neck. I reach around to the small of his back and pull him against the fence separating us. Our lips open to each other. At first, Miles's body is tense and taut, but as our kiss continues, he relaxes into me. And me into him. The nervous energy is eventually pushed aside and all I feel is the explosion of excitement in my stomach, the beat of my heart, and every amazing thing all at once.

Because yeah, when I wake up from those nightmares about Easton where the gun isn't loaded or I can't free myself—in the darkest parts of the night—I think maybe I should have just stayed with my real family, and we would have avoided all that trauma.

But in moments like this, where I'm being more myself than ever before, it's worth it. Despite every awful thing, I can finally be who I really am.

Valencia and I beach the kayak on the island and hop out. This time, we brought backpacks with water and tied the shovels to them. I untie the shovel on my pack and lead her into the woods in silence.

We reach the clearing with the felled tree, and it's kind of a mess. The holes Miles and I dug six weeks ago are still there, and the broken fort is shoved against the tree.

Valencia looks back at me, and I take her to the hole where Nate still lies.

I expect her to react like Miles did. Knowing Nate is out here is one thing, but *seeing* what's left of Nate makes it all so much more real. But all she does is sigh and crouch down at the edge of the hole. She reaches out carefully to put a hand on the center of Nate's chest.

Then she closes her eyes and holds it there.

This feels like a private moment, like I shouldn't be here. But I *am* Nate now. We're brothers. So I stay.

"Okay," Valencia says. "Let's get him buried." I help her lift what remains of Nate's small, nearly weightless body out of the hole, and Valencia wraps him in the baby blanket she brought him home from the hospital in. We carry it back to the clearing, where we gently set him down. Valencia points to the hole by the tree where the fort originally stood, and we start digging deeper.

It takes a few hours to make the hole wider—and we don't go a full six feet down—but we get a decent-sized grave dug for Nate and then lean the shovels against the tree. We carefully move him again, placing him in a grave that feels more purposeful than the one Easton left him in.

"What if someone finds him?" I say. We talked about what to do several times over the last few weeks, but this was the only solution we came up with. We thought about cremating him ourselves and mixing his and Marcus's ashes together, but Miles told us how hot the flame would need to be and that there would still be bones left without a crematorium doing the work.

Valencia shrugs. "They won't unless they dig. And it's not like the island is big enough for real estate development. Besides, climate change will have this all underwater in a few years' time."

She reaches into her backpack and takes out the urn with Marcus's ashes. Then she unscrews the top and slowly pours them next to Nate's body.

Now she starts to cry—silent, almost dignified tears. I crouch down next to her and she lets me hug her. My mom. My brother. My dad.

"What do you think about selling the house?"

I turn away from loading the dishwasher to look at Valencia. We finished dinner and were cleaning the dishes when she got quiet. I glance back at Gramma Sharon, who sits at the kitchen island playing solitaire. She gives me an *I'm staying out of this* look. So I reach for the plate in Valencia's hand and shrug, because I honestly don't feel like I can make that decision. This was never my house. It's always been hers. And Marcus's, and Easton's, and Nate's. Yes, I'm part of the family now, but I wasn't when they spent the majority of their lives here.

"If you want to."

"I don't know." She continues rinsing our forks and knives. "It felt a little big when Easton went to school and it was Marcus and me. We talked about it, but decided to stick around and see how we felt once he was done with college. We built the boathouse thinking it would be a nice investment to help us stand out in the market. Then when you came into our lives, we never really got the chance to talk about it again."

She's been doing that more. Acknowledging that I'm not the real Nate when it's just the family. Unfortunately my kidnapping case is still open, but with Miles's help, I've been telling Dr. Zapata a story about a woman kidnapping me and telling me I was her nephew. We used the gas station video as evidence, and said that eight months before I was arrested, she finally told me the truth and I ran away. But I don't know the address or her real name.

Miles said the cops and Dr. Z will probably think I'm trying to protect the woman because I still feel a familial connection to her. And since it's not a child abduction ring, they'll let the case remain open. They might come back every once in a while, but they haven't so far. They have plenty of open cases to focus on where the kids haven't come home.

Is it weird that I kind of appreciate how Valencia makes sure I know she sees the real me? She was lying to herself before because she wanted her son back. Now that she knows both her real children are dead, she wants me to understand she knows who I really am, and that she still loves me.

That she tells me all the time.

Something I *really* appreciate. And I love her, too. She's the polar opposite of my parents, who seemed to never want to have kids; it was like they were stuck with me.

Valencia was never stuck with me; she chose me.

"Well, what are your thoughts now?" I ask her, closing the dishwasher and grabbing a towel to dry my hands.

"Sell the damn thing." I turn to look at Gramma Sharon. Her mouth has healed pretty well since the glass incident, and she's moved on to soft foods.

Valencia chuckles and takes the towel from me as she looks around the kitchen. The crime scene cleanup crew took care of everything quickly once we were allowed to let them in. And now it doesn't look like a dead guy had been lying five feet from where we're standing.

"I'm not sure. I mean, you're going off to college in a couple years, right? Do you want to go to college?"

"College is expensive," Gramma Sharon says. "You can sell this place and buy a smaller one—maybe over in my neighborhood! Then put the rest in a savings account for school."

We didn't need money. Easton's life insurance paid for Nate's, which we did have to pay back. And Marcus's now sits in an investment account that Valencia said I could have when I turn eighteen.

But going to college, I'm not sure about. "Before, I wanted to go, because I knew it was the only way I could be myself." I remember what I told Miles. I do want to help kids like me in the future, and that requires plenty of expensive schooling for not a lot of pay.

Valencia smirks and leans on the island. "It might still be, *Nate*."

I laugh. "No, I think I'm through reinventing myself. As long as you're good with calling me Nate, I'm good with being Nate."

She reaches out and rubs my shoulder. "I'm good with that. Well, we don't have to decide now—"

"Sell it!" Gramma Sharon says again, looking up from her cards. "Am I invisible?"

"No, Mom, we just don't trust your opinions."

She scoffs at us and goes back to her game. Then Valencia turns back to me. "But maybe we'll think about it."

The thing about Valencia is that she means it. My bio parents never would have asked my opinion on something so big and life-changing. Valencia cares about my thoughts and feelings the way she cared about Easton's. And Nate's, of course.

We're a family, and for the first time since I can't even remember, I feel loved. Real love. Valencia still loved Easton despite everything he did—and knowing the truth might make that harder for her, but she still does. It's something she'd never admit aloud to anyone, but I believe it. And that's how I know she'll always love me, too. It doesn't matter who I am or who I love or what I believe.

This is what my life should have been. It's what everyone's life should be.

Acknowledgments

WHEN DOES WRITING A BOOK GET EASIER?

Asking specifically for me and no one else. This is my fourth published book and you'd think I'd have it down by now, but you'd be wrong! There are so many challenges in writing and publishing, but I am so thankful to everyone I'm about to tell you about for their guidance, knowledge, and support as I worked on this killer story.

My agent, Michael Bourret, never seems daunted by the crazy ideas I pitch him, and I'm not sure if it's because he's a professional or I'm not trying hard enough. . . . To be fair, the reason I queried him in the first place is because he represented one of my favorite books, *Grasshopper Jungle* by Andrew Smith. It's about a bisexual teen figuring out life while his town is destroyed by giant, horny, man-eating praying mantis creatures. So I guess if anything, my ideas haven't been wild enough! Note taken, Michael. I'll see what I can do for book six. (I feel like we've already decided on book five and fingers crossed for that one!)

Thanks also to everyone on team Dystel, Goderich & Bourret, including assistant Michaela Whatnall, and Lauren Abramo and Gracie Freeman Lifschutz, who are responsible for making sure my books are available overseas and in different translations, and thank you, Anna Carmichael at Abner Stein, who represents me in the UK.

Thank you to my US editor, Kristin Rens, who always manages to make sure every one of my books has a beating heart—and in cases like this, that I rip it out perfectly. Christian Vega was the editorial assistant for my last three books as well as *Better the Devil.* He came to one of my book events—I think it might have been for *Lose You to Find Me*?—and said he was excited for the day I write something scary. Well, Christian? Did I deliver or what?

Chris Kwon designed the amazing cover and Nicholas Moegly brought it to life with his artwork even better than I imagined! Thank you to production editor Caitlin Lonning, Melissa Cicchitelli in production, Michael D'Angelo and Matt Maguda in marketing, Abby Dommert, who handled publicity, Monica Shah and her team in sales, and Patty Rosati and her team, who focus on school and library sales.

I do owe an apology to my UK publisher, Hachette. I know I'm responsible for the spike in turnovers during the past year or so while we were working on *Better the Devil.* It was so horrifying and brutal that my editor Katherine Agar, Alexandra Haywood in marketing, and my publicist Lucy Clayton all *quit*!

Okay so they didn't actually quit—they went on leave, got promotions, or changed positions . . . but I like to pretend it was all my doing. "Erik J. Brown: terrifying publishing since 2020."

That being said, my editor Georgina Mitchell and editorial assistant Noah Grey braved all the blood, guts, and eye-trauma to make sure I could still successfully jump into the thriller genre without totally alienating the readers who loved the comfort and coziness of *All That's Left in the World.*

Joana Reis designed and created the UK cover and interior. Thanks also to desk editor Laura Pritchard; Joey Esdelle in production; Nils Jones, who took over marketing for Alex after I scared her off; and Karis Pearson, who filled Lucy's shoes in PR. Thanks to Siobhan Tierney who is the Group Sales Director for Hachette Ireland and to the whole sales team at Hachette UK.

And as always, thank you, reader. If you bought this book, received it as a gift, checked it out from the library, or even borrowed it from a friend, you have helped keep all the people above—and me—employed and doing what we love: sharing stories with the world.

Thank you to the authors I've somehow managed to con into being my friends, and those who have heard me pitch this story, helped me work through a plot snarl, or even just talked and provided emotional support: Jennifer Dugan, David Fenne, Anna Gracia, Amy Ignatow, Brian D. Kennedy, Naz Kutub, Susan Lee, Alex London, Gretchen McNeil, Rex Ogle, Adam Sass, Eliot Schrefer, Zachary Sergi, Josh Silver, Eric Smith, and Tig Wallace.

Thanks to Dr. Leah Freilich, who not only answers vet questions to keep my dog, Charlie, healthy but made sure Chardonnay's brush with death was realistic as well. Dr. Mark Tingey helped me out with a lot of the forensic science, and his wife Angela Tingey answered all my dental questions. Mark and Angela, after reading this book, you'll both realize I ignored large parts of what each of you said because it didn't help my plot . . . but I appreciate the hard work anyway! Thanks also to Supervisory Special Agent Raymond Hall at the FBI who answered my questions about kidnappings, investigations, and all the tiny details around Nate's disappearance and reappearance to keep this story as close to reality as fiction can be.

A special thank-you to my family, who understands what unconditional love is and has always loved and supported me in every aspect of my life. I'm always thankful for you. But especially my nephew Nolan Brown, who called me to ask about my books and reminded me I had to write these acknowledgments.

If you're a reader who has made the unfortunate discovery that your family's love was in fact conditional, know that you can not only live but thrive without it. Yes, it's awful, and no, it's not fair, but it isn't about you.

It's always about *them*. Something in *them* is broken, not you.

You are deserving of love, and you'll find it from the people in your life who see the real you and stick around when things get hard.